WHAT GOOD MEN DO

JOY MOY

First published in Great Britain by
Gardenview Publications in 2019
Martock, Somerset
gardenviewpublications@gmail.com

Cover photographs © Andrew Moy 2019

For Andrew – for everything

For Andy and Matt – for friendship and memories

Good men all!

CONTENTS

FOREWORD

'With permission, Mr Speaker, I would like to make a statement on a legal settlement the Government has reached concerning the claims of Kenyan citizens who lived through the emergency period and the Mau Mau insurgency from October 1952 to December 1963.'

As he rose to his feet in the House of Commons on 6th June 2013, Rt Honourable William Hague MP, then Foreign Secretary, was attempting to draw a line under events. A settlement sum of £19.9 million was paid in respect of 5,228 claimants.

'I would like to make clear now and for the first time, on behalf of Her Majesty's Government, that we understand the pain and grievance felt by those who were involved in the events of the Emergency in Kenya. The British Government recognises that Kenyans were subject to torture and other forms of ill treatment at the hands of the colonial administration. The British government sincerely regrets that these abuses took place. Torture and ill treatment are abhorrent violations of human dignity, which we unreservedly condemn.'

Many of the records were destroyed at the time and many were 'migrated' to a secret archive at Hanslope Park, the home of 'Her Majesty's Government Communications Centre.'

The facts are horrific. Why did no one do anything at the time?

What follows is a work of fiction – perhaps an answer to that question.

1

Kenya, Rift Valley – 1961

Christmas Eve. Theo glances at his watch in the half-light. Coming on midnight. Lake Naivasha is behind them now and up ahead, against a backcloth of stars, Mount Longenot looms in the darkness. His jaw is clenched, his parched lips tight. Beside him, she has slipped into a fitful slumber, the horrors of her dreams erupting in bouts of heart-breaking whimpers. The tunnel of light along the road draws him onwards, mile after mile across the Rift. His own struggle is with his heavy eyelids.

The flashlight waving in the centre of the road is hard to miss but Theo almost does. Too late, he remembers the curfew. The men – in the shadows Theo can make out four, maybe five of them – are dressed in military style uniforms, heavy with guns. They are standing now almost nose-to-nose in the darkness with the clicking Land Rover. Cautious, he lowers the window and greets the Kenyan – large, gleaming black in the lamplight, probably Kikuyu – who seems to be their leader. His greeting is returned. But the others are pacing around the vehicle now, predatory. Theo hears a noise and turns sharply towards the passenger's door. One of them has come close, peering nose-on through the glass, rattling at the door handle. Startled, she sits up, wide-eyed, panic-stricken, caught in the glare of the ragged soldier's hateful gaze. Horrified she watches as recognition dawns in his yellowed eyes, hears his sharp call to the other gunmen.

'Who is she? Who is the woman?' At the window, the commander's question is curt.

'She is my wife. She is in pain. She will have the baby soon.'

Theo's reply is quick, unthinking. 'I am taking her to the hospital at Kijabe. This is an emergency!'

The big man at the driver's window scowls. There is menace in his eyes. He raises his weapon. 'What do you have for me?' His voice is rough, his intention plain.

Theo reaches into his breast pocket, pulls out his purse. 'I have some money, not much. Here.' He extracts the cash that he has, shoves it through the window into the man's grasping hand.

'Wait! Wait! I know her. She was at the school. She is not his. She is the wife of *Kernowi*.' From the far side of the Land Rover, the skinny would-be-soldier's frantic shouts slash the darkness. In un-laced, oversized boots he is dashing around the front of the vehicle towards his commander, banging on the car, brandishing his rifle. The others are racing to join the fracas, weapons at the ready.

'Theo! I remember him. He was at Gilgil, at that cricket match. I saw him. He poured tea. We must get away! Theo!' Her tone is urgent. She is gripping at his arm, her fingers tight, pleading.

'Your watch.'

Beside him, the big man has not yet grasped the significance of all the noise. He gestures towards Theo's wrist. He wants more. Without a second thought Theo hands over the precious timepiece that was his father's.

'Can we go now?'

He demands an answer and in response the man steps back, shouts something to the others, gestures with his gun. The Land Rover's engine springs to life first time. The escaping vehicle accelerates into the night, covering the gaggle of militia in a hail of tiny stones. Within minutes, headlamps ablaze, they are back to speed, the familiar trail of dust barrelling in their wake across the valley floor. Beside him, Theo catches her sigh. He glances side-ways and in the darkness can just make out the shape of her, knees pulled up, arms embracing her belly. He hears her groan; imagines her pain. Eyes on the road he urges the vehicle to greater speed. He must get her to Kijabe.

And then, with a shock, he sees it: in the rear-view mirror, the lights of another vehicle, approaching at break-neck speed. The gunmen are giving chase. Heart pounding, Theo stamps his foot down harder on the accelerator – faster, faster. Fear consumes him. Caution thrown to the winds, he rounds the bend at full speed.

Caught in the light, the donkey's eyes are as stunned as his own. The collision overtakes them both. It collapses them; catches them up; rolls them high, over the thorny acacia branches. It hurls them back down along the moonlit road, bounces them over the verges. It casts them belly-up, lifeless together in the stony ditch.

The chasing vehicle, screeching to a halt beneath the stars, can only take in the carnage. The ragged young soldier lowers his readied gun as he stares, black-eyed, down at the mangled heap, the twisted metal and the bodies. He scrambles back into the truck. There is nothing left here to kill. Compassionless, the commander turns the vehicle around and they head off, back the way they have come, back into the midnight valley.

It is the woman who stirs first, roused by the waves of pain as her child struggles to escape her damaged body. She opens her mouth in a scream, but there is no sound. Instinctively, she attempts to roll over into a crouch, but her limbs do not seem to be under her control. She tries again, and this time her body responds. She is kneeling on metal. With a shock she realises that it is the upended roof of the vehicle. Another wave of pain drags her head down over her knees. This time the scream is primal and real. It reaches Theo in the depths of his blackness. His eyelids flutter as he begins his long struggle back towards the stars.

The child's cry pierces the night air and Theo is awake. Eyes open at last, he stares up at the blanketing sky. Memory floods back with the pain and he drags himself to a sitting position, looks around him, searching the dark for some sign of her. Where is she? He struggles to his feet. He has been thrown from the vehicle, but not far. He uses it to support himself as he shuffles around to the other side of the twisted metal carcass, desperate to find the woman he has sworn to protect. And then he sees her, slumped in the shadows, leaning back against the lifeless body of the donkey. Lying on his mother, nestled between her breasts, he sees her son.

Like her mother before her, she has given birth alone.

Close now, when he speaks her name, she moans softly, lifts her eyelids. He touches her cheek, speaks again, but this time she does not respond. He reaches for her wrist; feels a pulse. Her hold on life is not strong. Regardless of his own pain, he moves back towards the abandoned vehicle, needing the blade, the binding, remembering the blanket. Returning with it and with a *kikapu,* he gently separates the newborn from its mother, sets it safe in the *kikapu,* the basket meant for vegetables. Back up on the moonlit verge he spreads the blanket, then drawing on some untapped well of inner strength, he returns to find her, picks her up into his arms, carries her out of the ditch and lays her on what he fears will be her deathbed.

He lowers himself down beside, takes her hand in his and she opens her eyes. Her grip on his fingers is soft, but insistent.

'His name is Daniel. You must take him with you, Theo, take him home … to Kernow … keep him safe.' Her voice is a whisper.

He sees she is bleeding. There is nothing he can do. He nods, but there are no words.

'He is your son now.' She has no strength but she must speak. There is more she wants to say. She strains to raise her head. Her eyes are large, fixed on his face. 'You must be careful, Theo. Kenyatta … he is your friend, but you have enemies because of him.' The effort has drained her. She falls silent; her hand lies limp in his. He fears that she has slipped away. Still, beneath the stars he keeps watch over her.

Suddenly her fingers are tight again, gripping his. In the vast silence her whisper is urgent. '*Uhuru* … beware of *Uhuru, the mzungu,* the white man. One day … he will come … for you … for the boy.'

He nods, attempts a smile to calm her. Believing her message understood, the young night-mother sighs, closes her eyes.

Somewhere in the distance a lone dog yips and a jackal calls into the darkness.

2

England, Sussex - 1979

'Is everybody ready back there? Mary? Joseph? The donkey?'

And so it begins, the final rehearsal for the first Christmas Concert in the school hall at Lind'n Lea Sussex, sister school to Lind'n Lea Nairobi, established by the Lind'n Lea Charitable Trust. The project has been a long time in the making but for Theo, the new Headmaster, it is the realisation of a dream, the fulfilment of a promise made a lifetime ago to a very dear friend. From the dais at the front of the hall, he watches as the rows of young faces are lifted with their voices:

'O come let us adore him, Christ the Lord.'

A discreet hand-signal from the music teacher in charge, and the shuffling children settle in classes on the newly polished floor.

The Headmaster remains standing, glancing down at the programme in his hand, then up towards the double doors at the rear of the hall. These have been opened wide to reveal the familiar tableau. As Mary and Joseph are ushered in by the deputy head and begin to make their way down the side aisle, he sees that they are leading a very excited Gary Roberts, who is wearing the painted donkey's head for the very first time. Despite the gravity of his role in the proceedings, Theo grins. Right on cue, the infant classes began to sing the song that they had been practising since half term:

'Little donkey, little donkey, on the dusty road,
Got to keep on plodding onward
with your precious load.'

He looks out for and then spots Mara, his own little daughter, sitting cross-legged at the front with the reception classes for her first Christmas nativity play.

'Been a long time little donkey,

there's a star ahead...'

The lump in his throat catches him unawares as he watches her beloved innocence. His precious girl is returning his smile. And then, in a flash that sets his heart thumping, he recalls that other donkey. His mouth is parched. He swallows hard. He can almost taste it on his tongue, the thick dust from the road across the Rift Valley. His pulse is racing. He can see the stars ...

'Are you alright, sir?'

He hears the whisper over his shoulder and turns to see the concern on the face of Mrs Kershaw the head of 'Early Years'. His knees have buckled beneath him and he has come down sharply onto the carved wooden chair. He nods in a way that he hopes is reassuring.

'I'm fine. Thank you.'

The older woman, reassured, returns to her seat and the Headmaster comes once again to his feet, smiling his encouragement to the young couple with the donkey as they make their way towards the stable, where the baby – a swaddled plastic doll – waits silently amongst the straw in the makeshift manger.

'It was the donkey that did it!'

A quick smile flickers, slips to a frown as Theo settles behind his desk. He sighs. Another time, another place it might have made an amusing headline, something from a pantomime – but not here, not now, not for him. The donkey was real, it had just appeared, stepped out in front of the Land Rover. There was nothing he could have done. It is even now the stuff of his nightmares. His study is cosy, warmed by the fire in the hearth, but he shivers, recalling his moment of weakness at the dress rehearsal. He has been feeling unsettled since then, all over Christmas and New Year. Several people have suggested he might be going down with the bug that seems to be going around. He shivers again. Maybe he is.

At least the meeting with his sister Rose, a few days ago up in London, has gone well. He'd been anxious about her reaction to his news – that he was planning to return with his young family to Nairobi, in the next school year, but she'd taken it in her stride. Thinking about her now, Theo is surprised that he'd ever expected otherwise. Rose has always been the strong one. Since their parents' too-early death she has been his strong centre. Without her he is certain that things would have fallen apart. A memory of a childhood game makes him smile – toe to toe, crossed-hands clasped tight, they would lean out and twirl each other round, spinning ever faster and faster. He was always the one who had called a halt, laughing and spluttering, freed his hands. She would never let go. And she never has.

Without hesitation, she has sheltered, protected and loved the child he that he brought back to her from Kenya, from boy to youth, to young man. And it seems that her love for the boy is returned as fiercely. Geographically distant, the legendary 'father' figure has become an ever more distant memory for the lad, so that now not even curiosity remains. Surely that is for the best. It is what he wanted; this is what he had planned all those years ago. At that time it had seemed there was no other way. The boy would never have been safe in Kenya. To have taken him back there would have flouted his mother's last wish and put the child in mortal danger. In Kenya they would have found him sooner or later. At the family home in Cornwall – for him it will always be 'Kernow' – the boy would be safe. And he has been safe. According to Rose, he has grown to be a fine young man, a Cornishman. Theo leans back in his favourite leather chair, smiling broadly beneath his full moustache. A Cornishman. Well fancy that!

'Know where you came from ...'

His father's friend Jomo Kenyatta gave him that life-advice a long time ago, when he was just a boy, and as a man he has come to understand exactly how much that matters. Theo shifts in his chair, nodding. In his life, where half-truths and imaginings have become the fabric of his identity, the fact that he was born in Cornwall, that his ancestors were Cornish is absolutely the truth, the bedrock of reality. He sighs.

So the boy thinks of himself as a Cornishman. That's what Rose said. It had come as a surprise. Though the child has been raised in Cornwall, he was certainly not born there. The circumstances of his birth will be forever etched in Theo's memory. Removing the glasses that he needs now for seeing things close up, he draws in a long breath and closes his eyes, massaging the bridge of his nose between the thumb and forefinger of his right hand. The horrors of that night: the killing knives, the moonlit dash across the Rift, the donkey's eyes, the carnage after; birth, death … the scenes flash across his inward eye with an immediacy that makes his stomach lurch. Alone, in the privacy of his study, Theo allows himself to remember.

Kernow; Kenya. He has loved them both with a passion that has rarely characterised his personal relationships. He is well aware that there are those who think of him as a cold man, an aloof man, a man of few words. He has heard it said and indeed had been told so on more than one occasion. A rueful smile twitches at his lips as he replaces his glasses and comes back to the present. Shifting in his chair, he begins, absent-mindedly at first, to twirl the tip of his moustache, when an unexpected memory of his father doing the same draws his attention to the gesture and he stops, clasping his hands tightly, lacing his fingers. He has often thought that he resembles his mother, with her auburn hair and her curls, but the moustache is his link with his father. He likes to think of it as distinctive; that it will always characterise his appearance. So is he a vain man? He considers the question, raising his eyebrows as he unclasps his hands, lifts himself from his chair and moves over to the window with its view out over the winter garden. It is true that he is a self-contained man, a private man … and with good reason. Idle gossip and what people like to call 'small talk' are things for which he has neither taste nor talent. Again the rueful smile. He is well aware that this particular quality has never endeared him to the folk who do. But he does make a very good Headmaster – many of the parents had shaken his hand enthusiastically at the end of term after the Christmas Concert and told him so. Is he a good man? Now that is a much harder question. He frowns. He has always tried to be, whatever 'good' means. He draws in a deep breath and holds it on the rising thoughts, remembering as clearly as if it were yesterday the time when he had challenged Uncle Charles on that very point.

'All that is needed for evil to triumph is that good men do nothing.' He can almost hear his young-man's voice, brave, strong, passionate. It sets his heart racing. But has he done more harm than good? Eyebrows raised in the familiar gesture, considering, older now, maybe wiser, who knows – Theo blows out his hopes and they mist on the cold windowpane. One thing he is sure of. He will always be a true and fiercely loyal champion of those whom he counts as his friends.

He turns back towards his desk and his eyes fall on the collection of framed photographs that he keeps there. A smile of genuine warmth lights his face as he takes in the well-remembered faces of friends and family and he is drawn as always to his favourite – his wife and his two little daughters, beaming beneath a glimmering Christmas tree. Reaching out, he lifts it with tenderness, his fingers toying with the tooled leather frame. In those closest to him he knows that he inspires love verging on devotion, though he acknowledges to himself that he is not the easiest, nor the most demonstrative of men. He holds the photograph close to his chest now in a gesture that would have surprised them. This devoted husband and father will always provide for and protect this precious woman whom he loves and the children that they share.

Setting the photograph carefully back in its place, it is of his children that he is thinking as he sits down and pulls open the drawer of the desk ... his little daughters ... and the boy ... his son. Reaching in towards the back of the shallow drawer he pulls out a small brown leather folder, like an old wallet. He opens it and the little boy smiles out at him from the fading black and white photograph that was taken all those years ago on his first birthday at the Old Rectory. Theo leans back in the chair and closes his eyes, remembering.

'Are you alright, Daddy?'

With a start he comes to, disorientated in the gloomy room. He must have dropped off – drifted away he certainly has, just like the day. His little daughter is at the door, bathed and ready for bed in her pink pyjamas.

'Mm, yes, yes I'm fine. Just nodded off for a minute. Are you ready for bed now? Come on in and give daddy a kiss, then off you go. Mummy will be waiting to read you a story. I'll look in later.'

The little girl runs to him and, standing on tiptoes, plants a kiss on his cheek.

'Who's that, Daddy?'

She glances at the photograph in his lap and he closes the folder quickly.

'Oh, just a little boy I used to know. Now off to bed, there's a good girl, and close the door behind you.' Mara squeals as her father ushers her out of the room.

The door closes with a click and the headmaster flicks a switch. The glow from the desk lamp pools on the folder in front of him, creating an illusion of safety from the storm that is blowing in on the wind outside in the darkened garden. He opens the folder once more and from the old photograph the child seems to be watching him, waiting for his next move.

The boy knows little or nothing about his past, about his mother, nor anything at all about his father or his country of birth. How could he? Who could answer his questions? There is no one who could explain. No one, that is, except the one person who was there, the one person who saw it all, Theo himself ... the Headmaster. In that moment he makes his decision. He will write it all down. He will write to the boy ... a letter. But he won't send it. He'll leave it with Jack or perhaps with his agent. Or maybe he should hold on to it himself, keep it in his special box along with the others, keep it until the right time comes. The boy will not know yet. But he will know.

3

Cornwall – 2008

'You know what this reminds me of?'

Mara flicked a sideways glance at her mother. Beside her in the passenger seat, Ellen seemed oblivious, eyes down, intent on the map spread out over her lap.

'Safari. I was thinking about safari. Those game drives when we were kids. Dad driving; you in the front with the books and the binoculars; Rosy and me in the back with the picnic.' Good times. She was grinning as she tapped the horn in warning to anything that might be oncoming and rounded yet another bend in the single track Cornish lane.

'Are you sure we took the right turning back there, mum?'

Several minutes had passed in silence. Driver now, Mara flared her eyes over the steering wheel. 'This is definitely getting narrower and all these potholes – it's looking more like a farm track, like that track around the back of Buffalo Camp, remember, where we saw Dad's rhino?'

If Ellen heard her daughter's overtures she gave no sign. The new OS Explorer map had all her attention as she wrestled to bring it under control, opening out, turning over, folding up, and folding again.

Mara happily left her to it. Ahead the narrow lane was dappled, sunlight shafting through overhanging branches, pockets of deep shade. A gritty dust was lifting in their wake, despite their nigh on walking pace and in the rear-view mirror she saw it. Just past sunrise, an early morning game drive, dusty mist mingling with wood-smoke in the chilly air. The rhino stepped out from the bush, right in front of their old Land Rover. The little girls had panicked but her father had calmly put the vehicle in reverse and 'saved the day!' It was an oft-told story – a favourite of his. It made Mara smile as, scanning the Cornish trail for signs of big game, she edged the Clio between the high hedgerows. Limey ferns brushed the flanks of the vehicle, clumps of late bluebells and wild garlic leaned in close.

'Well I don't know, dear.'

So her mother had been listening after all.

Ellen drew a deep breath and blew out her frustration, lifting her fringe in the process. 'It's so hard to tell on this map, but I think we should see a crossroads soon – probably just around the next bend. We're going in the right general direction anyway.' Her tone was hopeful, but she was frowning. 'Why don't you find somewhere to pull over and we can both take a look? Is it just me or is it getting very warm in here?' So saying she pressed down on the button at her side. The air that slid in through the lowering window was warm and earthy and heavy with garlic. Horse dung up the centre of the track lent a gamey note and the sharp scent memory caught her unawares. Her sigh drew a quick anxious glance from her daughter.

'Okay?'

'Mm, I'm fine.'

Ellen nodded slowly. And she was fine. She was there at last, on the safari. Gazelles grazing, short tails flicking in the umbrella shade of thorn trees and Theo, her man, young again, strong hands on the wheel, sunlight lifting his hair, like a nimbus. She sighed. Beside her, Mara was relieved to see that her mother was smiling.

'How about I pull in up there?'

Mara's question broke into the stillness that had descended. Without waiting for a response, she made the obvious choice. She eased the car into the wide grassy gateway.

'You should see this view, Mum.'

Mara was already up at the gate, fingers laced, pressing hard against the sky, arching out her spine as if in homage to the landscape that rolled away in shades of green towards the south coast and the sea. Gathering her flyaway curls into a makeshift ponytail, she turned back to her mother who was still sitting half in, half out of the car.

'I'll be right there.' Ellen watched for a moment as her daughter climbed up to sit on the top rung of the wooden gate, then leaving the car doors wide open to the air, she picked her way over tufty grass and dried-out car tracks towards the promised view.

'Look, there's the river, and over there, that's that church where we went to the flower festival yesterday.' Mara was gesticulating excitedly now, like some kind of tour guide. Her mother smiled.

'Your father would have loved all this, you know.'

Theo's absence hung between them, like an anniversary balloon, string dangling. Ellen drew him in and Mara nodded. He would.

'He was never happier than when he was here, in Cornwall. In fact, I think the older he got the more Cornish he became. I was looking at that video clip just before we came away ... the one of him singing 'Trelawney' at the Helston Flora Day last year ... or maybe it was the year before. He was singing his heart out, standing there in the crowd right next to the man waving the black and white Cornish flag. The way they were singing you'd have thought they were about to march on London then and there... an army of old Cornishmen rallying to the battle cry.' Ellen laughed then, but softly, to herself. She recalled saying exactly that to her husband at the time and the way they'd laughed together at the very idea.

Mara was still. The nod to her own inner voice was almost imperceptible. Her father's love for Cornwall was certainly the stuff of family legend. It was why they were here – the reason she'd agreed to come.

It was Rosy's suggestion. She and her sister had been reminiscing together over a bottle of red wine after the funeral when Rosy had come up with the idea. 'I think it would do Mum good to get away for a bit. She's looking tired. She's been under so much pressure what with Dad's illness and now all this. Graham was talking to her earlier and apparently she said she'd like to go back to

Cornwall again.'

Graham and his mother-in-law were close. The seed had been sown. And now Mara and her mother were in Kernow, staying not far from the seaside town of Looe, at Duloe Manor. Mara was a writer, freelance; she had a couple of weeks free between projects so she and her mother were exploring the unfamiliar area together. Lostwithiel was at the top of their agenda today. An advertising flier for the town's annual arts and music festival had caught their imagination but the cross-country route they'd chosen was not going quite to plan.

'I just can't get used to that new map. It's too big for me.' Ellen was feeling better now. She was smiling, ready for the task in hand. 'I know what your Dad would say.'

'A bad workman always blames his tools!' The two women quoted Theo in unison, mimicking his tone, laughing together at the memory.

'I'll go and have another look – I'm sure I put his map book in the bag. I don't think Lostwithiel can be too far from here.'

Ellen turned and made her way back to the car. Setting the offending OS Explorer map firmly to one side, she reached into her basket and pulled out Theo's leather-bound map book. The book had belonged to her husband for as long as she'd known him. Before that it had belonged to his friend, a man called Daniel as far as she could make out from the signature inside the front cover. Theo had rarely travelled without it. She smoothed the soft brown leather. Now it had passed to her; she would use it. Without more ado she turned to the correct page and located Lostwithiel, easily, as it happens, since Theodore had already circled the name with his pencil ... strange, since as far as she could remember, they had never been there. It took her just a moment to find their current position and then she set about tracing a route with her finger, glancing only momentarily at the wedding band that she knew she would always wear.

Still at the gate, Mara was in reflective mood. It was so strange being back in Cornwall without him. Glancing back, she saw that Ellen was already sitting in the car, doors wide open, poring over the map. Her mother was endlessly resourceful. She would find her way. On that thought, Mara shut her eyes against the tears that seemed never far away these days. Lately she had begun to wonder if she was losing hers.

'What do you think, Dad? Am I losing my way? Am I lost already?'

In the quiet afternoon, she heard her own voice. She had spoken the words aloud ... not too loud, but real words, as if he might answer. She shook her head. Despite all appearances to the contrary, despite the face she put on for the world, Theo's brave daughter was bereft. She was no good at this, no good at dealing with death, not this death. He was gone. He was not coming back. Not ever. Door slammed. Abandoned. Again. Fatherless, she felt herself altered, adrift somehow, like her anchor had shifted.

Her phone 'buzzed,' breaking the chain of her thought. 'TIM' wanting 'face-time.' Mara frowned, pressed hard on the red button and shoved the phone back into her pocket. Huffing, she looked over her shoulder to where her mother, eyes closed now, mouth open, seemed to be dozing in the sunshine and for a moment she watched, imagining the gentle snoring that Ellen would deny when awake. Fond, Mara turned her face to the sun and closed her eyes too.

A sudden image of her father, lamp-lit, glimpsed through the half open door of his study, sprang sharp to her mind. She was five or maybe six. He'd been looking at some old photographs, something about a boy. She blinked, opened her eyes. Her thoughts had been wandering. Now they were back, in Kernow, with him. This place, or at least, his sense of the place, had defined him somehow. Mara frowned. That whole 'family heritage' thing – it had been so important to him but she'd never really given it much thought, not until recently. She was part of his story: 'Headmaster's daughter,' 'my eldest,' ' my daughter the writer.' It was how her father spoke of her, how she thought of herself if she were honest. But now his story had come to an end. She sighed. Perhaps it was time – time that she sorted out her own story.

'*And about bloody time too!*' She knew exactly what Tim

would say if he knew what she was thinking. He'd told her, once too often, that she needed to grow up, get over it. '*It's not all about him! Think for yourself! You can't go on blaming your father forever!*' She remembered the anger, the frustration in his voice, but for her it had been the last straw. She'd walked out then – left him '*forever!*' And '*no*' she would not be returning his calls. This time away with her mother was doing her good, giving her space to think. She drummed her fist on the unsuspecting gate and determinedly went back to doing exactly that.

So, if the Cornish ancestors were his, then as far as the 'family tree' was concerned, they were hers too. Mara tapped on the bar of the gate again, as if in a court of law and she making the case. So, was she Cornish? And what would that mean anyway? She hadn't been born in Cornwall. Her parents were just back from Kenya, staying in Uncle Jack's country house somewhere on the outskirts of Bristol, when she was born. But Theo was a Cornishman, through and through. 'Trelawney' was his anthem:

'King James' men shall understand
What Cornish lads can do!'

Eyes closed she could almost hear it, his fine tenor, bouncing up through the branches of the Jacaranda tree, in the garden of their home on the green edge of Nairobi. He'd loved Kenya too – Kenya and Kernow.

The photograph of his grandmother Theodora, all curls and pearls, outside The Old Rectory, the family home in Kernow, had been on display in every home that Mara could remember. Even she could see the likeness that her father was fond of pointing out between the young woman in the photograph and his own eldest daughter. But, now that she thought of it, despite all that talk, all those childhood tales about secret gardens and swings in the orchards, all the Cornish holidays, he had never once taken them to visit The Old Rectory nor introduced them to any actual relatives. In fact she had no idea at all whereabouts in Cornwall the family home might be. He was always so evasive when pressed on the details, defensive almost. There were those stories he'd told when they were children, but otherwise nothing, nothing real anyway.

She knew that his parents had died when he was young in a tragic road accident, somewhere in Egypt or was it East Africa, and that he had been brought up by an old couple, or was it an aunt, in the family home until he was sent away to school. There were a few school photographs – rugby and hockey teams and things like that – but nothing much else. Thinking about it now, she realised that the rest was a blank – a mystery – a mystery he had guarded with his silence, taken to his grave. His grave. Mara shuddered.

'What was that about, Dad? Why were you always so secretive? Was there something to hide?' She realised she was clenching her teeth and forced herself to relax. But the questions were out there on the winds, and a cow browsing nearby paused, turned its head towards the sound. Her pale-blue eyes met its dark-eyed stare. She was not the first to turn away, though her mind was already somewhere else.

'Are you okay then, Mara? Shall we make a move?'

Ellen was awake; her voice broke into the moment. Mara brushed the hair back from her face. She would be 'okay', but she would have to deal with this in her own way. She was a writer. She would write about it, about her father, losing him, finding herself, maybe discovering lost family, something like that. It would make an interesting feature – Kenya/Kernow – the symmetry was perfect – plenty of opportunities for photographs too. Her professional antennae were twitching already. She knew how to do the research. She would 'dig out her roots', 'climb her family tree.' Mara grinned at the easy clichés.

Stepping back from the gate and calling a cheerful farewell to the still champing cattle, the young woman made her way back to the car. Settling into the driving seat, she smiled across at her mother.

'You're using Dad's old map-book. That's nice.'

'It's strange you know. He'd already circled Lostwithiel. I can't imagine why. Here ... look.' Ellen held out the page and they studied it together.

'It must be a sign. We were meant to go there today.' Mara was only half joking as she started up the engine. Ellen adjusted her seatbelt and turned her attention once more to navigation. Theo's leather-bound guide lay open on her lap. The brand-new OS map had been consigned to the basket at her feet.

4

Kenya, Rift Valley – 1961

From the basket meant for vegetables, the night-child's bleating draws on the scrawny sheep and ragged flop-eared goats dawn-grazing the dusty verges. Shouts and whistles from the barefoot goat-boy chafe the morning air, rousing the figure lying slumped at the roadside. The burst of coughing startles the boy and he watches, transfixed, from the safety of a rocky outcrop as Theo sits up and stares around him. Scrambling to his feet, he rubs at his beard, his moustache, his eyes, with bloodied hands. The sickly scent of death makes him gag. Behind him, the twisted metal of the vehicle in the ditch clicks in the rising heat and on the spread blanket, flies are gathering around the eyes and nostrils of the new mother's lifeless body. Somewhere in the distance a lorry sounds its heavy horn.

Grinding and crunching, black smoke belching, the ancient lorry struggles onward up the snaking road out of the Great Rift Valley. Down in the basket, the baby, close-swaddled now in a dusty head-scarf, is sleeping fitfully. Beside the driver, Theo stares blank-faced through the cracked windscreen. Behind him, in the open back of the lorry, half-buried amongst the mounded sacks of charcoal, her body lies shrouded in the blood stained blanket. In the cab the child stirs and he looks down at the tiny boy. His words are soft, scarcely audible above the noisy engine; they might have been a breath: 'Mwanangu … My son.'

'Dust to dust, ashes to ashes.' the brief ceremony plays over and over in his memory: the young priest's voice, the wandering goats, himself beside the hasty grave, in the basket at his feet her child sleeping.

Head in hands, he exhales his sorrow on a long sigh. In the small round hut, acrid scents of wood smoke seep into the mud walls, settle thick over the mattress at his feet. He shifts his weight on the low three-legged stool and his foot prods the empty basket, prompting the question. What will he do now that she is gone? He knows the answer. He must leave too and take the boy, keep him safe from those evil men who would have seized the mother, killed the son. It was her final wish, as she lay dying. She had squeezed his fingers, extracted his promise. He will return to Kernow. Once more he weeps for the terrible loss.

Somewhere not too far away on the Mission Station at Kijabe the motherless child nestles, new-fed, in the arms of another young mother. Her own son, born on Christmas Eve, is sleeping peacefully in the cradle at her feet.

5

Cornwall, Lostwithiel – 2008

From the far side of the stream of weekend traffic heading for the coast, Frank watched wide-eyed as the man in the black leather jacket shook his brother's hand. The two men seemed to know each other – at least it was clear they'd met before. Intrigued, he saw his brother's shaggy-haired nod and caught his quick shout of laughter.

'What the …!' Heedless of the drama unfolding across the road, a white van slowed to a halt, completely blocking his view. Shrugging ruefully, Frank exchanged a grin with the unwitting driver and nudged his wooden handcart out onto the crossing that his mother still called a zebra. Up ahead he caught the ping as the green door of 'The Secret Garden' was opened from the inside, but before he reached the opposite pavement, the two men had disappeared into the depths of the new 'Interior Design and Antiques Emporium'.

As the flow of traffic resumed behind him, Frank stopped, staring up at the artfully scrolled sign over the green door: 'Emporium'. Just a fancy name for a shop as far as he was concerned but, he had to admit, a lot of people seemed to like it – incomers mostly, not locals. Whatever was his brother doing in there?

Frank approached the window and glanced in, but the two men were nowhere to be seen. He was sorely tempted to peer up close through the glass, but thought better of it. Whatever Dan was up to, he certainly wouldn't appreciate being spied on and anyway there wasn't much time to spare for that kind of detective work. He glanced at his watch. The day's schedule for the various groups of musicians and dancers was quite tight and he didn't want to miss his slot outside the church.

Everybody loved a one-man-band. He'd got his programme sorted out but he could be flexible too. He'd try to catch the mood as he usually did – actually he enjoyed the music as much as the audience. That was why he was so popular, or so they said, the people who booked him up for all the local fairs and festivals. Today it was the Lostwithiel Festival or 'Lostfest' as they'd taken to calling it these days – nicely close to home and the sun was shining, for the moment anyway.

Turning the corner into the high street, he saw that it was already buzzing with people. Bunting and balloons decorating the shop fronts and lampposts gave a festive air to the narrow street and rising from somewhere further towards the centre of town, probably from down on the green under the trees beside the river, he could hear the strains of a lively fiddle and an accordion. It was almost certainly one of the groups of Morris dancers that he often met on these occasions. From this distance he couldn't tell which one but they'd be sure to meet up before too long.

As the one-man-band made its way through the festival-goers, an infectious cheerfulness broke out on every side. A group of giggling youths in droopy jeans and identical trainers fell in be-hind him and within minutes he was the Pied Piper pursued by a noisy crowd of youngsters – many with parents and grandparents in tow.

Frank was in his element now, beaming as his two-wheeled handcart bumped ahead of him on the cobbled street. He could hear the drum that he would strap to his back jostling about inside. In fact all the tools of his trade, including his precious banjo, were contained in that trolley. His mother always said it reminded her of the old stop-me-and-buy-one ice-cream sellers from her child-hood. This one he had designed himself and had it made especially so that he could carry with him everything he would need for his performances. The musical notes and motifs painted in gold across the sides were his own handiwork but the rainbow coloured capital letters of his name 'The Music Man' had been painted by Maisy, his brother's Cornish pixie of a daughter. She must have been about nine or ten back then, just before her mother had packed up one night and taken the beloved girl away with her back to London. Six, nearly seven years it must be, or perhaps it was even longer than that now that he came to think of it. He sighed.

Ahead of him now he could hear the claps and cheers of the crowd who had just been enjoying the performance by a group called Barefoot Jazz. They were good. The trombone player Baz was an old friend of his. They'd known each other from way back.

'Hey, mate. How're you doing?' Baz called across the square as Frank steered his 'Music Man' box into position, lowering the red handles, which neatly turned into front legs and kept everything upright and secure.

'Not bad. Yourself?'

'Yeah. Good, thanks. Great day for it. Not like last year. Remember that downpour? The day was an absolute wash out.'

'Sure was.' How could Frank forget? The soggy top hat, the spoiled drum… Things could only get better as far as he was concerned. He lifted the lid of his box of tricks and started to set out the props for his performance: the small black amplifier, his CDs and the advertising stand he'd made, his banjo case in which he collected the money and the painted sign saying 'Thanks!'

'See you later then, down at the Red Lion?' The rest of the Barefoot Jazz band had left the square now and were well on their way to their next venue. Baz went to follow after them then turned back.

'Oh, by the way, I was surprised to hear about your mother's old place, the sale and all that?'

Baz had not expected the reaction he saw now on his friend's face. Shock was it? Surprise certainly. 'What d'you mean … sale? What sort of sale? Who told you that?'

'Betty Roper, you know, she works down at the Co-op now. She said she saw the article about it in the free paper, and an advert with the date, some of the items for sale, that sort of thing. I haven't seen it myself.'

Frank could think of nothing to say. There was nothing he could say. He knew nothing about it at all. There must be some mistake. He had to speak to Dan. An expectant crowd was gathering in the square, attracted by the colourful spectacle he made, unaware that the music had been knocked right out of their favourite 'Music Man'.

Dan shifted awkwardly in the gilded chair that looked like some kind of throne. It creaked as he moved and, with his hands gripping the arms, he leaned forward to look down through his own at the chair's gold-painted legs. 'Pretentious rubbish,' he muttered under his breath, recognising the piece for what it was despite its price tag. He righted himself, raked his fingers through his curls and coughed to clear his throat. His mouth felt dry. He could really do with a drink; a coffee would be good. How much longer were they planning on keeping him waiting?

There were no windows in the room and he supposed the lighting was designed to be subtle. The velvet of the matching throne glowed from the other side of the marble fireplace, reflecting the light from a standard lamp in the corner and on the polished wooden writing table another lamp radiated a welcoming bonhomie. An artist himself, Dan recognised artifice when he saw it. Glossy magazines fanned on the glass-topped coffee table and amber liquid glinted in a cut glass decanter alongside other expensive-looking bottles on the sideboard. There was even sparkling water. Dan knew that the drinks were simply window dressing but if they didn't come back soon he was going to help himself.

'Right then, Daniel.' The door was opened and swiftly closed behind him by the speaker, who entered just in time to prevent Dan raiding the drinks tray. 'It seems he's interested, very interested. In fact ...' and on this point the left eyebrow arched disconcertingly, '... he even went so far as to say that one or two of the items on your list ... well, he's been keen to get hold of them for a very long time.' The nod in Dan's direction was strangely suggestive. Settling himself briskly onto the vacant throne the man adjusted the sleeves of his black leather jacket and absently flicked a piece of fluff from the knee of his jeans. Dan was certain they were 'designer' as was everything about him, right down to the neat little beard.

'So he's agreed the prices – and the deadline.' Dan could barely conceal his relief. 'He knows the deadline's critical?'

The snort of amusement was nasal, almost a sneer. 'Now hold on; hold on just one moment Daniel. He didn't exactly go that far. He merely said that he would like to meet you, to see what you have. He's interested in the artwork particularly, and one or two pieces of the jewellery, I think, also some of the Lamu furniture. Apparently his daughter has a new house that she's keen to furnish in that dark wood, carved African style. It's very desirable at the moment.' Again the arched eyebrow, though the smile he flicked across at Dan was pinched. The manicured finger waving back and forth was definitely irritating.

'Fine. But there's been a lot of other interest, you know, since it went on-line. I need to know he's serious, your client, Mr Uhuru, did you say his name was?' Dan was not to be intimidated.

'Actually, his name is Freeman, John Freeman. 'Uhuru' is the name of his company.' The man smiled tightly, amused at the joke. Seeing no sign of appreciation on Dan's face, he spoke again, as if to a child – or an idiot. '*Uhuru* is the Swahili word for *Freedom*. Clever don't you think, his name being *Free*man?'

Dan was unimpressed. 'Well whatever his name is, he needs to understand, there's a deadline here, and he's in danger of missing it.' The flash of adrenaline had spoken; it left him weakened. He drew in a long breath, folded his arms across his chest. The two men eyed each other. It was not Dan who blinked first.

'Give me a minute.' The man rose and made for the door. Once more Dan found himself alone. He let his arms flop to his sides, flexed his fingers. He considered the sofa, but decided to remain standing. After a few minutes the door opened and the man was back.

'I've spoken to his agent in London. He is flying in from Nairobi next Friday. He'll be in the country for about a week, perhaps longer. He has some personal business to conduct. But he is very keen to meet you while he is here. I'll call you to arrange the meeting – if you're still interested that is.'

Dan nodded, buttoned his jacket, preparing to leave. 'I'll wait to hear from you then.' He moved towards the door. The man in black nodded in acknowledgement and they exited the room together.

'The town's really busy today. Good day for the festival.' They were making small talk now as they moved out into the central, more public areas of the 'Secret Garden' antiques emporium. Through a stone archway Dan could see the garden and courtyard that gave the business its name. The display of weathered statuary and other garden features was certainly impressive and he had to admit that, apart from its size of course, the garden looked like something that might have belonged to the National Trust. Strolling in the sunshine, admiring the items on display, were some very well-heeled couples. They looked more comfortable in this setting than Dan felt at the moment and, today's business having moved closer to a successful conclusion, he was now keen to leave.

'Mr Stevens, excuse me, Mr Stevens.' From a small reception area off of the entrance foyer a young woman's voice called to catch her boss's attention. 'The envelope, sir. Have you forgotten the envelope?' The smart-suited Emily – she was wearing a name badge Dan noted – was waving a large official-looking envelope and smiling her question towards the man in black.

'Ah, Emily. Thank you. What would I do without you?' He smiled at her, condescendingly Dan thought, and she blushed. 'I almost forgot.' This time he was addressing Dan. 'There are some papers in here for you to sign. You know the sort of thing, confirming provenance, your right to sell, that sort of thing. We must make sure that everything is done properly mustn't we?'

'But of course.' Dan's reply was business-like. He straightened his shoulders, standing taller, like he did this kind of business every day of the week. 'I'll have everything completed in time for our next meeting, don't you worry. Mr John Freeman – 'Uhuru' – has nothing to fear from me.' He laughed. The man in the designer outfit didn't. A brief nod, a handshake and he found himself once again out on the pavement, clutching the official looking envelope and feeling more than a little pleased with the way things were coming together. Turning on his heel, he walked resolutely in the direction of the High Street.

Flags, balloons, crowds of people. For a moment Dan was confused. Caught up in his own affairs he had temporarily forgotten about the festival. The pub across the road looked crowded and he couldn't face meeting up with Frank at this point. His brother was sure to be in the thick of it somewhere. He turned his back on the noise and bustle and made for the crossing that was the only way on a busy afternoon like this one to get to the other side of this river of traffic.

'Come on, come on. Don't you know you're meant to stop at these things?' Dan glared his frustration at the unwitting drivers as they kept resolutely nose to tail over his crossing. They really should put lights here. He considered stepping out onto the crossing anyway. They'd have to stop then. Just as he was about to do something desperate, the green Clio drew to a halt. From the passenger seat, the older lady smiled in his direction and beside her the young woman driver nodded patiently.

'Well, thank you ladies.'

He nodded back and with a wave of his envelope he crossed to safety. He would fetch his car and drive for a bit, clear his head before going to see his mother.

'Look! There's one, over there, on that telegraph pole, by the bus shelter.' The bright red posters were unmistakeable, with a Royalist cavalier pointing the way to the Festival. They'd spotted the first one as soon as they had pulled out onto the main road.

'I don't think it's far now. I reckon that this is West Taphouse – yes, there's the sign. So Lostwithiel should be just a couple of miles down the road.' Ellen had sighed then, shut the map-book and settled back to enjoy the rest of the journey. But now with their destination in sight, the cavalier seemed to have abandoned them. No more posters. The road that had brought them to the town of Lostwithiel seemed to be fast taking them out the other side.

'I'm going to have to pull in somewhere or at least pull off of this road or we'll miss it completely. I'm taking the next turning left.' Up ahead, a sign said 'Antiques Fair'. Was that part of the festival? They would soon find out – the turning was just after the zebra crossing. Mara slowed the car to a halt and she and her mother watched as the man in the green corduroy jacket stepped out in front of them, lifting a large white envelope and nodding briefly in their direction.

'Nice jacket.' Mara grinned, nodded back. The car behind tapped his horn. 'Alright, alright, be patient.'

Mara pulled forward over the crossing, resisting the temptation to look back to see where the man in the green jacket was heading. For some reason he had caught her interest. Perhaps they'd see him again somewhere around the festival, if they ever found it that is. The left turn seemed promising. She took it and was rewarded with a red cavalier pointing the way to the Community Centre.

But the car park at the front of the Centre was completely full - even the grassy verges were parked up. There was no room to turn round either. Mara was on the point of reversing back up the narrow lane and out of the whole affair when her mother touched her arm.

'Look, I think they're leaving, over there in the corner.'

A wave from the couple getting into to a muddied Land Rover stopped Mara just in the nick of time. She returned the nod as the driver edged past, and with some relief she eased the Clio into the space he had just vacated.

Ellen tucked the map-book underneath her seat. She was ready to explore now and the sign over the entrance to the centre promised: 'Antiques and Collectables.' There was nothing she enjoyed more. The prospect of an hour or two's browsing filled her with delight. She said as much to her daughter.

'I'll stay up here, if that's all right with you, dear. I'll enjoy having a potter around the sale. You go on down, have a look around the town, see what's going on. What do you think? Shall we meet back here at four o'clock, say, for a cup of tea?' Ellen was keen to get going.

Mara knew that her mother could spend hours amongst the antique stalls but for herself she liked to wander, to go with the flow. She fancied listening to a bit of country music. Dancing – she would find some dancing and have a browse around the craft stalls that were meant to be down by the river.

'Good plan. Look, I'll follow that sign over there, that's where everybody else seems to be heading.' She leaned forward and gathered up her red satchel bag, checking for her purse and sunglasses. 'I'll see you back here at four, in the teashop and then if there's anything interesting going on in the centre later on, we can walk back down together after tea if you feel like it.'

The plan suited them both and, leaving the Clio safely ensconced in the shade beneath the oak tree, the two women happily set off on an afternoon of exploration.

'Leave them alone, and they'll come home ...'

Rose was humming softly. Sometimes her lips moved. But were the words in her head or was she singing out loud? She could no longer be sure. Through the window, she studied the clouds as they drifted, insubstantial, like lambs in blue fields of sky. 'Little Bo-peep has lost her sheep and doesn't know where to find them, leave them alone and they'll come home, bringing their tails behind them.' Rose smiled. They always came home. She remembered. But where would they come now?

Shaking her head, she closed her eyes, opened them again, wide, like windows onto this strange new world. Where were they? Where was she? Suddenly, she was afraid. 'Home, come home ...' She felt the cry in her voice as tears spilled over, wet on her cheek.

'What's the matter, Rose? You're crying, my love.' The nurse in her blue uniform bustled into the room, carrying some towels.

Rose smiled at the young woman whose name she thought was Rachel through the tears that she herself didn't quite understand.

'You remember me don't you? I'm Rachel. Look, here are some tissues.' She passed the box across towards the chair where Rose was sitting by the window. 'Wipe those tears away and I'll fetch you some tea. Is your son Dan coming to see you this afternoon? He often pops in on a Sunday afternoon doesn't he?'

Rose couldn't be sure about who was coming to see her. She felt so confused these days. Who was Dan? The nurse had said Dan might come … Dan. Then she remembered little Danny, her brother's boy. 'Boys and girls come out to play; the moon doth shine as bright as day.' The nursery rhyme played through her memory and she smiled as she watched them playing – Theo, Frank, Dan, Maisy. There they were dancing about on the lawn outside of the old house, her house, The Old Rectory. The Old Rectory, her parents' house, her brother's house, her home. But where was her home now? She frowned, shook her head. She was afraid again. Panic rose tight in her throat. She could taste it, thick and dry on her tongue. Where were the children now? Where was she? Wide-eyed, she looked around the room with the single bed, the pink bed cover, the bedside table, the deep pink carpet, the coffee table with a big pink plant in the middle, the two small armchairs. She looked down at the plum-coloured armchair where she was sitting. It looked as if she lived here now. She could see some of her dresses through the slightly open cupboard door. When did she come to live here?

The door opened.

'Here he is. I told you he was coming, didn't I.' Nurse Rachel eased her way into the room balancing a plastic tray on which Rose could see two white mugs of tea and two pieces of fruit cake. Behind the nurse, his hand still resting on the door handle stood a tall man in a green corded jacket, his grey-flecked curls tucked behind his ear. He was carrying a large white envelope. He entered and seemed to fill the room, as the heavy door closed behind him. She watched him as he stepped around her coffee table then leaned forward to kiss her. Rose offered him her cheek. She remembered his spicy fragrance. He sat down warily into the small armchair. He seemed tired.

'How're you feeling today then, Rose?'

Rose looked across at him, surprise dawning behind her blue-grey eyes, a slight frown on her wrinkled forehead. No, she was not his mother, this was not her son. She could not remember his mother. She had held him as a baby but he was Theodore's boy, her brother's son. The old woman shook her head. 'No! No! No!'

The young nurse and the man in the armchair looked on as Rose shook her head again and again. She was becoming agitated now, waving her hands, trying to push them away. They both stood and the man leaned forward, reaching out to touch Rose gently on the shoulder. The touch seemed to steady her and she relaxed under his hand. Her eyes were closed now. She leaned back into her chair and seemed to doze. The man and the woman waited. Sensing that the moment had passed the nurse slipped out of the door, shutting it softly behind her. The man leaned back into his own chair. He would wait a while.

He opened his eyes. He must have dropped off. She was watching him, alert now.

'Dan. I'm glad you came. Drink your tea. Would you like some cake? They make very nice fruit cake here. Did you bring little Maisy? I haven't seen her for such a long time. Are you taking me home today? I want to go home now. I want to see the roses, my beautiful roses. I was named for the roses, you know. Rose, rose-red, red rose. Ring a ring of roses, a pocket full of posies.' She was smiling at her memories, lips moving, talking to her dreams. But were the words in the room or inside her head?

Rose felt them, the questions, the answers … rolling around in her mind, bouncing off each other. Words and phrases, bubbling up from somewhere deep inside cascaded unchecked from her lips. She was a river, a flood, a waterfall. 'Many waters cannot quench love neither can the floods overcome it.' The old words sang through her memory. Rose was the river, she was the flood, now she was falling, falling. She cried out for help but there was only silence.

As Rachel and another young nurse lifted the old lady from the chair and settled her under the pink cover on the single bed, smoothing the pillow, touching her cheek, Dan slipped out of the room, taking the envelope with him. He would look in again tomorrow and check to see if she was all right. He was confident that all would be well. It had to be.

For the first time in his fifteen years as a one-man band, Frank had found it a real struggle to get himself going. The easy banter that was key to his relationship with his audiences just wasn't flowing. Of course he had still played his set like he always did, and the crowd had laughed and clapped and danced in the usual way, but the music man's jollity had been an act – an empty act that he was glad to have finished. He had fifteen minutes free now before his next slot down on the green beside the river. He should just about have time to pick up a copy of the free paper from the Co-op and check out the article that Baz had told him about.

The Old Rectory had been in his mother's family for generations. It was filled with memories and memorabilia collected over the years, treasures brought back from their travels in Africa, and with so many photographs. Despite his current mood, Frank grinned at the thought of all those photographs, large and small, in frames and albums, all around the house. Rose should give guided tours. She knew the names of practically everyone, down to the tiniest African toto. How could anyone be thinking that these things would be up for sale by public auction? There must be some mistake. He knew that a certain well-known property company had made approaches in the past, a few years ago now, with a view to purchasing the land for some kind of upmarket holiday complex, but their advances had been rejected in no uncertain terms by his mother. Even now he smiled at the memory. She had certainly given them short shrift. She was a force to be reckoned with when roused, a strong-willed, feisty woman, passionate in the defence of all that she held dear. Her home was her heritage, her family's heritage. He knew that she would never have knowingly sanctioned a public sale, not in a million years.

Nevertheless the mention of the article had worried him.

Circumstances had certainly changed in the last year he had to admit that, and since her illness his precious mother Rose had never really recovered. In fact, as her old friend Esme who specialised in clichés had said, she was left a shadow of her former self, and indeed the change had been heart-breaking to see for all those who loved her. It was getting on for a year now since her doctors had reluctantly suggested that it would be best for her to spend some time in the nursing home down in the town and to their surprise she had agreed, with no argument whatsoever. If he was honest, he doubted now that she would ever be able to return to her own home and the thought made him sad to his heart.

Bumping his barrow down the narrow high street, his thoughts with his mother, the Music Man did not notice until too late the young woman who stepped out directly into his path. She was scrabbling about for something in the depths of a huge red shoulder bag, which now spilled its contents on the pavement around them.

'I'm so sorry. Are you all right? You just stepped out, right in front of me.' He didn't know quite what to do next, shocked, unsure whether to be apologetic or angry.

'Ouch!' The young woman grimaced, rubbing at her left ankle and on her shin there was a trickle of blood from the graze where the sharp corner of the music box had knocked into her. 'What are you doing, charging along with that thing without looking where you're going?' She scowled up at him.

'What do you mean, me not looking where I was going? It was you who just stepped out in front of me!' He propped up his barrow and bent to pick up some of the items from her bag that were strewn haphazard under its wheels: tissues, lipstick, hairbrush, car keys, a black moleskin notebook, some pencils ... a couple of interested onlookers had stooped to help now and soon all of her personal effects seemed to have been returned to their rightful owner. She was dabbing one of the tissues against the graze on her shin and seemed to be gradually recovering her equilibrium. She looked up and even managed a smile as she returned the thankfully undamaged pair of sunglasses to the reassembled red bag.

'I guess you're right. It was probably my fault. But I just didn't expect to be run down by a speeding runaway one-man band. You should be banned you know.' She chuckled at her own joke. 'I was just trying to put my purse away safely before getting out into the crowd again. I bought some Cornish fudge. Here, would you like a piece?' She was standing in front of him now with her peace-offering. He accepted a piece of the fudge.

'Thanks. You made a good choice. I happen to know that they make the best fudge in town.' He grinned and struggled to stop himself from dribbling – it certainly came in very large chunks.

'It's a great day for the festival. The music's good too.'

He nodded, chewing on the sweet, sticky fudge. He glanced at his watch. His fifteen minute break was nearly up and he still had to get to the riverside pitch and set up. There would never be time to go to the Co-op now to pick up a paper. He would have to do that later. She spotted his time-check.

'Sorry. I've delayed you enough already. Where're you playing next? I'll come and watch. It's a long time since I've seen a one-man band.'

'I'm playing down by the river in about three minutes from now. I'll be a bit late starting but you take your time. I'll look out for you.' He began to move off.

'Watch where you're going now – you might bump into someone,' Mara called after him and he waved as he disappeared into the crowd. Actually there really was quite a crowd now, bustling about the pavements, spilling over the roadway like a multi-coloured millrace, making their way downstream to hear their favourite band.

Clutching the red bag in front of her – she didn't plan to scatter the contents for a second time – Mara stepped off the pavement and was at once swept up in the flow. She grinned up at the baby face bobbing along in front of her, over its daddy's shoulder and was rewarded with a smile. Nice. She liked kids, got on well with them, made a great aunty – she was even Godmother to a couple of her friend's children – but she had never really thought she would have any of her own. The truth was, she supposed, that she'd never met the right man. A memory of Tim's face sprang to mind and she wrinkled her nose. Actually, there'd been one or two who had come close, but somehow they'd never really matched up.

Looking about her, across the busy street, Mara noticed the bright window display of draped velvets and black and white photographs. She decided to make her way over and have a look. Old photographs always fascinated her. One of her favourite childhood pastimes had been exploring the family albums. Her mother was a great compiler and the albums had a whole bookcase of their own, even back then. But, though Ellen took such care with the photos themselves, she was completely care-less of the volumes in which they were bound. The ones that had been bought while they were in Nairobi were particularly garish, covered with Swiss mountain scenes, improbably bright blue waters of Norwegian lakes and Germanic looking castles perched high on fluorescent green hillsides. But it was between these unlikely covers that their African adventures were stored. At that time her father had been very fond of photography and his young family seemed always to be smiling.

Mara was smiling now, at memories first, and then at the recollection of her more recent collision with the one-man band. She would just have a quick look at these photographs and then she would make her way down towards the river, where he would be performing. He seemed nice – at least he seemed to have a sense of humour, which was more than you could say for a lot of men these days, or the ones she had met anyway.

The men in the old photographs all seemed very serious, not a smile between them. Mara leaned in so that her forehead was almost touching against the glass, as her attention was caught first by several interesting images grouped together in shades of grey on the velvet cloth. Swarthy, oil-skinned men, mostly thick-bearded, beside what she took to be an old lifeboat; weathered fishermen in front of tilting beached boats; neck-tied men in tight-buttoned coats grouped outside of the church – members of a local male-voice choir according to the label – and several photographs of what looked to be a young squire, or perhaps it was a clergyman, with various groupings of men who seemed to be labourers, in front of a large country house.

Mara was just wondering where all the women were, when something snagged at her attention. She stopped and looked back at the last group of images. There it was. One of the men was black, an African. She peered in closer and read the label: 'Members of the Cornwall Workers Educational Association with Jomo Kenyatta at the Old Rectory – 1938.' Jomo Kenyatta, the first president of Kenya. She stepped back, looking around her at the festive crowd. Then, once more, she leaned in towards the window, only this time she was trying to get a closer look at the detail, not of the men, but of the house that was their backdrop. Surely she had seen it before. The name was the same certainly, but then, there must be plenty of big old houses called the Old Rectory in Cornwall. But how many of them had been visited by Jomo Kenyatta?

In her father's boyhood story, before Kenyan Independence, long before he'd become president, Kenyatta had visited the Old Rectory in Kernow. And this really did look familiar – so much like the old house that had been the backdrop for the lovely Theodora, even down to the roses. It would be an improbable coincidence indeed, Mara realised, if just a few hours after she had decided to explore her Cornish connections, she should have made such a significant discovery. Nevertheless, despite the fact that it was improbable, it was still possible.

Excited at the prospect, she headed for the doorway, determined to find out more about the old house in the photographs, only to discover that that the shop was closed until the following morning at ten o'clock, according to the hand-written notice on the door. The disappointment was irrational, but there was nothing she could do about it now. All she had to do was to persuade her mother that they should return to Lostwithiel tomorrow, or at least, sometime soon. Mara wondered whether she should explain her reasons for wanting to come back – maybe Ellen would not want to become involved in this kind of thing so soon after his death. Perhaps even to suggest it would seem insensitive. Still mulling it over, she moved away from the shop and headed downstream in the direction of the one-man band.

The Old Rectory looked sad, in the original sense of the word that is, not 'sad' as in 'totally embarrassing' the way his daughter had used it to describe the green corduroy jacket that he'd been wearing the last time he'd seen her. Dan grinned. He remembered he'd caught the early train up to London just for the day to meet up with her and that was the first thing she had said, after the hug they had shared on the busy station concourse.

'Dad, that jacket is so sad.'

Maisy was laughing as she said it, teasing, and he had reached out, ruffling her curls as she squealed and grabbed at his hands. He remembered that her mother had hardly met his eyes as she'd handed over their daughter – her instructions about the time and place for meeting up at the end of the day had been conveyed to Maisy in his hearing rather than directly to him. It was so strange; hard to think now of the things they'd once thought they'd shared. A kiss for her daughter, and she'd gone, almost before he knew it, just like the day she'd left him, taking Maisy with her, and him all alone.

But that day had been his to spend with his little girl, not so little now. They'd had a great time. His daughter was really good company and the hours had passed by in a flash of trendy clothes shops and coffee shops, picking favourites in the National Portrait Gallery and applauding some amazing open-air opera singers in Covent Garden market. He realised with a shock now that it was well over a year ago. Things had become difficult, complicated, since then he told himself.

Dan breathed in deep and slow as he looked about him now. This place was in his bones. He knew it. It knew him. All at once he was overtaken by images from his childhood. He saw himself with curly-hair, short-trousers, little blue duffle coat. He heard his six-year-old voice: 'Wait for me Frank, wait for me!' as he ran behind his big brother over the gravel drive and across the grass, towards their favourite tree and the morning's haul of shiny conkers. Dan grinned. Wherever Frank was, his little brother was never far behind. He frowned. He'd have to face Frank soon, but not yet.

Thinking about the conkers, he reached down into the pockets of his grown-up green jacket and his fingers caught the rounded edge of a piece of turquoise sea-glass. He was always doing it, picking up bits and pieces, collecting conkers, acorns, sometimes pebbles, stones, shells, anything that caught his imagination. Now he picked out the piece of sea-glass and held it up to the light. Even through the turquoise eyeglass, the old place did indeed look sad, lonely he thought as he looked up towards the high gabled window of his childhood bedroom. His treasures were still there, stored in jars and bottles, in cardboard boxes and on wooden shelves, collections of shells and pebbles that were dearer to him even now than the more costly toys stored alongside had ever been. The carriages, engines, scenery and track of the old Hornby train set, still with all the original boxes would, he knew, fetch a lot of money at the forthcoming sale as would many of the other mechanical toys and teddy bears – a couple of them Steif – that his father, or at least his father's agent, had regularly sent him for birthdays and sometimes Christmas. They had not brought him joy. They had not brought his father. Now they would bring him what he needed. He was the father now. He needed funds – for his daughter, for Maisy.

From his left hand pocket he took out the familiar bundle of keys and sorting through them he quickly isolated the one that he wanted. He knew it, even without reading the little white sticky label: main door. The stone porch was cold and it smelt damp as Dan fiddled with the key in the lock. There was a knack to making it turn and he hadn't lost it. Grasping the black metal door handle, he pulled it firmly towards him and turned the key clockwise, not anti-clockwise as people usually did to unlock doors. Sure enough he felt the release and the heavy door opened inwards.

6

Cornwall - 1962

The sitting room at the Old Rectory is decorated for Christmas, in reds and greens and lots of white candles. Garlands of holly and ivy are strung across the mantelpiece and lying along the top of the piano. Crepe paper trimmings are hanging from the picture rails and the candles have been lit. There are even balloons. The little boy's laughter fills the room in celebration of the season and of his own first birthday. Beating on a bright tin drum beside the festive tree, he is a picture of delight.

At the piano, a young lad of about four or perhaps five years of age, has clambered onto the music-stool and is rehearsing with one finger what sounds to be the opening notes of 'Happy Birthday to you'.

'Well done, son.'

Standing with his back to the fire his father, a tall man with a full black beard lifts his pipe in greeting to the young woman who nudges her way into the room and heads towards the festive table. She sets down her tray and, off-loading plates of sausage rolls and sandwiches, smiles across at her husband.

Beside the fire, the younger man, her brother Theo, has settled himself into the armchair. He seems thoughtful, twirling at the edge of his moustache, flicking his foot to the rhythm of some inner dialogue. A grin lights his face as the birthday-boy holds out the drumsticks towards him. He jiggles his fingers and the little boy laughs. The child is happy here. It helps. This decision has not been easy. In other circumstances he might have made a different choice, but for now he can see no other way. His silence and his absence are the debt that he owes. The letters that arrived from Nairobi just yesterday via his agent in London have simply confirmed things. The old school out in the Rift Valley has been sold. Uncle Charles will not be returning to Kenya and there are matters to be sorted. Jack has found some land on the edge of Nairobi for a new school, out near the Ngong Hills. It is fitting and it is time. And there is other work to be done. Theo is resolved. He will leave Kernow without delay. After one final meeting with his solicitors, he will return to Kenya.

His sister beckons. She offers food. Her smile is warm. Theo nods and makes to rise, but there is no smile in his eyes. His thoughts are with the child. The boy will stay.

The two men push back the dark leather chairs and rise almost simultaneously. The older, stepping out from behind the wooden desk approaches Theo who offers his hand in anticipation of the handshake.

All is in order. The child will be raised by the young man's sister Rose and her husband Edward at the family home in Cornwall. Each year on his birthday and at Christmas the boy will receive a gift via his father's agent, but there will be no further communications. A more-than-adequate financial provision has been made for this and for the boy's subsequent education. All the necessary arrangements for his inheritance are established in the pile of recently signed documentation, which lies on the desk of the solicitor who is an old and trusted friend of the family.

The firm will also retain custody of the package, including the wooden box and one or two letters, plus a few other items for security, until such time as the younger man sees fit.

Their business concluded, the portly solicitor moves across to a side table and pours them both a drink from the crystal decanter. In response to a nod from his young friend, he adds a splash of water from the matching jug. The older man, drinking, anticipates lunch. As Theo sets his glass back down onto the tray there is a look of something like sadness in his eyes.

7

Cornwall – 2008

It was the silence that bothered him most. He coughed – the air inside the old house was chilled and dusty. The sound jangled in the silence, like the bunch of keys that he still held in his hand. With the heavy door closed behind him, Dan stood as if stranded on the faded Persian rug that he'd known since childhood. The grown man imagined himself marooned in shark-infested waters, steel-grey stones lurking. He shivered. He tried to remember if he had ever been in the house alone. Surely he must have been, but he knew that he had never felt this loneliness before. The life had gone from the place; even the air felt emptied. He coughed again, a shallow cough, clearing his throat. The noise was too loud. He wanted to call it back before someone heard and demanded to know his business. The idea was ridiculous of course. No one was here.

'Hello!' His voice came out croakily. He called again, this time with more confidence. 'Hello! Anybody there?'

He waited. No answer. Of course there was no answer you fool. He laughed nervously, but he felt better, now that the awful silence had been broken. He stepped off the rug onto the flagstones; caught himself trying not to step on the lines. He smiled. Today's business was actually up on the first floor but he was drawn as always down the hallway towards the big family kitchen at the back of the house.

Nothing had changed. The long oak table still stood, right there, in the centre of the room. But something was different. The heavy wooden chairs were all tucked in along the sides and one at either end. Someone had obviously been in and cleaned up the place. The chairs would never have been tucked in neatly like this when Rose was there. They would have been pulled out, random, as if the previous occupant had just left, ready to welcome the next. Someone was always sitting at the table, usually with a mug of tea, a slice of cake, or something else that Rose had offered.

Dan had a sudden, unwelcome memory of Rose as he'd seen her earlier – so changed, smaller somehow and vulnerable in ways that were hard to understand. She'd scarcely seemed to recognise him at first. That had really caught him by surprise, knocked him off balance. Frowning, he pulled out one of the heavy chairs and sat down at the end of table.

Rose was not his real mother. When she had first told him, he'd felt confused. It was his seventh birthday. At that same kitchen table, she had shared with him the little she knew of his birth and of his father, her younger brother. Together they'd opened the parcel that had arrived earlier in the post, his father's birthday gift. His father had sent gifts regularly throughout his childhood and the occasional postcard, but as far as Dan could remember they had never met. All Rose told him about her brother was that he was working in Africa. The last time Dan had heard anything from him was on his thirteenth birthday.

Dan had hardly thought about him at all after that. As a child he'd looked in the old atlas in the library and realised that Africa was another continent, much too far away to visit. He couldn't imagine that the Royal Mail would be able to deliver any letters he wrote to thank his father either so he didn't think about it anymore. Rose had already explained to him that the birthday presents were sent from his father's agent in London. How else could the gifts have been purchased in places like Harrods, which even Dan knew was a massive store in London? The young boy had listened quietly as Rose had explained that the hot, far-distant place where his father was working would not be suitable for a little boy – and anyway she wanted Dan here in Cornwall, with her, because he was precious.

Rose was Frank's real mother but there had never seemed to be any difference between them. Frank was his older brother, his hero, back then and still today, if he was honest. A lot of water had certainly gone under the bridge since the days when they had played and fought and practised their music together – Frank on the piano, later the guitar, and young Dan on the flute – but the friendship between them was still strong. They were not the same of course – Dan knew that he would never be as steady and strong, as reliable, and definitely not as good a musician as his older brother – but each had always known that they could depend upon the other.

Thinking about Frank now made Dan's heart beat faster. He felt suddenly hot and the familiar tension churned his stomach. The feeling was guilt – he acknowledged it. He felt guilty. There it was – guilt. He knew that none of this should be happening behind Frank's back. He should have talked about it with him. He knew that he should. In the silent kitchen he wished he had. There would certainly have been an argument. Frank would not have agreed to anything without Rose being consulted. Not at first. But when he understood how important it was for Maisy, he might have come around. Anyway, it was too late now. Frank would find out and there might be trouble but until then Dan knew that he would try to stay as far away from his older brother as possible.

The chair legs scraped across the flagstone floor as Dan stood up. He would not tuck the chair back in like the others – he left it out, waiting. Back in the hallway he felt the nervous feeling again – as if somebody might be upstairs, watching him through the banisters, like he had used to watch when he was a boy. He looked up. Nothing stared back at him through the wooden rails on the galleried first floor landing. At the bottom of the broad stair-case, the door to the sitting room was ajar. He hesitated, his foot already on the first stair.

Even the dark brown chips in the layered cream paintwork were familiar to him as, in response to his nudge the door swung open, revealing chintzy cushioned sofas and armchairs, the broad tapestry footstool, the coffee table strewn with gardening magazines, in the far corner the piano.

Dan's eyes slid over each familiar detail, as he moved

towards the mantelpiece, drawn as always to the family photographs. From amongst them, he picked up the silver-framed image of his father as a young man standing at the doorway of a hut made of mud with a grass roof. Beside him was a short, black-skinned man – the elder of the tribe according to Rose – wearing a leather apron around his waist, on his head a feathery headdress that Rose had said was made from the black and white skin of a Colobus monkey. It had seemed to Dan at the time that Rose knew more about the African than she did about her brother. All Dan could tell from the black and white image was that his father had quite light, rather bushy, perhaps curly hair, that his nose was long and straight over a full moustache, that he was not particularly tall – not what you'd call thin, but not fat either – and that he was nothing like his son. Dan set the picture back down in its place on the mantelpiece and glanced at his reflection in the large gilt-framed mirror that had always hung above the fireplace. No. He was nothing like his father.

Turning from the mirror, his eyes fell on the familiar photograph of Rose's grandmother, with her flowing curls and warm smile just like Rose. She seemed to be dressed up for some special occasion, wearing pearls, posing in front of the rose-covered stone porch. He smiled, and then, leaving the door ajar as he had found it, he stepped back into the empty hallway and set his foot on the bottom stair.

Ellen almost missed it. It was the blue jug that had first drawn her towards the tables, squashed in right up next to the stage. Everything about the little jug was a delight, especially the price. Reaching into her bag for her purse, Ellen glanced down and it was only then that she spotted the stack of watercolours, propped up against the leg of the old dining table that had been used to display the items for today's sale. While the lady popped across to the neighbouring stall to get change for the proffered ten-pound note, Ellen knelt and flipped idly through what seemed to be a collection of largely amateur paintings of beach and countryside views.

In this company, the picture of the old house stood out. Ellen picked it from the stack and held it up to the light. She didn't recognise the artist's name – it looked like Daniel something or other, the signature was scarcely legible – but as she took in the detail of the house with its gables and its central stone porch, there was definitely something familiar. The pink and red roses rambling over the front of the old house seemed captured in sunlight. This artist was certainly in a class of his own.

'You've picked a good one there.' The lady was back with her change and now she interrupted Ellen's inspection of the painting. 'I don't often get pieces of his. Once folk get hold of them they usually hang on to them ... especially his coastal scenes and the seascapes. Old Cornish houses too ... that's another of his specialities ... they're often commissioned by the owners, but people love his flowers. There are always flowers.'

'Yes, these roses are really good, the detail's fantastic. But I was also interested in the house itself – it seems familiar. Do you know it?' Ellen had already decided to buy the painting but her curiosity was aroused.

'Course I do. Everyone around here knows it. It's the Old Rectory.' She paused but there was no recognition in her customer's eyes. 'You haven't heard of it then? Goodness, I remember going up there when I was a girl. They used to hold the Sunday school picnics up there in the gardens every summer. I remember those roses too. Always a real picture they were.'

'Did you say 'the Old Rectory'?' Ellen was looking more closely at the picture now.

'Yes. That's its name, but people round here often call it the Manor.'

'Is it far from here then?'

'Not far. Have you got a car? It's a bit off the beaten track, you know. You'd never get there by bus. We used to go up on the farm cart when I was little, but later they sometimes booked a charabanc – what fun that was!' She grinned and tapped her hand lightly against Ellen's arm.

'My daughter drives. She's off enjoying the music down in

the town. I'm meeting up with her later.' Ellen paused, looking back at the painting, trying to make out more of the detail. She reached for her purse again. 'I'll take the picture. I really like it and the house reminds me of something I've seen in a photograph. It might be nothing – I might be quite mistaken but it's interesting none the less. How much do you want for it?'

They were quite friendly now and haggling was hardly worth the bother. She would write a cheque if necessary. A reasonable price was agreed and Ellen became the unexpected owner of a very attractive watercolour of the Old Rectory, along with some rudimentary instructions about how to find the house itself. The picture was soon wrapped in brown paper and securely tied with string, which the lady tied in such a way as to create a sort of handle since Ellen's basket was already bulging with her earlier purchases. She was grinning as she made her way through the bustle towards the back of the hall; her family had always called her a magpie, collecting her treasures. The watercolour was a bit out of character though. She didn't usually buy pictures but this one had really caught her imagination.

'Tea, please, and a piece of that flapjack. Thanks. It looks good.'

A young woman in a flowery apron smiled across at Ellen from behind the trestle table. Members of the local Women's Institute were running the refreshments for today's fair and they had certainly been busy. Ellen had spotted a free table in the corner and with some relief had set her basket down on the plastic bucket-chair. Now from her place in the queue she could see the brown-paper parcel lying on the chequered tablecloth. No-one was going to walk off with it here, she knew that but she tried to keep her eye on it anyway as she counted out the coins for the tea and, balancing the tray, edged her way around the other tables back to her own oasis.

The tea was just what she needed. Ellen sipped it and picked at what was undoubtedly an excellent piece of flapjack, while around her the hubbub milled and chattered.

The Old Rectory had taken her by surprise. The name of the

house certainly, but it was the stone porch and the roses that had convinced her that the house in this painting was likely to be the same Old Rectory, the backdrop to her husband's grandmother's photograph, his family home. Her heart fluttered and she coughed, took another sip of the tea.

Somewhere along the line she had stopped expecting it to be a real place. He had never taken her there, had never returned himself as an adult as far as she was aware. She had only suggested it once, way back in the beginning, when they had first ventured together into his beloved Cornwall. But the shadow that had passed across his face in the bedroom of the little B and B in St Ives, his tight-lipped reply, had left her in no doubt that she should leave well alone. And she had. Ever since that day she had never questioned him again. The photograph was always one of his treasures and she had heard him describe the Old Rectory to the children. But his stories about the place had become just that – stories; his personal legends that seemed to have no place in real life. Certainly they'd often been to Cornwall as a family but he had never made any attempt to take them to the places he had known as a child and, strangely now that she came to think about it, the girls had never asked. She wondered what he would he have said if they had. But it was too late now. He was dead. She picked up the cup. Her hand was shaking. Swallowing the hot tea, she set the cup down with exaggerated precision onto its saucer. She glanced at her watch. It was still a little while until she was due to meet up with Mara, but she was feeling tired now. She couldn't really face the crowded hall again. Perhaps a bit of fresh air would be better.

Picking up her shopping bags and hooking the string of the parcel over her fingers, she edged her way back through the tightly-packed tables and out into the entrance hall where a few people were browsing the notices on the boards. On the table in the corner, amongst an array of tourist leaflets, Ellen noticed a pile of the local free newspapers. Leaning across she picked one up, tucked it into the top of her basket and made for the door. She would find somewhere to sit down out in the sunshine and read the paper while she waited for her daughter to return.

The article caught her eye straightaway. A house sale was always interesting. You never knew what you might find, especially at these large country houses. She pulled the page closer to read the detail.

'I never thought I'd see the day.' The woman, who had just settled herself into the empty seat on the bench beside Ellen, fiddled with the scarf at her neck and nodded towards the headline that had attracted her attention. 'I never thought I'd see the day that that place would be up for sale.' She shook her head. Ellen waited; there was clearly more to come. 'That house has been in that family for centuries. It don't seem right, really it don't.'

'You know it then?' Ellen asked, turning to meet the grey eyes, narrowed now in disapproval. The woman frowned and drew in her chin.

'The Old Rectory? Course I do. Everyone around here does.'

'The Old Rectory? Is that where this sale is then? I've only just started to read the article. I do like country house sales.' Ellen's voice betrayed her interest.

'It's the Old Rectory, you know, where the parson and his family did always live for years and years. At least it used to be. My granny used to tell us stories about the place; she worked up there when she was a girl. There's no parson these days of course but that house has been in the family for generations. It's a lovely house mind, beautiful old stone place and the roses were always lovely too. It's a regular piece of our history coming to an end and no mistake. It's a real shame, that's what I think – we all do. It'll get turned into holiday flats before long, you mark my words.' The woman narrowed her lips and shook her head again. The prospect of more holiday flats seemed to offend her almost as much as did the loss of an important piece of local history.

'If the house has been in the family that long, why are they selling up now? Has something happened – did someone die or did the family die out or something like that?'

Ellen was good at making conversation with strangers. Her family had always teased her about the way she talked to people on bus stops and on park benches, but this time she was really interested in the answers. This Old Rectory was probably the one in her painting and, who knows, it could be the one in her husband's photograph. The family in question could be his ... could be hers. Her heart was pounding as she waited for the woman's reply.

'No they didn't die out!' She chuckled. 'Why, one of them's probably down there in the town playing his heart out right now!'

'Why did you laugh?' Ellen was really curious.

'He's the one-man band. He's sure to be down there at the centre of things. I like him myself. He's always friendly to every-body. You'd never think he was from the Rectory if you met him.' She was smiling now just thinking about him. This one-man band was clearly a local favourite.

'You said one of them – are there more then?'

'I don't reckon I know all about the family – he's got at least one brother that I know of, but I did hear that the old lady had been very ill a while back. I think I heard that she had had to be put in some kind of home. That could be why they decided to sell I suppose.'

'I think I might try and get to that sale. I'd be interested to see the old house. I wonder where I could find out more information about it.' Ellen was looking back at the article. Perhaps there was a phone number.

'I reckon you could ask in the tourist information place when they open tomorrow, that's if you're still around of course. They've got a phone number though – it's usually in there somewhere, at the back I think.' She watched as Ellen turned towards the back page.

'There it is.' They found it together and shared the smile of satisfaction.

Ellen was pleased. She would definitely phone them in the morning and find out as much as she could about the house itself as well as the details of the sale. They might be able to tell her some more about the family, or at least make some suggestions about how she could find out about the history of the place. She could feel herself getting quite excited about the prospect. What a strange coincidence that she should spot the painting and then see the article about the sale on the same day and on this first holiday without him. She knew that Theo would never have let her pursue this – in fact Ellen dreaded to think how he would have reacted if she had even suggested it. It made her feel quite hot and bothered just to think about it – the paling around his eyes, the grey, tight-lipped look of suppressed irritation, the frown, the moody silence. The nervous sensation in her stomach now was familiar. She would never knowingly have gone against his wishes. The indrawn breath, the long sigh that followed it, caused her new friend to look side-ways with concern.

'Are you all right, my dear? You've gone all pale, like some-thing had upset you?' She rested her freckled hand on the arm of Ellen's cardigan. 'Here, would you like one of my mints?' She was rustling in her handbag now. 'They always help me when I come over a bit queer.' Finding the opened green tube of sweets she held them out towards Ellen. 'Go on. Have one. These extra strong ones are just the job when you're feeling a bit queasy.'

Actually, she was right. Sucking the strong white mint did seem to make Ellen feel better. She felt calmer already and her breathing relaxed.

'It's silly really. I was just thinking about my husband. I think he came from this area – at least it was somewhere in Corn-wall. I don't really know exactly where. He never liked to talk about it much – the detail that is. I never met any of his family. There might have been some difficulties – I'm not sure. He died … quite recently.' She hesitated a moment, swallowed, cleared her throat. Her voice wavered as she continued. 'Actually this is my first time away without him.' Ellen lifted her hand to hide the tears that took her by surprise. She paused and glanced down at the newspaper on her lap. 'The Old Rectory seemed familiar that's all and it made me start thinking about him.' She realised that she was babbling now. Why was she telling her private business to someone she had just met? Theo would definitely have disapproved. She felt embar-rassed. 'I'm sorry.'

'No, I'm sorry, my dear. I know what it's like. My lad – I always called him that – he died getting on for four years ago last

February. His heart it was. I still talk to him sometimes you know. You can't help it, can you, after so many years being together. It's early days for you though. My Jack, he was from around here. They might have known each other, do you think, gone to the same school even?'

'Oh no, I don't think so. My husband told me that he was sent away to school when he was very young. His parents had both been killed, in an accident I think – somewhere in Egypt, Cairo if I remember rightly.' Ellen had never talked about Theo like this with anyone, let alone a stranger, but she couldn't seem to stop herself now.

'Poor thing! Didn't he have no brothers or sisters?'

'I don't think so. He never spoke about anyone else ... except his nanny ... or aunt ... I can't quite remember ... the one who looked after him that is.'

'So you don't know anything about the rest of his family then? Didn't any of them come to his funeral?' The woman stopped suddenly, flustered. 'Oh, I am sorry. There I go again. Nosey Parker, that's what my lad used to call me – always sticking my nose in where it's not wanted he used to say.' She paused. She really did look sorry now. 'It's none of my business, my dear. Don't you mind me.'

'Oh, don't apologise. Actually it's been good to chat with somebody. As I said, the Old Rectory took me a bit by surprise. That was the name of my husband's old family home. Of course it may not be the same one – but the old house in this painting that I bought at the sale does look very much like the house in one of his old photographs and the lady said that it was not far from here. I think it's probably the same one as the Old Rectory in this article – where the sale is.' As Ellen explained, the woman's face registered her concern and her growing interest in the story.

'D'you know what, I just had a thought myself. My Jack, he had a story about that place too. He used to say that it was up there that he first saw a black man, when he was a boy, up there with his Dad. His dad used to go to evening classes you know, with the WEA. They all got invited up there once, to meet this man from

Africa ... his name was Jomo, or something like that. If I remember rightly, he went on to become the president ... I can't quite remember where.'

'Kenya – it was Kenya. Jomo Kenyatta. He was the first president of Kenya.' Ellen's excitement was in her voice. 'Your Jack met him? My Theo met him too, at the Old Rectory, when he was a boy.'

'Well I never ... fancy that!' The woman's face was a picture of disbelief. 'Here, I just remembered something else too; something else my Jack used to say ... he used to think it was funny. He reckoned that his Dad found out that that man, you know, the black man who became president, that his wife was called Edna.' She laughed then, almost a giggle.

'Edna?' Ellen was beginning to feel a bit confused.

'That's right. Edna, Edna Clarke as was. Apparently she was one of the lecturers, like he was too, for the WEA, somewhere over in Sussex I think, but I can't be sure about that.'

'Well, I hadn't heard anything about that. I don't know anything about his wife called Edna ... but I really am beginning to think that this might be the one, the house, that is, the Old Rectory, my husband's family home.' Ellen breathed deep. She was trying hard to stay calm, but her pulse was racing.

'I reckon that you should go along to the sale, at least to have a look at the house. Who knows, you might find out more about the family history.' She raised her eyebrows and nodded in Ellen's direction. 'You might even see some of the family themselves.' Once more she reached out her hand and touched Ellen's arm. 'Of course there might not be any connection at all – disappointing, but at least you'd know.'

Ellen nodded. 'You're right. I'll definitely ring that number tomorrow and I'll try to get to the sale.' She folded up the newspaper and tucked it into the side of her shopping bag. 'I'm glad we met. My name's Ellen by the way. I enjoyed our chat.'

'I'm glad too.' She laughed. 'Actually I am really Glad – my name's Gladys.' They laughed together. It was funny after all. 'Oh, look, there's my Jeannie.' She said she'd try and get down with the car to fetch me instead of me getting the bus back.'

A blue four wheel drive vehicle – Ellen couldn't recognise the make – was pulling into the curb beside them and from behind the wheel a younger woman with a floppy fringe, a heavy dark blonde braid and a big grin was waving at her mother.

'I'll be going then. She'll be in a hurry as usual. But it's been nice. Who knows, perhaps I'll go to that sale myself – if I can get her to give me a lift up there.' She gestured towards her daughter with shopping bags that she had collected up, standing now.

'That would be good. I'll look out for you.' Ellen waved as Gladys climbed up, not very elegantly, but thankfully, into the car. 'Bye then.' The dusty blue vehicle pulled off and the new friends waved.

Well, what an afternoon this had turned out to be. So much seemed to have happened in such a short time! Ellen was quite taken aback, as she sat, alone once more, on the wooden bench outside the village hall. Inside, the sale was still in full swing. From the town she could hear the sounds of music and around her the chattering groups of festival folk were heading towards the fun. Ellen watched them idly. A plan was taking shape – but how to tell her daughter?

He was good. Mara was smiling. Actually he was very good. All around her in the crowd, people were clapping, singing along. The young couple beside her were laughing, practically dancing, swaying to the beat, feet tapping. She half remembered the song herself, something about San Francisco bay, and before long she was joining in with the rest of them. At the end of the song, she was swept up on the wave of clapping and cheering. She even whistled through her fingers. She hadn't enjoyed herself like this for ages.

The one-man band seemed to be having fun too. Despite the top hat and the patchwork trousers he still managed to look quite interesting she thought. She tried to guess his age – older than her definitely but not as old as her mum. Perhaps in his late forties, maybe early fifties – she laughed. She wasn't much good at this really. He was taking a short break between songs and she watched him as he raised the chequered hat, ruffled his hair – blondish, light brown, floppy – before replacing his headgear and grinning at a familiar face in the crowd. His long face was tanned, his manner easy. The sleeves of his denim shirt were rolled back at the wrists and he held the banjo at the ready as he bantered now with a group of young guys who were sitting on the grassy bank behind him.

A festival mood was in the air – wafts of onions frying, of hot-dogs and grilling burgers mingled with candyfloss and cookies from somewhere further along the green. Jingling bells on the ankles of a troupe of Morris men caught Mara's ear and she turned just in time to catch sight of the colourful band as they made their way back up through the town.

A fresh outburst of applause greeted the start of the Music Man's next song. Mara was fascinated as she watched him making his music, playing the banjo, the big drum strapped to his back, a mouth organ somehow suspended to his side and through it all keeping time on some other percussion and cymbals that he seemed to be working with his feet. It was certainly an impressive feat of coordination and of musicianship. That he managed to sing as well – and engage the audience at the same time – filled her with admiration and intrigued her too. The man was clearly a very competent musician. It would be interesting to discover what had made him decide to become a one-man band. She found herself hoping for another chance to chat. Perhaps she could catch him at the end of this session and ask him if he would like to come for a drink. No – that was not really her style and anyway he might get the wrong idea. She was only interested in the music after all. Grinning, Mara looked around her at the crowd, which was building steadily, drawn by the sound of people having fun. And suddenly she was singing herself – 'Lala dida … you're my … brown-eyed girl …' She was dancing too, and laughing. The young man dancing with his partner next to her reached out and took Mara's hand – she twirled under his arching arm, singing and laughing and dancing – happier than she had been in ages. When the song came to an end the cheering crowd begged for more.

'Come on, Frank. You can't stop now!'

Many of the people in the crowd seemed to know his name and called out to him for their favourite songs. Mara watched him – Frank – finally agreeing to sing one more song. Then, just as he seemed to be settling on the tune, just as he was about to begin, she heard the church clock begin to strike the hour. She looked down at her watch. Four o'clock. She should be up at the hall right now, meeting her mother. How could the time have passed so quickly? How long would it take her to get back up there? Was there a quicker way than going back up through the High Street?

'I've just realised I should be meeting up with my mother, up at the hall, the community centre. I'm late already. What's the best way to get there, the quickest way?' The locals might know a short cut. She decided to ask the guy who had twirled her around just a few minutes earlier. He must be from around here. At least, he knew the one-man band's name.

It was the girl who answered, pointing on along the road towards the bridge. 'If you go on down to the bridge then turn up left, past the pub, you'll soon see a footpath signposted on your right. Head up there, past the Ambulance station and the hall is just up the lane, by the car park.' She smiled.

'Thanks. I'd better go then. He's great though, isn't he! I wish I could stay till the end.' Mara's reluctance to leave showed in her face.

'He'll be on again later, you know. At about six o'clock I reckon, up outside the church, in the open bit there.'

'If I know Frank, he'll be in the pub up the road with the rest of us before then. We'll make sure he's on time.' The man behind them laughed, friendly like everyone around here seemed to be, thought Mara, turning round and smiling.

'Thanks. I'll see how things are with my mum, but I'll try and get there. I'd certainly like to hear him again. I can't remember when I last enjoyed myself so much!' She meant what she said.

'We might see you later then.'

Mara parted from the young couple like old friends and,

clutching her red bag close, she nudged her way through the crowds in the direction of the bridge. She would be a bit late but she wouldn't have missed this for the world.

In vain his blue eyes searched the dispersing crowd. She must have slipped away during that last song. Frank sighed, then, hitching the strap of his banjo up and over his head, he leaned forward and started to pack it away in its case. He'd not let on but he'd spotted her – the girl with the red bag – the moment she'd emerged from the crowds and tagged herself on to the back of his audience, just behind that young couple who were renting the caravan up at Lane's Farm. At first he wasn't sure if she was enjoying the music. She'd seemed hesitant, a bit watchful, detached somehow. Perhaps she just wasn't the type to enjoy a one-man-band … but before long she'd joined in the clapping with everybody else and he'd even seen her laughing, dancing too. Nice girl.

'That was great! Thanks!'

A middle-aged couple called their encouragement, waving across at him as they strolled back along the path, sharing a bag of chips from the van parked up by the bridge. He grinned and waved back.

'Go on, that's right – put it in the basket.'

Behind him Frank heard a woman's voice, gentle, coaxing and then the chink of coins dropped into his basket. He turned to smile at the blonde-haired little boy who was smiling back at him, still holding tightly on to his mother's hand.

'Well, thank you. That's very kind. Did you like the music?' The child nodded coyly and Frank laughed. 'Here, would you like to bang on the drum?'

The little boy reached for the drumstick and his mother reached for her camera. The next few minutes of delighted banging and snapping kept everybody happy.

'Nice work if you can get it!' Jeff, who'd been a joker as long as Frank had known him, waved, laughing as he approached. These days he worked in the kitchens at the new bistro at the bottom of the High Street and was pushing it a bit to be there in time to start his shift. He checked his watch.

'How's it going, mate?' He and Frank went back a long way – they'd been at primary school together.

'Good, thanks. I'm enjoying the chance to cook a bit more, develop my ideas like ...'

'See yourself as one of those celebrity chefs then, do you?'

'Ah, you just wait and see. You never know.' They laughed together.

'Don't forget me when you make your money then. It was me that taught you how to cook sausages – remember, that time we camped out in our back field.'

'Strikes me it's you who'll be making money before me then. What's this I've been hearing about you lot selling up to that posh holiday company? You'll be making millions so they were all saying down at the pub the other night.'

'I don't know where they got that idea – I don't know what they're talking about.' Frank was not laughing now and Jeff could see that something was wrong.

'Well I saw it myself in the free paper – the sale and all that. An auction it said. I didn't read it all though. Perhaps I've got the wrong end of the stick. Perhaps there's some mistake. I don't know. You'd better have a look for yourself and see what you make of it.' There was concern in Jeff's voice. Frank really did seem a bit perplexed – it was not like him.

'I'm just about finished here and I'm not due on again until about six up at the church. I reckon I'll go down to the Co-op and see if I can get hold of a paper for myself. Something obviously needs sorting out.' Frank was packing his gear into the handcart as he spoke, clearly ruffled by what Jeff had told him.

'Well, I hope you can get to the bottom of it mate. You take care of yourself – and give my love to Rose when you see her. It's really sad how things have turned out.' Jeff flipped back his ever-flopping fringe and scratched his forehead, concern showing on his kindly face even as he glanced down to check his watch once more. 'Anyway, mate, I'd better be getting off or they'll be giving me the sack before I've really got started.' He grinned and clapped his hand on Frank's shoulder.

'Yes, see you mate. You take care yourself.' Frank was ready to go now. He picked up the red handles of his cart and moved off in the direction of the co-op. Goodwill followed him as he pushed his way over the grass, past refreshment tents and handicraft stalls. But, nodding and smiling to admirers and well-wishers as he went, Frank was deeply preoccupied.

What in the world was going on? Where did that paper get the idea that they were selling up? What did they mean by a sale? How could he find out what it was really all about? Now that Rose was in the home, who was handling her business affairs? And, now that he came to think about it, how stupid of him not to have thought about that before. But Rose had never let him get involved in the running of the place or anything like that. When Edward, his dad was alive, Frank imagined they'd done it all together. Edward and Rose had been such a great partnership; they relied on each other. Frank sighed. He'd been lucky. He'd never been the slightest bit interested, if he was honest, and they'd taken care of everything; let him do his own thing. Rose was so capable and she always sorted everything out with George Harper the family solicitor if there was a problem. Actually as far as Frank was aware, there had never really been any problems – at least Rose had never talked about any. As far as he knew, she'd inherited the house from her family. He'd never inquired, nor been told about the details. The house and the 'estate' had seemed to manage itself. As far as what might happen when Rose wasn't there, he'd no idea – he'd never wanted to talk or even think about it. Now that he was thinking about it, he'd presumed that the solicitors would just sort it all out and that things would just go on as before; that the Old Rectory would stay in the family and that one of them would go back and live there. Actually, now that he had his own place 'Rock Cottage,' he thought that Dan should probably go back there, hopefully taking Maisy with him. For himself he was not ambitious. He was a One-Man-Band now and he was very happy. But family mattered. That the family home or its contents would be sold, without him knowing anything about it had never crossed his mind. He would have to find his brother. Perhaps he knew something about it. It was unlikely that Dan would have anything to do with solicitors and suchlike – he was an artist after all – but maybe he had heard something. Now that Frank thought about it, he could imagine that Dan might well have some scheme or other going on, but he just could not believe that his brother would go so far as to put the house up for auction on a whim. It wasn't his to sell after all. No, that was crazy. The idea was unthinkable.

Frank shook his head. He stopped and set down the back legs of his handcart to take a breather. Only then did he realise that he had already reached his goal – he was standing right outside of the little Co-op supermarket.

'Keep an eye on that for me for a minute, would you Jessie?' Frank parked his cart up against the wall by the shop doorway and called to the two young girls who were leaning there chatting. He had known them both since they were babies and they grinned back at him.

'Sure, Frank. Just leave it there – we'll fight off anyone who tries to walk off with it.' She laughed. Jessie was the daughter of the local postman, another one of Frank's old friends. She'd always liked the one-man band – he'd played at more than one of her childhood birthday parties. He smiled his thanks and the two girls resumed their perusal of the teen magazine they'd just bought from the shelves at the back of shop to which Frank now headed.

The free papers were kept in a separate rack beside the shelves, which held the other newspapers and magazines and Frank leaned down to collect what seemed to be one of the last few copies. He did a quick flip through the pages in search of the article about the house, although he wasn't really quite sure what he was looking for. Just before the biggest section of the paper, the houses for sale, he spotted the photograph of the Old Rectory. The photographer must have been standing outside, across the road from the main gates. Frank was relieved to see that the article didn't seem to be in the 'Properties for Sale' section. Thank goodness for that at least.

'Holiday Property Company plans to develop local Manor.' He frowned. There had certainly been an offer and they'd definitely been interested, but all that was ages ago. Rose had turned them down flat. How could they still have any 'plans'? He closed the paper. He needed to read this properly when he could sit down and take it all in. It was then that he saw the advertisement on the front page, bottom right, for the 'Sale of antiques and collectables' at the Old Rectory. There it was in black and white – time date, even a little map of how to get there. Whatever was all this about? Whoever was organising the sale? He had absolutely no idea. But it was there in the paper, right next to the photograph of the local headmistress's wedding to her 'childhood sweetheart', so it must be true.

'Sorry. Could I just get through there?'

Frank realised he was blocking the way and he stood to the side to allow the young woman to pass; then he folded the paper, tucked it under his arm and walked towards the door. He had to find Dan.

'Hi Mum. Sorry to keep you waiting.'

Mara's greeting was warm as she squeezed through the gap between an old jeep and the ice-cream van, still doing a brisk trade in the afternoon sunshine. She'd kept a steady pace all the way back up through the crowds on North Street, past the overflowing Red Lion Inn, along the narrow stony lane and out into the public car park area by the Ambulance station. Hurrying up the slope past the playing fields, from the far side of the Community Centre car park she'd spotted her mother on the bench with a couple of other ladies.

As Mara approached, Ellen gathered up the basket that she had set down on the seat beside her and made space for her daughter to join them.

'Come and join us. Sit down and get your breath back.' She patted Mara's knee then turned to the ladies. 'This is my daughter Mara, the one I was telling you about, the writer. She's been so good – she's the one who organised everything for this holiday. She's the driver. I don't know what I'd do without her.' Words were bubbling again and Ellen knew she was talking too much.

'It's very nice to meet you, my dear. Your mum's been telling us all about you.'

Mara grinned, earnestly hoping that she hadn't, but suspecting that she had. The ladies were sisters she thought, probably even twins they were so much alike, blue eyes crinkling in almost identical smiles.

'How did you like our little town then?' Two pairs of eyebrows arched in unison on the question mark.

'Actually, I've had a great time. It's really bustling down there.' Mara nodded back in the direction of the town centre. 'The town looks beautiful and the atmosphere is great.'

The ladies grinned, taking her praise personally. 'And what did you think of the music? Did you see our one-man band?'

'He was really good – everybody's favourite obviously. You would have liked him, Mum.' Mara turned to her mother.

Ellen picked up her daughter's enthusiasm. 'Someone I met earlier was telling me about him. It's a shame I missed his performance – perhaps we could catch him later? But I've had a nice time myself, up here at the sale. I've seen some lovely things.'

'And bought quite few I see.' Mara pointed laughing in the direction of Ellen's basket.

'Just one or two bits - you know me. I can't resist a bargain. I'm especially pleased with this though.' She reached down and picked up the package that had been propped up against the leg of the bench, resting it on her lap. Carefully peeling back the brown paper wrapping, she opened up the parcel to reveal the picture. Mara and the twins regarded it with interest, Mara enjoying the colours and the skill of the artist, the twins exclaiming in recognition.

'It's one of Dan's. It's the Manor!'

'You know the artist?' Ellen was excited.

'Yes of course we do. You're lucky to get hold of one of his in a sale like that. Actually that's his home he's painted there. It's the

Old Rectory – or as people from around here call it: the Manor.' The twins seemed delighted to pass on their local knowledge to these new friends.

'Did you say The Old Rectory?' Mara and Ellen spoke in unison, just like the twins. It must be catching. Their burst of laughter was tinged with something like relief. Each had been wondering how to bring up the subject of the Old Rectory and now there it was, out there in the open. 'The Old Rectory?' Again they spoke in unison; the emphasis was firmly on 'The'.

'Ah, you know about it then?' Just one of the twins asked the question this time and it was Ellen who answered.

'We certainly know about *an* Old Rectory, somewhere in Cornwall, but we didn't realise that it might be here, in Lostwithiel.'

'That's right. We've seen an old photograph of *an* old rectory. It might not be anything to do with the one in this painting. The roses are there though, all over the porch, just like in our photograph and actually it does look quite similar, don't you think, mum?'

Ellen nodded as she leaned in, looking more closely at the picture. The artist was really good. As to whether this was the same Old Rectory that had meant so much to Theo she could not be certain – yet. But, if her plan to go to the sale came together they might know soon. On that thought, her stomach flipped. Maybe it would be better to let things from the past just stay in the past – perhaps she should forget the whole idea – maybe they should just leave well alone. But, even as she folded the thick brown paper carefully back around the painting and re-tied the string handle, the roses lingered in her memory.

8

Kenya, Rift Valley – 1963

He has visited this place so many times in his dreams, driven past it since his return in the company of others. But, standing here alone at the roadside, Theo knows he should not have come back, not like this. Despite the heat, he shivers. He inhales and the dry heat prickles the tiny hairs on the inside of his nose. His tongue sticks to the roof of his mouth and he imagines himself desiccating like the earth beneath his feet. Red dust is gritty between his teeth.

He tilts the heavy sun-hat and, pulling a handkerchief from the pocket of his cotton jacket, mops the sweat from his eyebrows, his forehead. Unsteady, he lowers himself onto a boulder. Stored heat burns through the seat of his trousers. This is the exact spot, he is certain of it. The rusting carcass of the vehicle, scattered bones in the ditch, the outcrop of rock where the goat boy was hiding, over there the scrawny umbrella shade of the thorn trees. He narrows his eyes, peering into the scrub. He half expects the donkey to appear on the road as it had that night; still dreads the sound of that other vehicle, clamouring in hot pursuit.

Squinting against the glare, he lifts his eyes towards the rim of Mount Longenot's crater, checking his bearings. From this distance the sleeping volcano seems to shimmer in the rising haze, purple, grey, green, out in the centre of the valley floor, basking in the midday heat of this Christmas, as it had that other day in that other December. Nothing changes. But everything has changed, for him and for this country.

Just a few nights ago, on the twelfth of December up in Nairobi, in the makeshift 'Independence Square', he had stood in the pouring rain alongside those men and women, fervent campaigners, sometime freedom fighters, many of whom had become his friends. Like them he had been caught up in the excitement of the crowds who had gathered in their thousands to witness this moment. At midnight, the lights in the square were dimmed. The silence, the tension was palpable. When the lights were turned on again, the British flag had been taken down and in its place was hanging the black, red and green flag of the new Independent Republic of Kenya. The crowd had erupted. 'Uhuru' – freedom – had come at last, the precious freedom that they had fought for together, the freedom that she will never know, the freedom that he prays he has procured for her child.

Reaching into his pocket, he takes out the small rectangle of cloth, rolled around a stick: the flag of Independence – red for the blood that was spilt, green for this beautiful land, black for its people, for the dark earth. This thing he will do. Bending low, he plants the flag in the rough soil at his feet, beside the boulder ... a token, an offering.

9

Cornwall – 2008

Holmes and Barratt Solicitors, London, 20th Dec. 1970.
Congratulations on your ninth birthday!
Your father has requested that we convey to you his good wishes along with this gift.
With kind regards,
Ernest Holmes.

Dan frowned as he replaced the letter – more of a note really – in the long narrow envelope and added it to the pile on the floor beside him. There had been plenty more like it from the same Ernest Holmes but his father had never written to him personally.

Kneeling on the faded-blue carpet of his old bedroom he felt all over again the child's loss. He sat back on his heels, removed his wiry silver-rimmed spectacles and, eyes shut tight against the rising tears, slowly massaged the bridge of his nose between the finger and thumb of his right hand.

Haphazard around him, cardboard boxes of various ages, shapes and sizes lay opened. The bedroom floor had by stages become a veritable treasure trove for any collector of old toys, games and puzzles, as Dan had lifted out, one after the other, the gifts that had arrived '*in loco parentis*' throughout his childhood. A poor substitute! He had felt it then and affirmed it now with a sigh. Looking around at the array of models and playthings, Dan hoped that he had been a better parent to his young Maisy. He had certainly always tried to listen to her, to be there for her in ways that his own father never had been. That was until her mother had taken her away to London. Even then he had made sure that she always knew that he loved her – would always love her.

Had his father ever loved him? The question would have to remain unanswered. Probably not, was his own honest thought. If the man in the old photograph downstairs, the initiator of all these expensive gifts, had cared about him at all, surely he would have found some way of returning to the family home, some way of looking into the eyes of his son. Now, after all this time, Dan knew that the chance had been lost forever. His father was dead.

The letter had been delivered to his studio in Polperro. The news was imparted in the same succinct prose by the same 'Holmes and Barratt Solicitors' who had managed his father's affairs throughout his life. In just a few brief sentences Dan was offered their condolences and an invitation to attend a meeting, the date of which to be confirmed later, in their offices in London. He had promptly written to accept both. He was still waiting to hear the date of the meeting.

Dan had long ago come to think of himself as fatherless. For as long as he could remember, Rose and Edward together had been the centre of his life and after Edward's sudden death in the accident, Rose on her own had given him all the love and support that he could have wished from any parent. He missed her presence more now than he would ever mourn the loss of the father that he had never known.

The tears had taken him by surprise though. The loneliness, that feeling of being abandoned, had settled over him like a dark cloud from the moment he'd entered the empty house. It struck him that it was the house itself that was overcome by loss: loss of its heart, loss of its precious Rose.

Dan fumbled the crumpled navy blue handkerchief from his back pocket and began slowly rubbing each lens of his glasses, before replacing them, tucking first one side then the other through the curls that always bunched behind his ears. He looked around him, his eyes taking in the threadbare candlewick bedspread that he remembered had once been a warm royal blue; the forget-me-not wallpaper patterned with little sprigs of blossom and now flecked with unmistakeable patches of damp. Casting his gaze towards the ceiling, he could still make out the dark ink blots, up high near the coving, where he had long ago flicked blotting-paper ink pellets at wandering bluebottles. The purple-pink sunset hues of his two wildfowl paintings by Peter Scott were still hanging high on the wall beside the single bed and on the shelf at its foot the battered Chambers' encyclopaedia and matching dictionary that Rose had given him just before he went off to school. Bottles and jars of his collected treasures – coloured pebbles, shells, crab-claws, and smooth brown conkers – still clustered atop the small chest of drawers in which he knew he would always find his clean white underwear, his grey school socks rolled up in balls and his neatly folded games kit. Dan breathed in deep and his imagination filled his nostrils with the fresh scent of clean laundry. This house was full to the brim with his memories. It was his home.

But what would happen to the old house now, with Rose in that other home and unlikely ever to be well enough to return? He had not thought about it before nor he was sure had Frank. Neither of them had any head for business, not that kind of business anyway. They would have to get together and talk about it for sure and probably sooner rather than later. When all this business with the sale was sorted he would get in touch with his brother – but not before. He could not afford to be talked out of this – he needed it to happen – he needed the money.

Dan shoved the handkerchief back into his pocket and tried to stand up. He had been kneeling in one place for too long and had to lean heavily against the old bed as he struggled to his feet, grimacing as he rubbed the life back into his calves and shins. He sat down heavily on the bed and looked at his watch. This was taking longer than he had thought. If he was going to get all these boxes sorted he would have to get on with it, and there were more in the attic.

He would have to find the rest of the letters too – they would prove that the toys and things really were his to sell. His father had been generous and the gifts had been well chosen by Ernest Holmes – or whoever it was that had actually done the selecting. Dan had already made some enquiries, done a bit of research here and there, and he had a good idea of the prices he might be able to get for several of the pieces. He permitted himself a smile. The gifts had given him no pleasure as a child; in fact he had flatly refused to play with any of them so Rose had packed them all away. The teddy bears, the train sets, the mechanical toys were in pristine condition, all in their original boxes, absolutely as new. A treasure trove indeed that only now would bring him some joy. He imagined the look on Maisy's face as he handed her the cheque that would make possible the trip of her lifetime and hopefully help with her fees for university.

The toys would certainly fetch a good price in the sale – he had actually already received several substantial bids for the blue-grey Steiff teddy bear and some of the other more exceptional pieces were also stirring up quite a bit of interest. But there was more and he planned to sell it all: the carved ebony chests and the antique chairs from Lamu, along with the malachite chess sets, the David Shepherd originals and all the various examples of ethnic art that had arrived at the Old Rectory shipped directly from Kenya in his name. These now formed the bulk of the collection that he was planning to sell – part of his own inheritance that he would pass on to his daughter, not on his death but now, when she really needed it. Several more valuable items of jewellery that had passed to him on his twenty-first birthday were however still kept in the bank. Rose had been their custodian on his behalf – an arrangement which had always seemed appropriate to them both – until now. Things had become more complicated. Her signature would be required before they could be released into his care.

It was thinking of getting things signed and sealed that reminded him of the envelope. That chap from Kenya, 'Uhuru', Freeman, or whatever his name was, the one who had been so interested when he'd put the details of his Kenyan stuff on the internet … he should be getting in again touch soon, or at least his agent should. He'd seemed really keen, had asked a lot of questions, about Dan's background, how he'd got hold of the items … that sort of thing. The guy from 'The Secret Garden' had said he'd call, but so far Dan had not heard anything. He checked his phone. There were no messages.

Dan glanced at his watch and then out of the window. He had spent longer at the old house than he had intended and afternoon was settling into evening. It was too late now to go back to Rose Lawns. The staff would be serving meals and then all the bedtime routines would be clicking in. No, he would leave it until tomorrow. Rose was usually better, more herself, in the mornings and the nurses would be bustling about with their general business. He would be more likely to find her on her own she would be much more likely to sign the papers for him if he could explain the situation calmly – if he could make her see that this was all for Maisy.

Rose had adored his daughter from the day that she was born – 'my precious granddaughter' she had always called her and Maisy had found in Rose everything any little girl would ever dream of in a 'grandma'. They were practically inseparable and from the time that Maisy was taking her first steps she was following in Rose's own. Rose would do anything for Maisy. She would do this now – if he pushed her that is. The thought shocked him, made him uncomfortable. How could he even contemplate manipulating Rose like that? He raised his hand in an involuntary motion, raking through his unruly hair, bunching the thick curls behind his ear.

Dan turned away from the window and surveyed the piles of letters and opened cardboard boxes. He knew that he should be making lists of everything that had come out of storage, lists that would help him do the research and arrange the valuations, that would help him to set guide prices for the sale. It all needed to be catalogued, everything had to be done properly – he had to make as much profit as he could after all. It was a daunting thought. He wasn't really much of an organiser – he had learned that much about himself years ago when he had first tried to start his own business. He could do with a secretary. With the thought came a plan.

'Hey, Jeannie. How're you doing?'

How did we ever manage without these things? Dan wondered to himself as he listened to his friend's surprise to hear from him at this time on a Sunday evening. It had actually taken him a while to get used to this new mobile phone but Maisy had convinced him that he should persevere and now that he had worked out how to use it properly he felt lost without it.

'Sorry? ... I didn't catch that ... Yes, I'm good, thanks ... its ages since I saw your mum ... give her my best too ... Plenty to keep me going ... Actually, I was wondering if you might have a few hours to spare ... I need some help with a project ... secretarial ... lists and that sort of thing ... photocopying ... for the sale ... yes, in the free paper ... a brochure? Yes I suppose I do ... quite a bit of work actually ... a week, maybe two ... Do you know of anybody who might be able to ... Yes, let me know ... a.s.a.p. ... Oh, right ... the Red Lion? Maybe I'll drop in myself later then ... yes, it'll be good to catch up ... Alright, Take care ... speak soon ...bye.'

Dropping his phone back into the pocket of his jacket, he stood up. It was too late to start fiddling about in the attic and he was beginning to feel a bit peckish. Perhaps he would stop in at the Red Lion on his way back through – the food was always good and it might be nice to have a bit of company. He would leave things as they were for now and come back tomorrow afternoon after his visit with Rose. Hopefully Jeannie would have some good news for him too by then and the whole thing could move forward.

As Dan picked his way carefully across the cluttered blue floor towards the door a question suddenly occurred to him: had anyone told Rose about his father's death? He considered for a moment then thought probably not.

The place was buzzing, absolutely jam-packed. Frank let the double-doors swing shut behind him. The wall of colour and noise temporarily stopped him in his tracks as his eyes searched the crowd. There they were. He grinned and began edging his way through the good-natured throng, nodding as glasses were raised in greeting.

'Thought I'd find you lot here already – propping up the bar as usual.'

Frank reached the bar at last and was glad of the drink that his mate Colin pushed over in his direction. Colin and brother Chas had done some landscaping work with their Dad up at the Old Rectory during school holidays when they were lads and they'd all been friends since.

'Thanks mate. Cheers. Hey Dave, hey Alan.'

Dave with the ginger beard and the be-spectacled Alan completed the crew that few people now remembered used to call themselves the Fearless Five, roaming the countryside in search of adventures, making dens in the woods behind the Old Rectory.

'Anyone seen Dan?' Frank asked the question.

'I haven't seen him in ages. What's he doing with himself nowadays?' Alan had been working away in Plymouth for a while and was afraid he might be losing touch.

'Oh, you know him … this and that. He's had a few commissions as far as I can tell and last time I saw him he told me that a gallery in London is interested in an exhibition. He's got a studio down in Polperro, down near the slip, by the harbour.'

'Has he now? It should be good down there come the summer.' Colin nodded and set down his glass, wiping the foam from his moustache with the back of his fisherman's hand.

'Yes, he was saying that he's having some print runs done. Apparently his work is really popular with the tourists – numbered prints and the like.' Frank paused and sipped thankfully on his beer. 'His originals are bit pricey for most people just buying souvenirs from their holidays. He's sold quite a few of his more recent harbour pieces, pictures of boats and the like though. It seems that he's begun to make quite a name for himself.'

'Good for him.' Colin raised his glass in salute of his old friend's success. 'When're you on by the way? That's what this crowd's all about you know really. They heard that the one-man band's playing later.' He grinned across at Frank who was looking a bit jaded, tired around the eyes he thought, though he wouldn't have said anything.

Frank leaned his elbow on the scrubbed wooden bar, turned and looked over his shoulder at the noisy hubbub. Several people caught his eye as he scanned the crowd and grinned in recognition. He nodded in their direction, acknowledging friends and fans alike.

He was well known here both for his music and for his good nature – a really nice bloke, a good guy, a true Cornishman if ever there was one seemed to be the general opinion. He smiled to himself as he turned back to pick up his glass.

In that moment he spotted them as they edged in through the heavy door, the younger woman holding it back to allow her companion to enter ahead of her. He saw their hesitation, just a flicker of indecision as they stood on the edge of the throng, eyes scanning the crowd as he had himself just minutes earlier. They seemed lost. He didn't want them to leave.

He stood and waved, catching the young woman's eye. He raised his eyebrows and his glass in the question – 'Fancy a drink?' He mouthed the words, lifted his glass – there was no way she would hear above the background noise. She grinned and nodded, turning to her companion then pointing in his direction. He watched as she led the way through the crowd, taking care, encouraging the older woman to follow safely behind her. He wondered about their connection. Could it be her mother? There was a slight resemblance but not the age difference surely. They looked more like friends.

As they approached he smiled warmly and greeted them like old friends – in fact that's exactly what the other members of the 'Fearless Five' took them to be as he settled them into the group and asked what he could get them to drink. This done Frank began some introductions:

'This is Colin, his brother Chas, the ginger one is Dave and the quiet one's Alan.' Everybody grinned and nodded and the guys waited.

'Yes, Frank – come on then, introduce your friends!' Colin was laughing.

'Do they have names?' Chas nudged his brother; they grinned at each other and then at Frank, who turned himself and looked at the women.

'Oh I'm Mara and this is Ellen.' More grinning, nodding and passing drinks and soon everybody relaxed, allowing the general noise to swirl around them as Ellen began a friendly chat with Colin who offered her his perch on the bar stool and Frank turned to Mara who was squashed in at his side.

'So you liked my music – decided to come back for more then?'

Mara had to lean towards him to catch what he was saying. She laughed.

'You certainly know how to keep your audience happy. It was great. I had a good time. Mum was keen to meet you too.'

'Your mum?'

'Yes, she met some people up at the antiques fair who were talking about you, about your house actually. She bought a really good painting of a local manor house called the Old Rectory and she's fallen in love with it – the painting that is – but she's also interested to find out more about the house.'

'The house? How does that connect with me? I'm just a one-man band after all. I'm certainly not a painter.' He laughed and sipped his drink.

'She met these ladies, twins we think they were, they were so alike, and they filled in some details about the house and the family. One of the family members is apparently the famous local celebrity, the one-man band.' She raised her glass in his direction. He bent his head, grinning, acknowledging the point she made.

'Alright, alright, I humbly accept your flattery, if that's what you're offering.' They were both laughing now.

'It sounds like the artist is my brother. He's actually the talented one. His work sells for good money. Your mother was lucky to get hold of one, especially one of the house itself. Does it show the front porch, with the roses?'

'It does. They're lovely.'

'Those roses are my mother's pride and joy – and her mother's before her.' He paused and took a sip of his drink. He seemed lost for a moment, somewhere in his memories.

'Is she still alive, your mother?' Mara posed the question tentatively and he nodded his response.

'Yes, she is, but she's not well at the moment, not the woman she used to be.' He shook his head. 'She's called Rose. Her name is Rose.'

Mara sipped her drink, unsure how to respond. She was definitely interested to find out more about Frank's family or at least to know more about the history of the Old Rectory, but she didn't want him to think she was being nosey and she didn't know him well enough to ask too many personal questions after all. If the house was indeed the same as the house in her father's old photograph there could well be some connections between their families but it was too soon to bring her suspicions out into the open.

She glanced around her, giving Frank a moment to collect his thoughts, waiting to see where he would take their conversation from here. She grinned across at her own mother who was becoming quite animated, enjoying the banter about tourists that seemed to be developing around her.

'Your mum seems to be enjoying herself over there.' Frank smiled and nodded towards Ellen who was laughing now and looking more relaxed than Mara had seen her for ages.

'She certainly does.' Mara laughed. 'I haven't seen her like that for such a long time. Things have been difficult for the last few months, probably longer actually. This holiday's really done her good.' It was Mara's turn to become thoughtful.

'Are you in Cornwall for long?' Frank seemed interested.

'We're down here for a couple of weeks ... Mum needed a break – this is the start of our second week. We're staying in a cottage in the grounds of an old manor house just outside a village called Duloe.'

Frank nodded in recognition. 'I know where you mean. It's nice over that way – there's some lovely walking in the woods all around there at this time of year. It's well known in the area for its bluebell valleys. We used to go there for picnics when we were kids.'

'Mum and I followed a trail yesterday morning – it was meant to be the easy walk but we got lost once or twice coming back up through the Forestry Commission paths. It was so beautiful though ... so many bluebells, carpets of them and all the wild garlic ... amazing ... like another world ... it was so peaceful.' She smiled and sipped her drink.

'You and your mum seem to get on well. What about your dad ... is he in Cornwall with you or did you leave him at home?'

His question took her by surprise. She had forgotten that he didn't know. 'My dad died – quite recently actually – that's the main reason that mum and I have come away right now. She needed a rest, needed to get away for a bit, and we thought that Cornwall would be a good idea.' Mara paused and looked over in her mother's direction.

'I'm really sorry for your loss.' Frank's expression conveyed his sympathy and she was grateful.

They sat in companionable silence while the general buzz of conversation ebbed and flowed around them. It was Frank who spoke first. 'Do you know Cornwall well then or is this your first venture over the border?' He smiled at her as his accent deliberately thickened.

'Oh no, I'm an old timer – I've been coming to Cornwall since I was a child – not this part though, more over in the St Ives area. My dad seemed to like the market at Helston too so we went there a lot.' She hesitated. 'Actually my dad was a Cornishman.' There, she had said it.

'Really? So I reckon that makes you a Cornishwoman then?' Frank was using the same thick Cornish accent. He laughed and raised his eyebrows. When she was slow to reply he continued with another question. 'So you've got roots down here. Which part of the Duchy did he come from then?' He was still grinning, enjoying the banter, but Mara felt suddenly out of her depth.

'I don't know.'

Frank looked at her, surprised at the sudden change in her expression and the finality of her response. He was about to question her further when their circle was suddenly interrupted by a new arrival.

'Hi, Jeannie ... Haven't seen you in ages ... how've you been ... how's Robert ... how's your mum ... you still working down at the library?' The woman with the floppy fringe and thick blonde plait was welcomed into the group in a flurry of questions and friendly kisses.

'Hi everyone ... Robert's over there with my mum. She heard that the famous one-man band was playing at the festival this evening and she wanted to come down with us.' Frank grinned and glanced at his watch as they all laughed.

'Tell Gladys we'll get her his autograph if she'll sing some of her old songs back up here afterwards.' It was Colin who spoke but they were all smiling their agreement.

Jeannie laughed. 'Actually I think she's already been asked to sing a couple later. I'll get her to sing 'Trelawney' if you like, especially for all you old Cornishmen.'

Her mum had always been a fine singer and she'd quite a reputation in the area – 'Lostwithiel's very own Brenda Wootton' was how the man on the mike had often announced her. For as long as she could remember Jeannie had been entranced by her mother's voice, flushed with pride at the clapping, the cheering and then that moment of hushed silence just before the deep velvet voice seemed to capture the air and hold the audience spell-bound. She sang the old songs, the old folk stories – not necessarily the kind of thing that went down well at the big festivals but the locals liked to listen and join in too over a few drinks.

'Did you say your mum was called Gladys?'

They all turned towards Ellen who was asking. The young woman had seemed familiar when she first came over, but Ellen couldn't think how she would have met her before. As soon as they mentioned Gladys, things had begun to drop into place. Could this Gladys be her new friend, the woman she had been chatting to outside of the village hall? Indeed now that she looked closer, Ellen was sure that this was the same Jeannie who had picked up her mum in the blue 4x4.

Jeannie seemed a bit surprised at Ellen's enthusiasm, but the young woman was friendly, interested.

'That's right. Do you know my mum? Have you two met before?'

'We just met today, on the bench outside the village hall. You collected her there; I remember you now. I was showing her the painting I had bought of the Old Rectory and she was telling me about the artist and about the old house itself. I liked her.'

'Funny you should mention the artist. I had a phone call from him out of the blue, just now, about half an hour ago.' She turned towards Frank. 'Your brother Dan – I hadn't heard from him for ages but he just rang me on my mobile. He wants some secretarial work done … something to do with a sale … lists, catalogues, brochures, that kind of thing.'

'I read about a sale in the free paper, in fact we were talking about it, Gladys and I. She seemed to think that the old house was going to be sold too … to a holiday company I think she said … of course that might have been just local gossip … I don't think it actually said that in the paper … just the sale of items … 'antiques and collectables' from the house.' Ellen spoke, her voice filled with enthusiasm. 'It sounded interesting. I thought I might like to go.'

She looked hopefully towards her daughter but Mara was looking at Frank. Frank was looking pale.

'Oh look, talk of the devil.' It was Alan, pointing over to the door, lifting his glass as he caught Dan's attention. 'Here he is then … over here.'

Grinning broadly, Dan approached the group. Then he spotted his brother. He frowned. Frank looked up and their eyes met, held just for a moment. It was Dan who turned away.

Maisy dropped the letter onto her rumpled duvet and leaned over the bed to draw back the curtains. Across the street the blue and white plaster Madonna gazed down from the red-brick frontage of the Catholic school at the early-morning city-workers hurrying to and from Waterloo station. From her own vantage point Maisy spotted a few umbrellas and sure enough the tell-tale raindrops were soon speckling the double glazing that thankfully protected her from at least some of the noise that was one of the few disadvantages of living right in the centre of the capital city.

In the early days she had done a lot of that – weighing up the advantages and disadvantages of things. She had always made lists, dividing up the pages of her notebooks with neat pencilled lines, always drawn with a ruler, top to bottom, with titles neatly written at the top of each column: 'Living with Mummy/Living with Daddy', 'Cornwall/London', 'Like/ Dislike' … foods, friends, bands, boys. Over the years it had helped her to make up her mind about all kinds of things. It also helped with sorting out her thoughts for the essays that she'd had to do in her course work. Her teachers commended her organised mind. It should stand her in good stead in the upcoming exams too so that she could secure her place at University and then take her year out.

That was what the letter had been about, her year out. She sat down on the bed and picked it up. It was from her Dad, hand-written in his lovely curly writing. She smiled as she read:

My darling girl.

How can it be that my little Cornish pixie has grown up so fast and is now talking about travelling the world all by herself? Any university you choose should be proud to have you as far as I can see and if they have to wait a year till you're ready to take up the place they offer then I'm sure they'll be glad to do that.

You say that you're planning to go to Kenya. What a surprise that was to me. What does your mother think? I would like a chance to meet up and talk about it with you. There are some things I'd like to show you, letters, old photographs, that type of thing. It might help you in your exploration. When can we do that? Could you come down here? It might be easier in the circumstances.

Your grandma is still not too good. The old house is strange without her – in fact no-one is there now. There are some developments in that area too that I'd also like to talk to you about. Hopefully by the time we meet I should have some good news for you on the financial front. How much did you say you expected your trip to cost? I'd really like to be able to support you in this venture you know. I'm hoping to sell some more of my work – there's a London gallery that is really interested in an exhibition – and I've also got something else on the go that is really exciting. Can't wait to tell you about it, but we'll talk about that when you come. Call me on my mobile if you can. That would be easiest as I'm moving about quite a bit at the moment. Call me SOON please my dear.

With love as always

Your Dad

Maisy smiled. Despite the impression that he'd always tried to give, the Kenya thing was obviously important for him, for them both. She understood that. For as long as she could remember the safari-suited Englishman and the African chief clad all in monkey skins had stared down at her from the mantelpiece in her grand-mother's sitting room. Her dad had answered her questions as far as he could, but actually even he didn't seem to know very much. Where was the picture taken? Does the old man live in those mud huts? Who is he? What's his name? Why is he wearing those funny clothes? What's that on his head? If that man with the moustache is your father does that mean he's my granddad? Why doesn't he look like you? Why can't he come to visit? Where does he live now?

As far as Maisy knew, her dad had never met his own father, had not even heard from him since he was about ten or eleven years old, had no idea where he lived now and had no interest at all in finding out. In fact he didn't really seem to care whether his father was alive or dead. Whenever she had tried to have conversations about it, her dad had always seemed uncomfortable, moved the conversation on to safer ground, away from the subject of his birth or his family history. Nevertheless, she had managed to find out that he had been born in Kenya but that he had been brought back to Cornwall when he was a baby and as far as she could tell had just been abandoned there by his father who had returned to Kenya without him.

As for his birth mother, Maisy had no idea at all. Nor, it seemed, had her dad. It was hard to remember now who it was had told her that Rose was not actually his mother – was it her dad … or her mum … or Rose herself … or could it have been Uncle Frank? Anyway, once her child's mind had got used to the idea, it didn't matter at all. Rose had always been as good as a mother to him, and to his daughter she was the best grandmother any girl could ever have. Throughout Maisy's childhood that had been enough but now that she was becoming a woman herself, somehow it had become important to her to find out more about the mys-terious woman who was surely a part of her own family as well as her dad's. In fact it was this need to know, to discover more about that side of her history that had been behind her plan to travel to Kenya, maybe to work there for a while to get the feel of the place. Was her real grandmother still alive, did she still have family in Kenya, what kind of woman was she, how could she possibly have allowed her baby son to be taken to England and just left there? Maisy had so many questions and now seemed to be the right time to find some answers.

The plan was that she and her friend Agnes would travel together. Agnes and her family were from Kenya. In fact it was Kenya that had brought the two girls together when they had first got chatting in the playground at primary school and they had been best friends ever since. Agnes Mwiti had actually started kindergarten at Rusinge School in the old colonial suburb of Nairobi known as Lavington. Maisy loved to look at the photographs that the Mwiti family had brought with them from Nairobi, whenever she spent time at her friend's home. The girls had fun giggling over pictures of baby Agnes strapped to her ayah's back, swaddled in the bright pink and orange kanga; toddler Agnes wobbling across the grass at the family's home in Lavington; school girl Agnes beaming in her blue-and-white-checked school uniform at various school events. Her parents were very proud of their only daughter. Her mother was a nurse and her father an up-and-coming hospital doctor and it seemed that neither had had any trouble finding good jobs in London. The family was enjoying their life in England but they kept in regular contact with their extended family back home. Agnes had spent several long summer holidays with her grandparents in Nairobi and now she was delighted to be able to travel back to Africa with her best friend.

Maisy had already done some research and she was really excited about their forthcoming trip. It would be good to be able to stay at Agnes's grandparents' home in Nairobi for the first week or two. Agnes clearly adored the old couple and it would also be a great chance to acclimatise, to get used to the heat and the altitude – the city of Nairobi stands at five thousand feet above sea level and the change in altitude can be a challenge for new arrivals, or so Maisy had read on somebody's blog. Then there was the food – she had tried some of the *irio* that Agnes's family seemed to love and the *ugali* was not too bad but Maisy could not understand how anyone could actually enjoy the slimy texture of okra. The two girls had laughed together about Maisy's preference for 'normal' food like fried chicken and chips and Agnes had reassured her that, if she was really desperate, she would be able to get Kentucky fried chicken down in the centre of Nairobi.

As soon as they got themselves sorted out, the girls had decided that they would like to go down to the coast for a few days. They planned to travel on the overnight train to Mombasa, which Agnes's mum had said was an experience not to be missed, as long as you travelled first class that is – like a trip back in time when dinner was served on white china from silver platters and the steward would make up your beds while you enjoyed a three course dinner in the dining carriage. Of course it was all a bit 'former glory' nowadays but still worth the ticket. From the station they would get a taxi out over the long bridge that links the island of Mombasa to the beaches of the north coast, to spend a few days at Nyali Beach Hotel which Maisy had found on the internet and Agnes remembered from a childhood visit. After that they would just go with the flow and see what happened next.

She picked up her dad's letter and read it through once more – he'd mentioned some letters, old photographs. How interesting ... perhaps he knew more than he had already told her, or perhaps he himself had recently discovered more that would help her in her search for her mysterious 'other' family. She was intrigued and it was definitely too long since their last meeting. She would call him later today. The young woman glanced over at the little clock on her bedside table. There certainly wouldn't be time now. She was already late.

Grabbing her old school sweatshirt from the back of the chair by her desk, Maisy made for the door and headed downstairs to have breakfast with her mother.

'What do you fancy for your breakfast this morning?'

Ellen posed the question as her daughter nudged her way in through the door to the kitchen of the large open-plan living space of their holiday cottage, still fixing her watchstrap. Mara came up beside her mother who was pouring glasses of orange juice for them both. The scent of Ellen's shampoo lingered, fresh and clean, like cologne. Mara knew it well.

'Mmm … you smell good. So does the coffee. Did you just make it? Can I pour you some? Have we got any eggs? I could just fancy some scrambled eggs … and some toast too, and orange juice. Let's do the whole works shall we?'

Mara chatted while she went into action, moving towards the large double-fronted fridge/freezer and producing eggs, butter, marmalade, setting the various cartons, packages and jars out on the wooden worktop. The next few minutes passed in easy silence as their breakfast took shape – Ellen scrambled the eggs in a glass bowl in the microwave, Mara cut the bread and dropped two slices into the stainless steel toaster, before setting two places at the long wooden table that could actually have seated eight. She sat down and poured coffee for them both. Before she had finished adding milk to hers, Ellen had set down two plates of scrambled eggs and seated herself opposite her daughter.

'So what do you reckon then, should I do it?'

Ellen asked the question and, not seeming to expect an immediate response, picked up her fork in her right hand and started on her eggs. 'Mm … that's not bad, though I do say so myself.' She set down her fork after a moment and began to butter a piece of toast before glancing up at her daughter. Mara was still sipping thoughtfully at her coffee, obviously giving the question serious consideration.

The previous evening, in fact the whole day really, had been totally unexpected and surprisingly enjoyable. Mara could hardly remember the last time she'd felt so much a part of things, so connected. And what a surprise it had been to see her mother looking so relaxed, laughing and chatting with such a light in her eyes – no one looking on would ever have suspected the group had only just met.

'Well, come on then, what do you think?'

Ellen interrupted her daughter's reverie. She was impatient now, eager to share her excitement, apprehension too. She had finished her eggs and was now cradling her mug in both hands, an unconscious mirror image of her daughter across the table.

'Would you like to? He seemed really keen when you were asking him about it. He obviously needs help and it does sound like interesting work, cataloguing items for the sale, preparing leaflets, brochures that sort of thing. Yes, I think you'd enjoy it – if you want to do it that is.' Mara's tone was definitely encouraging. She raised her eyebrows in a question as she set down her mug, lifted her fork and made a belated start on her own breakfast.

'Mm ... I always said you make the best scrambled eggs!'

Ellen acknowledged the praise with a smile. 'I liked him – and yes, I was fascinated by the house from the moment I first heard about it. The Old Rectory – I love the painting, the roses, the colours. The more I found out about it the more interested I became. And then to meet the family, the artist himself just like that ... I don't know, it just seems a bit strange. What do you reckon?'

'I know what you mean. I'd been thinking the same thing. What a coincidence that I should bump into Frank, then see the old photograph of the house – the Old Rectory, his family home – at the same time that you're buying one of his brother's paintings of the place and finding out all about the family.'

'Yes, and what about Gladys and Jeannie turning up? I could hardly believe it, meeting up with them again too.' Ellen shook her head in amazement, picking up her orange juice.

'It seems a bit like a soap opera, doesn't it, like 'Eastenders' or 'Emmerdale,' when you think about it ... too many ominous co-incidences ... or even like something out of Thomas Hardy. I reckon we'd better start watching out for letters that arrive in the nick of time – or more likely, don't!' The two women laughed together at the idea of themselves as characters in Coronation Street or as *dramatis personae* of a classic novel.

'I'm so glad we decided to go back in the evening though, aren't you? Frank makes a brilliant one-man-band don't you think? He's got such a way with him. He really gets the audience going and he's a talented musician too ... the way he plays all the instruments and sings at the same time. I don't know how he does it. Everyone was joining in. You were nearly dancing, Mara ... yes you were … I saw you!' They were giggling, like schoolgirls, as they recalled the fun of the unexpected adventure.

'At one point though, I wasn't sure whether he would actually be able to go on. He looked so pale when we were all talking about the sale at the Old Rectory. I got the impression that he didn't really know much about it.'

Ellen agreed. 'I thought the same. I felt a bit awkward having mentioned it at first. And then when his brother turned up … they didn't seem too pleased to see each other either. It looked like there was some talking to be done there I thought. Frank didn't seem to know anything at all about a sale if you ask me'

'I got that impression too. Under the circumstances I reckon Frank did really well to carry it off. Actually I liked his brother – very arty looking and a bit intense, but nice, I thought. He's obviously got a lot on his plate, getting everything ready for this sale that he's planning and he certainly seemed to need some support with it all.' Mara looked at her mother.

'I reckon I might be able to do something about that, to help him get things organised – a bit of typing, cataloguing, that sort of thing, and it's definitely the kind of work I'd like to do, but what do you think? It would mean staying on down here for another week or so. I don't even know if this place would be available.'

'Well, I suppose we could stay on, for a bit anyway – although we do have to be back for that meeting with dad's solicitors … about the will and whatever. What was the date of that meeting? I've got it written in my diary upstairs. Can you remember when it was?'

A shadow passed across Ellen's face. 'Oh yes – in all the excitement of yesterday I had forgotten about that arrangement. Everything should be quite straightforward though – it's just a matter of the legal bits I think and it's only the two of us, and your sister of course, who would be affected. Perhaps we could get in touch with them and delay the meeting for a few days – maybe a week or two – it can't make that much difference. I'll give the solicitor's a ring later if we decide to stay and see what can be arranged if you like.'

'Actually, I think I would like to stay down here in Cornwall for a bit longer too. I could use the time to do a bit of research for a piece I've been thinking might make an interesting feature.' Ellen was looking interested as her daughter continued. 'I've been thinking a lot about Dad recently, about all the things he'd done in his life, the things that were important to him, who he really was, that sort of thing.' Mara looked closely at her mother who had turned away, and was now towards the cattle in the field on the far side of the valley. She remained silent, listening or thinking, Mara was not sure but she decided to push on anyway.

'Mum, we know that he was Cornish – that his family home was in Cornwall – but that's about all I know really. She paused and looked at Ellen who seemed to feel her gaze and turned back so that their eyes met.

'And what about Dad's 'Old Rectory'? Is it the same 'Old Rectory' that we were hearing about yesterday, the one in your painting?' Now it was Mara's turn to look away from the questions that she saw in her mother's eyes.

Ellen reached across the breakfast table and touched her daughter's hand. 'Do you know, I've been wondering the same sort of things myself. From the moment I first saw the painting, I've had my suspicions. Your Father would talk about his Cornish roots to anyone as we all know – but as for the detail … I'm sorry to say that I don't really know any more than you. He did say once that he wanted to make a fresh start, put the past behind him … something like that. He would never discuss it with me though, right from the start he would just close himself off if I asked him any questions about his past. You know what he could be like. I hated that cold, closed look of his, so I'm afraid that I simply played the game by his rules. I just stopped asking.'

They sat for a moment in the uncomfortable silence.

'Mum, I really think it's time now. In some ways it's a bit late, I suppose, but I do want to ask the questions. I want to try to find out more about his – about our – family. I want to try to find out if this is the same Old Rectory, if Dad's family actually came from this place, from Lostwithiel. I just want to know … I guess I just want to give myself a bit of time to think about it all … who he was … who I am … what it is that makes any of us who we are. I think I need to do this now … sort out the past, before I can get on with the future.' She grinned suddenly. 'And I reckon that with some strategic shots of the stunning local scenery there should be plenty of interest in the finished article I'm planning too – a good opportunity to combine the professional and the personal don't you think?'

Ellen laughed. 'So it looks like we might both be glad of the excuse to stay on a little longer, then.' Her daughter nodded her assent. 'Then I'll call the solicitors later and see if we can rearrange that meeting. Would you see if you could arrange for us to stay on in this cottage for a bit? I think the paperwork with the phone numbers on is in that blue file over there on the coffee table. If things seem to be to be working out then I'll give Frank's brother a ring and offer him my services – such as they are – for a few days later this week and we'll see how we go from there.'

'You certainly don't let the grass grow under your feet once you've made up your mind!' Mara was teasing now. 'I haven't seen you like this for a while, Mum. I'm glad you're feeling excited about something again.' She reached out for her mother and pulled her into a hug as they stood together from the breakfast table.

Ellen pulled away first. 'Come on then, let's get this show on the road.' Picking up her empty mug and plate and moving towards the dishwasher, she grinned at her daughter; 'there's work to be done.'

Mara laughed. 'I'll get right on it!'

Making his way down Lansallos Street towards the slip, Frank had the purposeful stride of a man who meant business. It was about time that brother of his told him what was going on. This morning he was definitely off-duty and a comfy navy blue fleece jumper and a pair of baggy old beige chinos replaced the bright uniform of the one-man-band – today he was intent on blending in. Despite his best attempts to travel incognito however, a few people greeted him as he passed. Old Bill stopped his sweeping and leaned on his brush on the cobbles outside the Noughts and Crosses Inn.

'Good day to 'ee lad. Down 'ere to see that brother o' yorn?

'Morning Bill. That's right. I haven't been down here for ages … too long. How're you keeping these days?'

'Not too bad – can't complain.' The old man reached down and rubbed the back of his right hip. 'Old bones a bit stiff of a mornin' but what can you expect at my age.' He laughed and coughed noisily. 'Young Dan seems to be doing a good trade down there. There's always plenty of comin's and goin's around 'is place anyway. From what I 'ear, his stuff is really good. I reckon I might even buy one meself, for the missis – if I could just afford his prices that is …' he broke off into another fit of laughter.

Frank grinned despite his own mood; he never could stay down in the dumps for long. 'I'll put in a good word for you if you like – perhaps he's got something on special offer.' This time the two men laughed together at the unlikely prospect.

As he moved off down the street, Frank was smiling again and beginning to feel more like his usual self. The morning was another bright one and the air smelt brisk and clear with a tang of the sea. He glanced up at the gulls, scribbles of white against the blue sky, soaring and gliding in some kind of glorious game, judging by their screeching as they dived to pick at the in-creeping waters. He stood now on the edge of the wall by the slip and watched, enthralled as he had been since a boy, as the incoming tide crept around and under the wooden hulls of a strung line of painted rowing boats, buoying them up until all four were bobbing, red, white, blue, yellow on the silky water. Magic … it had been worth coming down here today just for this.

On either side of the harbour, the morning sun was lighting the clusters of white-painted fishermen's cottages climbing the hillside. Frank breathed deep. He loved all this, the familiar salty tang of the sea, of fresh caught fish and nets ready for mending, of oily rags and boat engines, of freshly brewed coffee. He turned and smiled across at a couple of holiday-makers sitting on a bench cradling mugs of coffee from the flask that was propped on top of the opened rucksack at their feet. Great place for a holiday! Whistling as he walked back towards the gallery on the corner of the slip, he was a Cornishman and proud.

Dan was already sitting at the desk in the back corner of the shop as his brother pulled the door closed behind him. He seemed to be searching for something amongst the piles of assorted paperwork and looked up with an anxious frown on his face which soon turned to a grin as he realised who it was who had entered the gallery before the official opening time – after all the sign hanging on the door was still showing 'closed'.

'Frank – what a surprise! You haven't been down here in ages.' Dan rose quickly from behind the desk – he seemed really pleased to see his brother and Frank could not have escaped the warm fraternal embrace even if he'd wanted to.

'Welcome to my humble abode – here, sit down.' Dan pulled over and opened up a bright red-painted wooden chair that been folded and leaning against the wall beside the piled desk. His green jacket was slung across the back of the chair that he had recently vacated and with the deep cornflower blue of his rolled-sleeved denim shirt and the sunflower yellow of the large ceramic mug balanced precariously on a stack of card files, the colourful scene certainly befitted an artist's studio. Just for a moment Frank felt himself dowdy. He sat carefully on the rather rickety chair, settling his large musician's hands on his knees, looking around with undisguised admiration at the canvases that were his brother's trade.

'How's business?'

'Quite good actually, can't grumble. There's been a lot of interest recently – a few commissions and suchlike – and this kind of thing seems to appeal to the tourists.' Dan waved his hand around at a range of dynamic images depicting the sea in various lights, groups of bright boats in the harbour, ducks on the water just off the slip out front.

Frank liked what he saw and said so. His brother smiled. It was too long since they had last sat down together – this felt good, like old times.

'Can I get you a drink? I can do tea or coffee, instant that is. I might have a beer out back if you want one but I guess it's a bit early for that.' Dan blustered. He was not used to playing host at this time of day.

'No, nothing thanks. I just thought it was time we had a chat. I'll get straight to it. What's all this about a sale? It's in the paper. How can the old house be up for sale when Mum is still in that place? It's her home – she would never let it go like that. And what were you talking about last night? What are you selling? What's going on, mate?' As he spoke Frank was becoming increasingly agitated and Dan was looking more uncomfortable.

'All right, all right. I'll answer your questions, but I don't know anything about the house being sold I swear to you.' Dan placed his hand on his heart as he said this but Frank did not find the melodramatic gesture at all reassuring. 'Where do you want to start?'

'Tell me what you do know. The sale that you were talking about last night at the pub for example – what are you selling that needs catalogues, lists, all that sort of thing?' Frank's tone was confused, cross even. 'Have you talked about it with anyone? Does Rose know? Are you holding the sale at the house? You can't just go in there letting people buy up the stuff, whatever they like. It's family stuff. It doesn't belong to you. You'll never get away with it.' He was really on a roll now and Dan could see that he was getting angry.

'Hang on mate, hang on. Let me explain, will you? Of course I won't be selling anything that's not mine to sell. What do you think I am?' Dan actually looked offended and Frank began to wonder if he had allowed his imagination to run away with him. He leaned back on his chair and allowed Dan to continue.

'I don't know where to begin really. I guess I first started thinking about selling stuff to get some money together for Maisy.' He paused.

'How's she doing?' Frank's expression warmed at the mention of his little niece who he found hard to accept was not so little any more.

'She's fine, great actually.' Dan beamed, every bit the proud dad. 'She's planning to take a gap year before going to university.'

'University? How can Maisy be old enough for university? Where did the time go?' Frank's surprise was genuine.

'It's as much a shock to me as it is to you. Still, that's what she's planning. I know I haven't always been able to be there for her and there's some who think I've let her down, but I want to be able to support her now. I want her to know that her Dad is proud of her, that she is so very precious to him.' Dan rarely spoke with such emotion – it surprised them both. He pulled a handkerchief from the pocket of his trousers and blew his nose. He dabbed at his eyes before shuffling the handkerchief back into his pocket.

'Sorry about that. I got a bit carried away.' He grinned sheepishly, clearing his throat before continuing with the explanation that his brother had demanded. He looked straight at Frank.

'We both know that although Rose treated us both equally, like we were both her sons, brothers … we are actually cousins. Rose is really your mother, not mine. Edward was your father and he was like a father to me, but my real father was not part of my life. I never knew him.'

Frank could see that Dan was not finding this easy. 'You were my little brother in all the ways that mattered; and my mother – and my father too when he was alive – loved you like a son.' Both men nodded – they knew that this was true.

'Well, every year on my birthday my father sent me gifts, toys and things, bought from expensive shops in London by that agent of his. I never wanted them, and never played with any of them. Rose just packed them away and kept them for me. There was a lot of other stuff too – paintings, artefacts from Africa, quite valuable things some of them that he collected on his travels, things that he told Rose to keep for me, for when I got older. I reckoned he was trying to buy my affection or something like that and I never wanted to know about any of it. But now I do. I reckon that I can sell it all and make enough money to finance Maisy's trip and hopefully be able to pay for her fees at university.' Dan had been staring out of the large display window as he spoke but now he looked back at Frank. Frank returned his gaze.

'Right, I'm beginning to see where you're coming from. Will it really raise much money, this stuff you've got?'

'I think it will. I've been doing some research, talking to people, you know the kind of thing. It seems that because the toys were never used, still in original boxes, and because the agent made particularly wise purchases, quite a lot of the items are very collectable, rare even, and you would not believe the prices the right people are prepared to pay for these things. I've already got buyers lined up for some of the items, queuing up actually, bidding against each other before we've even started.' His face was becoming ever more animated. His deep brown eyes were bright below raised brows. He nodded his assurance. 'Yes, you could say I'm feeling optimistic that the final total will be more than enough to give my princess the start in life that she deserves.' Dan was smiling broadly now. 'She's planning to go to Kenya, you know.' He paused and watched the expression on his brother's face – he would always think of this man as his brother despite what they had both just acknowledged.

'She's going to actually go to Kenya?' Frank asked the question with as much awe in his voice as if his niece was about to travel to Fairyland, to the land beyond the rainbow. Kenya had always been part of his brother's legend, hardly a real place at all while they were growing up. As far as he was aware, Dan had never even considered travelling to that dark distant continent that had held his father enthralled – to have accepted that Africa could be visited would have been to raise the question that no-one was brave enough to ask. Why did his father not come back to visit him?

'She's set her heart on it. It seems she's got a friend who's home is in Nairobi and the girls are planning to travel together, in the beginning at least. They're going to have a bit of a holiday at first, so it seems, acclimatise, hang out for a bit around Nairobi then go down to the coast by train and spend a week or so at a hotel that they've seen on the internet. Actually I think that Agnes – that the friend's name – has stayed there before so it should be alright.' Dan was clearly trying to convince himself here as well as the concerned uncle sitting opposite.

'Kids these days, they get around so much more than we ever did. They seem to think that the world is their oyster – no sense of danger ...' Frank's tone was rueful and the two men found themselves nodding as one. 'Hang on a minute – listen to us – anyone would think we were getting old or something.' They laughed together at the moment of self-knowledge.

'I'll make us a cup of tea shall I?'

Dan stood and made as if to go towards the low archway in the far corner of the studio that seemed to lead off into some kind of kitchenette.

'Oh go on then – strong, milk no sugar.'

Frank leaned back on his chair and looked around him, listening to the familiar sounds of tea-making drifting in from the beyond the archway: an electric kettle being switched on, mugs rattling, spoons clinking, fridge opening ... shutting. He was feeling a lot better now that they had talked, more relaxed, less out of control somehow. So ... Dan was selling his own stuff, his own past, releasing equity you could say. Well there wasn't much he could say about that was there? It was nothing to do with him really. He hadn't realised that there was so much stuff though – it must have been stored away somewhere. His mum was good at that sort of thing – business-like, taking control once she was sure that that was the right thing to do, that it was best for her family, for her boys. Her boys ... that's what she had always called them: 'my boys' ... and usually with a note of pride in her voice.

As if on cue Dan emerged from the archway balancing two large mugs of tea on a small round metal tray. He set it down on top of a rather precarious pile of papers and Frank watched somewhat anxiously as the yellow mug was offered to him. He reached across to take it carefully – it was hot and he moved some papers on the corner of the desk to make space to set it down.

'I was just thinking about mum ... about Rose. Have you

been to see her lately?'

'I called in yesterday. She didn't seem too good actually – a bit confused, sad, not like her old self at all. I found it a bit upsetting to tell you the truth.' Dan sipped his tea carefully, holding his mug with two hands. The two men sat for a moment in silence, the steam from the hot tea drifting between them like their shared thoughts of Rose.

'Do you think she'd be okay about you selling your things like this? I mean, won't she feel that she should have some say if you're bringing out from store all the things that she packed away for your future? What about papers, that sort of thing? Will you need to have something to prove that you really do own this stuff? If it's valuable like you say, there might be some documentation you'll need, authentication to prove its provenance – I think that's what they call it – at least they do on Antiques Roadshow.' Frank grinned and looked across at his brother.

'You're right actually. There are some papers that I need her to sign. Some of the really special items are stored in the bank. I can't get hold of them unless Rose signs to release those particular things to me. And yes there are some papers too that I will need, papers that will confirm, authenticate, prove 'provenance' as you suggest.' For the first time a note of uncertainty had entered Dan's voice. He was sitting on the edge of his chair, leaning forward. He seemed suddenly tense.

'What sort of things do you mean? How will mum be able to sign for them in the state that she's in? It probably wouldn't be legal if you could get her to do it, would it, with her being like she is at the moment?' Frank paused before he continued. 'We should have thought of this kind of thing sooner, shouldn't we? We should have arranged for one of us – it would probably have to have been me as her oldest son but I don't really know – to have a power of attorney I think it's called, so that we could have taken responsibility for her affairs properly.' They looked at each other, both of them suddenly aware of their shared concerns.

'What about her solicitors? Perhaps we should speak to them. I'm a bit surprised that they haven't contacted us already, actually. Could you call them later today? After all it probably should come from you, as you say – especially since in actual fact you are legally speaking not her oldest son but her only son.' Dan seemed relieved that the responsibility for this important official duty could be offloaded to the older man.

Frank sighed, reluctantly accepting the inevitability of it all. 'You're probably right. I'll find their number when I get back and give them a call. It'll be helpful to chat through any issues and then if there's anything that needs to be done I can make sure it happens – or at least they can. I'll let you know what they say about releasing your stuff too if you like.'

Dan nodded. 'Sooner rather than later if you could – there's a lot hanging on it.'

He turned and glanced towards the window where the couple Frank had spotted earlier were standing, obviously admiring the large water-colour of Polperro harbour at sunset that was propped on an easel to catch the light as well as the attention of passers-by.

Frank nodded to the couple through the glass and they waved back in recognition. He stood as if to leave. 'Reckon it's time for me to move off so that you can meet your public.' Dan rose too and the brothers moved in the direction of the door. Frank suddenly stopped, turned back: 'Oh I just remembered – there was something else. Did you see that article in the paper about that holiday property company still wanting to purchase the manor? Actually it almost seemed to be implying that they had already bought it – took me by surprise I have to admit.'

Was there a hint of suspicion in his voice? Dan thought there just might be. He held up both his hands against his chest, barring the way for any notion of that kind.

'I promise you that I haven't any idea what that's all about. It's nothing to do with me. That would be Rose's decision wouldn't it? She owns the place after all. It's a dead cert that she's done nothing about it recently anyway so they must be just flying a kite. Don't worry about it mate. There's nothing in it.' He clapped his hand reassuringly on Frank's shoulder and the two men hugged briefly before going their separate ways, Frank to make a phone call in Lostwithiel and Dan to welcome in the day's first customers.

It was not until later, sitting at his desk in a snatched moment of stillness amidst the all the business of his art, that Dan remembered the other important bit of news that he had thought he should share with Frank. With all the other things they had talked about it had completely slipped his mind. His father was dead.

Becalmed, he sat, his thoughts drifting with the ebb and flow of his breathing. And who knows how long the moment might have lasted, had his phone not suddenly set up a buzzing and jiggling across the table, demanding his return to the real world.

'That's right. Yes, it's Ellen ... we met yesterday evening at the pub ... that's right, she's my daughter ... yes, he nearly knocked her over apparently ... yes, he's really good ... we really enjoyed the whole evening ... mmm. Actually it was about the work you wanted doing that I called, the typing, that sort of thing ... if you're still looking for someone, I think I could help you out ... yes, if this place is free for another week, possibly two, we could stay on down here and I could do your work ... She'd be fine about it. It was she who suggested it actually ... yes, she encouraged me to call you, see what you thought about the idea ... she's decided that she wants to do some research for a piece she wants to write, an idea she's got for a feature ... something about Cornwall, our family history, I'm not really sure, but she seems quite excited about it ... Oh good! That would be great ... it sounds to me like just the sort of thing I'd be interested in. I love sales like that myself ... yes, I'd really like to do it ... yes, I could meet you there if you like ... what time would suit you? ... If there are any problems, I'll let you know ... yes, I'll look forward to it. See you there. Bye.'

Ellen was smiling as she put the phone down. She was still smiling when Mara entered the room a few minutes later.

'Well, what did he say? How did he sound? Is he interested? Have you got the job? When do you start?' She flopped down into the armchair facing her mother.

'So many questions! Yes, he sounded nice. Yes he is inter-ested. Yes, we've agreed that the job's mine if I still want it, when I've found out more details about what it is exactly that he needs. We've arranged to meet up tomorrow to talk about it.' Ellen was clearly relishing the prospect.

'That's great – where're you meeting him?'

'Well, that's the really exciting thing – he wants to meet at midday tomorrow, up at the Old Rectory itself.' Ellen clapped her hands together. 'This old house has really caught my imagination, you know.' Enthusiasm for the project was writ large across her face. But all at once her expression altered. 'Oh no … I completely forgot … I'm getting ahead of myself. What if we can't stay on here after all?'

Mara was glad to be able to put her mother out of her misery.

'It's ok. Don't panic. I've just spoken to the office and they've agreed that we can stay on for two more weeks. The next week was free anyway and they've managed to move the couple who were due in the following week by offering them an upgrade to one of the feature apartments in the old house – so everybody's happy.'

'Oh Mara, that's such good news.' Ellen sighed her relief, as she settled back into the armchair. 'How kind of them to go to that trouble for us … I'll call them myself later and thank them.' The smile was back. She couldn't help it; she was so looking forward to having something to get her teeth into again. Lying awake during the night she had even begun to plan the layout for an advertising flyer, to imagine a logo for the sale catalogue.

'I'll give you a lift up to the house, if you like.' Mara was on the edge of her seat. 'I'd love to see it myself – after all if I'm going to write this article, I need to start my research somewhere. We've both been curious about the Old Rectory, haven't we, to know if it's the same as the one that dad used to talk about … I mean, it's probably not … but wouldn't it be an amazing coincidence if it did turn out to be the one …'

Ellen rose and moved towards the window. Looking out over

the garden, she spoke softly at first, as if to herself. 'Yes, it would, especially when you think of all those holidays … all those times when we were so close. Why didn't your father bring us here? Why did he keep us away? Why didn't he want us to see the places where he grew up, to meet the people?' As she turned to face her daughter, Mara thought that she saw a tear.

'I don't know, Mum. It doesn't make sense to me either. But I'm sure it made sense to him. It had to.' She was at her mother's side now. She took her hand. 'Dad would never have meant to hurt us … to hurt you.' She squeezed Ellen's fingers. 'He loved you – he loved us all. He would have done anything in his power to protect us. You know that. So there had to have been a reason – a jolly good reason – for his decision to keep us in the dark.'

'I do know that. You're right.'

Ellen was nodding, her eyes closed. Mara waited, watching her mother's face as the frown passed over and the corners of her mouth lifted.

'Alright then!'

There was a new note of determination in Ellen's voice as she pulled her hand free and stepped away. She had made her decision. 'I'm sure that Theo thought that what he was doing was for the best. But I'm sorry. He can't protect us any longer. I'm the one who needs to step up now, to take responsibility.' She raised her hand, just in time to prevent Mara from interrupting. She was not finished yet. 'No. It's time for us to make choices for ourselves. I want to do this job, and I want to know about the house. You want to discover more about your family. You should do that. It is important for you. If you need it, you have my blessing.'

Mara was grinning, watching as her mother swung into action.

'Now, we need to get on. That solicitor's letter – I think it's upstairs, in my travel folder. I'll fetch it. We have a meeting to rearrange.'

Ellen's new resolve carried her briskly up the stairs and into her room where she located the folder easily. But, sitting down for a moment to catch her breath on the edge of the bed, with the solicitor's letter in her hand, Ellen slumped forward. *'Please accept our condolences on your sad loss.'* Her loss. Her terrible loss – like a weight, she felt it.

Reaching out, she picked up the leather folder from the bedside table. She had been looking at it earlier, the small album she'd made up of their photos before she came away, hers and Theo's, small enough to carry with her, keep him close. Snapshots – his arm around her shoulders outside of their tent in the Masai Mara – the ranger had taken that one, on their first safari. Their wedding day, his brown suit, her white hat, both of them smiling, happy, who had taken that one? Her fingers touched the image and she closed her eyes.

10

Kenya, Nairobi – 1969

'Sorry I'm late sir. The warthogs were out on the playing field again. The little children were chasing them.'

Breathing an apology, the young Kikuyu woman slips into the last remaining seat at the table. In Lind'n Lea School Nairobi, staff meetings start promptly. Several of the other teachers are grinning their sympathy in her direction. The sight of the baby warthogs, tails up, running behind their mother with the younger children giggling in hot pursuit is a familiar one. Even the Headmaster is suppressing a smile behind his moustache.

'Right. Well, as long as everything is in order then perhaps we can get started. I trust that someone is out there supervising or have the children been left to their own devices?'

'Mrs Kitoto is out there sir, with Patience.'

'Good. Well let's get down to business then. We don't want to leave poor Mrs Kitoto at their mercy for longer than necessary, do we?'

So saying, the Headmaster adjusts his spectacles and his papers and surveys the assembled group of young teachers.

'First things first – I'm sure that you've all already met our new member of staff,' he pauses nodding towards the young English woman, smiling and blushing at the far end of the table. 'Miss Ellen Taylor has recently arrived from England. She is new to Nairobi and new to teaching – lots of enthusiasm to share with us all. I trust you'll make her welcome.'

And so, introductions over, the first weekly business meeting of the new school term at Lind'n Lea gets underway. Set on the green edge of Nairobi, at the foot of the Ngong Hills, it is a constant and quiet joy to the Headmaster that on the far side of those rolling peaks, the precipitous landscape plummets vertically to the floor of the Great Rift Valley itself.

Miss Ellen Taylor turns her head, catching him unawares. She smiles and lifts her hand in greeting. From the shaded veranda, the Headmaster has been observing her at her work. Awkward for a moment, he feels himself blush, averts his gaze.

Still smiling, Ellen turns back to the task in hand, shepherding her students into the cool stone classroom, enjoying their playground chatter as they settle at wooden desks. From this distance Theo can hear the sound and then the silence.

She has settled in well, quickly popular with the other staff and with the children. He has been pleased to see her quiet confidence, her friendliness. Her teaching skills have impressed him too. Her lessons are well planned and the pupils keen to learn. He has noticed that she sometimes takes her class outside under the shade of the big tree to

study and he has been intrigued to see for himself the colourful display of work that they have produced about their new 'secret garden' – a quiet reading place behind their classroom. She plays the guitar; she's even started a choir. He was telling Jack about it only yesterday. As Theo turns back to his study, he is grinning. It has occurred to him that he is as taken with the new teacher as are her students. 'Ellen.' Her name feels easy on his lips.

The small private ceremony takes place on the morning of 20th December 1972 at the District Commissioner's office in Central Nairobi. In attendance are the groom's best man, Mr Jack Davidson-Lea and his wife Theresa. Mrs Wood the school secretary and Alice, the bride's best friend and housemate, who also teaches at the school, are the only other guests. The bride is wearing a pale blue dress and jacket with white hat and gloves and the groom beams throughout the whole proceedings in his brown suit, set off at the lapel with a white rose. After the District Commissioner has pronounced the couple 'man and wife' and the assembled friends have wished them well with kisses and handshakes, the small party adjourns to Lind'n Lea where a reception awaits them at the schoolhouse.

The wedding feast has been planned and prepared by Festus the cook. It is laid out along the veranda on trestle tables covered with white tablecloths and decorated with jugs of purple and crimson-red bougainvillea. As the returning party is welcomed in through the school gates, they are greeted on all sides by the smiles, cheers and laughter of the young staff and their pupils.

Everyone enjoys the occasion immensely and the Headmaster and his new wife Ellen, who will surely be called 'Miss Taylor' for a long time yet by her students, declare themselves to be delighted to have been able to share their special day with such a wonderful group of friends.

My dear sister Rose

It is with a degree of surprise as well as delight that I write to let you know that I have married. My wife's name is Ellen. She is young and it is my hope that before long we will be blessed with a family of our own. For me this will be a new beginning.

I am grateful beyond words for all that your love for me has cost you. Please convey my gratitude to Edward also. I know that he is your rock. To me he will always be a dear friend and brother-in-law. I feel myself to be forever indebted to you both.

Give my regards to the boy if you think that would be appropriate, but I can well understand that he may by now think me dead or even wish me to be.

Your ever-loving brother

Theo.

The wooden bench clacks, seesawing on uneven legs as Theo sits down heavily at one end and leans back against the whitewashed blocks of the classroom wall. In the shade of the overhanging thatched roof, the opened letter from his sister lies in his lap:

'Cornwall, May 1975. There has been an accident. Edward is dead.'

From somewhere over behind the staff quarters, the sounds of old Kikuyu women's voices raised in shrill laughter drifts in on the dry air. He shifts, sits upright away from the wall. For a long moment he is motionless, staring straight out across the parched games fields down country to the horizon where the smudge of white cloud marks the far distant summit of Mt Kilimanjaro, over the border.

Coming to his feet, he refolds the letter, tucking it back into its envelope. Just a few days ago the letter containing the formal announcement of the death of Sir James Lind in Sussex, England, had arrived in the post, along with all the attendant official documentation. The implications of that death have yet to be fully understood. But now this … this shocking news from his sister … an accident. Edward is dead and Rose all alone.

The shaggy thatch brushes against his hair as he ducks out of its shade and stands tall in the sun. Turning, he comes to face the Ngong Hills, their purple rolling peaks like knuckles of a giant fist, clenched against the African sky. At his side, his own hand draws up into a tight ball. Without shifting his gaze, the Headmaster raises his fist and presses it hard against his pursed lips. It seems that he might remain that way for longer, but the sounds of children's voices are soon mingling with the scraping of stools on concrete floors, signalling the end of the lesson.

'Good afternoon sir.'

'Good afternoon to you David.'

The young boy and the Headmaster exchange their polite afternoon greetings then they each move on – the boy to change his shoes ready for the games lesson, the man to make plans for himself and for his family that will change everything.

Ellen sits back on her heels and surveys the scene. She makes to stand, then thinks better of it and settles sideways into something like a sitting position, reclining against the sofa. The heat and the pregnancy are sapping her strength.

She is an island, surrounded on all sides by boxes and packing cases, bright kangas and local cloths, piles of folded bed linen, her dresses draped over chairs, shoes and sandals lined up in neat pairs, toe to toe with piles of her books, her guitar. The move back to England is actually happening. She reaches around her thickening middle and massages the muscles behind what was once her waist in an effort to relieve some of the tension there. Her left hand rests lightly across her belly in the familiar stance of the pregnant mother.

'Here, drink your water, Madam. You will feel better.' The young housemaid has come up quietly behind her and now offers the glass.

'Asante sana, Esther.'

The condensation on the glass moistens her fingers as she lifts it from the tray and sips at the cool water. Esther has been her housemaid since her marriage to the Headmaster and the two have become close during that time. If only Esther could accompany them on the trip to England. It would be such a blessing. But no, that would be impossible, unwise and probably unkind too. How could she ever expect the young African woman to leave this beautiful place for the bleak prospect of an English autumn and winter that even she herself is not relishing? Despite the warmth in the shuttered room, she shivers.

England. Ellen had not expected to be returning so soon. Theo's decision to transfer the Headship of the school to Jack, his business partner, school bursar and old friend and leave the country at the end of the summer term, has completely taken her by surprise. Despite her questioning, he has been disinclined to discuss his thinking or explain his reasons further. He has simply said that the time is right, that the move will be good for them. He will oversee the setting up of a new Lind'n Lea School in a former country estate somewhere in Sussex. It will be a boarding school, for both girls and boys – and then she'd seen a glimmer of a smile – it will be perfect for their sons and daughters too. The plural made her smile. He'd added, almost as an afterthought that they would need to leave soon. He wants their first child to be born in England.

Born in England? Ellen is smiling again on that thought. Born in England, but not begun there. She nods slowly, recalling their last safari together to Masai Mara, their tent beside the Mara River. Wherever her daughter is born – for Ellen is sure that this precious baby is a girl – her name will be 'Mara'. Still smiling, she reaches out a hand and Esther helps her rise to feet.

'*Asante sana*, Esther. Thank you. I think I'd better get started on with sorting out some of those school papers next, don't you?

11

Cornwall – 2008

Incongruous amongst the usual mix of bills and gaudy junk mail, the cream envelope came early to the harbour-side studio.

Emerging from the galley kitchen at the back of the shop, Dan was still in pyjamas, with an old fisherman's jumper pulled-over and a breakfast mug of coffee cradled in both hands. Drawn as always to the picture window, he paused, sipping, as he watched the sun creep over the clustered roofs of this fishing village that he was learning to call home. One or two folk were already up and about on the cobbles, the usual suspects tinkering with boats at the water's edge. Seagulls wheeled and squabbled overhead as he unlocked the door, stuck his head outside and breathed deep. The salt air smelled of oily rags, of fish, and of seaweed – it lifted his mood. He was humming one of Frank's songs as he pulled the door shut, clicked the latch, bent to pick up the bundle of mail and returned to his cluttered desk and his coffee. From the kitchen the familiar jingle heralded the news on the hour, and somewhere beneath the piles of papers in front of him his mobile phone buzzed into life. As he scrabbled to locate the source of the disturbance, the morning's mail was shuffled first to this side and then that, finally coming to rest at the back of the desk beneath a pile of brightly coloured catalogues.

'Yes!'

Triumphant, Dan located the mobile phone and snatched it up from beneath the piles of papers, setting off an avalanche of assorted mail that slithered over the edge of his desk and settled around his feet. Barefoot, he almost slipped as he stepped across the fliers and plastic-wrapped brochures to reach the chair by the window, where he sank down, smiling at the sound of his daughter's voice.

'Hey, Maisy … is that you?'

'Dad!' She was shouting as if she had to make herself heard all the way from London to the far western rim of the world. He could hear the smile in her voice too.

'It's so good to hear you. How are things?'

'Good thanks.' There was a crackle on the line, a pause. He waited. 'Are you still there, Dad? I got your letter.'

It was his turn to pause. It seemed a long time since he wrote. 'I'm still here. Listen Maisy … there's something I need to tell you first. I had a letter … my father died.'

'Your father? I'm so sorry, Dad. Did he die in Africa? Was he sick? Had he been ill? What happened?' The questions bubbled up now. She had more.

He has no answers. 'I don't know yet. There's to be a meeting … in London … with his solicitor's … I'll go … I guess I'll get some answers then.'

'I'm sorry, Dad. It must be really strange, not knowing your dad, what he was like and all that. Do you feel sad … knowing that he's dead, I mean?'

'Yes. I think I do. I feel different anyway … it's strange … disconcerting. And with Rose being so poorly too …' his voice trailed to a halt.

'How is grandma? Is she any better? Have you been to see her? Did she ask about me? Is she coming home soon?' There was real anxiety in her questions now.

'I don't think she'll be coming home soon, my love. She may not be well enough to come home at all, you know. I'm not sure if she even recognised me when I saw her the other day.'

'Oh Dad, that must have been awful.' Father and daughter shared a moment of silence that acknowledged things so often unsaid between them, like love, loss, sadness.

'Anyway how are your plans coming on, for your travels?' He is the first to begin again, to move towards her future. 'I wanted to talk to you about funding, about my plans to help you with that. Did I mention about the sale in my letter? I think I did.'

'You said you had something 'on the go' ... that's what I think you said in the letter, but you didn't give any details. You know, it's really great of you to want to help financially dad – and I could definitely do with some help – but you don't have to. I've got a job Saturdays and holidays helping out at the local hairdressers and I've been doing some baby-sitting ... things like that. Mum's going to help me too.'

'I want to support you. I always have and I always will. I'm having a sale ... at the Old Rectory ... of my stuff ... old toys, paintings and suchlike ... apparently some of it is really valuable ... there's already been a lot of interest, locally and from further afield ... I've been making enquiries, getting the word out ... you know me.' She could hear that he was excited. There was enthusiasm, hope in his voice.

'I do know you Dad, and I love what you're trying to do. Look, I'm free next weekend. Can I come down and visit? I could go to see grandma, go up to the old house, hear about your plans, help you even ...'

'That would be fantastic. I'd love to see you ... so would Rose, and Uncle Frank. And you will be able to meet my new assistant.'

'New assistant? What's this? You've never had an assistant before. What's she like? She must have some very special skills to have won you over.' This news was definitely a surprise. She was teasing him now.

'You'll meet her when you come.'

They were laughing together now as they made their plans for the weekend, she gazing out at the painted Madonna across the road and he watching a pair of seagulls tussling over a couple of cold chips on the cobbles outside his studio window.

'Love you too ... Bye.'

As he turned, still smiling, back to the things of the day, his eye chanced on the cream envelope, exposed now atop the spread pile of junk mail. Curious, he picked it up, tried and failed to guess the sender from the handwriting, studied the postmark: London. Intrigued, he carried it back to his desk, remembered his appointment up at the old house and glanced at his watch. Time enough. Adjusting his glasses on his nose, he started to read:

> *'Dear Dan,*
>
> *We haven't met, but I have heard a lot about you, from Maisy. Our daughters are planning to travel to Kenya together – I am the father of Agnes. I understand that you were born in the Rift Valley on Christmas day, 1961. So was I – at least I was born on Christmas Eve – at Kijabe Mission Station …*

Dan stopped reading, looked up frowning, then came abruptly to his feet and moved across to the window. Outside on the cobbles a lone seagull was finishing off the last of the chips.

The church clock from the village back down the lane chimed another quarter hour.

'He definitely said midday. I'm sure that was what we arranged.' An edge of uncertainty had crept back into Ellen's voice. After the surge of confidence, the excitement of a new challenge, she was beginning to doubt herself again. 'Do you think he's forgotten? Perhaps he's decided I'm unsuitable, or too old. Perhaps he doesn't need the help after all.'

Her daughter's tone was reassuring. 'Relax, mum. I'm sure he'll come. He must have been delayed. He'll be here any minute now, I'm sure of it. Why don't we go and sit own over there, on that seat, look.' Mara nudged her gently with her elbow. 'I reckon we'll have a great view out over the valley from there.'

'Just look at those roses. It looks like they're cascading down over the stone wall and the porch rather than climbing up, doesn't it.' Settled on the wooden bench, Ellen was feeling calmer now.

'They're really beautiful. Somebody has obviously taken very good care of this garden. I like it. It has such a peaceful atmosphere too, don't you think, loved, really safe if you know what I mean …' Mara's voice tailed off. She was beginning to feel a bit emotional for some reason. Why did she say 'safe'?

'Strange isn't it, the way the house, this garden, feels sort of familiar, even though this is the first time we've been here.' Ellen paused. When she continued her tone was thoughtful. 'I don't know what you think, but I think that the porch with the roses all over it looks exactly like the porch in that old photograph of your father's, you know the one of his grandmother, the one we always had on the mantelpiece.'

The sudden crunch of tyres on the gravel prevented any further discussion.

Ellen seized her daughter's hand. 'He's here.' The tension was back – in her vice-like grip and in her voice.

Mara turned and smiled what she hoped was a confident smile as the two women made their way over to where the new arrival was clambering out of his car, an apologetic grin stretched beneath his shaggy curls.

'So sorry to have kept you ladies waiting ... one phone call after another ... a letter ... you know how it is. I'm glad to see you making yourselves at home.'

'Oh, I hope you don't mind but that bench was beckoning, with views over the valley and in this lovely sunshine ...' Ellen was flustered again.

'Of course I don't mind. Why would I mind? The view is great isn't it? In fact the whole garden's a real treat. Rose has done a fantastic job with it over the years ... she's an absolute natural. She would love that you're enjoying it too ... and I mean it. Feel free to explore. There's no one around at the moment, you needn't worry about disturbing anyone.' He lifted his hands in an expansive gesture, smiling broadly.

'Thanks for that. I'm sure Mum would love to have a look around later, but it's about the job, the one you need help with that we've come really.' Ellen nodded her encouragement as Mara continued. 'At least, Mum's come about the job. I'm just curious to see this old house that everyone seems to be talking about.' Her eyes crinkled in a grin and the man responded in kind.

'Ah, I like your honesty, and I can't say that I blame you. It's a fantastic old place. Come on in. I'll give you a guided tour if you like before we get down to work.' He leaned back into the car and took out a large bunch of keys, which he fiddled with as the three of them made their way towards the entrance to the Old Rectory.

Despite the warmth of early summer outside, in the hallway of the old house the atmosphere was surprisingly gloomy. Ellen shivered, rubbing her hands together, tugging the sleeves of her cardigan back down over her wrists. There was a definite chill in the air. Mara had already moved across to look at some old photographs displayed one atop the other on the wall just inside the door. The man was occupied for the moment, checking through a small pile of mail that someone has placed on the hall table.

Ellen was still by the door, her eyes wide as she took in the spacious hallway. From the rug at her feet, out over the flagstones, along the passageway towards a door that stood tantalisingly ajar, probably the kitchen, her gaze swept over her new surroundings. She glanced up at the galleried landing then back down the staircase to the other doors, cream painted, leading to other rooms – dining room, study perhaps, definitely one of them is a sitting room – she guessed at what might lie behind each door. How she would love to wander, to explore this old house. Turning, she realised with a start that she was being watched, and raised her hand ready to apologise.

'It's fine.' Dan shook his head. He had set the mail back down on the table and was smiling, seemed to be enjoying her reaction. 'It's a lovely old house, isn't it, but I think it feels lonely now, empty without Rose, sad somehow. Sorry if that sounds a bit whimsical, but that's how it seems to me. When Rose was here everything sort of lit up. The house came alive – it was a proper home.'

'Rose is your mother.'

The man tucked his hair behind his ear, an unconscious gesture. He turned his attention towards Mara and nodded. 'Yes. She is. She's not well at the moment. She's in hospital … a care home down in town actually. They don't think that she's going to recover fully … not really, not back to her normal self.' He cleared his throat, embarrassed. He was saying too much. 'I'm sorry, I didn't mean …'

Ellen reached out, touched her hand lightly on his sleeve. 'Don't worry – its all right. We understand what it is to worry about the people you love.'

'Thanks. Well, anyway, let's get on. I promised you ladies a guided tour didn't I? Perhaps we could just do the shortened version today? Let's start at the back, with the kitchen.' And so saying he turned and led the way to the open door at the end of the hallway. Mara glanced towards her mother and raised her eyebrows.

'After you.' The two women exchanged a smile and followed on behind him.

'This is such a lovely house.' Ellen paused. 'Actually you know, its more than that – it's a lovely home. I really like all those jugs that your mother ... that Rose has collected. I do the same. I collect interesting jugs, bowls, plates, and things like that. My kitchen is full of them.' She was back to herself now, chattering happily as she walked ahead of the others back along the hallway. The tour was going well. The kitchen was a great success and upstairs was beckoning.

'She does ... and it is. In fact it's not just the kitchen that's full of her trophies.' Mara laughed. She was enjoying the easy banter.

'Trophies?' Dan was entering into the spirit too. 'Can this woman be trusted?' He smiled on the question, eyebrows raised as they paused at the foot of the staircase.

'She buys them at sales, junk shops, antiques fairs, that sort of thing. And she usually manages to get them for a good price – she chats, makes friends with the vendors so that they don't like to disappoint her.'

All three were laughing as another key turned in the lock. When Frank opened the door and stepped into the hallway, three faces turned towards him, caught somewhere between shock and a smile.

'Hey, mate. I didn't expect to see you again so soon. You didn't mention anything about coming up here today.' Dan's surprise at seeing his brother was clearly a pleasant one. He moved forward to welcome him, took his arm as if to introduce him to the two women.

'This is my brother, Frank.' The smiles and nods of the others seemed familiar. He suddenly remembered. 'Oh, sorry ... yes of course ... you all know each other. You met ... we all met ... down at the Red Lion.'

'We did. It's good to see you both again.' Frank grinned.

'You look quite different without your costume, the red and white hat, the colourful trousers ...' Mara was happy to see him too. Her tone was light. 'You look quite normal now, quite nice actually.' She flushed. She hadn't meant it to come out quite like that.

'Well thanks for the compliment.' Frank was enjoying the moment. But then, as he remembered what had brought him to the Old Rectory so unexpectedly this afternoon, his smile faded. His tone was serious as he addressed his brother.

'Actually, Dan, I've got some news ... about the house ... and I thought I needed to tell you about it as soon as possible, and in person. It's all been a bit of a surprise really.'

'What is it, bro? You look as if something awful has happened. Come on, let's go into Rose's study for a minute . You can tell me what's going on in there.'

He gestured towards the door to the sitting room.

'You ladies make yourself at home in the sitting room while we get this sorted out, if you don't mind. Have a good look round – enjoy yourselves, but,' he turned towards Mara, 'keep an eye on your mother. We don't want her walking off with any of the valuables ... taking any more trophies.'

Laughing, the women made their way through into the sitting room and Dan ushered his brother into the little room at the front of the house that Rose used to use as her study.

'It's the house, Dan, The Old Rectory. It's not for sale after all.' Frank paused and his brother blew his relief through pursed lips. 'But,' and here Frank raised his hand, 'our old stables are, and the gardener's cottage along with the paddocks. And here's the really surprising thing, so are those three adjoining cottages and that big stone building further down the road, the one that looks a bit like a chapel, you know it, the one that was refurbished a few years ago, with the terrace gardens up the hill, the Old School House.' Dan was nodding, waiting. 'Well, apparently, they're all being sold by the same vendor, the official owner of The Old Rectory, and that's not Rose.' The brothers shared a look of incredulity and Frank shook his head. 'It's true. This house doesn't belong to Rose at all; it never belonged to her, though she is allowed to live there throughout her lifetime.'

The two men shared another look of total disbelief as Frank continued. 'It seems that the Old Rectory actually belongs to her brother, as does the Old School House and those cottages. The whole estate has belonged to him, the eldest son ... ever since their parents died. And now it's all being sold, to that holiday property company, just like it said in the paper – although they got the name wrong, it's not The Old Rectory that's being sold, it's The Old School House.'

Frank had slumped onto Rose's little settee, Dan was sitting on the swivel chair at her desk, hands on his knees, leaning forward towards his brother. Their faces were close, so different from each other, yet mirror images of disbelief.

'What? What do you mean? How can the house not belong to Rose? There must be some mistake. Who told you?' Dan was frowning, his tone incredulous.

'The solicitor, mum's solicitor. I called him like I said I would, you know, about the power of attorney and that. Well, he asked me if I'd seen the letters and I said 'What letters?' And he said 'The letters about the properties ... about the sale...' and I told him that no, I hadn't seen any letters and he said that Rose had had several letters and that she was going to talk to us about it, show us the letters ... all that sort of thing ... and I said no. Didn't he know that Rose had been ill, is still ill ... or at least not recovered ... and we don't know anything about it. That's when he told me.' The words came in a rush. Frank's elbows were on his knees and he dropped his face into his cupped hands. The shock of it all had left him drained.

Dan was leaning back into the swivel chair. He was staring out through the small window onto the garden at the front of the house – or was he looking at the sky – soft blue with scudding clouds, as he spoke. 'To be honest, I never thought that Rose would sell the house. She would have talked to us about something like that. I know she would. But what about all this other stuff? The Old School House you say, and the cottages, the paddocks too? And they're being sold? Why? What's it all about? Who made the decision to sell? Did her brother decide? Why would he just do that?' Dan's questions tumble out into the space between them.

'It seems that he didn't … just do it, I mean. He and Rose have sorted it all out together. It was his idea. But they talked about it and she has agreed. It looks like it's all going ahead, though I don't think anything's been signed yet. They've agreed in principle to sell to the property company who have agreed to build a cottage, all mod-cons, adapted to Rose's own specifications, down near the rose-garden where she will have those views that she loves out across the valley. According to the solicitor she was, is, really happy about it, and he, her brother that is, wants the money. It seems he has plans to refurbish this place. 'Bring it into the twenty first century,' were the solicitor's words. He said he had the impression that Rose was expecting, at least hoping, that her brother might move back here himself one day.' Frank stopped. He was done. The silence grew between them as each tried to digest the astonishing surfeit of information.

'But he's dead.' It is Dan's turn to drop the bombshell.

'He's dead? When? How do you know?'

'I had a letter … from his agent … there's a meeting at the end of the month I think it is. They want me to go.'

'Oh listen, I'm really sorry, mate. I had no idea.'

Frank reached out, placed a hand on his brother's knee. 'He was your father.' He hesitated. 'Was he sick?'

'I don't know anything about it. I don't know him … I never knew him. I don't know what I should feel. I don't feel anything much at all.' Dan was staring once again out of the window, up at the sky. His voice when he spoke had the sound of someone reasoning with himself. 'So – my father owned this place – as well as all that other stuff, but he is, or he was, selling. What is that all about? What was he trying to achieve? Was he really planning to move back here?' Dan shook his head. 'And what happens now that he is dead? Who is responsible now?'

'This whole thing just gets more and more weird. We'll have to get an appointment with the solicitors ... with mum's solicitors ... they might be able to help us make sense of all this. It was strange enough to begin with, but now, with her brother dying, and Rose being as she is, will the whole thing go ahead? Could we stop it? What happens next? Should we stop it, Dan, at least pause it anyway?' Frank was suddenly certain that he wanted the sale to be stopped. It was a gut reaction, but he trusted it.

There was a look of urgency on his face as his brother turned and their eyes met, held for just a second. Dan made his own decision.

'Yes! We need more time. Make the call!'

'Come and look at this view Mum, over the garden and across the valley.' The sun through the square bay window was lending gold to Mara's curls and lighting the pale roses on the arm of the sofa where Ellen was sitting back, making herself comfortable. She seemed to be listening, but not necessarily to her daughter.

'Just imagine having a garden like this, mum? Look at the way it's been terraced, those roses, that old grey-stone wall. There's a door there – look. I'll bet that leads into a walled garden, a secret garden with apple trees ... and a swing.' Mara turned back into the room, eyes bright. Unable to resist any longer, Ellen moved to join her and soon the pair of eager gardeners were pointing out plants, guessing about colours, reminiscing about the gardens that they had worked on together.

'And look, over there, I think that's a fountain in that pond, amongst the water lilies. I wonder if there are fish. I love the effect, with that little bridge and look, there's a hammock between those trees. Wouldn't it be great to have a really good look around the garden? Perhaps we could go out, through those French windows. Look the key's here in the lock. Shall we go?' With her hand already on the key, Mara looked to her mother.

'Wait, Mara, wait. I think we should wait until Dan comes back, don't you? It's his house. He might think it's a bit presumptuous of us, don't you think, to just go wandering about wherever we want. After all, it's the first time we've been here. I'm sure there'll be other opportunities. He did say we should have a good look around in here though. Come on, look at all those photographs on the mantelpiece. You'd love those, I'm sure.'

The painting of a young girl sitting reading in a cane armchair surrounded by roses caught Ellen's eye and she moved across for a closer look.

'I thought so. Look, Mara. This is one of Dan's, see, his signature, just like on my painting. He's got it just right. That's exactly how you used to sit, all curled up lost in a book. I do like his work. He has such a talent for faces, the expression's perfect. He's great with colour too. I'd like to buy some more of his work. What do you think?'

Mara was standing over by the fireplace. Maybe she had not heard the question. She seemed to be studying a framed photograph, holding it close with both hands. When she turned towards her mother, all the earlier animation was gone from her face.

'Mum – you should come and see this.'

'What is it Mara? What have you found?'

In response, Mara offered the photograph. Curious, Ellen took it. Looking down, she found herself face to face with the familiar black and white image.

'It's Theodora. It's your father's grandmother, your great-grandmother. But what's she doing here?' Confused, she looked up.

'And look at this one.' Blank-faced, Mara offered another framed image.

'It's Theo.' Ellen paled. There was no doubt. It was Theo, her husband.

'Come and sit down, Mum. It's a shock, I know, seeing him here, like that.' Mara felt it too as she led her mother back over to the sofa.

The two women were still sitting side-by-side, when Dan

entered. Their strange silence caught him unawares. Looking from one to the other, he saw that they were each holding one of the photographs from the mantelpiece.

'So sorry to have left you ladies like that. Is something the matter? Your mother looks pale. Is she all right? Shall I fetch some water?'

It occurred to Dan that, from the look of her, Mara might need of a glass of water too. But she did not answer his questions. She came slowly to her feet and faced him.

'It's these photographs, Dan. We know them. We have a copy of this one on our mantelpiece at home. It is my great-grand-mother, Theodora. And this one ...' She took the second photo-graph from her mother and held it out towards him. 'This one ... this one is of my father.'

'I'm sorry ... what? What do you mean? There must be some mistake ...' Confusion was in Dan's voice as he scanned the faces of the two women. There was no mistake. He moved across to the armchair, sat down as Mara handed him the photograph of the young man with the moustache. For a long moment he was silent, studying the image. He had paled. His skin had taken on a greyish tone. He closed his eyes.

'Dan, what is it? Are you all right? Is something wrong?'

He looked up then, met Mara's eyes, turned to face her mother. When he spoke, his words left the two women speechless. 'This man ... this man is my father.'

The sofa was an island of safety in an insecure world. Mother and daughter sheltered there.

Dan got up and moved away, slowly, as in a dream. Alone at the window, he was caught in the same light that had earlier gilded the young woman, his unsuspecting sister. His sister? Frowning he surveyed the garden. Those reddish curls, the pale-blue eyes ... She couldn't be. He looked down at his own hands, seemed to study them; shoved them deep into his pockets. And then he thought of Rose and the man who just might be a brother released the long breath that he had been holding unawares.

The photographs were still on the coffee table. In the fractured air of the room, they alone remained unchanged – Theodore, Theodora – facing the camera with the same blithe self-belief, heedless of the altered universe in which these three people now found themselves.

'Do you know something? I had actually wondered about your name ...' Dan turned back into the room. 'Mara. It's a place, a game reserve I think, and a river too in Kenya isn't it? It's such an unusual name. I was even wondering if your family had connections with Kenya. To think ... I might have asked you about it later.' He was staring straight at Mara. She met his gaze. His look of incredulity was reflected in hers.

'Yes. You're right, Dan.' It was Ellen who broke into the building silence. 'Theo and I named her Mara, our first daughter, after that most beautiful of places. It was where Theo and I spent our honeymoon, our special place. We would go back there whenever we could. In fact, you know, I've always believed that her life really began there, beneath the African stars, beside the Mara River.' The older woman was finding her voice. Memories were bringing life back into her face though she seemed quite unaware of Mara's blush at this surfeit of information.

Coming to the Old Rectory, Ellen had already begun to suspect, perhaps hope for, a link with her husband's past. Even so, seeing the photograph of Theo as a younger man had given her a jolt. Then when Dan had dropped his own bombshell, everything in her suddenly blanked ... as if her inner hard-drive had crashed. She might have swooned like some Victorian heroine had she not already been seated.

But now, with her daughter at her side, she was visibly rebooting. After all, she was the parent, at least the grown-up, here. Her sense of the shape of things had certainly taken a knock but she would not be a victim. There were things to be sorted out, things to be investigated, things to be understood. And then there was the man to consider, this man who might even now turn out to be her husband's son. Her pulse quickened at the thought, but still she smiled, raised her hand in a gesture of something like welcome.

'Why don't you come and sit down here Dan. It's been a

shock for us. It's been a shock for you. I think we've all got things to talk about, questions to ask. Let's look at those photographs again shall we? Are there any more in here?'

As Dan moved to respond to her suggestion, she looked around the room, continuing to talk, trying to bring some normality back to the situation.

'That picture of Theo with the chief … it's one we've never seen before.' She reached out to take the photograph from the table, as Dan settled himself in the armchair beside them. For a long moment she studied the familiar features, younger but unmistakeably Theo.

'Do you know how old he was here, or when it was taken? It was obviously in Kenya and, by the look of it, quite a while before I even met him. Do you know who took the photograph?' Ellen was looking to Dan for answers. Dan was looking bemused. The afternoon's events had simply added to the sum total of things that he did not know about his father. As she looked into his face, Ellen fancied that he was near to tears.

'How old are you, Dan? When were you born?'

At this he brightened. He did know the answers to these questions at least.

'I was born in Kenya, on Christmas day, 25th December 1961. Actually I was born just after midnight, out under the stars – so the legend goes – in the Great Rift Valley. There was an accident. My mother died, or was killed. That's all I know.'

Mara had seemed preoccupied but at the mention of his birth, the date, she looked up, her expression quizzical. She had thought him younger. She had questions, many questions, of her own – but where to begin? Shifting in her seat, she turned to face him, seemed about to speak, but then she hesitated. Ellen was watching them both. She waited while her daughter struggled to find the words.

'So, Dan, if, as you say, my father was your father … then … who was your mother?' Mara blurted her question. She looked to her mother, then turned back to face him. 'Dan, if my … if Theo was your father … then … your mother must have been …'

Dan nodded, finishing her sentence for her: 'My mother must have been black.'

12

Kenya, Rift Valley – 1938

Late-born after many brothers and many sisters, Njeri has always known that she is precious. In the mud-and-grass huts of her father Chief Njoroge and his three wives, she is an ever-welcome visitor, petted and played with by sisters and aunts alike. But Njeri is not a toy. She is a girl, a five-year-old girl who wishes that she were a boy - her given name means 'daughter of a warrior'. She likes to race about, to chase chickens, to stalk the skinny goats. She follows after the herd-boys in the long grass around the *shambas*, and she talks – she talks to everyone. Gap-toothed old women bent double like ostriches, raking over the stony soil pause in their labours to gaggle with the little girl. Young women thrashing the field-ripened beans stop from their work to banter. Mothers milking goats in the trodden-earth spaces between the huts squirt milk into her opened mouth. The *mzees*, the old men of the village, greet her like an elder as she joins their circle and sits playing with stones at their feet.

There is much wise talk at these *mzees'* gatherings and much complaint. What the child Njeri has not yet understood is that her people are squatters. They hold just a few acres on a white man's farm, and in order to stay on the land they must work for the owner for one hundred and eighty days out of each year for which they are paid twelve shillings for each thirty days. They must also pay a hut tax to the government – twelve shillings for each hut, which the landowner collects on the government's behalf. Many of the squatters have been born on this land and but for the hated hut-tax have come to think of it as their own. Njeri certainly knows this land as hers. It is in her eyes and in her feet – if it were taken from her eyes, her feet would surely find their way back home.

Alexandra, or Alexa as her husband calls her and as she now thinks of herself, is hot, really hot. Beneath the wide-brimmed hat, her sandy curls are plastered to her head. She can feel them damp with sweat, sticky on her forehead. Her mouth is dry. As she makes her way through the long grass towards the Kikuyu village, dry stalks swishing, crackling under her boots, she wonders how it would feel to be barefoot. She has watched the Kikuyu women walking freely over the rough ground – perhaps they feel nothing. Their smooth, peat-coloured skin is certainly easy in the harsh sunshine as hers is not – her pale, freckle-dusted cheeks and nose seem to blush deep pinkish-red at the very thought of the sun. But the long sleeves, the culottes that she is forced to wear for protection, the heavy sunhat ... surely these are simply adding to her discomfort. In a moment of devil-may-care she takes off the offending hat and shakes out her hair.

'Hah! That's more like it!' Better already, she uses the hat as a fan to move the air, cooling her face – not quite cooling, but at least the lifting air feels refreshing. A noise on the path behind her catches her attention. She turns. The tiny girl is frowning, seems intrigued by the strange spectacle. Alexa meets the child's gaze. She tilts her head, smiles. This *toto* is brave. She does not scamper screaming away, but tilts her tiny head in sharp imitation, returning a tentative smile of her own. Alexa uses the sunhat to fan her own face then flaps the hat towards the little girl, fanning the air onto her face. The girl wrinkles her nose, giggles. Alexa fans again – more giggles. And soon they are both enjoying the unlikely game – the English woman and the African child, strange playmates, both grinning from ear to ear.

'Hat' – Alexa sets the hat upon her head, removes it, points to it, 'hat' sets it once more on her head. The little girl watches as the white woman turns, waves her hand and resumes her walking towards the twists of smoke drifting up into the blue haze from the shambas just beyond the shaggy stand of gum trees. Scampering barefoot over the rough, dry stalks, the child follows in the woman's wake, pausing, statue-like, every now and then, nostrils aquiver at the strange scent lingering on the air. It reminds her of the smell that comes from the tall white flowers after the rains.

Alexa is well aware that she is being followed, and by whom. She is grinning as she comes upon the cluster of grass huts. Moving more easily now over the smoothed mud paths, she passes between *shambas* planted with maize and sweet potatoes, raising a hand in greeting to the old woman bent from the waist raking over the rough soil. Since their arrival at the school just a few weeks earlier, Alexa has become a familiar face here. She likes to sit and talk to the women, watch them at their chores, hold their babies. She tries to use Swahili words that she knows, to learn more from them, to teach them some words of English.

She understands that her behaviour might well seem strange, that her interest in these native women, their life and their work, is not usual amongst settlers or their wives in this British Colony. Nevertheless, being a woman of strong opinions, she is determined to make her own choices. Lifting her chin, Alexa smiles at the thought of herself as an independent thinker who likes to challenge her husband with extracts from her reading. 'All that is needed for evil to triumph is that good men do nothing,' from Edmund Burke, is a current favourite. It is a game they both enjoy.

'*Jambo*, Njeri.' Alexa is still smiling as she calls back over her shoulder now to her little shadow, inviting her closer: '*Kuja hapa* – come here,' holding her un-gloved hand out behind her. In moments, she feels the small dry fingers touch against hers and she enfolds the little hand in a warm clasp. By the time they come to a stop in front of a round, grass hut where a young woman is sitting on the threshold, suckling her baby, the two are holding hands like old friends. The young mother invites the *mzungu* to sit on the low three-legged stool and soon the talk, with much sign language and laughter, is of children and husbands and weather. Alexa tells of her own children and wishes they could be here to see how different life is for these people, to discover for themselves how much there is to be gained from time spent in this way.

She says as much to her husband one evening as they are

preparing for dinner up at the house. 'She is such a bright little thing Teddy. She follows me everywhere. We're becoming quite inseparable. I showed her a picture book yesterday and she was really interested. I'm sure Theo would love her – they'd have great games, stalking each other through the long grass. I think they must be about the same age – perhaps he's a little bit older, but not much. She's quite charming, so full of fun. Rose would adore her – little Njeri would be treated like a doll – our lovely daughter would have her all dressed up in ribbons before too long.'

Turning from his own toilette, her husband is smiling as he watches his young wife dressing, picturing her children in this strange and exotic place. She misses them, would have brought them if she could, but, knowing they are well looked after, she had been eager to accompany him on this trip.

The meeting with Jomo Kenyatta, at their home in Cornwall had come at a crucial time for her. His wife was a passionate woman of sharp intelligence – she had always been an avid reader and at that point some of her reading and thinking was causing her to raise questions about the Empire, about Britain's role in its Colonies. He remembers with fondness their lively discussions over supper during that period, when she had challenged him about his British public school attitudes, about the arrogance of young men from schools such as his who thought it their God-given right to go out and rule the world. Often he knew that she was teasing, but still, her questions had provoked his own thinking and he had been at pains to defend his own position on more than one occasion. They'd finally come to some agreement over the government's White Paper of 1930 in its assertion that 'Primarily Kenya is an African territory … where the interests of the natives must be paramount.' Like himself she was becoming interested in the African perspective and so, when a friend had introduced him to the delegate from Kenya at one of his meetings in London, he had invited the young African down to Cornwall for a few days. The opportunity to talk with this articulate young Kikuyu and to listen to his views had proved formative for them both. They liked the man too – had enjoyed his company – and he had been so good with the children.

This invitation from his old friend Charles to visit him and his wife Catherine at their school in out in Kenya's beautiful Rift Valley had come at just the right time. And now here they are, stepping out along the lamp-lit veranda in the warm African night, surrounded by the buzz of cicadas, the whooping of frogs, the scent of distant wood fires on the air. As his lovely wife hooks her arm through his, he knows himself to be a happy man.

'I hear you've been down to the village again, Alexa. You're making quite a name for yourself. The red-haired *memsabu* is becoming a favourite amongst our Kikuyu neighbours.' Charles is beaming, the affable host, as he welcomes them, pours drinks for his guests and his pretty wife beneath the gently whirring ceiling fan in the candlelit dining room.

'I just love to be down there, Charles, to watch them, to listen. There is so much to learn. This is such an amazing place – you are so fortunate you two.' Alexa is smiling, raising her glass to her host and to her hostess. 'Thank you so much for these opportunities ... for your kind hospitality.' The friends happily drink to each other, to their friendship, to their future, as canapés are passed around and another pleasant evening unfolds in the flickering candlelight.

Beyond the candle-glow, beneath the star-spangled African sky, the uninvited guest, the girl Njeri sits, knees up, on the warm stone of the steps, nibbling on a maize cob, listening to the rise and fall of their voices. She pictures the red-haired *memsahib*'s quick smile, her eyes blue like the sky, her white hands like butterflies as she speaks, soft to the touch like a baby bird. Njeri holds out her own hands in the borrowed light – not begging but remembering that hand-clasp, her small brown fingers held firm by the kind white woman who had reached out to take her hand.

'But I don't just want her to go to school, Charles. I want her to go to your school!' Alexandra is standing in front of the headmaster's desk. Her face is set firm, lips pulled in tight. From the look of her, it seems she might stamp her foot. A curl has slipped loose over her forehead; another has escaped the clip in the breeze created by the ceiling fan. She lifts her hand and tucks the offending strand behind her ear. With the same hand she slaps down on the edge of the desk. The headmaster turns in his swivel chair, away from her, towards the open window.

'Charles, she is bright. She has learned to read the books I have been showing her from your schoolroom as quickly as any white child I have ever taught ... more quickly than most I should say. She wants to learn. I believe that she would make an excellent student if you would just be brave enough to give her a chance.'

Charles swings his chair back around to face her. His face is flushed; he has taken her bait. 'Brave enough? Brave enough you say! It's not a question of being brave enough.' Despite his strong inclination to behave in a gentlemanly manner towards this woman, his guest, he can feel himself beginning to lose his temper. He is not accustomed to being told what to do, not in this tone, not by any woman. He takes a deep breath.

'Look Alexa, this is not anything to do with bravery – it's just that I am not sure how the other parents would react to a Kikuyu child studying in the same class. Njeri would be the first Kenyan child to be educated in a school like this ... in this school I should say, since it is only in this school that I am Headmaster. I don't know ... I really don't know.'

'Oh Charles. So you are not saying 'no'. If I can convince you ... We have two more weeks here, 'till the end of the month. If by then she can show you that she can settle in class like the other students; behave with good manners; listen and learn her lessons; then you might say 'yes'? Teddy and I will pay her school fees, send money, set up a trust ... whatever you want ...within reason of course. Please say that there is a chance.'

Alexa's hands are clasped in front of her now, beseeching. For a long moment Charles meets her eye, unblinking. Then, all of a sudden, his face relaxes and he is smiling.

'All right then – you have a deal. She is on trial. Convince me. Actually I know that you and Catherine have already been talking about this. She feels the same way as you do about Njeri. She can see her potential like you can … although I know that it's you who is the object of Njeri's devotion not my darling wife. Still … Catherine assures me that she will give Njeri any extra support she needs as long as the girl continues to want to make the most of this opportunity.'

'Oh, thank you … thank you Charles. I assure you that you will not regret this. I will speak to Njeri, talk to her father … her mother. I'll sort out her school uniform and I'll make sure she knows how to behave in class. I'll do all I can to help her make a success of this, I promise you.' Alexa is positively glowing in her enthusiasm.

'I will sort out the details with Teddy … financial contributions that sort of thing. We men are still good for some things you know.' Charles laughs as he stands up from his chair. It is her cue to leave him to his work. She takes her cue and moves towards the door, waits while he opens it for her, bowing slightly as she moves past him into the sunlight.

Alexa feels like dancing, whooping for joy, but just in time remembers that she is an English lady. She turns, walking lightly across the grass towards their guest room annexe. Once inside she kicks off her shoes, twirls like a child, then, suddenly exhausted by her successful mission, sinks down into the basket chair and lets out a long sigh – not sad but smiling broadly. She closes her eyes, imagining Njeri's delight, the difference that this opportunity will make. She, Alexa, may not be able to change the world, but she can make a difference in this one child's life and who knows where that will lead.

Her thoughts turn to her own children, her Theo and her Rose. If only they could be here to share in this moment. Alexa imagines them all laughing, playing together, dancing, singing songs. She leaps up and moves towards the small writing desk; she will write a letter to her children and tell them all about the little girl Njeri. She will send them a photograph of her so that they can think of her as their friend, almost like a sister. Alexa imagines Njeri visiting their home in Cornwall when she is older. How lovely that would be!

'My darling children

Your father and I are having a lovely time here in Kenya. I hope that you are both being good for your Aunt. Daddy and I are missing you both very much and we are looking forward to seeing you very soon. My darlings, I want to tell you about a little girl called Njeri. She has become my friend and I know that she would like to become your friend too. She is a Kenyan from the Kikuyu tribe. She is about the same age as you are Theo but we are not quite sure because people here do not remember birthdays like we do. I am sending you a photograph of her so that you will recognise her when you see her one day when she comes to visit us in Cornwall ...'

And so the happy mother's letter to her own young children back home in England, in Cornwall, continues with more details about the heat, the holiday, about the school and about this great opportunity for Njeri. At its conclusion she urges them once more to be good children and then she sends them all her fondest love.

13

Cornwall, Old Rectory - 1939

Just as he does every night before he settles down to sleep, Theo is reading his mother's last letter. Her special message to him: '*Mwanangu*', my son; her fond '*Kwaheri*' goodbye to them both. He whispers again the closing sentences, imagines her voice, speaking the now familiar words, sending her blessing :

'Be good children for your Aunt and remember always to be the best that you can be. Daddy and I are looking forward to seeing you both very soon now.
With all my love to you my darling children from
Your Mother
P.S. Daddy sends his love too and Njeri says 'Jambo' to you both.'

'*Jambo.*' Theo whispers the strange word into the silence. He has learned that '*Jambo*' is a greeting, the Swahili word for 'hello'. '*Kwaheri*' is the word for 'goodbye'. '*Mwana*' is the word for 'son'; '*Mwanangu*' is just one word in Swahili, but it has two words in English. It means 'my son.' From his mother, '*Mwanangu*' is precious.

He folds the letter neatly along its well-worn creases and tucks it back inside the envelope. He has read his mother's last words so many times that he can recite them by heart – he knows that he can do this because he has been practising, night after night in the long sleepless hours, sometimes with his eyes closed and sometimes with them open, staring up into the darkness, watching the slow change through shades of grey to morning.

Alone in his single bed Theo has finally worked out a way to manage the pain of his great loss. If he draws in a long, deep breath through his nose, holds it very tight for a count of twenty – at first he could only do ten – then lets the air escape very slowly through his lips until it is all gone, at the same time imagining that the pain – he pictures it deep purple – is flowing out with the breath into the darkness, through the gap in the curtains, out through the opened sash window into the night and away with the wind. If he does all that then the ache in his throat and in his chest, the pain that makes him want to explode into uncontrollable sobbing is not so hard to bear.

But now, turning back the thick candlewick bedcover he climbs out from the warm sheets. Padding across the cold floor to his dressing table, he replaces his mother's letter in his special box with all her other letters from Kenya, alongside the first letter that he received from Aunt Catherine, the one which had included the note from Njeri. Closing the box carefully he returns to his bed and slides back down in under the covers.

Theo knows that he has a good memory. He heard Aunt Grace saying as much just the other day to one of the visitors who came to take tea with her, to offer their condolences. He heard her say that, for a child of his age, he is exceptionally bright and has an excellent memory for facts. She went on to say that she expected that he would do very well at St. Andrew's school for boys when he started there after the Christmas holidays. Just thinking about being sent away to boarding school makes Theo's insides lurch. He is tempted to start his 'purple pain process' all over again but decides against it – he can handle this one by himself. This pain is only a blue one – they're not so bad.

He has been working out his own colour code for pain ever since he and Rose were first called into the sitting room by Aunt Grace. There she had told them, in her quiet voice, that their parents had been involved in an accident on their way back home to England. The accident happened in Cairo, which he now knows is the capital of Egypt. They were both killed instantly. He can remember speaking the word 'instantly' in his mind, hearing each syllable, wondering what it had meant for his mother, his father ... they were killed 'instantly'. He remembers looking into Aunt Grace's grey eyes, watching the tears trickle down over her pink cheeks. He remembers the lace handkerchief crumpled in her hand, dabbing at the teardrops, wiping her nose. He remembers how she reached out and pulled Rose to her chest in a tight embrace, how she laid her hand on his shoulder. He recalls her words: 'You'll need to be a brave boy now for your sister.'

But Aunt Grace does not understand that Rose is the brave one. It is Rose who is not afraid of hairy spiders, or wild horses, or barking dogs, or big waves, or high walls or dark cellars. Rose is not afraid of anything. It is Rose who takes care of him. It was Rose who gave him her special box so that he could keep his treasures safe.

Lying under the covers in the quiet darkness he thinks about his mother's letter tucked up safely in his special box. He thinks about where she was when she was writing it – he tries to imagine her curly hair, her smile as she waited for the ideas to come, her tongue between her lips as she writes on the tissue thin paper. He thinks about the girl Njeri.

Njeri was in the letter. She was the last child his mother had played and read with, the last child she had sung to. In her short letter Njeri said that she loved his mother too – that she had cried when Aunt Catherine had told her that memsabu Alexa was dead. There is a small photograph of Njeri in his special box. He yawns and pulls the bedcovers up to his chin. Perhaps tomorrow he will write a letter to Njeri. He might send her a small photograph of himself and Rose in the garden with Sam the dog. She might write back to him; she might become his penfriend. Rose has a penfriend who lives in Sussex. It would be fun to have a penfriend – a penfriend who lives in Africa. That would be something to tell to the boys at school – an African penfriend with black skin just like that friend of his father's. What was his name? Theo searches his excellent memory … Jomo … yes that was it, a bit like '*Jambo*' the Swahili word for 'Hello' … Jomo Kenyatta … a nice man. He rubs his eyes, yawns once, yawns again. When he goes to school he will take his special box with the letters and the photographs in it; he will put Jomo Kenyatta's photograph in the box too.

'Theo, are you still awake?'

Rose is at the door in her pink dressing gown, her shadow, her beloved retriever Sam, at her heels. She whispers her question, watches her brother come up onto his elbow, enters on tiptoe and perches herself on the corner of his bed, pulling up her feet as the old dog flops beside.

'Theo, do you think he'll come? Father Christmas I mean? Do you think he'll know where to find us? What if he thinks we're with Mummy and Daddy? He might not know where to look for us ...' Her round face with its halo of sandy curls, so like their mother's, is a picture of despair in the pale light that seeps under the door from the landing.

'He'll find us Rose. I'm sure he will! Mummy and daddy will tell him about us. They will tell him that we're still here. Aunt Grace has left him a drink just like Mummy usually does. Everything is going to be all right Rose. Don't worry.'

His words bring reassurance. She nods. 'I expect you're right. They'll probably meet him in heaven. Goodnight then Theo, sleep tight ... I'll see you in the morning. Happy Christmas to you.' So saying, she plants a kiss on his cheek as she leaves, tiptoeing with her shadow back along the landing to her own bedroom to wait, more peacefully now, for this first Christmas morning without Mummy and Daddy.

As Theo slips at last into sleep he is smiling. The sooner he gets to sleep, the sooner Father Christmas will come, and then after Christmas, if he has a penfriend, maybe school won't be so scary after all.

14

Kenya, Rift Valley – 1951

Theo can hardly stop grinning. He is here, at last, at the Old School out in the Rift Valley. He can scarcely believe it. Alone in the guest cottage, he dances a jig, like a schoolboy - but he is a teacher now, at least he will be once the new term begins. Composing himself again with some effort, he sits back down at the desk. At the very same desk where it was written all those years ago, he folds the last letter from his mother and tucks it back into its envelope. Holding the tissue-thin memories between finger and thumb, the young man takes a moment to draw breath, closes his eyes. In the lamp's glow, a hint of a frown suggests concentration as he listens to the strange sounds and scents of the African night. He opens his eyes. On the desk in front of him, his special box stands open. It seems silly to have gone on calling it that, childish really. But when his sister Rose first gave it to him soon after their parent's death, that's what she'd called it. He can still hear her voice. Closing his eyes, he can see her.

'Theo this is my special box. You can have it now … to keep mummy's letters in … all of your precious things … anything you like really. If you feel sad you can look at the things in it and they might cheer you up. Anyway, it's yours now. I want you to have it. You can keep it for ever.'

He remembers being filled with gratitude, humbled by such a precious gift. In that moment he had understood for the first time how much Rose loved him. Her commitment was 'for ever.' And so he continues to treasure the special box, replacing the precious letter amongst the photographs and other letters, which have become his treasure trove. He locks it in the secret way known only to himself and to his sister. That done he turns his attention back to the task in hand: settling himself in and getting ready for dinner.

The brown leather travelling case that was his father's stands opened beside his bed in what is actually the guest room, but which is to be his for the Christmas period. When school re-starts after the break he will transfer to a *rondavel,* a small round bungalow, staff accomodation which he will share with another young man, Jack Davidson-Lea by name, Mathematics teacher by profession. Apparently, Jack's parents have a farm up near Limuru.

Thinking about the coming term brings a grin to Theo's face. His old friend from school and university, Daniel Lind, has promised to visit soon. He has even agreed to teach some art classes, although he has made it clear that it is the chance to paint in this glorious Rift Valley setting that is his real motivation not the students nor Theo's precious 'cause' of 'education for all'. The pair have been friends ever since they started at boarding school on the same day. They were in the same House, had adjacent beds in the same dormitory and discovered quite soon that they had both lost their parents in accidents. The further discovery that these separate accidents had happened in East Africa sealed the bond between the two boys. Neither had shared details, but young Theo gradually came to understand that Daniel's parents, both the offspring of very aristocratic early settlers, were killed in a hunting accident. During school holidays the two lads have spent time in each other's homes – at least Daniel has stayed at The Old Rectory in Cornwall. Theo has often visited his friend at the home of his grandfather Sir James Lind, a large country estate in Sussex. But what Daniel has always talked of as his 'real' home, his parents' farm on the outskirts of Nairobi in East Africa, was being man-aged by an aging Uncle on his mother's side. Recently Theo was delighted to hear that Daniel is planning to return to the Colony in the New Year, to take over from his uncle and run the farm himself. His arrival can't come soon enough for Theo. His friend has even joked that he will be travelling out with Princess Elizabeth and her husband – at least Theo thinks it is a joke – with Daniel you can never be quite sure.

'Theo, are you all right in there? Supper is almost ready. Njeri has just come over too.' It is Aunt Catherine. Her gentle knock on his door, her soft voice … it is not hard to understand why his mother counted this kind woman amongst her best friends.

'I'm fine thank you, Aunt Catherine. I'm so sorry to keep you all waiting. I'm just coming.' Theo rises quickly and opens the door to his Aunt. She is dressed up for this special supper, smiling warm in the lamplight. Insects are thronging in the bright beam of the lamp – he must remember to take his medicine against malaria. There are risks living out here – he must not forget that.

'There's no hurry really my dear. I just wanted to make sure that everything was alright.' He stands back and she enters so that he can shut the door against the flying creatures that are beginning to turn their attention to the oil-lamp inside the room. Theo offers her the chair and she sits.

'Everything is more than all right, Aunt Catherine. I am so grateful for this room; for everything that you and Uncle Charles have done to make all of this possible. After the travelling to get here … it was so good to see you both on the platform at Nairobi Station.' He grins at the memory of his arrival.

'That train journey is quite an experience isn't it? The service is so good in the dining car and the food is generally quite acceptable too if I remember rightly.' She smiles at the young man she has almost come to think of as her own son. 'The bunks are quite comfortable too aren't they?' She looks across at the bed in this guest room. 'I do hope that you will sleep well here. You won't forget to secure the mosquito net will you? We don't want you to get bitten … although one or two are perhaps inevitable on your first nights here I'm afraid my dear.' She comes to her feet. 'Anyway, I mustn't keep you here chatting. Uncle Charles and Njeri are awaiting us. Njeri has been looking forward to meeting you. I understand that the two of you have become friends, penfriends that is. I am certain that neither of you will be disappointed to meet each other in the flesh, as it were. She has become a fine young woman. Your dear mother would have been proud. Your Uncle and I certainly are.'

Theo feels himself blush in the wave of heat that has suddenly made his skin prickle. He is definitely looking forward to meeting Njeri after all this time … but he is also feeling quite nervous, very nervous actually. He adjusts his necktie, pulls at the knot and tucks a pesky curl back behind his ear, clearing his throat as he does so. The older woman smiles, watching his preparations as he comes to his feet, lowers the flame in the lamp and moves to escort his Aunt in to this special Christmas supper. Closing the door behind them, Theo has a sudden image of his parents setting out together along this same veranda. In his imagination they are smiling their encouragement. In the warmth of this East African Christmas night, their well-beloved son smiles too, believing in their watchful goodwill.

15

Kenya, Rift Valley – 1952

'Look at this one. They're really good, Daniel.'

In the late afternoon sunshine, the two men are standing, shoulder to shoulder, before an array of colourful artwork set out to dry along the veranda.

'I'm so impressed. It's all you, you know. You've shown them how to do it – to catch the movement, to blend colours. You should definitely consider teaching as a full-time option. Uncle Charles would employ you. I'd employ you. You're a natural.' The young schoolmaster nudges his old friend.

'Well thank you for that glowing endorsement, but you know I'd go mad if I had to teach all the other boring stuff like you do. It's the art that I love. It's all that I'm good at really.' Daniel's laughter is infectious. 'Anyway, the energy all came from the pupils themselves. They were just full of it: the trip up to Nairobi, that reception at Government house, marching past the dignitaries with all those other schoolchildren and their teachers cheering and waving their flags, not to mention seeing Princess Elizabeth herself and her handsome young husband. I just told them to close their eyes and remember what they'd seen, to focus on the colours and movement of the flags, to imagine the hats and heads as pauses. When they opened their eyes, we talked a bit about colour and dynamic, then they just got on with it. It's your students who are naturals.' This time it is the turn of the artist to nudge the schoolmaster.

'Well, whatever the reason, this was their best work yet. We'll have to get some of it up around the school. They'll be so proud. Uncle Charles ... sorry ... 'Sir' will be really pleased with them.'

The young men turn and together make their way down over the steps and across the grass towards the wooden bench from where they can continue their conversations, whilst still keeping an eye on the groups of children who are enjoying some free time before the bell rings for supper. Most of the students are boarders – during term time this is their home.

'It's a good thing you're doing here, Theo. Whatever you say about me, you are definitely cut out to be a schoolmaster.' Daniel claps his friend on the shoulder and Theo smiles, his eyes surveying the scene with real satisfaction and a degree of pride.

'By the way, how is Njeri? I haven't seen her around today.'

Despite his efforts to make it sound so, this is clearly not a casual question for Daniel. He shifts his position on the wooden bench. His tone has altered and his demeanour is more serious as he continues without waiting for his friend's reply. He has something important to say.

'Theo, I know that she goes up to meetings in Nairobi, but she's going to have to be careful. There's trouble brewing, big trouble. The fact that she works here with you, that she's been to a white school ... Things could get very difficult for her. If this Mau Mau thing gets going it won't just be the whites who are targeted. Apparently, even loyal Kikuyu are being forced to swear the oaths, you know, under threat of reprisals against their families, torture, even death.' He swallows hard; turns to face his friend. 'I've heard that these forced oathing ceremonies are being held at night, inside huts, sometimes on European farms too, for fear of being discovered. Who knows where it's all going to end?' His question is rhetorical but the answer he fears is in his eyes. 'I was hearing just the other night that a farm not too far from ours was attacked by a gang. Nobody was badly hurt thankfully, but the property was wrecked and the Kikuyu house staff have all disappeared, scared for their lives apparently.' His sigh hangs in the air, mingles with the children's voices. Minutes lapse in silence, as the men reflect on the implications of this news.

'My uncle is getting out you know, going back to England, now that I've arrived – he's too old for all this and he's not been well either.' Daniel's elbows are on his knees now as he shares this last news, his head in his hands.

'What will you do? How are you going to manage on your own?'

'You're right, Theo. I don't know much about farming and nothing at all about managing the estate. I reckon I'll just have to rely on Freeman, the manager that my Uncle's employed to do the job for a while, but not for long I hope. The chap seems quite good on the farming side, but there's something about him that I just don't like.'

When Daniel continues he is speaking into the distance. Theo can hear the concern in his voice and see it in his clenched hands.

'Apparently this guy's got plenty of experience managing big farms like ours, from the time he spent down in South Africa, but I just don't like the way he is ... with me to some extent ... he's surly, only just the right side of downright rude ... but mainly with our African workers. He's cruel, Theo. I don't trust him, or his son for that matter. The boy John's just a lad, he looks about thirteen or fourteen, maybe fifteen, but he's got a mean streak, just like his father. The Kikuyu women are definitely frightened of him, of them both. There are stories going round, rumours of beatings and other very bad stuff, talk of rapes. I'm going to have to do something about it – I just hope it's not too late.' Daniel is sitting forward on the bench now, his fists drumming on his knees. His fear is real.

Theo can feel it too. He has worries of his own and he is relieved to be able to share them with his friend. 'Njeri is actually up in Nairobi at the moment, staying with friends out at Kangeme. And yes she is still going to meetings. In fact she has even spoken at one or two rallies recently. I tell you Daniel, she is a fiery public speaker, one of the few women I've listened to who can inspire the men.' Despite his fears, Theo turns and they share a grin of recognition.

'She's still helping out with classes here at the school but recently she's become very involved with the Kenya African Union.' Theo pauses and glances over his shoulder. He lowers his voice and his tone is conspiratorial. 'Since Jomo Kenyatta became its president she has been working quite closely with him, supporting him at meetings and suchlike, rallying more women to the cause, the struggle for freedom. She talks endlessly about Uhuru, self-government, getting rid of the hut-tax. It's the land issue that's at the root of it all, that's getting them all fired up ... and who can blame them? There's little justice in it as far as I can see.' He sighs, shrugs his shoulders. 'Aunt Catherine, bless her, is really proud of Njeri. I'm certain she thinks of her as her daughter ... but lately I have the feeling that she is becoming more and more concerned for her safety, especially when she's out overnight.' At this, Theo shakes his head, frowning. Daniel can see that it is not only Aunt Catherine who is worried about Njeri. Theo is concerned for her too.

'What does she have to say about the oathing then ... all these rumours about secret societies, getting naked and drinking blood out in the forests, vowing to kill all Europeans and their collaborators? All that sort of thing doesn't really seem like Njeri to me. She's passionate about her causes I know, but she's not a killer surely.' Daniel is smiling now in an effort to lift the mood, as he looks straight at Theo. He has only met Njeri a couple of times but he likes her.

'You're right; she's not. She's always arguing for the political way forward ... some agitation perhaps, like strikes, demonstrations, protests ... you know the sort of thing. But she's not in favour of the kind of violence we've been hearing about. As far as I can tell, neither is Kenyatta. She was saying the other day that he's against the savagery and violence of the Mau Mau response, despite the rumours about him. I know that my father held him in high esteem. He spoke and wrote of him as a man of rare insight, of natural wisdom. I was only a boy when I met him first but he seemed like a kind of hero to me even then.' He pauses, seems to hesitate, then, decision made he leans in toward his friend. ' I was going to tell you, later. Njeri arranged for me to meet with him.'

'What? And you thought that was a good idea ... in the

current circumstances I mean? You're one of the white settlers that they're all vowing to kill, you know.' Daniel's tone is sharp.

'It was okay actually. She told him about me. He was interested in meeting me again. He said he'd come if it was safe ... somewhere out in the Aberdares ... in the forest. Njeri got it all sorted. I just wanted to do something, meet him again, talk with him about the way things are going. I took my photograph with me ... you know, that one that he signed.'

'Of course I remember the picture ... but did you really think it would make a difference? Did you think he'd remember?' He pauses, but when no response is forthcoming he continues. 'I know that he's been special for you; that he was a friend of your father's. The people that my grandfather knows in Sussex, the ones that own the nursery near his estate, Lindfield I think their name is ... where Kenyatta was working for a while during the war years ... they all used to speak very fondly of him too ... everyone liked him. But times have changed; things are different out here. You must be careful, Theo.'

'Don't worry. It was fine. After all, I might be white but I'm not really English.' Mischievous now, Theo is grinning. 'I'm a Cornishman ... remember, we fought the English too!' The proud Cornishman leaps to his feet and starts to sing, his strong tenor voice taking everyone by surprise:

'A good sword and a trusty hand
A merry heart and true
King James's men shall understand
What Cornish lads can do.'

Despite his determination to be serious, Daniel is dragged into the merriment. As boys they have sung the Cornish anthem together many times. They even performed it once on stage, dressed in period costume and fake beards, at the age of about ten or eleven.

'And shall Trelawney live?
And shall Trelawney die?
Here's twenty thousand Cornish lads,
Shall know the reason why.'

The commotion catches the children's attention. Soon they are streaming over, laughing, clapping, and dancing as the grown-ups continue with the performance then take their applause. Theo, laughing too, shoos them back to their own games and collapses next to his friend. 'It was *Trelawney* that saved me actually.' Theo is still panting.

'What do you mean? *Trelawney* saved you?' Daniel is incredulous.

Nodding slowly, breathing deep, Theo talks softly to his friend beside him, eyes still on the playing children. 'We were there, somewhere out in The Aberdares, deep in the forest, I don't know where exactly. I'd been blindfolded most of the way – for my own safety they said. To be quite honest with you, I was beginning to think I'd made a mistake then. Men just appeared out of nowhere, and yes, when they saw me, a white man, they just went crazy. There was a lot of shouting, threatening talk and gestures – they thought I was an English spy … all that kind of thing. But when Kenyatta arrived, I showed the photograph and he remembered me. He asked about my parents, offered his condolences when I told him about their death. He said he was sorry that I had come to his country at such a time. Although I was definitely scared, I told him that I still believed in the ideals that he and my father had talked about, the vision they had shared. He shook my hand then.'

'He shook your hand? Just like that? Theo, I had no idea that you'd done this, taken such a risk!' Daniel is sitting up, staring back in horror. 'Why didn't you tell anyone?'

'They'd never have let me go and it was something I needed to do. Anyway, it was all right. I'm all right. Like I told you – *Trelawney* saved the day!' He is grinning again as he goes on with the story he has decided to tell.

'Just listen, let me finish and I'll tell you how. One of the men would not let it go. He kept coming up close, really close, threatening, leering right into my face.' He grimaced at the memory. 'He kept shouting, 'You *Mzungu*! You English! I kill you!' and poking his *panga* knife into my chest. I don't know where I got the courage from, but I looked him in the eye and I yelled, 'I am not English! I'm Cornish! I am from Kernow! Kernow!' and you'll never guess what I did next …' He sat up abruptly and turned to face his friend. He seemed about to laugh.

'Okay. What did you do? What did you do next, you fool?'

'You'll never believe this, but it's true. I started to sing. Out there in the forest, surrounded by Mau Mau fighters I stood there and sang '*Trelawney.*'

'You sang *Trelawney*? Are you mad?

'I sang Trelawney. I told them it was my Anthem. I told them it was our Battle Song against the English … King James and all that! They were convinced. They wanted me to teach them the song. You'd never believe it! There they were, dancing about in that forest-clearing in darkest Africa, in the middle of the night singing:

'And shall Trelawney live?
And shall Trelawney die?
Here's twenty thousand Cornish men
Shall know the reason why.'

Theo stopped singing. 'They called me *Kernowi* then, the man from *Kernow*. They liked me. They liked the song. They thought I was funny. It had made them laugh. They said I was brave. That was my name: *Kernowi*. That's what they call me now.'

Daniel was silent. Theo waited.

'You might have been killed.'

'But I wasn't. I'm all right. I will be all right. And if I'm not, you can sort out all my affairs … my last will and testament.'

Theo is laughing now, joking with his friend. But Daniel is not smiling. For him, this is all too much to take in. And this subject in particular is no laughing matter. 'Don't joke about things like that, Theo. I don't like it, not when the situation is getting so serious out here. It's not funny my friend. As far as I can see, we'd all better be sorting out our 'last Will and Testaments'. In fact I've already been thinking about it, I'm going to do mine very soon. You can look after it for me.'

Theo is still smiling but Daniel shakes his head. 'I'm not joking, Theo. If anything happens to me, there's no one, no family, except for my grandfather of course, but he won't be there forever and I'm his only heir too … no heirs of my own … not yet anyway

... no one to pass it all on to ... the farm out here ... the house in Malindi ... grandfather's estate back in Sussex, in England.' He turns, looks directly at his best friend. 'There's only you, Theo. Will you take care of things for me? Will you be my heir? Can I leave it all to you? If something bad happens you'll know what to do? If I die out here?'

'What are you talking about? You're not going to die any time soon. You don't need to worry about all that yet.' Theo is taken by surprise, but he can see that Daniel is serious, that he is actually considering this as an option. His friend really is waiting for an answer. He turns away. The answer when he gives it is playful. 'Of course I'd be your heir.' He laughs. 'I'll be your Cornish heir ... fresh ... smelling of the sea! Don't you get it? Cornish heir ... Cornish air! Come on ... you're meant to laugh! It's funny!'

'Cornish air? As far as I remember, Cornish air is fresh, that's true, but it smells of farmyards and cattle dung!' Their laughter causes another outbreak of hilarity amongst the nearest groups of schoolchildren.

The sombre mood has lifted now as Theo finishes the thought. 'If I was your heir though, I'd use it all to found a series of schools, really good schools, you know, with scholarships, funding for those children who really need support ... all in your name ... can you imagine that?'

Any further conversation is precluded by the sound of the bell, rung loud and long by one of the older students. This is the bell for teatime, one of the several bells that mark out the day for pupils and staff alike. For Theo it is a call to duty. Leaping to his feet, he turns to his friend; 'Come in and get a cup of tea and some fruitcake if you like. I need to be in there for a while ... routines you know. You just make yourself comfortable. I'll see you later. We'll chat more about this over supper, if you still want to that is.'

Daniel watches his friend go, cheerfully rounding up the dawdlers, shepherding the chattering groups of children towards the dining room. He might just stay out here for a while. He is comfortable in the shade and the mosquitoes are not biting yet. The paintings along the veranda catch his eye and he smiles. It was definitely worth the journey down from Nairobi. He is glad that he came after all. He is planning to stay here overnight – it would be too dangerous to travel after sunset – and then return to his farm in the morning after an early breakfast. Later this evening, after supper he plans to raise the issue of his Will once more. It has been niggling away at him for a while, since soon after he arrived in the country.

Panic is in the newspapers and in the air. Behind all the bravado, all the Colonial pomp and circumstance, there is a definite sense of looming disaster. As far he has been able to gather from talking to the owners of nearby farms and then listening to the Jacksons and some other old friends of his parents at a dinner party last weekend, the recently retired governor Sir Philip Mitchell has simply been turning a blind eye to the upsurge of Mau Mau violence. But there is no ignoring it now.

According to the talk at the club, Henry Potter the acting governor will be more than glad to hand over to the new man for the job, Sir Evelyn Baring, when he arrives at the end of the month. With all the rumours going around Nairobi of horrific Mau Mau attacks on white families and on loyal Kikuyus ... surely hyperbolic tales of crazed violence lurking out there in the dark ... savage murders ... Daniel is feeling anxious. Some of the farmers he met just a few days ago in the men's bar at Muthaiga were talking about banding together, fighting back, sorting out the natives in their own way. They want him to join them. They all have guns. He has a gun himself. There are guns everywhere. No one feels safe. He wouldn't dream of mentioning all this to Theo. Theo is sure that things will be sorted out peacefully. But he, Daniel, has not been sleeping much at nights, out there on the farm. He is wondering about moving in to Nairobi, perhaps staying at the Muthaiga Club for a while. He is ... he can scarcely admit it to himself ... beginning to be afraid for his life. And if he dies without making a will, then what will happen to his affairs? He has already spoken to the family's solicitor in Nairobi, asked all the questions. Now that he has finally hit on the solution, he will not let this opportunity pass.

16

Kenya, Rift Valley - 1953

Atop the young pine tree, lopped and decorated for the festive season, the large silver star that travelled with Catherine and Charles all those years ago from England is listing precariously to the left, bowing under the heavy burden of their expectations.

'It was all a sham, a show trial. 'The Kapenguria Six' that's what they're being called you know. Kaggia, Karumba, Kubai, Paul Ngei, Oneko and Jomo Kenyatta – they're Nationalists, not criminals. The charges were trumped up, the witnesses were bribed and so was the judge. Locked up in Kapenguria! Seven years hard labour! What do they think all that says about British Colonial justice?' Theo's question needs no answer in this company, but nonetheless his eyes are challenging as he takes in his audience.

'Kenyatta might have been leader of the KAU but I tell you he is not behind the Mau Mau uprising.' On the 'not,' he slaps the back of his right hand across his left palm – for emphasis. 'Sir Evelyn Baring ...' there is disdain in Theo's voice as he enunciates the name again, '... Sir Evelyn Baring and the whole Colonial government just wanted him out of the way. Declaring a 'State of Emergency' – it just gave them an excuse to make the KAU 'an unlawful organisation,' round them all up. Kenyatta was against the terror attacks, the forced oathing ceremonies all along. I heard him say it myself. I was at that meeting, with Njeri when he spoke out clearly, told them it was against Kikuyu law and custom. If only they'd listened. His grievances were always about the land, saving the land, protecting the Kikuyu customs, the integrity of their traditional way of life. In the midst of all the savagery and violence, his at least was a voice of reason. None of this needed to have happened. Now they're rounding the Africans up, treating them like animals ... why should they be surprised when they start acting that way?'

The young speaker is pacing the room, gesticulating with his right hand, a gin mixed with tonic water is thrust into his left by Uncle Charles as their other guests look on.

Reverend and Mrs Cookson from the nearby Church of Scotland mission have been invited to stay the night, as has Joyce McElroy, a young American nurse from the mission hospital up at Kijabe. Daniel is here too. He has become a frequent visitor to the school of late, 'practically a member of the family,' according to Aunt Catherine when she introduced him to Joyce earlier. Jack Davidson-Lea the young mathematics teacher is also here, debonair on this festive occasion in silk cravat and matching waistcoat. He has not gone home to Limuru for Christmas this year as his family is in England, at their country house just outside of Bristol, ostensibly for his mother's health. The last guest has not yet arrived and it is this absence that is contributing to their hostess's agitation. Njeri has finally given way to pressure from her beloved Aunt Catherine and has promised that she will try very hard to make it back in time for the special Christmas supper. Catherine has not asked 'from where?' She is only too well aware that Njeri's commitment to the cause would make it hard for her to share any information and even harder for her Aunt to hear. And then there is the curfew.

Since the new Governor declared the State of Emergency at the end of October last year everything has spiralled out of control. Any hope of a peaceful transition to Independence has surely been lost. Nairobi has seen terrible violence, with mass arrests of suspected Mau Mau rebels by the police and the army. And now the Colonial government has recruited thousands – about 20,000 if the rumours can be believed – of so called 'loyal' Kikuyus as 'home guards', given them guns and uniforms and sent them out to round up more rebel fighters; practically a civil war. Around the country whole Kikuyu communities have been herded like cattle into 'protected villages' surrounded by rolls of barbed wire. Conditions inside these villages are deteriorating fast and, from the detention camps, horrific stories of beatings and torture are emerging. Anyone caught breaking the curfew is shot dead on sight.

Aunt Catherine swallows hard, blinks back her fears, glancing anxiously from her mother's big clock on the mantelpiece to her adopted nephew.

'Theo, why don't you come and sit down over here, my dear? It's Christmas and you're frightening our guests. Let's at least try to have a peaceful Christmas supper ... while we still can. Njeri will be here soon, I'm sure.'

Reverend Cookson, tall, buttoned-up in his best Sunday suit behind his young wife's chair, coughs, adjusting his spectacles. Mrs Cookson simpers in her flower-sprigged cotton frock and sips at her lemonade as her hostess continues.

'Things aren't too bad for us out here at the moment are they, although there are soldiers everywhere, the King's African Rifles ... I haven't been out but I was hearing from one of our parents that they're stationed somewhere around Gilgil.' Aunt Catherine looks towards Joyce for confirmation. She has driven through that way on her way from Kijabe.

Before Joyce can either confirm or deny the rumours, a scuttling in the dark, a barking of dogs, a sharp whistling and a flurry of Kikuyu drags all eyes to the door. Uncle Charles is on his feet, reaching for the rifle that has been standing in the corner, against just such an eventuality. Daniel is at the door as it swings open and Njeri, clutching at her side, stumbles forward into his arms.

'Ambush ... men with pangas ... out in the trees ... he's bleeding, must get help.' She is gasping, her words barely audible. There is blood spattered across her face, oozing from a gash on her forehead. Joyce, unruffled and competent in the face of danger, surges forward to help, her strong shoulders supporting Njeri as they limp towards the armchair. Theo and Jack are out on the veranda, around the garden, eyes and flash-lamps searching the night, checking for intruders, calling to each other, to anyone who might be lurking amongst the trees. Moses the ancient askari who has been on watch at the gate appears through the darkness, clutching his wooden club, his eyes shine bright, caught in the beam of the lamp. Fear is written large on his leathery face, panic in his laboured breath. Relieved to find reinforcements, he joins forces with the young men as they complete their sweep of the area around the house.

It is only as they return across the grass, having found nothing, that Jack spots the body slumped at the bottom of the veranda steps. The man, at least it seems to be a man, was not there when they left; he must have dragged himself out of the bushes while they were searching the grounds. Moses is dispatched to guard the gate. The two young men are soon kneeling beside the body, turning him onto his back. The man's eyes are closed, but he is breathing. There is blood staining his torn shirt, running down the side of his face. Theo reaches out and turns the man's head. He recoils in horror at the gory mess where the man's ear had been.

'Whatever is this? He's been slashed – by a *panga* I'd say, probably in the skirmish. His ear has been practically severed.' Recovering himself, Theo is already attempting to lift the man. 'We need to get him inside.'

As Jack takes the man's other arm, Reverend Cookson appears on the veranda. He is unbuttoned, in shirtsleeves now, bloodstained. He has carried Njeri onto the couch, assisted Joyce with cleaning the wounds. He spots Theo and speaks urgently. 'She says there's a man ... out here somewhere ... injured ... badly ... you've found him. Quick, let's get him in here.' He is down the steps, lifting the man's legs and between them they carry the limp body up onto the veranda, through the doorway, onto the wooden floor of the dining room.

Mrs Cookson and Aunt Catherine are busy, clearing away the festive table, carrying everything through into the lamp-lit kitchen at the back of the house. Uncle Charles is emerging from there with tea for the shocked and the wounded. Daniel is sitting anxiously beside Njeri, pressing a thick wad of some kind of dressing against the gash on her forehead, across her eyebrow. He is holding her limp hand in his. Her eyes are closed, her face strangely ashen.

As the men arrive with this new patient, Joyce, completely the nurse now, moves swiftly to assess his injuries. She directs the men and they fetch water, cloths, antiseptic from the store cupboard in the kitchen, dressings.

Aunt Catherine, returning from the back of the house, pauses by the table, surveys the shattered festive scene. Christmas night and the crisis has burst right into this room ... room at the inn? Catherine's smile is fleeting, not in her eyes. She looks over to where Joyce is organising the care of the injured man, cleaning, dressing wounds. He is groaning now, moaning in a language she cannot understand. There is one word he keeps repeating, over and over again: 'Kernowi ... Kernowi ...' it seems to have meant something to Theo but the word is strange her. It is not Swahili. Perhaps it is Kikuyu, perhaps it's a name, perhaps it's his own name. Who is this man lying bleeding on her wooden floor? Where has he come from? And Njeri ... thankfully her wounds this time are not life threatening, but Catherine has feared for a while that something like this would happen. Lord, protect her. Mrs Cookson appears quietly by her side. Catherine turns, hostess again.

'Come with me dear. We'll need blankets ... pillows. I think that the patients will be spending the night in here and I guess several others will need to be in here to take care of them. I think the young men will probably want to keep watch too, in case of any more trouble. We'll bring blankets from the guest rooms, and from our room. Would you help me carry them, my dear?' Catherine leads the way and Mrs Cookson follows on her heels, out into the warm night, along the lamp-lit veranda, through the onslaught of winged insects drawn towards the light.

Christmas night. For a moment Catherine stops, breathes deep as she looks up. The young minister's wife, standing at her shoulder, does the same. Overhead, the canopy of diamond bright stars seems to be looking down, perhaps watching to see what happens next, maybe waiting for the heavenly host to break into song. But not this Christmas. Not here. There will be no singing tonight. In the silent night, Mrs Cookson reaches for Catherine's hand and the two women stand together, gazing up at those stars, each in their own way offering a prayer. At that very moment, back inside the house, Daniel Lind is keeping watch over Njeri, silently doing the same.

17

Cornwall – 2008

'Did you say that you were born at Christmas? Christmas Night 1961?'

At The Old Rectory, they had moved into the kitchen and were around the table now drinking tea. Ellen's hands were cupping her mug, drawing comfort from the warm china. Across the table Mara was clutching a bright orange cup as if it were a life belt. Dan seemed more relaxed, leaning back in his chair, fiddling with the handle of the mug on the table in front of him. Several minutes passed in silence, before he answered Ellen's question.

'That's right. It was Christmas night 1961. As I said, all I know is that there was a car crash of some kind and my mother died. I think there was a donkey involved somehow. There'd have to be, wouldn't there, it being Christmas after all?' He glanced at the others but no one was smiling. 'The donkey just stepped out onto the road, in front of the vehicle; I think that was what Rose said. I'm not sure if my mother died as a result of the crash or of my birth or something else.' Dan sighed.

Ellen was nodding. 'If I remember correctly, it was in 1961 that Kenyatta was released from prison and became leader of KANU – the Kenya African National Union – and then there was a conference in London – Kenyatta led the delegation – just after you were born I suppose. It was all in the days leading up to Independence, the end of colonial rule in Kenya. I know that Theo was quite involved with a reform group at that time. Perhaps your mother was a member of that group. They might have been on their way to a meeting or something like that.' Ellen looked at the others. Both faces looking back at her were blank.

Dan lifted his shoulders in something like a shrug. 'You might be right, Ellen, but I really don't know. I do remember Rose saying one time that her brother couldn't stay in England for very long, when he brought me over, because he had work to do back in Kenya. She said it was important, that he was needed back there. I remember that, because I recall thinking at one stage that he was bloody well needed back here too! If you'll pardon my language?' He grinned his apology. Mara nodded. She could understand the sentiment completely.

'Aha, here you are! I was wondering where everyone was. Tea break already I see. And you've only just started work … that's if you have started. I don't see any evidence of it if I might say so.' Frank was grinning as he entered the kitchen. He stopped short when he sensed that he was out of tune with the prevailing mood. 'What's up? Have I said something wrong?'

'Help yourself to tea Frank. Something's happened. We've got some news.' Dan pulled out the chair beside him, making space for his brother at the table.

'I'll make tea later.' Frank sat and looked around at the others. 'Well come on then. What is it? What's the news?'

'Frank … meet my sister … my half-sister anyway.' Dan gestured towards Mara by way of introduction. 'And this lady here …' and now he turned to Ellen. 'This lady here is my father's wife.' He sat back, arms folded across his chest, watching his brother's reaction.

'What are you talking about? What do you mean? How can she be your sister? We've only just met.' Frank looked at Mara. He was clearly bewildered.

'It was the photographs, the ones on the mantelpiece in the sitting room.' Frank's attention switches to Ellen as she takes up the explanation. 'You see, we have a picture of Theodora by the Old Rectory on our mantelpiece at home. Theodora is my husband's grandmother. The young man in the other photograph, the one with the African chief – that young man is, or should I say was, my husband Theodore - Theo.' She picked up her mug and took a long sip of the tea, which was cooling already.

Frank turned to his brother. 'Are you sure about all this, Dan? There's no mistake?'

'No. I think they're right. As we've talked about it I'm sure that it's the same man ... the Kenya connection ... his being Cornish ... dying recently ... the dates make sense ... even if nothing else does.'

'So your husband must have been married before. Did you know about his first wife? Did you know he had a son?' Frank's questions were fired at Ellen. He had more for Mara. 'Did you know about any of this? Did he never mention that you had a brother? I thought you said you didn't know anything about your father's Cornish connections.'

In the face of this barrage of questions both women were speechless. Ellen had frozen. Mara looked as if she might cry. Frank was mortified.

'Oh, I am so sorry. I should not have said any of that.' Remorse was in his voice, his apologies sincere. 'I can see that all this is just as much of a shock to you as it is to us.'

Ellen recovered quickly. 'It's ok, Frank. It really is. And 'no' is the answer to pretty much all of your questions.'

'What about Mum? Dan ... what about Rose? Do you think she knows about any of this?' The brothers exchanged a look. Probably not. If only she was well and here to help them understand the past, find the way ahead.

Dan turned to Ellen. 'You should meet Rose ... and sooner rather than later. You would like her. She always spoke fondly of her brother, my father, even though we never saw him. I got the impression that they were devoted to each other, especially after their parents died. She would want to meet you, I know she would.'

'We would like to meet her too. And we will ... soon. We have a Rose too, at least a Rosy. She's my younger daughter. As soon as we get back to the cottage, we'll phone her and tell her about all this. I think she'll want to come down and be here with us, meet you all, be part of this whole new development ... I don't know what else to call it.' Ellen's sigh betrayed her tiredness.

'Perhaps we should be getting back soon Mum. You look tired. We can contact Rosy then and make a plan. What do you think?' Her mother nodded. Mara turned to the brothers. 'What about if we all meet up tomorrow?'

'Maisy's coming down for the weekend too. Maisy is my daughter. We can all get together, up here at the house, later, perhaps tomorrow afternoon. What do you think?' Dan was glad of a plan to grab hold of.

After some more discussion and a decision to postpone the detail – they would speak on the phone tomorrow – new friends, new family, bid farewell to the Old Rectory for now. As Mara pulled the Clio out onto the gravel, the scent of apple blossom drifted in through the car's open window and she caught herself humming the old Lind'n Lea School song as they moved off down the drive.

'And I be free to go abroad
Or take again the homeward road
To where for me, the apple tree
Doth lean down low, in Linden Lea.'

As the South West Trains connection from Plymouth eased in towards Lostwithiel Railway Station, Dan jumped to his feet. He'd arrived in plenty of time and had been sitting since then on the bench on the platform, switched into what he called 'waiting mode.' But he was back on full power now, his eyes searching the carriages chuntering to a halt beside him for any sign of his daughter. What if she'd missed the train? What if she hadn't made the connection in Plymouth? He still found it amazing that she was old enough to travel down from London on her own. What if … and then he spotted her.

'Dad…' Her face was alight. She had seen him too. Maisy hitched her rucksack down from her back and leaned it against her leg, opening her arms to share the hug that her father was offering.

'It's so good to see you.' They spoke at once.

'How was the journey? Here, let me take that?'

Dan lifted the rucksack up onto his shoulder and Maisy followed in his wake down the platform towards the exit, filling him in on all the interesting bits of her journey back to the West Country, into Cornwall, the place that even after all this time she still thought of as home.

'I thought you might like to pop in and see your Grandma first then we can call in to Uncle Frank's on our way up through to the old house. I'm in the middle of sorting through things up there and you did say you'd lend a hand didn't you? Uncle Frank's at home today sorting out some new music and working on his garden – and there are some things I need to chat to him about. When I told him you were coming he was really keen to see you anyway – he might even have baked you a chocolate cake.' They grinned one behind the other on the narrow pavement. Uncle Frank's reputation as a baker of 'exceedingly good chocolate cakes' was second to none.

` Like countless other travellers down through the centuries, father and daughter were making their way into the town of Lostwithiel across the medieval bridge over the river Fowey. History had it that this ancient bridge with its broad span of pointed arches and triangular support pillars had been the setting for the arrival of the Black Prince and his retinue en route to nearby Restormel Castle in 1345 and that it had seen the routing of the Parliamentary army by the Royalists in 1644. Now it was witnessing the homecoming of Maisy and the opening of a new chapter in the story of one of the town's oldest families.

'Hi Grandma – it's me, Maisy.'

In the quiet room Rose was dozing, head back, mouth lolling, in the armchair beside the single bed. Dan and his daughter had slipped in without disturbing her and now Maisy's warm brown fingers stroked, gentle over the pale blue-veined hand of the sleeping woman. Rose had faded. She seemed so frail in the enveloping chair, like one of her own roses, wilting petals held in place by the sun, ready to fall at the first breath of the wind.

'Grandma – it's me, Maisy.'

The young woman leaned in close; spoke softly, coaxing her

grandmother back from her dreams. Rose slept on. Maisy turned, looked towards her father, who was watching them from the other chair.

'Maybe we should just leave her to rest?' She whispered her question. 'We could call in tomorrow. She might be more awake then. It seems a shame to disturb her doesn't it.' She withdrew her hand.

Dan nodded, standing quietly, picking up the rucksack and gesturing with his eyes towards the door. They did not speak as they made their way back along the carpeted corridor towards the reception area. There was nothing to be said. Their shared sadness needed no words – not yet anyway.

'You've been to see Rose then? How was she today? Was she awake or dozing?' Nurse Rachel looked up, smiling at their approach. Her expression softened as she felt their silence. 'You mustn't worry. She has been sleeping quite a lot lately – but it's good that she's peaceful isn't it, not so many tears. Often she remembers my name – but she is still confused about where she is … when she's going home … that sort of thing. Also I was going to mention to you …' she looked straight at Dan 'Rose seems quite bothered about her house. She keeps saying they've sold the house … things like that about the house being sold. Of course she's confused … it seems to be preying on her mind though.'

Dan nodded. 'Next time I come, if she's awake and it seems like a good time, I'll try to talk to her about it – put her mind at rest, if I can.' He turned to Maisy. 'It's hard to know how much she understands, how much she's taking in.' Turning back to the nurse, he shrugged, helpless.

'Come on Dad. There's nothing more we can do here today. We'll call in again, in the morning. Maybe Grandma will be awake then and we can have a chat, spend some time with her.'

'You're right.' He looked at Rachel, 'that's what we'll do – we'll call in tomorrow – later in the morning. If you could tell Rose we're coming, it might encourage her to stay focussed.' As he said the words he wasn't sure that it would make any difference. He just couldn't get his head around it, the whole idea of dementia … what it might mean for Rose, for anyone trying to reach her. He shook his head. No one could explain. There was no cure. It was so unpredictable. What a mess! He swallowed hard, turned away.

'We'll see you tomorrow then.' Rachel smiled at Maisy and pressed the button to release the lock on the front door. Re-entering the outside world, father and daughter heard the click as the heavy security system reengaged behind them.

'I know it's to keep them safe, to stop people with dementia wandering out by themselves and getting hurt but I still hate the idea of Grandma being locked away in there.'

Dan reached out, comforting. 'Come on. Let's get on up to Uncle Frank's house. If he can't cheer us up then no one can.' Hooking his arm through hers, the pair made their way across the small car park to where he had left his car. It wouldn't take long. A cup of tea and hopefully some of his brother's chocolate cake would be just what they needed.

Frank was in his garden when they arrived – not working, just sitting beside his pond, playing his guitar, singing softly to himself, looking at the sky.

'What a picture! So peaceful – it's a shame to disturb him.' With his hand on the garden gate, Dan whispered grinning to his daughter as they watched, unobserved.

Frank's home – and his garden – fit him like a glove. When his paternal grandfather died, Frank was the only beneficiary of his estate and he'd known at once what he would do with his legacy. He loved the Old Rectory, but owning his own home had always been his dream, his own kitchen, his own garden. Refurbishing these old farm cottages had been his joy and his hard labour for the last several years. Dan had helped out some weekends along with a variety of Frank's friends. And now it was everything Frank had hoped it would be. The downstairs living space was open-plan, airy and light, wooden floors, big open fireplace at the far end with a solid oak beam as a mantle, two comfy leather armchairs and a sofa, a lovely old rug that was a gift from his mother, and his piano.

Smiling, Dan raised his eyebrows and signalled to Maisy. 'Okay? Enough. Let's surprise him.' His voice was a whisper and she nodded.

'Uncle Frank!'

At Maisy's call Frank turned, a quick smile flashed to his eyes. He set down his guitar and walked forward, arms outstretched, into her bear hug.

'It's been a long time. You look great!' He was happy to see her again and she him.

'Your garden's looking lovely too!' She was soon wandering about the garden, looking at all the changes, enjoying the sunshine, the country air.

'We called in to see Rose on our way up, but she was asleep – we didn't stay long. I've told them we'll call again tomorrow.' The brothers hugged, stood watching their precious girl as Dan passed on the nurse's news about Rose. 'Rachel said that Rose seems bothered … about the house … she seems to be half-remembering something about the sale.'

'I'll tell you later what I've managed to find out. Let's not talk about it yet with Maisy … there's going to be so much for her to take in. Let's take it slowly, shall we? Perhaps we should wait till we get up to the house. It'll be easier for her up there. What do you think?' Frank was talking quietly. Dan understood and nodded his assent.

'Maisy, guess what I've made, especially for you …' Her uncle called her and she came back to join them.

'Let me guess – chocolate cake?' She was grinning, the happy child she had been, the woman she was becoming.

They transferred to his kitchen and while Frank made tea his guests made themselves at home, lounging on his sofa, looking at his pictures, picking up his new CDs, playing on his piano, reading his newspapers. He was happy, watching them, his family, in his home.

'Come on then. Come and get this cake. If I've slaved in the kitchen all morning making this for you, the least you can do is come and eat it.' Frank was laughing now as they gathered around his table, waiting to be served the generous slices he was cutting.

'Mmm … this is as good as ever!' Maisy was enjoying the

cake – chocolate frosting smudged at the edges of her mouth, on the tip of her nose.

'You always were such a messy eater!' Frank offered a paper napkin. 'So how are you doing? I've been hearing that you're planning a trip, that you're going to Africa … that you're going to university. I'm with your Dad! I think you should stay at home here. You're far too young to travel on your own.' Maisy giggled and made as if to thump him. It was so good to be back.

And in the comfort of Uncle Frank's home the threesome relaxed together – the men mostly listening and asking questions and Maisy mostly answering, sharing news of her life in London, her ideas about university courses, her plans for the upcoming trip.

Watching his daughter talking so easily about visiting Kenya, going on safari, travelling to the coast … it struck Dan afresh how strange it all was, this thing with his father, with Africa. And in that moment, for the first time in his life, he had the germ of an idea that he might travel to Kenya himself … not with Maisy, he wasn't thinking that at all. It was important for her this independence thing. No, this would be for himself, for his mother.

His mother? Where did that come from? And the sudden idea took shape in his mind like it had been 'beamed up by Scotty'. All of his life, all of his thinking about himself, his past, all of his anger, his resentment, all of it … everything had been about his father. Nothing, none of it, had ever been about his mother.

'What do you think, Dad?' Maisy was asking him a question. He turned towards his daughter, dragging his thoughts back to the present. She watched it happening on his face. 'Dad where were you? You looked miles away.'

'Sorry – it was something you said, about Kenya. It just got me thinking, that's all. What was it you were asking me?' he smiled.

'I was just asking what you thought about travelling, the flights, booking the tickets, the best way to do it.'

'What does your mother think? She's good at that sort of thing.'

Maisy looked at him, astonishment flickering in her wide

brown eyes. What was that about? It was not often that he brought her mother into their conversation; in fact she couldn't remember the last time he'd even asked about her. It was true. Her mother was good at that sort of thing and in fact she had already given the girls lots of helpful advice. It was just that Maisy wanted to ask him, wanted him to feel involved – wanted him to be involved. She hesitated for just a moment before deciding to take his question at face value.

'Actually Mum was looking on line the other day. She got some useful ideas. A friend of hers is a travel agent too, so that might prove to be a good connection. We haven't actually booked anything yet. Mum's a bit like you though – one minute she's doing all she can to encourage us to go, the next minute she reads something about girls being attacked abroad or watches a film, like that one, 'Taken'... have you seen it? And then before you know it she's trying to put a lid on the whole thing. You parents are all the same.' She rolled her eyes in mock despair and they laughed together

Watching the pair of them, Frank smiled. When he thought about what might be ahead for them both, the word that kept coming into his head was 'compassion' ... strange old-fashioned sort of word, but that was exactly what he felt. As far as he was concerned Dan was his real brother. No physical connection or lack of it could ever make any difference to the way he felt. They were brothers. But looked at objectively, their family history was clearly not the same. Frank was very aware of his own craggy looks but Dan's lean handsome face with it's darker skin tone, his curls, not tight, nor frizzy, like most African hair, but looser somehow, softer ... must be something to do with his father's hair Frank supposed, and the unmistakeably East African cast to his features, the warm dark eyes, these were all very different to his own. And it was there too, that trace of the exotic, in his daughter. Dan considered himself a Cornishman – he often claimed it and sang '*Trelawney*' with as much passion as the next man, standing proudly beneath the black and white flag every 5th March on St. Piran's day – but in truth it was obvious that his heritage was not that straightforward. Frank could never be certain but it seemed to him that Dan had simply chosen not to think about it. Now he would have to … think about it that is. Mara had named it, brought it out into the open and now, for the first time, Frank had heard Dan talk about his natural mother and, what is more, acknowledge that she was most likely Kenyan.

'Am I boring you guys?'

Maisy was teasing them both. She had been in full flow, somewhere on the Mombasa coast, when she had suddenly become aware that both men were looking preoccupied, each lost in their own thoughts. 'Do you two old men need an afternoon nap or something?'

'We were simply carried away by your fantastic descriptions – imagining ourselves on some exotic beach, bananas, palm trees, the lot … at least I was.' Frank jumped to his feet and reached for the tray, gathering up the plates smeared with the remnants of the chocolate frosting, collecting the mugs. 'Are you two on your way up to the old house? If you are, I reckon I might join you.'

And so, in a clutter of tea cups and cake plates, they moved towards their rendezvous with the Old Rectory – Maisy blithely anticipating her return to the beloved old house; the two men each in their own way anxious, unsure how the young woman would react to the news that the future of their family home was anything but certain.

18

Cornwall, Duloe Manor – 2008

'Good morning, Mum. Did you sleep well?'

Mara, damp-haired, wrapped in a blue dressing gown, pushed open the door to her mother's bedroom and entered, carrying a tray with two large mugs of tea.

'It's a beautiful morning. It looks like it's going to be another nice day. I thought I heard some movement up here so I've brought you a cup of tea too.'

She set the mug down beside the photograph on the bedside table and opened the curtains as Ellen pulled herself up out from under the covers and settled herself back against the pillows.

'What a nice idea. I slept quite well thank you. I went out like a light. Did you manage to get through to your sister last night? I thought I heard you chatting on the phone but once my head was on the pillow I was so tired I think I must have just gone straight off. I don't remember anything else.'

She definitely looked rested. Her daughter was relieved. Taking the other mug from the tray, Mara perched herself on the edge of the bed.

'I did speak to Rosy last night. She'd been out all day but she'd picked up the messages I left earlier. She sends her love – hopes you're all right. As you can imagine, she was as shocked by the news as we were. We chatted for quite a while. She's going to pick up a few things from the house – some of the albums like you suggested, anything else that seems relevant – and then she's going to drive down tomorrow morning. She should be here by lunchtime.'

'What about the children – is she bringing them with her?'

'Graham's going to take a couple of days holiday – look after the kids – so she's planning to stay down here for a few days, at least until after the weekend when we might be a bit clearer about what's happening. No one really knows what to make of it all yet.' She paused, sipped her tea, as her mother tried to take in the new arrangements. Ellen reached out for her mug and a thoughtful silence overtook them both.

'It's such a shame, isn't it, about their mother, about Rose, that she's been so poorly and now the dementia. She was obviously the one who kept everything going for those boys ... for Frank and Dan, men I should say. It seems like, although they were each doing their own thing, she held everything together. They still seem quite dependent on her, don't they? It would have been so much easier now, with all this, if we could have talked to her.' Ellen's tone was wistful.

'I was thinking about her too, when I was awake in the night. If what we've been hearing is right then I guess Rose is my aunt. Do you think that our Rosy is named after her, even though we didn't even know she existed?' Mara's eyebrows lifted with the rising note of her voice as she faced her mother.

'Your Father always said that you were his Kenyan beauty and she was his English Rose. That's why we named you girls. You were so special, our first-born: 'Mara' – you began your life in Kenya. Your sister was born when we were living back in England. She was our English 'Rose.' That's what we said and that's how it seems to me. If he was also thinking of his own sister Rose, we shall never know now. It sounds as if his sister was – is – a fine woman anyway, so maybe it wouldn't be so bad if he did have her in mind, would it.' It was a statement rather than a question. Ellen smiled.

Mara watched her mother. All things considered, she seemed to be taking this quite calmly, on the surface anyway. Sensing herself studied, Ellen glanced up, meeting the questions in her daughter's eyes. She was ready with a plan.

'I've been thinking. If you don't mind dropping me over there, I might call in and see her later. After all, it seems that she is Theo's sister. I think I ought to meet her, don't you?' Ellen hesitated, set down her mug. She shook her head. 'But I just don't understand why he never told me about her ... why he never brought us here. I could have coped ... I know I could have coped with anything he might have told me about his past before we met. Why did he keep this a secret?'

It was Mara's turn to meet the questions in her mother's eyes. There were no answers. Not yet, anyway. Despite her own inner confusion, Mara managed a smile.

'Come on, why don't we get up and get ourselves washed and dressed? We'll feel better after we've had some breakfast. When you're ready we can make a plan, try to find some answers ... to some of the questions anyway, and we'll think about the rest later. Come on, let's get this show on the road. Remember that film we watched when we were kids, in Nairobi I think it was, you know, 'The Jewel of the Nile,' that song 'When the going gets tough ...?'

'The tough get going!' Grinning now, her mother sang the answer. They laughed together. And then that is exactly what these two 'tough' women did. They got themselves going, each making a determined effort to keep at bay the questions ... questions ... more questions that poured down with the water in the hot shower, loomed through the mist in the bathroom mirror and hung in the cupboard amongst their holiday clothes.

Over coffee later, they were still at the table, talking over their plans for the day when the phone rang.

'Hello?'

Mara moved across to the window, listening to the caller as her mother watched her. 'Yes ... yes we'll still be here ... yes ... but my sister is planning to arrive sometime around lunch time tomorrow ... yes, we'd like to meet her too ... we could come over to the Old Rectory later ... meet you there ... around five should be fine ... good ... that would be good ... Rosy will be with us ... yes ... fine ... see you tomorrow then.' Mara clicked the phone back into its holder, walked over to the sofa and sat down.

'That was Frank. He was inviting us to lunch at his house tomorrow with Dan and Maisy but I told him that Rosy would be arriving about then. He said that they were planning to go on up to the Old Rectory later and so I've agreed that we'll meet them up there. Is that okay with you?' Her mother nodded, moved away from the table to join her daughter on the settee. 'Sorry. I should have asked you first but I thought it would probably be a good thing to do. A chance for us all to meet ...' How strange this all was. How quickly everything was moving on.

'No, I think you're right and if we leave it until later like you say, Rosy will be able to meet them too. At least it will be a chance for us all to talk. Perhaps they might be able to answer some of our questions. We might be able to answer some of theirs. Maybe amongst some of Dan's letters, the things he received from Kenya ... maybe we'll find some clues. I don't know. It will be interesting to look at any photographs they have. If Rosy brings down some of the albums, we can show them ours. Oh Mara - this is all so strange.' Ellen leaned forward, covering her face with her cupped hands.

Mara reached out. Her voice was soft, but her question was hard. 'Did you never suspect? Did you ever have any idea that Dad might have been married before ... that he might have had another family ... before us?'

As soon as the words were out of her mouth, Mara wished they had not been spoken. But her mother did not flinch. She sat up and turned, looking straight into her daughter's eyes.

'No, my dear, I did not. In the early years of our marriage I did get the impression that there were some things about his life in Kenya, during the troubles, before Independence when he first was out there teaching at the school in the Rift Valley ... I did get the feeling that there were things that had happened, things he had seen, probably things he had done, that he didn't want to talk about, but I thought he was just being protective. You know what he could be like ... that whole 'man' thing, protecting his women. It sounds so old-fashioned now, but that was the sort of man he was. I just never asked him. I hated his silences, that closed look. I guess I simply chose not to go there.' Ellen leaned back into the cushions. She sighed; shook her head. 'But did I think he had fathered a son?

No, absolutely not.' She closed her eyes. For the time being at least, she was done.

Mara rose. Leaving her mother resting on the sofa, she pottered quietly about the kitchen, clearing, packing the dishwasher, getting some fish out of the small freezer to defrost in time for their supper. They could have that with some new potatoes and salad and there was plenty of fruit. She would need to pick up some milk and fresh bread later from the local shop or maybe in the town if her mother still wanted to drive over to Lostwithiel later. Mara was not sure if visiting Rose in the care home would be a good idea, either for her mother or for Rose at this stage. She decided that she would try to dissuade her if she could, encourage her to wait until they had talked it over with Frank and Dan.

Thinking of Frank and Dan, she felt it again, the tightening in her chest, the churning in her stomach. The tension was nothing to do with the men themselves. They were nice. She had liked them both straight away. There was an easy confidence, an open friendliness about them that she found comfortable, attractive even. In different circumstances ... she sighed. Now, just imagine it, there was a very strong chance that one of them was her first cousin and the other one ... she could scarcely allow the thought ... was her brother, her half-brother anyway. Mara was clutching the tea towel as she leaned against the sink. If she felt like this, whatever must it be like for her mother?

Ellen seemed to be dozing. Mara watched her, thankful for the peace that had crept over her like a blanket. Careful, she tiptoed from the room, crossed the small hallway and climbed the stairs, thinking to collect the forgotten teacups from earlier.

On the bedside table, beside the mug, Mara spotted the small photo. Curious, she picked it up and saw what her mother must have been looking earlier. It was a photograph of the three of them, Theo with his two little girls. They were holding hands, grinning at the camera, beside a lake. Standing in the shallows was a beautiful crested crane.

The crested crane. Mara caught her breath, dropped the photograph. She watched it flutter from her fingers and settle facedown on the carpet. She remembered. The fateful safari, the lake-side hotel, the door slammed shut.

'Daddy, don't go!'

The child's pain was real. She clutched her hands over her stomach. Dad, don't go! Please – don't go! Theo's grown-up daughter sat down on the edge of her mother's bed. She was rocking herself now, eyes clenched tight over the hot tears that welled up, squeezed out from beneath her eyelids. He was gone – really gone. He would not be coming back. Ever. The missing was physical, a boulder, a deep ache somewhere at the centre of the child she had been, the woman she had become. Without him, how could she make sense of anything anymore? Tears spilled down her cheeks, dribbled over her chin, dripped onto her hands. Her nose was running too. Sniffing, she picked up the pillow, holding it against her face, breathing deep. And then she was weeping, great wrenching sobs. Curled up around her terrible grief, for the first time since her father's death, Mara let go.

19

Kenya, Nairobi – 1981

'Look, daddy. These birds are wearing golden crowns, like a king and a queen.'

In the courtyard gardens of the Norfolk Hotel the aviaries were festooned with bougainvillea – reds, pinks, and mauves. Five-year-old Mara had been instantly entranced by the golden yellow weaverbirds, glossy azure-blue starlings with coppery-orange breasts and iridescent blue-green humming birds. Her new favourite pastime was drawing them and she was even learning to write their names. Every day since the family's arrival in Nairobi, Theo and Mara had come to visit the birds after lunch while his younger daughter Rosy was still napping with her mother in their room upstairs. The drawing book was bridging his knees as he sat on the bench, watching the little girl as she whispered to her new friends through the netting that divided them. Leaning forward the better to listen in on her storytelling, Theo was careless for an instant and the book slid from his lap. He watched it as it fell open onto the grass. Mara had turned back as he stooped to retrieve her treasures and come running to help him gather up the coloured crayons, which had spilled haphazard from their paper packet. Now she was holding out the leaflet that she'd picked up from the grass, pointing excitedly at a picture of two long-legged birds, whose necks arched towards each other, appearing to make the shape of a heart. Laughing, her father swept her up and swung her onto the seat beside him.

'Let's have a look then, shall we?'

The image was certainly eye-catching. He explained to her

that they were called 'crested cranes' and soon the majestic birds were joining the others on the pages of her drawing book. Watching his mop-haired five-year old, deep in concentration, tongue between her lips, he felt a wave of pure relief to see her relaxed and happy again after all the upheaval and disorientation of the last few days, perhaps longer.

The Kenya Airways flight had been difficult for them all. The narrow seats on either side of the cramped, disconcertingly shabby cabin were arranged in threes and since there were four of them, he and his wife had separated – she had travelled in front with their younger daughter Rosy and he had travelled with Mara in the row behind. The children had been fizzing with excitement throughout the long day and the late take-off had left them both hollow-eyed and fractious.

Once in the air he had discovered that no amount of jiggling, or eventually brute force could induce his stubbornly upright seat to recline even an inch. As a consequence he had barely slept a wink on the interminable journey through the night skies down over Africa, while his little daughter slept at last with her thumb in her mouth and her head on his lap.

In the row in front his wife had scarcely had better luck as her seat would only recline, lolling at an unnaturally relaxed angle, refusing even to stay upright for take-off, despite repeated warnings from the dour-faced stewardess. Their two year old daughter had been grizzling on and off throughout the flight but as the plane was preparing to land at Jomo Kenyatta airport she had set up a loud wailing. In the crowded, sleep-deprived cabin there was no escape from this wave of misery and his family had been on the receiving end of a storm of angry looks and tight-lipped frowns from the weary crew and fellow passengers. As the plane taxied through the early morning light towards the huge circular-concrete terminal building, Rosy had finally vomited, filling the already malodorous air in the cabin with the stomach-churning smells of stale milk.

The ensuing struggles from the slept-over aircraft and out into the echoing concrete building was now a vivid scent-memory. Damp vegetation, unwashed bodies in shuffling lines, sweaty customs officials, morose in thick uniforms, palm oil … He grinned. It was how Kenya had always reached him, through his nose.

In the hotel's tropical garden now, he breathed deep and caught the heady scent of frangipani and the lemony fragrance of the pink and red pelargoniums. Sun-baked, red-earth aromas reminded him of baking bread and from somewhere beyond the garden, sharp, smoky drifts from smouldering heaps of wayside rubbish wafted in. This last was all too familiar, this acrid smell of ash, of burning. A shadow crossed his face. Other echoes came unbidden on the smoke … that other Africa, that other time, that other life.

'What does this say, Daddy?'

His daughter had finished crayoning and was holding up the leaflet, pointing at the large red letters over the picture of the birds. At home in England she had begun to recognise some familiar words but these were strange. Startled back to the present, he smiled, leaned towards her, pointing as he began to read.

'This says, 'Jambo' – it's Swahili – it means 'Hello' in English. This says, 'Karibuni' – it's Swahili too – it means 'Welcome.' This next bit is in English. It's telling people about some lovely gardens at a hotel beside a lake called Naivasha. It's out in the Rift Valley, not too far from Nairobi. Look, there's a picture inside here of the lake … look and more birds too … that's what they call a heron, a goliath heron … and that's an ibis. Look at its long curved beak.' Pointing as he spoke, Father and daughter enjoyed the photographs together.

'Can we go there, Daddy? Can we go to see the birds? Let's go now.'

'Well, not today. We can't go today can we?' He chuckled at her childish enthusiasm. 'But yes, we can go, one day soon, when uncle Jack gets back from Mombasa and once we've settled into our new house.'

'We'll go soon, Daddy, won't we?' She was wriggling down from the seat, holding tight to the leaflet, leaving him to collect the crayons and the drawing book. 'Come on, Daddy, let's go and show Mummy and Rosy the birds on the leaflet.'

With the artist's gear tucked underneath his arm, he took Mara's hand and together they made their way back up to the room at the Norfolk hotel which would be their home in Nairobi for just two more days. Two more days until Jack and Theresa returned from their farewell trip to Mombasa. The plan was that Jack's driver would collect the couple from Wilson airport and, after dropping Theresa off at the Headmaster's house at Langata, they would drive back into central Nairobi to the Norfolk hotel where the 'new' headmaster and his young family would be waiting, ready to begin their life together in Kenya, this country that Theo already thought of as home.

20

Kenya, Rift Valley – 1982

'Look at that sign ... over there. Look, Theo! You must get a photo of that. Look, Mara, it says 'Fish and Chip Hotel' there, on that sign. It looks about the size of our garden shed back at home, doesn't it?'

In the front seat of the Peugeot, Ellen was pointing, laughing. 'Do you think we'll have to stay there if we can't find anyone to mend the tyre? Perhaps we could buy some fish and chips there for our lunch, what do you think, girls?'

They were on their first family safari to Lake Naivasha and she was determined that they would all enjoy it, despite this unscheduled detour. Behind her in the back seat, the little girls were all excitement. Beside her, Theo was frowning. His attention was all on the road ahead, as the saloon car bumped over the potholed dirt road into the small lakeside town of Naivasha. As they came to a scrunching halt alongside a makeshift wooden dukka, the rolling clouds of dust that had trailed in their wake caught up, hung heavy in the air then settled in thick layers over the vehicle, like frosting. Theo sighed.

Kneeling up on the seat, peering out through dust-caked rear window, Mara spotted something that she recognised. Two fluorescent-orange bottles stood proud beside a punnet of brown hens' eggs and a small pyramid of green-and-white striped tetra-packs of KCC milk, on the narrow shelf that served as the display counter for the small, wooden shop.

'Daddy, look – they've got Fanta! Mummy, can we have a Fanta? Please!'

The fizzy orange drink had become a favourite with the girls ever since their first taste, soon after their arrival in Nairobi. Its colour and its sugar content made it less of a hit with their parents, but now the sisters were hot and tired and the prospect of Fanta through a plastic straw revived their flagging spirits as the views over the Rift Valley had been quite unable to do.

'Go on then, you can share one ... if you sit back nicely.' Ellen turned in her seat and smiled at her daughters, who were now sitting up straight, arms folded in eager anticipation of the treat. 'See if you can get two straws, Daddy.' She grinned across at her husband who had already wound down the window, opened the car door and was even now stepping out onto the stony, corrugated dirt-road.

Shading his eyes against the strong sunlight, Theo scanned the cluster of shacks and shanties for anything that might resemble a garage, or even a local *fundi* – a jack-of-all-trades who might be able to do a quick repair-job on the damaged tyre. On roads like this, to go on without a reliable spare wheel would be foolish and they had already had to use theirs. If only he had not pulled off the road – he really should have known better but as ever he had been unable to resist the spectacular beauty of the Rift Valley. Snaking its way down over the escarpment, the tarmac road from Nairobi to Kisumu followed an ancient elephant trail and at every turn offered distant views of Lake Naivasha and the extinct volcanoes Suswa and Longenot. He'd stopped the car at frequent viewpoints on their descent, taking photographs and pointing out to the children the strange and exciting flora and fauna, but actually pulling off the narrow strip of tarmac ... that had been his big mistake.

It was their first free weekend since their arrival in Kenya and the family were finally taking the promised trip to the Lake Hotel at Naivasha. The sole purpose of the safari, as far as Mara was concerned was to see the crested cranes whose photographs were on the front of her treasured leaflet. She could hardly contain her excitement. After an early breakfast on the veranda of the schoolhouse, they had packed sunhats and sunscreen, swimming things and snacks, along with some bottles of filtered water into the back of the white Peugeot that had been Uncle Jack's and set off on their first big adventure.

All had been going to plan until that moment when he had pulled the car off the road onto the dusty verge to snap an absolutely irresistible image of scrub-grazing Thompson's gazelles, beneath a thorn-tree with Mount Longenot rising as a splendid purple-grey backdrop. He had encouraged his young family to scramble out alongside him so that he could point out the distant rim of the crater and the bouncing black-and-white stripes on the flanks of the young gazelles, as they bolted at the sounds of the children's voices. The air quivered with heat. The girls were giggly. It felt like they were in a giant's oven, with the musky smell of game browsing in the bush nearby, the crackling and scrunching of dry grasses against their legs and under their feet the powdery red dust baking memories that would last forever.

It was only after the couple and their excited children had settled themselves back into the vehicle for the final stage of their safari that his folly had become apparent. With Lake Naivasha glimmering in the distance, above the hubbub of happy chatter, the horror in their father's voice had grabbed everyone's attention.

'Oh no! Not now! Not out here!'

He was gripping hard at the steering wheel, clearly struggling to keep the car on the narrow strip of tarmac. The vehicle was slewing heavily to the left and the slack flapping of the flat tyre was unmistakeable. There was nothing for it but to pull up at the side of the road and they came to a stop in the sparse shade of acacia trees. While their father climbed out to look at the damage, the little girls fidgeted in the stifling heat of the car with their mother who had wound down the window and was leaning out to see what was happening.

'It's the tyre – it's completely wrecked – look at this!' Theo held up the thin branch, ringed with clusters of long thorns, sharp like nails and just as lethal. 'This was in the tyre – we must have pulled up right on top of this lot.' He waved the branch towards the window and the children recoiled in horror.

'What about the spare ... can you change it out here?' Ellen climbed out of the car now and was gazing helplessly around her at the scrubby plains, the craggy escarpment rising behind them, the dusty road snaking into the heat-haze ahead. They really were in the middle of nowhere. After closer inspection they discovered that, thankfully, the spare was fine and before long Theo had begun the job of changing the damaged wheel, whilst the children, in bright cotton skirts and floppy sunhats, pottered about in the meagre shade at the edge of the road, singing songs and playing 'I-spy' with their ever-watchful mother.

'Be careful by the ditch, Mara! Come on over here!'

Ellen's sudden sharp call was just in time to stop the little girl from clambering down into the thorny roadside ditch in pursuit of a turquoise-headed lizard.

'Just leave it alone ... stay over here by the car with mummy and Rosy... come on!'

'Mummy look!' Mara was pointing down into the stony ditch. 'Look – it's a dead car – it's upside down, on its back, all rusty! There, in the ditch! Look I can see some bones too – like a skeleton!' She was excited, pleased with the big word – it was a game. Her shrill young voice caused her father to look up sharply from the job in hand.

Shock thickened his throat.

'Leave it, Mara! Leave it at once! Come back, over here. I heard mummy tell you to come back here by the car. Come here, now!' His tone was harsh, urgent.

The little girl turned back to his call. She hesitated, confused. Daddy was cross – he sounded angry. Her lower lip wobbled as she ran back over the stones and buried her face into her mother's skirts.

'It's all right. Come on Mara – you're all right now. Daddy's not cross – he just wants you to be safe.' Ellen gently detached herself from her daughter's grasp. 'Come on let's see what Rosy's up to shall we? Oh dear, look she's picking up stones. No darling, leave them on the ground – no not in your mouth. Come on – take my hand both of you. We'll go and watch Daddy, shall we? Let's see if he's nearly finished.'

Ellen was good with the girls. She knew how to keep talking, to keep their attention and to redirect their interest rather than to scold. Theo was only dimly aware of their chatter as he had turned back to finish his task but his thoughts were somewhere else entirely.

In fact his thoughts were in the same place – it was the time that was different. At his daughter's mention of the rusted vehicle in the ditch, the scattered bones … the years had fallen away and the events of that terrible night flashed as clear in his memory as if they had happened just heartbeats ago. His pulse was racing as he saw it, felt it, all over again: the fear for her life, the panic, the heart-stopping terror when the donkey had suddenly appeared in the headlights, the screeching of breaks, her screams as the vehicle careered off the road, rolled over and over into the ditch, the pain, her agonised cries, the horrible stillness.

Theo sat back on his heels and raised his eyes to the cloudless blue over his head. Distracted, he scraped his fingers back through his hair, feeling the sun's heat on his hands, his face, but remembering only the stars, those stars that had thronged the night sky, the stars that had watched over the birth, the death. His hands were covering his face as he leaned his forehead against the hot paintwork of the Peugeot.

'Are you alright, Daddy?' Mara was beside him, watchful. She sensed the strangeness in his silence, saw the pain in his eyes as he turned and looked straight at her.

'Daddy's very hot. He's been working hard. He should have been drinking his water. How's it going?' It was Ellen's voice; she was talking to him. He turned towards the sound, his eyes focussing on her face as she leaned towards him, holding out the bottled water.

'Thanks.'

He reached out and took the bottle, unscrewing the lid and gulping the water, wiping his wet mouth with the back of his hand.

'I think it's done now.'

He came slowly to his feet, leaning back against the driver's door and finishing off the rest of the water, closely watched by his family. Passing the empty bottle back to his wife, Theo picked up the wheel with the damaged tyre and fixed it back into the boot of the car.

'Come on then, let's get everybody back on board and we'll get this show on the road again. Those crested cranes will think we're not coming after all.' He laughed down at Mara and pulled off her sunhat, ruffling her hair as she scrambled past him up into the back seat of the car. Relieved, she grinned back at her daddy as she settled into her place and he tossed the sunhat onto her lap – he seemed better now.

As the travellers had resumed their course across the sun-baked floor of the Great Rift Valley, the girls had dozed in the back of the car while their parents decided on a plan. The priority was to get the spare wheel operational and the nearest place where that might be possible was in the small township of Naivasha. This would mean a slight detour from the route to the Lake Hotel – perhaps they would be able to leave the tyre there to be fixed and collect it on their way back from the hotel on their way home to Nairobi later that afternoon. It seemed to be their only option.

But what had seemed quite possible earlier was beginning to seem less likely, now that they were confronted with the Saturday-afternoon reality of the deserted township. A lonely goat strolled out from between two wooden shacks, a black plastic bag rolled down the road followed by a stray breeze, and the sign for the 'Fish and chip Hotel' creaked on its lop-sided chain.

'Jambo, Mzee.'

The wizened old man was sitting in the shade at the side of the dukka, hunched up on a low three-legged wooden stool, idly chewing on a piece of stick. Moving towards the man, Theo addressed him now with the traditional Swahili term of respect for an elder. The mzee seemed reluctant to acknowledge the greeting. He continued to chew on the twig, scrutinising the tall white man through black beady eyes. He turned his leathered face away, spat in the dust then resumed his chewing.

'Jambo, Bwana.'

The woman's voice caught Theo by surprise. He turned to find her staring out at him from behind the orange Fanta bottles. A blue headscarf was pulled tightly over her wiry hair and tied at the nape of her neck; her round face shone behind the broad smile.

'*Jambo sana. Habari?*'

He was familiar with Swahili 'How are you?' and returned the greeting with ease, enquiring after her good health as he stepped towards the counter and nodded at her response, '*Mzuri*' – 'I'm fine.'

'*Waweza kuongea English?*' Can you speak English? He asked the question, knowing that he would find it easier if their conversation could continue in English. He was uncomfortably aware that his own Swahili had become rusty from lack of use.

'I can speak English sir. I have worked in Nairobi with a family from England. How can I help you?' She was friendly, keen to help; she smiled across at the car, waving at the little girl who waved back.

'Well first I would like to buy a bottle of Fanta for my daughters and then I need to find someone who can repair the spare wheel on my car. We had an accident on the way here.' He smiled as she passed him the Fanta and offered a packet of straws from which he took two. '*Asante sana*' ... He nodded his thanks as he handed over the shillings to the young woman and then handed the bottle and the straws through the car window to his wife.

'There is no garage here sir, but there are *fundis* on the rough land, over there behind the hotel. It may be that they will help you with the tyre. My brother will take you.'

The woman had stepped out from the shaded interior of the dukka to talk with him and now he could see that she was quite young, he thought about sixteen, scarcely more than a girl. Beneath the knitted cardigan, she wore the traditional kanga – bright red, yellow and green cloth – swathed tightly around her, tucked right up underneath her arms like a bath towel; on her feet she wore an old pair of unlaced plimsolls. As she turned to call to the barefoot young boy who was out on the stony scrub behind the dukka kicking a ball made of some kind of rolled up material – it looked like a pair of old socks – Theo noticed the small black head of a sleeping baby folded into the cloth on her back. He wondered if the child was hers.

The young footballer came skipping over at her call, eager to inspect the *mzungu* – even these days it was not often that a white man stopped at their dukka. The man and the boy exchanged brief grins as the older sister commissioned her brother in a quick dialect that Theo was unable to grasp, although its gist was apparent from the rapid hand signals. The lad nodded his understanding of the situation and, in a gesture that took the man by surprise, reached out and took his hand.

'*Kuja hapa, kuja!*'

This time Theo understood the Swahili command – 'come here!' – and he responded with amusement to the boys tugging, waving to his family as he found himself pulled off in the direction of the 'Fish and Chip hotel.'

The wooden sign that his wife had found so funny earlier dangled over the entrance to this strange concoction of wooden planking and concrete that proclaimed itself to be 'The Fish and Chip Hotel'. It hung now above Theo's head as he stood waiting in the doorway for 'Murungi the *fundi*' to come and inspect the spare wheel that was propped up against the *murram*-stained concrete pillar.

His young guide had soon lost interest and had scampered back to his football practice behind the dukka. Shielding his eyes against the sun, Theo could still see the boy who was lost in imagination, scoring the winning goal at a Cup Final. The headmaster smiled – children were the same the world over. He turned back towards the 'hotel' and, dipping his head, stepped inside.

In stark contrast to the glare outside, the interior was shady. The still air was heavy with the scent of sun-baked wood, of roasted maize cobs, musky unwashed bodies and livestock nearby – goats probably or piebald, lop-eared sheep. Trails of smoke drifted in from burning rubbish somewhere out back and mingled with tainted air from the insufficiently-distant pit latrine. Theo hoped that Murungi – whoever he turned out to be – would soon be able to sort out the tyre and that the family's stay in this place would be as brief as possible.

As his eyes adjusted to the dim light, he looked about him. He was standing in a room about the size of a large garden shed or perhaps a garage, sparsely furnished with a single Formica-topped table and a couple of off-white plastic chairs. Hanging on the far wall was the ubiquitous framed portrait of President Daniel arap Moi and beside it a poster on which the words *Uhuru* and *Nyayo* featured largely alongside the red, green, white and black Kenyan flag. The words he knew only too well … in this country, they were iconic: *Uhuru* – 'freedom' or 'independence' remembering Jomo Kenyatta, the first Kenyan President; *Nyayo* – literally 'footsteps' but lately with more specific connotations of Daniel arap Moi, the current president, following in the great leader's footsteps.

'*Uhuru.*'

Theo spoke the word aloud, rubbed at the corner of his eye, coughed the dry air, as his own dark memories of those days of struggle, insurrection and 'Emergency' rose unbidden. He attempted to swallow but his mouth was dry; his pulse had quickened. Reaching out, he rested his hand on the back of the nearest plastic chair. At his touch, its feet creaked on the concrete floor and just at that moment he became aware of the man who had entered through the opening at the far end of the room. The man was watching him.

'*Jambo, Bwana.*'

The Kenyan was quite tall, broad-shouldered in the unbuttoned, dark blue boiler suit often worn out here as overalls. He was shoeless and his feet were leathered and dusty, but generally his appearance was clean and the skin of his hands and muscled forearms gleamed as if recently rubbed with Vaseline.

'*Jambo, sana. Waweza kuongea English?*'

Again the question. If the man had no English Theo knew that they would have to resort to sign language.

'*Ndio.* Yes. I am Murungi. I speak some English. I have been to school. How can I help you, sir?'

The man smiled, stepped forward, seemed about to offer his hand. Theo offered his own and the two shook hands before getting down to business.

'This tyre is broken,' Theo lead the man to the wheel and pointed to the split in the tyre. 'We do not have a spare now to continue our safari. Can you help us?' He endeavoured to keep his explanation and his question clear and simple.

Murungi, the *fundi*, inspected the damaged wheel before replying. 'I think I can find replacement.' He paused and Theo nodded, pleased. 'You can come back later … in about two hours? I will fix it by then.'

'We are going to Lake Hotel. We will come back later to collect the wheel. Thank you very much … *Asante sana, Murungi*.'

The men shook hands for the second time. Theo's relief was immense. They could have made the return journey without a spare wheel but it would not have been wise. He would never travel again with just the one spare. How fortunate they were that this man seemed willing and able to do the work. They could sort out the price later. Theo hoped that he was carrying enough shillings in his wallet. He doubted that a cheque book would be any use at all out here.

After more nods and handshakes the deal was arranged and Theo turned to leave.

'*Bwana*, I think perhaps you remember my father?' Murungi's voice was soft, hesitant. The question took the Englishman by surprise. He turned sharply, looked hard at the questioner.

'Sorry … did you say I might remember your father? What do you mean?' He stepped back towards the shade.

'My father was for a long time cook at the English school over beyond Gilgil. Some time I stayed with him there. My father's name is also Murungi but *mzungu* called his name Samson.'

The two men were facing each other now in the *mkuti*-shade of a lean-to at the side of the 'hotel'. The younger by perhaps ten, maybe fifteen years, Murungi was smiling, tentative; the Englishman had paled behind his beard, around his eyes. He was frowning. Yes, he remembered Samson. Samson, the man who'd turned up bruised and bleeding that Christmas night with Njeri; the man who'd lost his ear; Samson, who'd later become the cook at the school. Theo would never forget Samson. He narrowed his eyes, studied the man standing opposite him. It was hard to tell. Maybe there was a resemblance. When he spoke, his voice was hesitant.

'That's all a very long time ago. But ... you are right. When I was a young man I was indeed a teacher at that school ... for a while ... I might remember Samson ... yes, I think I do recall a cook, called Samson.' His smile was thoughtful. 'If I remember rightly he was a good cook.'

Murungi nodded, accepted the compliment on behalf of his father. 'He is an old man now, a very old man.'

'He is well?' Theo asked the question.

'He is quite well. Thank you.'

'Then please give him my regards when next you see him.'

Theo raised his right hand in something that resembled a wave, made as if to leave. His heart was racing again. He had no wish to prolong this encounter with the past. He needed to return to the present, to his new life, his new family who had by now been left waiting in the car for far too long.

But Murungi wanted more. 'You can meet him ... when you return for your wheel ... he is here ... he will be very happy to see you, sir. This is your family?' He pointed, smiling, towards the car.

'Yes ... no ... maybe ...'

Theo knew that his hesitation was confusing the Kenyan but he had no intention of allowing his new family to encounter his past. He knew that his behaviour was strange. He felt strange, un-usually hot and short of breath.

'I will come back later to collect the tyre. If your father is here, I will be happy to meet him. *Kwaheri, Goodbye.*'

This time he turned with resolution and took his leave. Red dust kicked up in his wake as he strode across the parched *murram* road, back to the present and to his young family. The Kenyan stared after him.

Theo sank gratefully into the hot front seat of the Peugot. The air was stuffy, filled with sweet smells of the orange Fanta, crumbling digestive biscuits and homemade rock cakes, with per-haps a hint of banana skins. He revelled in the wonderful warm scent of his wife's favourite perfume and the washed-hair smells of his children, of Johnson's baby shampoo. How could he ever tell them how much he loved them all, how glad he was to be back with them in this safe, this glorious life? He leaned his head back against the headrest and closed his eyes.

'Is everything ok, Theo? Can they mend the wheel?' Ellen paused, waited for her husband to respond. 'Theo, are you all right? You look a bit pale. It must be the heat. You should have worn your hat. Come on – drink some water.' She unscrewed the lid and held out the bottle. He opened his eyes but did not take the bottle straight away. He turned to face her, finally accepting her offer of water, took a few mouthfuls, paused then drank again. The colour was slowly returning to his face.

'Thanks, I'm ok now – it must have been the sun – for a moment there I felt a bit faint.' He smiled, grinned over his shoulder at the girls. 'Yes. They can fix the tyre,' he was looking back at Ellen now, 'but they're not sure how long it will take. It may not be ready until tomorrow. I'll come back over in a couple of hours to see how things are going, see if they're able to get the spare today, but you girls can stay by the pool. You don't need to come at all. It will be best if you stay. Actually I think it would be best if we try to get a room at the hotel and stay overnight anyway. It would make more of a trip of it too. I understand that they have some lovely little guest cottages in the grounds. It will be fun.' He turned and smiled at the children once more, surprised how easy it had been to tell the story.

'But we haven't brought anything with us, night things, clean clothes, toothbrushes ... nothing like that. Also they will be expecting us back ... Esther, Vitas ... they'll be worried.' Ellen was not quite sure what to make of these new circumstances, her eyebrows were raised – so was her voice.

'It'll be fine – they'll have what we need for just one night there. I'm sure we won't be the first travellers out here to encounter such unexpected difficulties. Relax. I'll call the house, let them know we're stopping over at the hotel. It'll be fine.' He leaned across and rested his hand on her knee. He smiled into her eyes.

'We'll be fine. Don't worry, it'll be fun, won't it girls?' He grinned at them in the rear view mirror.

Engaging his children's support – and through them his wife's – with his stories of crested cranes and bird-walks, swimming pools and boat rides on the lake, Theo restarted the car and soon, with clouds of dust trailing in their wake, the family were back on safari heading once more for the Lake Naivasha Hotel.

'Oh, this is lovely, Theo.'

Ellen looked across the table at her husband and smiled. The Lake Hotel was proving to be all that they had hoped for, from the polite and friendly welcome at the reception desk, the accommodating response to their questions about an overnight stay, the helpful assistance by the room steward as they settled into the guest cottage, to the speed with which he returned to their door with toothpaste, toothbrushes and a little toilette bag for each of them. The two-bedroomed cottage also had a large, bright bathroom with plenty of big, soft towels and a sitting room with comfortable armchairs, a well-stocked mini-bar and glass doors onto a small patio with a view across the lawns to the lake.

Within thirty minutes of their arrival, the grownups were relaxing on the patio in white-painted cane armchairs enjoying Tusker beer and a bowl of home-made mixed sweet potato, banana and coconut crisps, while the children played quietly on the floor of the sitting room behind them. Mara was as usual lost in her drawing book and Rosy was playing an imaginary game with the little wooden animals that were her current favourites. Sunlight filtered down through thorny acacia trees onto the patio, flaming the fluorescent reds, purples and oranges of the bougainvillea that sprawled all over the wooden balustrade. The air was pleasantly fresh and warm. Ellen leaned back against the striped cushions of the cane chair and closed her eyes.

'Oh Theo, we must do this more often ... every weekend would definitely suit me! This place is amazing.' She sat up, grinning across at him, childlike in her enthusiasm. 'It's like being in an English country house, like in the Lake District, but without all the cloud and the rain. Those beautiful lawns rolling down to the lake … 'fringing the shoreline' … just like it says in the leaflet … and all the different greens, the thorn trees, the fever trees. See the hummingbirds at those scarlet canna lilies … and look at the bougainvillea … it's just heavenly.' She leaned back once more and closed her eyes, lifting her face to the warmth of the sun.

Her husband had taken out his binoculars and was focussing on the birdlife of which even back here there was plenty. He was watching a small group of white sacred ibis with their jet black heads and scimitar beaks foraging across the lawns and a couple of red-billed hornbills were lurking at the edge of the patio watching him, waiting to be thrown another crisp. Over in the nearby acacia tree a colony of golden-breasted weaverbirds busied itself noisily around its intricately-woven nest suspended from one of the highest branches. The leaflet that the family had been given on their arrival proclaimed that over 300 species of birds were known to inhabit the shores of Lake Naivasha; a birdwatcher's paradise.

'Mummy, there's someone knocking at the door.'

Mara calling from inside the room disturbed the reverie of both parents. They leapt up to receive the room service they'd ordered, a sort of cross between late lunch and early tea. A large plate of sandwiches, another of homemade scones, butter, jam, another bowl of crisps and a small plate of shortbread biscuits was all they needed to make their happiness complete. The stewards carried the two trays out through the general excitement to the table on the patio. The children were beside themselves with delight.

Lunch had gone well.

But now it was over.

'Daddy wait! Wait! It's not fair! Daddy, you said we could go and see them now!' Mara was wailing. Angry tears wet her cheeks as she hurled the crayons across the room. 'Daddy, don't go!'

Mara ran towards the closed door and was left staring helplessly out through the thick glass panel beside it, watching her father walk away. His binoculars dangled around his neck and he was reaching into his back pocket, pulling out the car keys. He did not turn back.

'Come on, Mara. Daddy will be back soon. He's only gone to check on the tyre like he said he would.' Ellen's tone was soft; her hands were light on the stiff shoulders of her angry little daughter. 'Come on, let's have a story and a little rest, then we can go for a walk ourselves, down by the lake, see if we can spot those crested cranes.'

Mara was bereft. She was still sobbing quietly as her mother lifted her up and carried her across to the sofa. Ellen cradled the little girl on her lap and began to tell the story, softly, whispering into the damp sandy curls. 'Once upon a time there was a little girl called Mara. One sunny day she set off with her mummy and her daddy and her little sister on an awfully big adventure to visit her friends the crested cranes ...' Soon the drooping eyelids, the gentle relaxing of the little body in her arms told the storyteller that Mara was asleep. Rosy had already settled for her afternoon nap. Sighing, Ellen leaned back into the soft cushions of the sofa and gazed out through the patio doors onto the gardens.

Her wandering thoughts soon returned, as was their wont, to her husband. She had committed herself so completely to this man, trusted his strength, respected his certainties, and yet there were times when she wondered if she really knew him at all. He loved her – there was no doubt in her mind about that, but often he would seem to withdraw somewhere inside himself, to exist in some other dimension which she was unable to reach. Sometimes he would just go off alone for hours with his binoculars, other times he would simply retreat to his study and close the door behind him. In the years since their marriage she had learned to spot the signs: the paleness around his eyes, the silences, the rift that seemed to open up between them. Only gradually had she come to realise that this had little if anything to do with her. Whatever it was that caused these strange episodes, once they'd passed, Theo would return completely to his normal, loving self.

Like today, when they'd had the puncture, when Mara had wandered off and shouted out about the dead car ... for a moment he'd changed, slipped away. It was hard for her to explain, even to herself, her feelings of panic as his eyes had seemed to glaze over, his voice become harsh, like someone quite other ... but then, just as quickly, he was fine again. The water seemed to have helped him pull himself together.

And then, when he came back from that 'Fish and Chip Hotel' ... when he'd first got back into the car he looked as if he'd seen a ghost. And just now, when he'd walked away from his distraught little daughter with scarcely a backward glance ... how could he do that? Surely it wouldn't have mattered too much if he had waited for a bit, talked to her kindly, stayed until she was resting like now. Ellen looked down at the sleeping child, planted a kiss on the flattened curls. Mara idolised her father. How would she learn to cope with this other side of the man who was the centre of her world?

In the sunshine, the weaverbirds were squabbling around their hanging-basket nest. Ellen watched them for a bit. Nesting – it was what she was good at, making a home for her family, keeping them safe. She shivered. The sudden sense of unease reminded her of one of her mother's old sayings – when you had that strange unsettled feeling it was because someone had just walked over your grave. What a horrible thought! No, it was probably something to do with the beer. She was not accustomed to drinking beer at lunchtimes ... it must be that. She closed her eyes. Soon the frown slipped from her face. She slept.

The loose gravel scrunched under the wheels of the Peugeot as Theo pulled the vehicle around, out of the hotel's driveway and back onto the open road. Dust trails kicked up in his wake as he forged along the raddled tarmac, swerving to avoid the deep ruts and potholes, bumping along the verges before clunking back up onto a tract of safer ground. He knew that he was driving faster than he had with the children in the car, too fast, straining to hold the steering steady. On some level he knew that he sought this struggle, this battle against the spirit of the place that held him back yet drew him on. All around him, vast arid plains stretching out to the far horizon made him small. Sheer escarpment walls, blue-grey in the distance, loomed in his imaginings. The Great Rift Valley held him in its grasp. The Rift was in his mind.

Trapped – that's what he was. He was living in the rift, the rift between the past and the present, between the man he had been and the man he wanted to become, between his old life and the new life that he had chosen with the young family that even now he had left behind. Theo balled a fist and punched the steering wheel. He was angry with himself. His daughter's cry tore at him:

'Daddy. Don't go!'

He should have stayed. He knew it. But here he was, driving as if the devil himself was on his tail, towards the past he was determined to leave behind.

Samson.

Theo slewed the vehicle off the road onto the scrubby verge and turned the key. Silence flowed back around him as the dust settled. He wound down the window and looked about. No sight or sound of life. He picked his binoculars from the seat beside him and swept the bush – nothing. It never ceased to amaze him how the bush could be so silent during daylight hours yet become so full of sound at night.

Samson. Samson had been there from the beginning, or at least not long after the beginning, however you reckoned it. He must be quite an old man by now. What would he remember? As Theo gave rein to his own memories, he felt it again: the tightening in his chest, the loosening in his stomach, dryness in his throat, bitterness on his tongue. He flung wide the car door and stepped out, breathing deep of the hot dry air. Bending at the waist he thought he might vomit, but nothing came. He reached into the car and was glad of the bottled water that his children had left rolling on the back seat. It was warm now, tepid, but it helped. He gulped at the water, emptied the bottle then tossed it back into the car on the floor behind the driver's seat.

Perhaps the old man would not recognise him – perhaps he would remember nothing at all, at least nothing important, nothing that could link him to Kernowi. How much had Samson really known anyway? Despite what Njeri had said about Samson's role in it all, Theo could not be sure. Samson had helped them with Njoroge. He had been there during the attack. He had been injured himself. But that was a time of violence. Many farms and homesteads had been attacked, schools even. Of course he would have his own take on it all, his own memories. And then there was Murungi. Murungi had recognised him certainly but only as one of the group of young men who had been at the school at the time. He was just a boy then – he could not have known anything about *Kernowi*.

The old man would certainly remember Daniel. He would remember his artwork – it was everywhere around the school, some landscapes, sketches of people, mostly Njeri. Daniel had been fascinated by the African face. He loved to capture nuances, particular features distinctive of different tribal ancestry. He might have even done a portrait of Samson. Theo could not be sure about that. But yes. It seemed that if Samson remembered any of them he would remember Daniel.

'Are you alright sir?'

The dark green land rover, emblazoned with the name of the nearby safari camp, pulled up in a screech of gravel and dust beside the Peugeot, catching Theo unawares. Its local driver seemed friendly, concerned.

'Thanks. I'm fine. I just stopped for a break on my way into town. It's ok.' Theo did his best to shrug off the man's attention.

'If you're sure then ... have a good day sir.' The vehicle pulled away in a cloud of dust and once more Theo found himself alone.

He should be getting on anyway. He looked at his watch, looked up at the sky. He didn't want to leave it too late – the children were awaiting his return. He climbed back into the car and restarted the engine. He was going to meet up with this man from his past, he was resolved – anyway he had to collect the spare wheel; they needed it for the journey back to Nairobi. There was nothing he could do at this stage to change anything. 'What will be, will be.' He spoke the words aloud as he pulled the Peugeot back onto the road.

Theo was calmer now; it showed in his driving. There was still the dust and the swerving around potholes, but the rage had gone ... the panic ... or whatever it had been. He managed to keep the vehicle largely on the tarmac for the rest of the journey into the town and arrived quite safely, even sedately – he was a headmaster after all – in front of the Fish and Chip Hotel. He switched off the engine and sat for a moment looking at the place. The sign was pretentious; how could anyone think of calling this ramshackle building a hotel? There was even a smile on his face as he got out of the car and made his way back towards this 'hotel's' reception.

Once more inside the building's shade he found himself alone. He called out: '*Jambo* ... is anybody there?' he waited. He walked over to the poster on the wall – was studying it as he heard a slight cough behind him. He turned towards the sound.

'*Jambo Bwana.*'

Murungi had entered and was standing by the doorway that lead further into the strange hotel's heart.

Theo walked towards the man, holding out his hand. '*Jambo sana. Habari?*'

'*Mzuri.*' The men exchanged the greetings. 'You have come to collect your tyre?'

'It is ready?' Theo was surprised.

'Yes, it is ready. The spare wheel is ready. You are lucky, sir, that we could fix it so quickly. There was another car ... it had been in an accident on the road ... you can have one of its wheels.' Murungi nodded towards the *mzungu*.

Theo smiled. He knew from experience that this was what happened here. One man's loss was another man's gain – or on this occasion 'car's'. '*Asante sana*. I am very lucky. Thank you.'

'I will go to fetch the spare wheel for you. You can wait here.' Murungi hesitated. 'My father ... he is here ... he says that he remembers you ... he would like to meet you ... can I bring him here?'

Theo's voice was more relaxed, more confident than he felt. 'Of course. If he would like to meet me I will be happy to greet him. Is he well?'

'He is an old man, sir. He has been through many things.'
Again the Kenyan seemed hesitant. 'My father was not the same
when he came back. He is scarred, sir. He does not hear well. They
took his ear.' Murungi looked down at his feet.

Theo felt his own heart sink inside his chest. 'I remember.
I am sorry.' He used the familiar phrase with feeling, not with fault.

'I will bring him, sir. Wait here please.'

The wait was brief, minutes only, but to the man who was
left alone, waiting, it seemed a long time indeed. The younger
man came back into the room, ushering in another man, smaller,
shrunken, swaying from side to side as he walked, like an elderly
vulture. His bent head was bald, skin in leathered wrinkles. He was
wearing dark trousers, a jacket seemingly from a suit; both had
seen better days. A blanket, tartan, red, was wrapped around his
shoulders. Murungi led his father across to one of the white plastic chairs and helped him sit. At the younger man's gesture, Theo
moved the other chair. He seated himself facing the old man that
he knew was Samson.

'I will fetch the wheel – you can talk with him. He remembers you.' Murungi bent close to his father's good ear, spoke to
him softly in a language that Theo could not understand. The old
man nodded, lifted his left hand from the blanket in a small gesture that might have been dismissal. Murungi turned towards the
Englishman, lowered his head briefly in something like a bow and
disappeared, leaving the two men alone.

Theo waited; he was not sure of the protocol. It was the
Mzee who broke the silence.

'I know you. You are Bwana Theodore. You have come
back.' The old man looked up. The eyes that held Theo's gaze
were heavy-lidded, black as obsidian, glassy, sharp. They seemed
to examine him for a long moment. Then the corners of the tight
lips twitched. He smiled. Theo let out a breath; he felt like he had
passed some test.

'My son has helped you. He has fixed your wheel. That is
good.'

'He has.' Theo nodded. '*Mzee*, I am pleased to see that you are well. Do you stay here with your son and his family?' He spoke slowly, clearly, making a show of the words.

'I do. He is a kind man – a good father to his children.'

'You were a good father to your family – a good cook, Samson. I remember you.' The old man raised his right hand towards his visitor, accepted the praise. The two men shared a smile. Samson looked down, seemed to be studying his hands.

'You were a good teacher. The children were happy with you.' This time it was Theo who raised his right hand to acknowledge the affirmation. Maybe the old man had forgotten.

But no; Samson had more to say. He was frowning now, fidgeting in his chair. 'No-one talks about those days any more but I cannot forget. I remember very bad things, Bwana Theo, at night I remember very bad things.' The old man shook his head, his eyes fixed on some point in the distant past. Theo was silent, watching, waiting. Several minutes passed before the *mzee* spoke again.

'I remember Kernowi.'

All at once his eyes were sharp, focused on Theo. Theo felt his pulse lurch. Under the old man's scrutiny, he blanched.

'Kernowi ... he was brave ... a warrior. He helped our people ... but he made many of his people angry. I remember him.' As he spoke, Samson's eyes had not left Theo's face. 'One of my sons is named Theodore Kernowi. He is named for you ... and for Bwana Daniel.'

Theo was taken aback ... so Njeri had been right. But why had Samson chosen to mention Daniel to him, like that, linking him with Kernowi? Was the old man testing him ... trying to find out how much he knew about the events of that terrible night? He made an instant decision.

'I am honoured. I hope that he is a good son to you.'

'He is a fine man. I am proud of him.' Again the *mzee* nodded. 'He is doing well. He worked hard at school. He is very interested in politics. He reminds me of you – also of Bwana Daniel.' There – he had mentioned his name again. And suddenly Theo was certain. Samson had believed back then, and still believed today, that Daniel was Kernowi. Kernowi had been betrayed. He held his breath; his heart beat loud in the uncomfortable silence. Outside the window, someone was working, hammering, listening to a local radio station, sometimes whistling, sometimes singing along to the lively African rhythm.

Theo's voice cut the air between them. 'Bwana Daniel was my friend. He was a brave man. He was a good man, a man of peace ... he was not afraid.' Theo had not spoken of his friend for a very long time. He stood sharply and the feet of the plastic chair scraped on the bare concrete floor. Turning his back, he moved towards the window.

'Our people have much to thank him for. Many were saved from torture and worse in those terrible camps. Without *Kernowi*, many of us would not be alive today.'

The old man stayed seated in the white bucket chair, head bowed beneath the weight of his memories. The horrors of those days, the struggles, they haunted him still, scarred his body. They had crippled his spirit. Emaciated and broken bodies hacked and abused during beatings and interrogations – these things he would never again speak of – not to anyone. Bwana Daniel had been there, in the camps. He was the one they called Kernowi, of that the old man was certain.

At the window Theo was also remembering Daniel. He shivered, despite the warmth in the room. Just thinking of those days brought it all back ... the noxious stench, the filth and depravity, the brutal conditions for the hordes of Kikuyu, many with no links at all to Mau Mau violence, shuffling in lines to be processed, screened by 'officials' with guns, before being moved on down the so called 'pipeline'. The system had been designed as a detention and rehabilitation programme for winning the war against the Mau Mau, but it was an abject failure that had led to the worst atrocities imaginable.

Like Daniel, he had written many letters to people he knew back in Britain, expressing outrage at the abuse being carried out in what was still a British Colony. Questions were raised in the House of Commons. Several MPs, old friends of his father's had weighed in. Barbara Castle had demanded answers, but no response had been forthcoming. When nothing had changed, he had been left with no choice. At the small window of the 'Fish and Chip Hotel,' in the dusty backwater that was Naivasha Town, the one-time freedom fighter 'Kernowi' shook his head and turned back to face Samson.

Unknowing, the *mzee* looked up, meeting Theo's gaze. In the white plastic chair, the old man pulled the blanket close against the worst horror of all. In the dark night he, Samson, had chosen his own way too.

'The spare wheel is outside. It is beside your car.'

Neither of them had noticed the return of Murungi. He was standing in the doorway to the street, watching them. Each seemed startled at his voice, turned towards the sound as if woken from a trance.

'Murungi. Thank you, *asante sana*. I will pay you. How much?' Theo moved towards the door; reached into his back pocket for his wallet; stopped beside the man sitting in the chair. Their eyes met, one last time. 'I am glad to see you, Samson. I hope that you will stay well.' He rested his left hand on the old man's shoulder and offered his right hand in farewell.

'I am happy to see you again, Bwana Theo. Travel safely to your family. Bring them my greetings.' The men shook hands across the years.

Soon Theo was taking his leave. As he drove away with the spare wheel safely in the boot of the Peugeot, he knew that his family would not be receiving the *mzee's* greetings. They would never know about this meeting. He would never tell them.

Turning the vehicle off the road into the broad driveway of the Lake Hotel, he caught sight of a gaggle of Kikuyu women selling souvenirs from big straw baskets that they had lifted down from their heads onto the verge. Charms and necklaces dangling from their outstretched hands, they were haggling noisily through the opened windows of a dusty white tour bus. He smiled. Maybe there would be some pottery, some soapstone carvings, perhaps some candlesticks for his wife. She liked that kind of thing.

21

Kenya, Nairobi – 1982

Ellen picked up the candlestick, one of a pair made of soapstone, pale as the skin on the inside of her wrist. With her fingertips, she traced its smooth, spiralled stem then set it back down onto the dark wood of the mantelpiece and held the base firm while she fixed a red Christmas candle into first one, then the other of the pair. Job done, she stepped back from the hearth, admiring the effect. Decorating for Christmas always made her nostalgic. There should be snow. But there was no chance of that here in Nairobi, just endless clear blue skies and unrelenting sunshine. She sighed, glancing towards the open doors to the veranda, where the swing-chair beckoned, then decided on the armchair closer to hand.

Those candlesticks had shifted her mood. Theo had brought them back that day, almost a year ago now, at Naivasha when he had gone out to fetch the tyre. He'd arrived noisily, in a flurry of gifts and greetings. The girls had been so excited to see him, all jealous rage forgotten in the joy of Daddy's return. Baskets, more carved animals, soapstone eggs painted with elephants and giraffes for the children and for her the candlesticks. Hugs and twirls for his daughters, a brush of his lips, his rough beard, on the cheek for his wife.

He'd been strangely full of laughs and smiles for the rest of the afternoon as they'd swum and explored the lake shore together, playing with the girls, pointing out birds and flowers, chasing them across the grass. She'd been happy too, watching them. But somehow, even in the midst of it all, she'd sensed that all was not well. He was trying hard, too hard, to be the perfect father, as if he felt guilty, as if there was something that he had to atone for. She'd noticed too that he seemed reluctant to meet her eyes.

Later, when the children were sleeping, a silence had grown between them. They were both reading in the lamplight but she recalled looking up to find his eyes watching her, thoughtful but somehow distant. He'd been quick to return her smile before turning back to his book, but the moment had lodged itself in her memory.

'You always make everything so nice, my dear. You're so good at that sort of thing.' Theo's voice disturbed her reverie. He was standing in the doorway. He'd been watching her. Now he came across and touched her lightly on the shoulder, leaning in to kiss her cheek. She flashed a smile, as he moved away, lowering himself into the armchair beside the coffee table, which was covered as usual with magazines and old newspapers. The latest copy of the Times from England caught his eye, over a week out of date, but no one minded that out here. Newspapers from home were very much in demand and anyone who had one, passed it on. Soon he was happily turning pages and scanning articles. Returning to the box of decorations, Ellen resumed her earlier occupation.

The girls were outside on the lawn. Rosy was lying on the grass playing some kind of safari game with her wooden menagerie and Mara was nestled amongst the cushions of the basketwork armchair, lost to the world in a book, fairy-tales probably, happy-ever-after endings. Kneeling beside the Christmas box, Ellen watched her children. It was good to see them peaceful now. The incident that morning at the Animal Orphanage had really shaken both girls. It had unsettled her too.

It was the start of the school holidays and they'd decided to take the children to the Animal Orphanage – 'something like a zoo really' was what they had been told – near the entrance to the Nairobi National Park. The girls were excited at the prospect and the trip had begun well. But they'd soon begun to feel uncomfortable. In some areas the boundary fences between the animals and the public looked less than secure and both she and the children had been upset to see a crowd of local people throwing lit cigarettes through the bars of a cage to a tired old ape, laughing uproariously when it copied the gestures of smoking. They'd moved swiftly on along the rutted track, she pushing the buggy with Rosy in and Mara walking beside, holding onto the handle. Turning to speak to Theo, she'd been surprised to find him gone. She'd stopped then and looked back down the track, scanning the sightseers for any sign of him. Out of the corner of her eye she'd finally spotted her husband in close conversation with a man in a shabby sports jacket, a Kenyan, probably a Kikuyu. Ellen remembered leaning forward over the handles of the buggy to speak to Rosy, then Mara's scream.

'Mummy, look! He's climbing out!'

Even now, the memory of that scream set her heart thumping. Looking up she'd watched in horror as the male baboon, standing taller than a man, clambered over the wooden barricade, his strong-muscled thighs straddling the barrier, powerful shoulders and arms swinging him out onto the path up ahead of them. Ellen knew that she would never forget those black eyes, the expressionless black-ape face with its halo of bristled khaki fur, as the creature strode down the track towards them. All at once Theo had been beside her, as the baboon, clearly with a mind of its own, veered across the track to the opposite barrier, cleared it with as much ease as it had the other and disappeared into the forest that formed the boundary with the game park itself. After the incident, there was no way that either she or the children wanted to continue with the outing. Even when they were all safely back in the car the feeling of menace, of threat to the family's security, hung coldly in the stifling air.

Ellen shivered at the memory as she returned to the present. Reaching into the Christmas box, she pulled out a couple of lengths of tinsel, in the process uncovering the pottery nativity figures wrapped separately in bubble-wrap. She lifted each one out carefully and set it down on the heaped tinsel, like onto a nest. First she un-wrapped the manger, then the baby and placed him gently on the pottery straw. The baby was blue-eyed, light-haired like Mary his pottery mother. Like mother, like son. Ellen smiled. She glanced through the open doors at her own children. Theo was out there with them now, sitting on the cane settee chatting to Mara. Still holding the Virgin Mary, Ellen moved out onto the veranda and sat down on the swing-seat. Unobserved, she watched them.

At her father's request, Mara began to sing one of the songs from her Christmas play:

> 'Little donkey, little donkey on the dusty road
> got to keep on plodding onward
> with your precious load'

As she sang, her sister joined in, climbing up onto Theo's lap. Ellen could see that he was smiling.

'You sing your song now Daddy. Go on ...go on.' The girls had jumped down onto the grass and were banging on his knees, laughing. It was not long before he gave in to their demands, and he began to sing, his fine tenor bouncing up through the branches of the Jacaranda tree over his head:

> A good sword and a trusty hand,
> A merry heart and true;
> King James' men shall understand
> What Cornish lads can do.'

Mara and Rosy had heard the song many times before. They were marching like soldiers around his chair as he swung into the chorus:

> 'And shall Trelawney live?
> And shall Trelawney die?
> Here's twenty thousand Cornish men
> Shall know the reason why.'

'Again Daddy... again!' Theo was marching with them now as he sang the song again about the twenty thousand Cornish men who would know the reason why the English would kill a Cornishman. The meaning of the song was lost on the children but they loved the marching and their father's voice as he sang. After a few more choruses of marching and singing, the three of them collapsed onto the grass in a heap.

'Tell us the story now, daddy.' As so often before, the girls were insistent and true to form, Theo soon gave in.

'Come on then, let's get up on the cushions. We'd better sit in the shade or Mummy will be after us, won't she.'

From the veranda Ellen watched as they settled on the big basketwork settee and listened as Theo began to tell the story.

'Once upon a time there was a handsome young prince – at least he was quite handsome. He lived in a rose-covered palace in the land of Kernow.'

'What colour were the roses, Daddy?' Mara would draw them later.

'Oh, they were red and some pink ones. Everybody in the land said how lovely they were. Anyway, one day he decided to go on a long journey, across the seas to another far away country to seek his fortune.'

'Why did he go Daddy?' Ellen smiled. Mara was always the one with questions.

'Well Mara, when he was a little boy, the king of that far-off country had come to visit Kernow and had stayed at his father's palace. That King was kind and funny and wise and the little prince thought that when he grew up he would like to be just like that. So, when he was nearly a king himself, he decided to go to that far distant country and find that King and ask him some magic questions.'

'Show us the picture Daddy. Show us the picture.' Rosy's voice carried across to her mother. Theo was reaching for his wallet. He pulled out a photograph, which he showed to his children while Ellen looked on from the veranda.

'Is that the King daddy? Is that you?'

'Yes, my love, that's the King; and that's me.' He nodded, tucking the photograph away into his wallet and the wallet into his back pocket.

'Now, have you had enough, or shall I go on?' Eager for more, the girls settled quickly and Theo continued with his story. 'Well, the journey was long and hard and on the way the brave prince had to do lots of daring deeds and had many adventures, but one day he arrived at the country where the kind King lived. Imagine his surprise to discover that some people from a country near to his own had got there first. They were not good men and they tried to stop the prince from seeing the King. The King was hiding from them to keep safe.'

'Where was the King hiding Daddy?' Mara's voice was anxious.

'He was hiding in a forest, near a magic mountain. The young prince was very sad. He wanted to see the King. One day, he met a man who was the king's friend. Because the brave prince looked quite similar to the baddies, the man thought he was a baddy too. But the young prince showed him the picture and the man believed him. So one day the man took him to the magic forest to see the King.'

'Did the King answer the magic questions, Daddy?' Mara wanted all the answers.

At that moment Theo looked up towards the house. He caught sight of his wife sitting on the swing-chair. She waved and he smiled.

'The rest will have to wait till another day, girls. Look there's mummy. Let's go and help her with the decorations shall we? She might even be ready for us to do the tree.'

'The tree! The tree! The Tree!'

So saying, the children ran across the lawn to their mother. The brave young prince stood and watched them for a moment before following them into the house.

'That photograph, the one you showed the children earlier.'

Ellen was at the writing desk in the corner of the room. Beyond the curtained and barred windows, quick, noisy darkness had cloaked the garden. Inside, the standard lamp from England pooled its light over the last of the Christmas cards, illuminating the pages of the address book at her elbow. She paused, pen in hand, to raise the question that had been puzzling her since she'd watched him with the children out in the garden earlier.

Theo looked up from his book. Unhurried, he removed his reading glasses and turned to face his wife. From the armchair beside the log-fire, he regarded her, his bearded face expressionless. He seemed poised, waiting for her to finish before deciding on his response.

'I don't think you noticed me, but I was on the veranda. The children were having such fun – you know how I love to watch you three together. You're so good with them.'

Ellen's words were warm and he relaxed visibly under her praise. In truth he'd been aware of her, watching from the shade of the swing-seat, and had sensed her curiosity. It had been a spur of the moment decision, to show them the photograph, out there in the garden. Like the girls, he'd been caught up, his imagination taking him back to those real memories that were so much a part of the child he had been, the man he had become. Couched in the language of fairy tale, there had been so much truth in his story that it had frightened him, to hear it out in the open like that. There'd been no *fundis* around for sure, no gardeners. He'd not thought himself overheard – until he'd spotted Ellen. Since that moment he had been on a knife-edge. Knowing her as he did, he was sure that she would need to voice the questions he saw in her eyes. She was not an artful woman; her openness and her honesty were qualities that he treasured. He would need to be careful, but he'd decided to answer her questions when they came with as much integrity as he could.

'Were you listening to the story? Would you like me to show you the photograph?' There was kindness in his voice and she nodded. 'Come over here then and I'll tell you what you want to know.'

He stood and reached into his pocket for his wallet, took out the picture, moved onto the soft, corded sofa and patted the cushions. Abandoning the Christmas cards, Ellen came to sit beside him. He offered her the photograph, which she took, as she brought her feet up beneath her and moved closer.

'How old are you here? You look so sweet, so serious.' She studied the picture of her husband as a boy, loving the child. She turned to face the man.

'I think I must have been about six perhaps, or seven. There's no date, but if you look on the back you will see that he has written on it.'

Ellen turned the photograph over and read the inscription: *'For Theodore, with best wishes from your friend* …and then he has signed his name, it says *Jomo Kenyatta.'* She looked back at the image. 'It's him, isn't it … it's Kenyatta, the first president.' She turned again to the dedication. 'He's written something else: *Know yourself and where you came from; know your parents and your country and be true to these things.'* She looked up at Theo. He was smiling. Reaching out, he took the photograph from her fingers.

'Before you ask me how this picture came about, let me just tell you that one day it saved my life. I'm not joking.' He paused, nodding at the surprise on her face. 'I'll start with that if you like.' And so he began his story, for the second time that day.

'Well, as you can see, I first met Jomo Kenyatta when he was in England and I was just a boy. My father had met him in London and he'd been impressed by the calibre of the man, his integrity, the things he had to say. Kenyatta was studying Anthropology at the time, at the LSE, and my father was interested to learn from him about the African perspective on land issues, about the traditions of the Kikuyu people, their sense of identity. He brought him down to Cornwall, to our home and Kenyatta stayed with us for a while – I can't remember how long, or much of the detail really. I just remember that he was kind and funny and clever. His voice was deep and warm – the kind that children respond to – and he played with us, my sister and me, in the garden. I know that he spent a lot of time talking with my parents, and they brought some of their friends, some people from the town, up to meet him too. My father took photographs – this is one of them. Kenyatta signed it when they met the next time and my father knew that I would like to have it. I have treasured it. I understood then that he was a good man and my father expected that he would be a great man, or at least that he would have a significant role to play in his country's future.' Theo paused, turned to his young wife. When she made no comment, he continued.

'As you can imagine, I was very influenced by my father. He would talk to me often, asking me questions, challenging me to develop my own thinking even though I was obviously just a child at that time. He was a thinker himself, and a good teacher. You said I looked serious and you're right, I was ... I suppose I always have been, still am really.' His wife nudged him in the ribs at this and they laughed together.

'Not long after this meeting with Kenyatta, my parents went on a trip to Kenya. They left my sister and me at home with an aunt and a nanny while they travelled to East Africa, to visit a school that had been set up by a friend of my father's from his university days. The school was in the Rift Valley – apparently they had taken over an old farm, some kind of estate that a fellow they knew wanted to sell in a hurry because he'd run out of money. I don't know all the history, just what I've gathered. My father's friend, my Uncle Charles, was a lot like him really – he believed with a passion that all people are born equal and he wanted to bring the blessing of a British education to the whole Empire, regardless of colour or tribe or race. My parents spent quite a while out there, at the school, getting to know the people, the area. Apparently my mother loved the local children and they loved her.' He smiled at his memory of her. 'She was just like my father; a passionate teacher ... reading, writing, singing, telling stories ... I can only imagine what it was like. There was one little girl she became especially fond of – her name was Njeri. It seems that Njeri was a happy child, particularly bright and eager to learn. When they left to come home, my mother gave money, committed herself to support Njeri's education at the school. My sister and I knew about Njeri because there were photographs and letters.' Theo paused, nodding.

'I never saw my parents again. They were killed in a car accident in Cairo – apparently they decided to stopover there on their return journey. I don't know much about it. We were just children and we were protected by the adults around us as much as possible. It was a strange time – a difficult time for everyone.' He stopped and Ellen reached out her hand, touching his cheek.

'Are you sure you want to go on? Shall I get us a drink? What would you like?'

'No it's fine … I'm fine. Now that I've started I think I'd better get it over with … that's if you'd like me to …' When she nodded her response, Theo returned to his story.

'I don't think you need me to go into all the details, but I reckon it's clear that the meeting with Kenyatta, and all the thinking my father had encouraged me to do had a huge impact on what I chose to do with my life. I enjoyed school actually. I was a serious and hard-working student, good at sport – which helped considerably as you can imagine – so I got on well with most people and generally made a success of the thing. I decided to become a teacher myself – despite some early pressure to follow my late father into the church. That was not going to be for me. I wanted to travel to Africa, to see things for myself and I guess, if I'm honest, that somewhere in all that was a feeling that I wanted to meet up with Jomo Kenyatta again. I think I imagined that I was as special to him as he was to me. Silly really – childish, at least childlike I suppose, but that's what I thought. I thought it would be that easy … to just call in and see him. I don't know … it makes me sound very nave doesn't it?' He smiled self-deprecatingly, before continuing.

'Well, skipping over the boring bits, I arrived in Nairobi not very long before the future Queen Elizabeth and her husband as it happens. It had been arranged that I could try teaching at the same school my parents had visited in the Rift Valley. I even got to see Princess Elizabeth and Prince Philip, along with some of the teachers and children from the school, at Government House when she met the children from all different schools. That was great actually. So many children, all different nationalities … cheering and waving flags, laughing and happy together. It seemed to be just what I had hoped to find, a place where everyone was treated with respect, happy. Little did I know!' He shook his head. His tone and his expression had become saddened.

'At first everything was fine. The weather was glorious. My parents' friends were happy to have me there, and I soon discovered that I had inherited my family's talent for teaching. The Rift Valley took my breath away as you can imagine and the setting of the school was really nice ... single storey buildings a bit like this one, verandas to shade the classrooms, nice gardens. I shared a room with another young chap not long out from England. We got on well – he taught Maths and games to the older children.'

'I know who that was. That's Jack isn't it? How nice for you both, that you started at the same time.' Ellen was smiling. She and Jack had always got on well.

'That's right. We were good company for each other. The thing I also liked about the school though, was that the students were quite mixed ... quite a lot of white farmers' and missionary's children but also some local children, Kenyans, Kikuyu mostly, even a few whose families had been displaced from their lands, tenant farmers, 'squatters' a lot of the English people called them. That was very unusual at the time ... very unusual. There was some sponsorship, I think, from like-minded friends of my uncle's, but still it was a courageous move. There was some opposition in the early days, but they stuck to their original principals, insisted that the school was for anybody. Brave of them really.'

'But it was not long before I realised that all was not well. There was trouble brewing in the country and most of it was about land, Africans being turned off their land, which was then sold to white settlers. You've heard about the Mau Mau rebellion – well that's what was about to happen.'

'At the school we started to hear rumours of violent attacks, horrible violence – the kind of thing that we could scarcely believe – and then we got the news that a white woman had been stabbed to death out near Thika. Just a week later we heard that one of the Senior Tribal Chiefs – a man who had been a strong supporter of the British in Kenya – had been shot in Nairobi, in broad daylight. I can tell you there was a real feeling of panic in the air. I actually considered going back home to Cornwall at that time – but then I remembered how kind Kenyatta had been, how measured his thinking and his arguments. I liked him and I couldn't bear to think that he would be behind any of this. I determined to meet him.'

'You tried to meet up with Kenyatta? But I thought that it was straight after that chief was killed that they declared the State of Emergency, those mass arrests, when the army rounded up all the Kikuyu in Nairobi into those detention camps. I thought that was when he was captured with the other leaders and there was that trial. Do you mean to say that you got involved in all that? You were still quite young then, weren't you?' Ellen was finding it hard to take it in, hard to connect the man she knew now, with those turbulent times. She was frowning as she shifted to face him. 'Did you get to meet him then? Is that when your picture saved your life?'

'I did meet him, several times actually, but the first time was just before he was arrested. I forgot to mention just now that I had met up with Njeri, you remember, the girl who had been special for my mother. She was grown up, of course; still at the school, working as a sort of part time teacher. We got on well – she had the makings of a really good teacher – I could see why my mother had taken to her. Anyway, Njeri had become quite political, believed in the cause. I suppose she was very like Kenyatta when I first met him in Cornwall actually – passionate about justice, equality, against oppression, that sort of thing. She had been attending rallies, going to meetings. She even joined the KAU ... that's the 'Kenyan African Union' ... Kenyatta was its president, at least I think she did, although I'm not certain about that. She was really against the secret societies like Mau Mau, the oaths people were being forced to take, the rituals, the vows to kill Europeans and their collaborators. She'd grown up with Europeans – she knew that they were not all bad. In the smaller meetings she was part of, I know that she argued for restraint, against violence. I know because on two occasions I was there with her. Her views, and I think Kenyatta's views, on these things were not in the majority.'

'I had shown her the photograph of me as a boy with Kenyatta. She knew of my affection for him, my sympathy with his opinions. She was able to make enquiries through the people she knew and one day she told me that it had been arranged. Violence was spreading like a fanned bush-fire; white Settlers killed, their farms and properties destroyed; murders of Africans loyal to the

Government. At the school we were trying to carry on as normal but it was a very difficult time. There seemed to be army, soldiers, and police everywhere.' He was upright now, his breaths short and quick, his shoulders tense.

'But the school was out in the Rift Valley. How did you get to where he was if there were soldiers everywhere? Surely it was really dangerous... you could have been arrested yourself, captured by the rebels, even killed.' Although he had clearly not been killed, she was caught up in the drama of his story, anxious for the man she loved. She watched his conscious efforts to relax as he sat back and continued.

'For the activists it was easier to move around at night out in the countryside. They knew the terrain better. The British were very threatened by this, very afraid of the primitive violence lurking in the dark. Njeri had arranged it and she was with me. We met some men. They had an old pick-up truck. We travelled some of the way in that ... but honestly, it was dark and yes, it was dangerous. Much of the detail of how we got there – even where exactly it was – I can't remember now and you don't really need to know anyway, my love. I don't want you having nightmares about it. I know what you're like.' He leaned his face down, smiling into her hair, kissed the top of her head.

'I will admit that I was afraid that night. We were somewhere out in the forest. I could hear that cacophony of night noises, animals hunting nearby, monkeys calling ... at least that's what I thought it was but I guess it could have been secret calls, people hiding in the woods. It was eerie, very strange. Men just appeared out of nowhere. There was a lot of shouting – they said I was an English spy, all that kind of thing. But when Kenyatta came, I showed the photograph and he remembered me. He asked about my parents, you know, offered his condolences when I told him about their death. We got on well. He shook my hand.' Ellen patted her husband's hand. Shaking hands – this was better. She relaxed a little, leaning in against the storyteller.

'But one of the men still kept shouting at me, 'You English! I kill you!' I don't know where I got the courage from, but I looked him straight in the eye, made one of my own horrible faces, and shouted, 'Oh no I'm not! I'm Cornish! I am from Kernow! Kernow!' and guess what I did next.' He sat up and turned to face his wife. He seemed about to laugh.

'What did you do, my darling? What did you do next?'

'I started to sing. I stood there and sang 'Trelawney.'

'You sang Trelawney? Whatever did you do that for?' She was aghast.

'I told them it was my Anthem, our Battle Song against the English! They believed me. They wanted me to teach them the song and soon there they were, dancing about in that forest clearing, in the middle of the night singing:

> 'And shall Trelawney live?
> And shall Trelawney die?
> Here's twenty thousand Cornish men
> Shall know the reason why.'

They called me Kernowi, the man from Kernow. They liked me. They liked the song. They thought I was funny. For a moment it had made them laugh. They said I was brave. That was my name: Kernowi. And, do you know, my love, from then on I actually felt it myself, that I was Kernowi, that I was one of Trelawney's brave 20,000 Cornishmen who would *'know the reason why!'*

All at once the proud Cornishman jumped to his feet and started to sing at the top of his voice:

> 'A good sword and a trusty hand,
> A merry heart and true
> King James' men shall understand
> What Cornish lads can do.'

In a moment of complete hilarity, his wife stood up too and started marching around him, following behind him, just like the girls had earlier. He sang the whole song and she marched and laughed and then they both laughed, noisily like children.

'What's going on Daddy? Why are you singing? Mummy,

why are you laughing? Did Father Christmas come already?' Neither parent had spotted their audience standing in the doorway. All sleepy-eyed and barefoot in pyjamas, the two little girls were watching their parents in disbelief.

'Oh my love, did we disturb you? Don't worry – mummy and daddy are just playing.' Ellen scooped up her youngest daughter and Theo swung Mara up high into her daddy's strong embrace.

'Come on – back to bed with you two. Father Christmas isn't here yet ... but your Daddy's here. Your Daddy will always be here to take care of his two little princesses.'

For once, sleep was eluding him. In the warm darkness that was never complete, Theo was wide-awake, staring up at the ceiling. An eerie orange glow from the security lights over the garden snuck in around the edges of the bedroom curtains while above him the fan turned softly. Beside him his wife slept, her breathing deep and regular with a whistle that he knew she would find funny if she could hear it. He turned his face to watch her, smiled. He found it funny too. Grabbing his crumpled pillow, he shook it, shuffled himself so that he was lying in what he imagined was a foetal position, facing what he liked to call his side of the bed.

Slipping at last towards sleep, Theo drew in a long breath, almost a yawn, held it then let it seep out slowly, like a long sigh. A childhood memory drifted but did not settle, as Ellen shifted behind him. He was relieved beyond measure that she had accepted his story earlier that evening, history now, though an abridged version, one that he knew she would be able understand, in which he was the hero. In this telling her husband had always acquitted himself with honour. There was some drama, some danger but nothing too disturbing. In the semi-darkness, the drowsy man smiled at her remembered face.

His story. A tightening frown replaced the smile as his brain refused to rest. His pulse quickened. Shoving the pillow from the bed, Theo rolled over on to his stomach. The past, 'another country' someone once said. Things were certainly coming back to him differently these days. Facts, details … he found he could not always recall exactly who'd been there, what they'd said, what they'd done, what he'd done. His restless mind was awash with images, of people and places, faces of his enemies, of his family, flickering like in an old film, forming and reforming like a kaleidoscope. There was blood. Struggling against the entwining sheet, Theo was suddenly upright, his heart racing. A heavy sense of nightmare gripped his chest, pressed down over his shoulders like a cloak, a heavy burden, a yoke. He must have slept. Like a man escaped from drowning, he sucked in deep gulps of air. He decided to get up.

Stealthy, Theo set his feet on the floor and eased himself from the bed where his wife was sleeping more softly now. Like a thief in the night, he tiptoed barefoot across the bedroom, slipping out through the partially opened door and across to the bathroom. Suddenly, urgently, he needed to pee. But after relieving himself as quietly as he could in the echoing darkness, he was not yet ready to return to the bed. Resuming his furtive tiptoeing, past his daughters' bedrooms and along the hallway of the single-storey schoolhouse, he reached the short flight of steps and descended into the sitting room.

It was strange to be out in this part of the house, alone in the darkness, or semi-darkness, for here too the orangey glow from the security lights seeped through the fabric of the full-length curtains. Theo shivered. Somehow he could never completely escape that vague sense of threat, the need for security. He padded over to the sofa. The cool wood-block flooring, so welcome in the heat of the day, felt chilled to him now, up through the soles of his bare feet and he was glad to reach the old rug that had travelled with him all those years ago from his parents' home. Settling himself on the sofa, he drew his feet up beneath him. What a strange sight he must make in his striped pyjamas curled up on the sofa like a child. He smiled, remembering his wife sitting just like that earlier.

Everything he had told her was true. He loved and respected her, had determined never to lie to her, but the details that he'd selected, episodes he'd chosen to omit, characters he'd mentioned, relationships he'd chosen to leave out from this version of the story – all these decisions had been made with his precious listener in mind. Some things he would never tell her, could never tell her.

Kenyatta's inscription on his photograph ... like himself as a boy, as a young man, she too had been inspired by the sentiments of loyalty, of faithfulness, of honour: *'Know yourself and where you came from, know your parents and your country and be true to those things.'* But what should a man do when the things that he knew about his parents, their values, everything they held dear, were so deeply at odds with the policies of his country, or at least of powerful and significant numbers of his countrymen? British Colonial Government? England? He was a Cornishman too. How could he stand by without demanding to *'know the reason why?'* When a man had to choose between his duty to his country and his commitment to what he knew to be right, that was where the real challenge came. *'All that is needful for evil to flourish is that good men do nothing.'* One of his father's favourite lines from Edmund Burke had made the choice plain. For a good man there were serious decisions to be made and he had made them.

Thinking about it now though, he was not sure he'd actually made decisions. He'd simply followed his gut instincts, more like. He shuddered. When the horrors had been right there in front of him, one man gouging another with a knife, cutting into the screaming man's flesh, hacking off bits of his body while another man standing with his foot on the squirming neck shouted obscenities ... what mattered then black or white? And when yet another is shoving stinking mud into the captive's mouth, urged on by a leering figure, the ring-leader, brandishing a loaded rifle, and all of those torturers wearing uniforms that should have guaranteed fairness, humanity ... how could any right thinking man not have got involved? Theo knew that it was not 'thinking' that had caused him to raise his own weapon, to shoot the leader, the commander, through the heart, to shoot at and wound several of the others ... it was pure rage, outrage. Reliving the madness, his breathing quickened. He shifted his feet out from under him. That was the first time, in the bloody aftermath of the *Lari* massacres and the reprisals that followed. There had been more.

He had made choices and because of those choices whole sections of his life had to be kept secret from those he loved … forever. Silence had become his companion. But even now he could not lie. He had told his wife of the mad Kenyan's threat to kill him in the forest. This was true, as was his battle cry, that crazy rendition of Trelawney. What he could not tell her was that his life had been under threat many times; that he had been attacked, captured once by a hard-core group of Mau Mau fighters who had no care for Kernowi's links with Kenyatta. He'd been tortured too. Even now he woke some nights bathed in sweat, filled with terror of the squirming soldier ants that swarmed over his body in the stinking pit. He had been rescued. He had not been killed. But he had killed … more than once … after *Lari*.

He swallowed. Even safe in this home, surrounded by the security of this new life, just thinking of those days made his stomach churn. Frowning, he straightened his back, rubbed his belly, burped. The taste reminded him of the time that he'd had food-poisoning after eating bad prawns at a barbeque. He scrambled to his feet and padded once more across the chilled floor to the kitchen for a glass of water.

Returning with the damp glass, he pulled up his feet, child-like in the corner of the sofa. He sipped the cooled water, but his mind was racing still. Atrocities … he whispered the word, felt it on his tongue – so soft, but what a multitude of evils it covered. Sighing, he shook his head. Atrocities had certainly been committed, on all sides, in those closing moments of Colonial rule in Kenya. He had managed to keep secret the true identity of Kernowi, continuing with his work during daylight hours as an earnest young schoolmaster out in the Rift Valley. None but a few of his closest friend had ever suspected his role in the struggles. He had never become politically involved – there had been Kenyans aplenty to take the cause forward in that way, Daniel arap Moi the current president being the obvious first among equals. He was never noticed at rallies or public demonstrations and the various edicts and government pronouncements during that period were only relevant to Kernowi when there were wrongs to be righted, captives to be freed or torture victims to be rescued. These people knew Kernowi … they knew that Kernowi was keeping account. The killings, the camps, the 'cover-ups' perpetrated by the colonial administration and its officials … Kernowi was keeping records. When this was all over, there would be a reckoning.

Theo shifted his feet, sighing into the orangey semi-darkness. In his innocence, in the early days he had conceived Kernowi to be rather like Robin Hood, a legendary figure standing up for the poor, the oppressed. But there was no glamour in it. For those he had rescued he supposed Kernowi was some kind of hero, but for those who felt they had been betrayed, for the majority of his own countrymen, he was an enemy who could be captured and killed with impunity … as Daniel had been killed. Swallowing hard against his rising stomach, the man who had been Kernowi took the last sip of water from the glass and set it down empty on the coffee table.

Daniel had been killed – that dreadful night, the attack out in the Rift Valley. Theo knew he would always think of it as the night of the Rift, the night his whole life fractured, like in some kind of seismic shift. Now he reckoned everything as being either before or after, like BC and AD. Because of Daniel's death, and because of the promise – more like a vow in his mind – that he, Theo, had made in those days after the Rift, Kernowi had died, and his legend with him. To his eternal shame, no one had been brought to account. The records he had kept, all the evidence, the photographs – all of it had been suppressed and the perpetrators had escaped the justice they deserved. And as a result, he too had escaped. He was able to pass unnoticed in their midst … until today.

Today at the Animal Orphanage he'd had a definite scare when that tall Kikuyu had tailed him, eyed him with suspicion, sidled up to him in the rowdy crowd tormenting that poor ape. '*I know you sir … you are Kernowi.*' The stalker's hissed accusation had sent shivers down his spine. He'd rounded on the man, affronted, angry. The vehemence of his response had hopefully been enough to convince the accuser of his mistake. Certainly there was no sign of the man when they'd left the park in a hurry after Ellen's panic over the baboon. He could not afford to be 'unmasked' – the consequences would be unthinkable for himself, for his family, for anyone at all with connections to Kernowi and also for those people whom he had loved. Daniel was dead and so was Njeri ... but her son ... her son was still alive. He had to be kept safe, to be protected from the past, protected for his own future.

22

Kenya, Mombasa – 1986

'Mummy, look ... they're waving to us ... look!'
Summer holidays at last. The girls were at the window, waving to other children who were running barefoot alongside the overnight train from Nairobi as it chuntered in towards Mombasa. Stately, as a galleon, or some kind of grand duchess, the heavy engine hauled its sleeper-coaches clacking over the final legs of the long journey down through the night from five thousand feet to sea level.

As the train trundled on through shanty areas, past sprawling rubbish tips where even at this early hour kids in ragged shirts and old women in tight-wrapped kangas were scrabbling through the detritus in search of something to eat or to sell, the stewards were about their business. In buttoned-up uniforms and 'white' cotton gloves they had already begun to gather up breakfast trays and blankets from the 'first-class' travellers who had enjoyed a silver-service supper followed by a good night's sleep on 'comfortable' beds. In fact, everything was very much 'former glory' – a throw back to colonial days – but the cost was only a few shillings extra and an experience not to be missed.

Ellen and the girls had certainly enjoyed their journey and were now looking forward to a holiday at the coast. Just north of Mombasa and an easy taxi ride from the station, the Nyali Beach Hotel had become a favourite of theirs.

'Will Daddy be at the station to meet us? Will he have my birthday present with him?' Seven years old tomorrow, Rosy could hardly contain her excitement. She was hoping for a mask and some flippers just like her big sister's. Bright-eyed and pony-tailed this morning, she was eager to see her Daddy. Though they always had a good time on these trips with their Mum, things never felt quite right, as far as she was concerned, until the family was back together again.

'All being well, Daddy will be on the platform waiting for us. He had a lot to do in Malindi, though, didn't he ... remember that's why he came down on the aeroplane, straight after term finished ... I heard him telling you about his old friend's house by the seaside that needs to be emptied now that it's been sold. The man was Daddy's friend when he was very young ... before I even knew him. Daddy's friend died a long time ago, but a lady was living in the house until recently. Daddy explained it to you, didn't he? Now that lady has gone back to her own country, and so everything from the friend's house, the furniture and things like that, needs to be sent back, to his family, in England.'

Throughout the conversation with her daughter, Ellen was folding up pyjamas, collecting toothbrushes, making sure that everything was safely back in the suitcase before their arrival at the station. This was the end of the line so there was not really any rush, but she liked to be organised. Seeing Rosy's still-expectant face, she continued.

'Do you remember, Daddy told you that he would be flying back down from Malindi in a small plane? If his plane's delayed for any reason and he can't get to the station in time, we're to get a taxi straight to the hotel and he'll meet us there later. So, if he's not there we won't worry, will we? We'll just quickly sort out our returns at the ticket office and then we'll find a taxi ... is that all right? Remember ... it's what Daddy told us to do?'

Ellen dropped a kiss on her daughter's forehead. She knew that if Daddy had said it would be all right, then it would be fine with his girls. 'And yes, I'm certain that he will be bringing with him a special parcel for a very special young lady.' Rosy beamed.

'Look Mummy, there's a dhow, look over there ... and another one ...' Mara was still at the window. The train was crossing over the bridge from the mainland onto Mombasa Island and it was a good place for spotting the trading boats, as well as little fishing dinghies and coracles. Ellen moved to join her daughter, pulling down on the leather strap and lowering the window. The breeze was exotic, warm and humid, heavy with the salty tang of the Indian Ocean. Spicy too, scented with coconuts and mangoes, blended with ancient plumbing and open drains. She grinned in anticipation of the break. But there was still work to be done.

'Come on Mara, have you collected up all your pencils and your drawing book ... look your reading book is still here, by your pillow. Put it in your backpack. Rosy, is this yours?' Ellen held up a pink hairband, which was soon snatched by her younger daughter and shoved into the top of her little bag. As the train drew into the station, they were ready.

After all the effort of getting the three of them and their luggage out from the compartment, bumping the suitcase along the corridor and negotiating the drop from the carriage onto the platform, disappointment awaited. Standing wide-eyed beside their bags, the children were in danger of losing their spirits. Daddy was nowhere to be seen.

It was Mummy who came to the rescue with a plan. 'Look, over there. There's the ticket office. We have to make our way over there. That's what Daddy said. Come on Mara. Rosy put your bag on your back and take my hand. That's right ... now off we go.' Wordless, the little girls obeyed and soon the band of three moved off, nudging through the noisy throng, buffeted on all sides by the swell of new arrivals and their entourages. At last the trio emerged through the archway into the high-ceilinged concourse. It was only marginally less crowded. Ellen kept her daughters close and battled on towards the ticket window. They arrived about sixth in the rapidly building line.

As the last of the passengers, with porters and piled luggage in tow pushed through from the platform and out onto the street, the tumult inside the station began to subside. The girls kept close, as they edged towards the ticket booth. Over their heads, searching for any sign of her husband's arrival, Ellen caught the eye of the smart-suited young Kenyan behind her in the line. Polite, he smiled, shifting his briefcase from hand to hand and checking his wristwatch. Behind him an Asian matriarch; a shy-eyed young woman in a burka; an elderly Kenyan, searching in the pockets of the jacket that he seemed to have been wearing since he was a younger, more broad-shouldered version of himself ... all these and more fell briefly under her gaze and most returned a fellow half-smile. Ellen sighed. No sign of Theo. Turning back, she smiled down to reassure her daughters.

'Stop! Stop! Thief!'

From the far side of the crowded concourse, a woman's screams shafted through the stifling air. Within seconds her cries were joined by others and soon the cacophony of screeching and yelling was deafening. From all sides, sloughing off the cloak of civilisation like superheroes transforming for the fray, the populace surged forward to join the fight, pushing past each other in their efforts to catch the thief. The girls were panicking now, clutching at her legs, but over their heads, Ellen watched in horror as the ragged man who had snatched the handbag was snatched himself by the mob, beaten, punched, kicked to the ground, dragged to his feet, beaten, punched and kicked again by many hands, many feet. Among the attackers she spotted the businessman who had been standing behind her in the queue, along with others whom she recognised. The mugger's screams and wails of agony were now added to the fury of the mob bent on blood, bent on vengeance.

Ellen drew her daughters in behind the barrier of their suitcase, talking calmly, shielding them from the horrors playing out behind her. One person only remained in front of them in the queue; there was no longer anyone in her wake. All were either partaking in the violence or egging on those who were. The experience was profoundly shocking. How thin was the veil of civilisation ... how visceral the desire for blood!

It was only later, much later, in the comfort of her husband's arms and with her daughters happily fed and settled to sleep, that Ellen allowed herself a tear as she recalled the incident, named her fears. Lately she had read the graphic accounts in the local press, seen the macabre images of what they called 'necklacing.' This primitive form of mob justice, meted out in the shantytowns and villages around Nairobi, was spreading fast. Suspected wrongdoers were set upon and savagely beaten by an avenging mob. Inflamed by bloodlust, the rabble-rousers would force a rubber tyre around the victim's neck, fill it with gasoline and set the whole thing alight. The crowd then watched and jeered as the victim burned alive. Such horrors had seemed scarcely credible until now. Today just such a vein of primitive violence had flared in an instant right before her eyes. She was shocked to the core – how close they had come to being caught up in it. Her desire to protect her family, and her husband's passion to protect them all, bound the couple close as they held each other beneath the stars. On the balcony of their suite overlooking the tropical night-gardens, he made his promise.

Later still as he watched her sleeping, Theo was at peace. Things were coming together. In recent days, his final promise to Daniel had been fulfilled. The house at Malindi had been sold and all the arrangements for the exportation of family furniture, paintings and other valuables back to England were now in place. Earlier that evening, his wife had given voice to her fears for her family in this country, which, though she loved, she could no longer trust. And on the last day of term, Jack had shared with him his feeling that the time was right at last, that he was ready to take up the reins of Lind'n Lea school in Nairobi once again, now that his long period of mourning for his wife was coming to an end. It was the time for moving on.

Sighing, but not sad, Theo shuffled his pillows and turned onto his side ready for sleep. All was as it should be. His family's time in Kenya was drawing to a close. He was taking his precious girls back home.

23

Cornwall, Duloe Manor – 2008

'Well, Dad, we're all here now.' Rosy turned off the ignition and sighed.

The journey down had gone more smoothly than she'd feared. She was not keen on motorway driving at the best of times and today she'd had a lot on her mind. Anyway, it was over now. She'd made good time and she had found the place without too much trouble. Reaching across for her bag, which was slumped on the passenger seat, she pulled out her mobile and called her husband's number. She missed him already, but knowing that he was on the end of the phone made all the difference on a day like today.

'Hi, Graham, it's me ... no, the traffic wasn't too bad ... I've only just arrived ... I haven't seen them yet ... I don't know ... no, not yet ... alright my love ... talk to you soon ... I love you too ... Bye ... I will.' She disconnected the short call and tucked the phone back into her bag. How did people ever manage without mobile phones? How would she ever manage without that lovely man? Smiling at the memory of him, she leaned her head back against the headrest and closed her eyes.

Rosy was still not sure what to make of this mission of hers, the things that she had found at the house, the things she had brought down with her. And on top of everything that her mother had already had to deal with, to discover that he'd been lying. All these years he'd been lying to them. A son ... he had a son? Just thinking about it made her blood boil. She drew a sharp breath, held it, narrow-eyed, before exhaling dragon-like, in a fiery burst of rage. Recognising the child's impulse to hit something, the grown woman leaned forward and thumped the leather dashboard. She longed to hammer against his chest, to sob loud and long, crying like when she was little in one of her tantrums. But, as so often back then, the frustration, the anger at her father soon dissolved into a need for her mother: comforting, reassuring, interpreting the man to his children.

On that thought, she gathered up her bag and, glancing around to reassure herself that nothing important was open to view, prepared to leave the safety of the car and go in search of the two women she knew would be eagerly anticipating her arrival. Making her way along the rough-barked path through the young birch trees, that she had been told would lead her to Lamorna Cottage, Rosy pondered the question that had been troubling her since she had heard her sister's news: Who would interpret him now?

They were at the door even before she reached the end of the path – one of them must have been on the look out. As she walked towards their welcome, a surge of relief flushed her cheeks to see her mother's usual smile. Ellen's irrepressible spirit was alive and strong in her as she hugged her younger daughter, bringing the girls together again, making everyone feel at home, just as she always had.

'That's better,' Rosy was smiling as she emerged from the downstairs cloakroom. 'This place looks really nice.' She was feeling more relaxed now, not sure exactly what she'd expected, but she was glad to see that an atmosphere of calm and normality prevailed. If her mother could handle this then Rosy knew that everything would be all right in the end. Leaning back against the kitchen worktop as her sister made coffee for the three of them, she looked around. 'I can see why you two like it here.'

Ellen was already at the table. 'We'll give you the guided tour later, then you can bring in your things and get yourself settled in your room. Come and sit down for a minute though. We'll have our coffee first shall we? It's good to see you Rosy. I'm so glad you were able to come down like this at such short notice. I do wish Graham could have come with you too, but I think it's probably best for the children to be at home this time.'

While Ellen was talking, Rosy moved some magazines, pulled out a chair and sat down at the table opposite her mother. 'I spoke to him on the phone as soon as I got here. He said to give you his love and to let you know that he is thinking of you ... and you too Mara.' Graham and his mother-in-law had been close ever since Rosy had first brought him home.

'Did you manage to get over to the house, pick up the albums, like you said you would?' Mara was carrying the mugs from the kitchen area, setting them down in front of the two women, returning for her own.

'I did and I've brought down one or two other things that were there, some notebooks, diaries that I found, that old wooden box of Dad's ... just things that I thought might be helpful, useful, interesting. I don't know how to call it really ... I'm not sure what this is all about ... what we'll need to be doing ... whoever would have expected anything like this to happen?' Overwhelmed at the sheer enormity of it all, she stopped. The lump in her throat made it hard to continue. She reached into the pocket of her jeans and pulled out a tissue, blew her nose and looked across at her mother. 'What does it all mean, mum? After all this time ... did Daddy really have a son? Do we have a brother? What are we going to do?' A tear slid from the corner of her eye and rolled down her nose. She wiped it away with the back of her hand.

Mara had taken the seat at the top of the table, between her mother and her sister. She reached out now, resting an arm on Rosy's shoulder, tipping her own sandy curls against her sister's smooth blonde hair that today was pulled back tightly into a ponytail. Ellen looked on in silence. After a long moment she set her hands flat on the table, reaching towards her daughters. Each covered one of hers with their own.

It was Ellen who withdrew first. She checked her wristwatch. 'Alright then.' She sighed. 'Well, if we're going to do the guided tour, get Rosy settled in and have some lunch before going up to the Old Rectory, then we'd better get on with it, don't you think?

'The Old Rectory? We're going up there today?' They had forgotten that Rosy had not been in on this plan.

'We've been invited up there, later this afternoon, to meet with Frank and Dan and Maisy. Maisy is Dan's daughter. She's down from London, visiting for a few days.'

Seeing the sudden anxious look on her younger daughter's face, Ellen moved quickly to reassure. 'Oh, Rosy ... you mustn't worry. They're really nice people. All this is as much of a shock to them as it is to us. And their mother, at least Frank's mother, is really poorly too. She was sick and now they've diagnosed dementia, I think it is, although of course we don't know any details. Rose is now in a care home in Lostwithiel. I was thinking I would go to see her later. After all it seems that she probably is your father's sister ... but Mara thinks that I should wait for a bit until we've had a chance to talk to the boys ... or should I say 'men' ... about it. I keep on wanting to call them the boys, just like I call you two 'the girls.' I'll have to be careful about that. They might not like it. They don't know me like you two do.' Ellen smiled.

Rosy looked across at her sister, eyebrows raised, uncertainty in her voice. 'Are you alright about this, I mean going up to the Old Rectory, meeting them all?'

'It's fine. Like Mum says, it's as hard for them as it is for us ... in some ways at least. As far as I can understand it though, Dan has never even met his father, except when he was very small, when he was brought back to this country. It seems like he was just abandoned after that, only birthday presents via the agent and the odd letter.' Mara shook her head and pushed back her chair. Collecting up the empty mugs she stood and moved towards the dishwasher. 'That's what I just can't understand you know ... the thing that I think I find hardest of all to accept ... that Dad, if of course it really was him, would have a son and then just leave him like that ... never go back to see him or anything. I mean I know Dad had his funny ways. He could definitely be a bit hard to understand sometimes. But he was a really kind man underneath it all. This whole leaving his son with his sister in England thing ... it just doesn't seem like him at all. There must be more to it. I'm sure there is. We'll just have to see if we can sort it out somehow.' Mara looked from her sister to her mother. 'I reckon we're like the three musketeers … our mission to defend Dad's honour … sort out his past … find out the truth … that sort of thing.' Nudging the door of the dishwasher shut with her knee, she swung her imaginary sword with a flourish.

'Well when you put it like that, how can we refuse?' Laughing, Rosy came over and linked arms with her sister.

They were still laughing together as they ran up the stairs to check out the bedrooms. Their mother followed more slowly, enjoying their bravado, hoping against hope that she would be able to keep her daughters safe. From the bedroom that was to be Rosy's, Ellen could hear the girls chatting away to each other. She pictured them sitting on the bed, catching up on all their news. They'd always got on well, ever since they were children. Reaching the top of the stairs, she decided not to interrupt them just yet. Shuffling around, she lowered herself down onto the top stair.

From this unfamiliar perspective, Ellen reviewed the strange circumstances in which they now found themselves. She wondered about the things her daughter had found – what she'd managed to bring from the house. Rosy had already mentioned the wooden box –Theo's special box. That box had travelled with him since he was a boy, his most private, probably his most prized possession, now that she came to think of it. As far as she knew, no one but Theo had ever been allowed access to it. And then another thought occurred – when you die, you lose more than your life. All the things that you've kept private, the things you've held dear … you lose all that too. As long as they have the key, anyone can just open your box, like Pandora's, and blow the consequences.

What would they find when Theo's box was opened? Ellen was suddenly certain that it would be, opened that is. She was not a jealous woman. She doubted that Theo had kept any secrets from her for any other reason than to protect her and her children. But protect them from what? She had absolutely no idea. It was inconceivable that the box would hold any secrets about dark sexual intrigues or erotic affairs. Theo was just not that kind of man, of that she was fairly certain. Knowing him as she did she'd begun to suspect that there had to be an 'honour' issue around somewhere.

Somebody's honour might be at stake, or something like that. It was much more likely that the man she had married would keep secrets for somebody else than for himself. But for whom? Ellen sighed. Until the box was opened she had no idea what the answer to all this might be. But whatever it was that Theo had been keeping from her, she had a strong feeling that his box might hold the key.

24

Cornwall, Old Rectory – 2008

'Dad, this is such a mess! Look there are boxes everywhere … these piles of letters … how are you ever going to get this all sorted out up here in this room? There's no space!'

Maisy turned and grinned at her Dad. Standing in the doorway of his boyhood bedroom, Dan looked suitably chastened.

'What a nightmare! Were you always this untidy?' She was teasing, but she was definitely making a point. She rolled her eyes to the ceiling. 'And what is that?' Now she was pointing accusingly at the ink blots on the ceiling. 'Don't tell me that you used to lie in bed flicking ink pellets up there. What were you like?'

Hands on hips, his daughter shook her head in mock despair. With exaggerated care she made her way across the room to the single bed and sat down heavily on the faded blue coverlet.

'Dad, you definitely need someone to take you in hand.' She grinned back across at her father who was still leaning against the doorpost, watching her.

'Aren't I lucky that you're here then?' He smiled.

'Is this all the stuff that you're planning to sell, the stuff you were telling me about?' Maisy looked around her at the piles, the half opened boxes.

'This is part of it. There is more in the attic – in the top floor storerooms – and there are some larger items, some chests, old wooden furniture that sort of thing apparently locked in the old gardeners' cottage down behind the walled garden. Before she was ill, Rose also told me that there was some jewellery – I'm not exactly sure what it is – held for me at the bank.' Dan frowned, trying to remember all that Rose had told him.

'Dad, what do you mean ... you're not sure what it is? Weren't you even a bit curious, a bit interested in all this stuff that was arriving for you?' Maisy was incredulous. It showed on her face and in her voice.

'It's not that simple. There's a lot of history here that you don't understand. When I was a boy, quite small, I had a choice. Either I was going to spend my life feeling angry, sorry for myself, abandoned ... all that sort of thing ... or I was going to count my blessings, accept the love of the people who offered it to me: Rose, Edward, Frank, my mother, father, brother, and get on with my life. I chose the latter. I consciously turned my back on whoever else might want to call himself my father, chose to ignore the gifts and all the other stuff that came. Once or twice he wrote me a brief note, but usually it was just from the agent. I didn't really let my-self think about it much ... hardly at all to be honest after that ... and it became a kind of habit. It still is I suppose.' He was standing up straight now, still on the threshold of the room. 'Rose under-stood. She took care of it all for me. I guess she thought, probably hoped, that one day I would get myself sorted out ... grow up ...' he flared his eyes. 'At least she hoped that I'd learn how to deal with things like grown up people do. I hope it's not too late.' He left the thought hanging out there. Maisy got up, came across the room and hugged him. He held her, accepting what she offered.

'I don't think you're a lost cause, Dad. We'll get you sorted out ... and we'll start with this lot.' She gestured at all the boxes at her feet. 'Why don't we carry them all downstairs to the sitting room? If we push some of grandma's furniture back to the side of the room there'll be plenty of space to lay this stuff out and get it sorted. Then we can start making lists.' She laughed. Her father knew very well how much she loved lists.

'That's a great idea. Why didn't I think of that? Let's do this lot first then we can bring down the stuff from upstairs – I'm not even sure what's up there – but apparently it's all stuff that was sent over from Africa. Rose thought it seemed like some kind of house clearance at the time – she told me about it. Anyway, first things first, that's a good idea of yours. Come down and help me clear the space … move the furniture back. I'm sure grandma won't mind. I'm sure she would think it was all in a good cause.' He turned and made for the stairs, Maisy hard on his heels.

'What's happened to Uncle Frank? He's just disappeared since we got up here.' Descending the stairs in single file Maisy spoke over Dan's shoulder.

'I think he's in grandma's study. There are some papers he needs to find, letters, that sort of thing. Since she went into hospital, nobody's been taking care of her affairs. Apparently there's a lady from down the road who's been doing a bit of cleaning, picking up the post and putting it in the study, on the desk, that sort of thing. But nobody's checked the mail. Nothing's really been sorted out for quite a while.'

They had been talking as they came down the stairs and the pair had now reached the door to the sitting room. Maisy went on ahead, pushing the door, stepping in to the room, and making her way across to the windows. Dan hesitated on the threshold. Maisy turned back, sensing his discomfort.

'Are you all right Dad? What's the matter?'

He stepped in to the room and she came towards him.

'Actually, Maisy, there's something else that I need to talk to you about … something that happened … in this room. That's why I hesitated. I was just remembering. You need to know. Come over here. Sit down.'

She was confused, but she did as he told her. Her father went across to the mantelpiece and picked up the two photographs. He was holding them when he sat down beside his daughter.

'Well come on then. What's all this about?' The young woman was impatient now, uncomfortable with the suspense.

'All right. Do you remember that I told you that I was thinking of taking on an assistant?' Maisy nodded. 'Well, I arranged to meet her up at the house so that she could see all the stuff, like you have, and we could make a plan about how to tackle the job … that was the idea. She brought her daughter with her and I was showing them around when Uncle Frank arrived. He had something important he had to discuss with me so I left the two women in here and Frank and I went into grandma's study.'

'Okay. So what happened next? Were they robbers? Did they run off with all the family silver while your back was turned?'

He continued with his story. 'No – not that. When I came back they were both looking kind of shocked, as if they'd seen a ghost. They were looking at these photographs.' He held out the image of Theodora. Maisy had been familiar with it all her life. 'They recognised this photograph. Apparently they have a copy of it in their home in Sussex. I can't remember if I told you, but they're on holiday down here. Anyway, I told them who it was and they already knew that her name was Theodora. It was this photograph really.' He took a deep breath and held out the black and white image of his father as a young man. 'This is the picture that had shocked the two women most of all.'

'This is your father as a young man – in Africa with the chief. I've always known it. Why were they shocked about it?' Maisy could not comprehend, not yet what all the fuss was about.

'Maisy, they were shocked because the man in this picture, Theodore, is the older lady's husband … the younger woman's father.' Dan sat back in the chair, Maisy stood up.

'What? How can he be? There must be some mistake?' She was struggling to take in the implications of what he was saying. 'Are you sure that there's not a mistake? Maybe the man they know just looks like your dad. Maybe it's not the same man at all?'

'No. I think they're right. It is the same man. They know some of the same details … but not about me. They don't know anything about me … nothing at all really about his life before she … Ellen, she's called Ellen … before Ellen met him in 1969 out in Kenya.' He waited for his daughter's response.

'So, he's the same man … but he didn't tell her anything about you? She didn't know. Gosh. Poor woman. That must have been a shock. Do you think Grandma knows, about this Ellen I mean? Do you think she knows anything about what her brother's up to now?' She paused, put her hand to her mouth. 'Oh, Dad I'm sorry – I forgot for a minute. Of course, he's dead.' She sat back down beside him.

'I felt sorry for the daughter too. Imagine finding out that you've got a brother … at least a half-brother … she's white, I'm not.' He paused. 'They're really nice people. I like them. I think you'll like them.'

'What?' Maisy interrupted him. 'I'll like them? I'm going to meet them?'

'You are. They're coming up here so that we can all meet, get to know each other. There's another sister … Rosy … she's coming too.' He watched her face as the strange news settled in.

'Dad – what's that going to be like? Will Uncle Frank be there?'

'I think it will be fine. As I said, they're nice people … and yes Uncle Frank will be there. He knew them already, just before I did. It seems they met at the Festival.'

'Oh Dad. If only Grandma could be there. She'd have all the answers wouldn't she, at least some of them I'm sure. I really miss her, Dad. What are we going to do without her?' The young woman leaned in to her father's side, rested her head on his shoulder. He put his arm around her, held her close. All at once she sat up out of his embrace, turned to face him. 'All that stuff … that furniture … paintings … those things that your father sent to you … do they still belong to you, Dad?'

'I think so. They were all directed clearly to me, care of Rose, as far as I'm aware. The bigger stuff and the jewellery I haven't even looked at yet, but that's what Rose told me. Anyway, I'm going to check through all my letters, documentation and that sort of thing, get myself organised. Uncle Frank is going to sort out all the official letters … deal with Grandma's solicitor. I'm going to get in touch with the agents who have been acting on my father's behalf all through the years and see what I can find out from them. But all that's for next week, after the weekend. There's a lot of groundwork to be done before then, before we start making it all official.'

Maisy looked at her father. She was surprised to see that he was smiling.

'So this is it, our ancestral home.' Rosy was only half joking.

Although Mara and Ellen had themselves only been to The Old Rectory once before, it was hard for them to remember that for Rosy everything was completely new. Their own first visit had been exciting. Back then it had all seemed like a game. Ellen found it especially hard to believe that 'back then' was in fact just a couple of days ago. Now as they made their way up the gravelled drive in Mara's green Clio, afternoon sun lit the stone to honey and flushed the pink roses with gold. With its trees and its lawns and its long views to the horizon, the house seemed to welcome them. Seeing it for the first time, Rosy was certain that this was the house of her dreams. As her sister drew the car to a scrunching halt and silenced the engine, in the front passenger seat Rosy seemed entranced.

'Mum, just look at the roses ... they must be the ones in Dad's photograph ... they are so beautiful, exactly as he described them ... and the lawns, and the trees ... I can just imagine Dad playing here as a little boy. And look over there. That must be the walled gardens. Mara, do you remember the stories he used to tell about his adventures in the walled garden? And the swing ... I bet there's a swing, tied to a tree behind those walls.' Rosy felt she had known this house all her life.

'Maybe you two can go and have a look later, but for now I think we'd better get ourselves sorted out and go and meet the others. It looks like they are here already.' Ellen was pointing across to where two other cars had been parked in the shade beneath the trees. 'Do you think we should take these boxes in straightaway or shall we leave them here till later?' Two of the yellow plastic boxes were stacked up on the back seat beside her.

Before they had left Lamorna Cottage, the girls had carried the boxes in from the car and between the three of them they had done a quick 'sort' of the contents. They had decided not to bring everything this time but they'd all agreed that the albums –

especially the Kenyan ones – would be interesting for the others to see. Some of Theo's diaries had come with them too – he had been a determined diarist, particularly in his later years – but Ellen had kept some of the early Kenyan ones back, planning to read them in private later. Rosy had not brought all of them from home anyway. There were also a few shoe-boxes of random correspondence which might be interesting to explore, a mixed box of old photographs and a long cardboard poster roll which seemed to contain large pictures, probably paintings. Theo's special box had been left behind for now – it was up on Ellen's dressing table. Somehow she had felt that when she opened it, for her husband's sake, she would like to be alone.

'Let's just leave the boxes in the car for now, shall we Mum? I reckon it would be easier to just go in and we can all meet and chat for a bit first, before we start trying to sort everything out. Dan's obviously got things we can look at too. It seems like the main purpose of today is to try and get a better sense of it ... the whole picture, I don't know. We can learn what they know about Dad. We can try to help them understand him from our point of view ... if you know what I mean ...' Her voice trailed off. Mara was trying to hold everything together but she was clearly not finding this easy.

Just at that moment, they became aware of voices behind them as the door to the Old Rectory opened from the inside and Dan and Frank appeared, in company with a young woman who had to be Dan's daughter. All three were smiling as they moved easily over the gravel towards the Clio.

'We thought we'd heard a vehicle. We thought it must be you. It's good to see you all. You must be Rosy. This is my daughter Maisy.' Dan was the first to reach them.

As Ellen, Mara and Rosy climbed out of the car, they were greeted as if they were old friends. Soon the group was chatting easily, moving away towards the lawns at the side of the house, out towards the gardens and the views over the valley. In the warmth of the afternoon, this meeting of strangers, who seemed to be family, was getting off to a good start.

'I knew there would be a swing. Dad told us so many stories

about that swing ... and the walled garden ... secret hideaways in the shrubbery...'

Ellen looked across at her younger daughter. Rosy was smiling, chatting easily to Dan and Maisy. Any inhibitions seemed long gone. The house appeared to have accepted her; she was at home. They were all in the kitchen now and Frank was making tea, assisted by Mara. Her mother watched as she organised the bright coloured mugs, selected a blue jug from the shelf, swilled it under the tap and filled it with milk from the carton, which one of the men had brought up from the village.

'Earl Grey or English Breakfast?'

Mara's question down the table was easy, as if she had been making tea in this kitchen with these people all her life.

In the midst of all this friendly chatter, Ellen permitted herself a moment's quiet. At least she was quiet on the outside. On the inside, the angry questions battered against her absent husband. 'Why, Theo? Why did we not do this when you were alive ... when you were here with us? Why did you keep us away? Why did you tell your children your stories but keep them from your home ... from their family?' She looked across at Dan, at Maisy. 'And why did you abandon this boy ... your son? Why, Theo?' She shook her head, frowning, lifted her hand to cover her mouth.

'Are you alright, Mum?'

Mara had come up behind her, whispered by her ear, placed a hand on her shoulder. 'Here's your tea. Drink it. It will help.' Her elder daughter could only imagine how hard this was, but she knew her mother. Mara never doubted for one minute that she would survive all this. 'Ellen: my strong centre.' That's what her father had called his wife. Despite all current appearances to the contrary, deep down Mara was certain that her father would never have done anything to harm this woman that he loved.

'Shall we take our tea through to the sitting room? The photographs, the pictures that we've got, some of the paintings ... they are all in there. What do you think? Shall we move on through?'

It was Frank who was taking the lead in his mother's home.

The others were grateful. It seemed like a plan. Picking up their mugs, they rose noisily from the table and Dan lead the way along the hallway towards the sitting room.

No one seemed keen to sit yet, as if to sit would be to start with the difficult part of the afternoon's agenda. Mara and her mother moved together to the mantelpiece and began to look at some of the other photographs and ornaments there. Frank and Dan were standing perusing a letter, which had been lying open on the top of the piano. Rosy and Maisy were chatting as they made their way across the room towards the window.

'That's you, isn't it?' Rosy had spotted Dan's painting of his young daughter, on the wall beside the window. 'It's definitely you. It's lovely. It's really good … it reminds me of Mara. She used to sit on her foot like that when she was reading.' She moved in closer, studying the painting up close. 'These roses are amazing, the colour, the detail.'

'Dad painted it. It's my grandma's favourite.' Maisy was beside her.

Rosy turned to look at Dan who had come up behind them. 'You really are very good, you know. This is great. You've captured that 'lost in a good book' expression perfectly. And Maisy, it's so you. I'm not surprised that your grandma loves it.' All at once, her face and her tone softened as she turned to Maisy. She reached out and touched her hand on the young woman's arm. 'I am so sorry about your grandma's illness. I should have said that earlier. It's such a shame that she can't be here with us today. Although what she would have made of us all I can't imagine.'

Frank put his hand on his brother's shoulder and the two men made their way across towards the circle of comfortable chairs that had been set around the large coffee table, beckoning to Mara and her mother to join them. Rosy and Maisy followed. As Rosy came to the circle, she gave voice to the questions that had been forming in her mind since the earlier talk of Rose.

'Do you think that Rose, your mother, your grandma, do you think she knew about all this? Do you think that she knew about Mum, about us?'

Without waiting for a response, she settled herself into a pink-flowered armchair, next to the sofa, shaking the cushions, pushing one in behind her back, making herself comfortable. When she looked up, all eyes were on her. Everyone in the circle was wondering the same thing. It was Frank who spoke.

'Rose, my mother, was ... she is a very strong woman. She is warm and loving, intelligent and kind. Once she's on your side, she'll stay there for always. What I mean is that she's totally devoted to the people she loves. She is loyal ... with a capital L.' He looked for confirmation from Dan to Maisy. Both were nodding fondly. 'From what I can understand, after their parents died Rose took responsibility for her little brother, for Theodore. She'd always loved him as her younger brother of course, but from then on she would have wanted to protect him, to take care of him too, like a mother. I think she felt that it was her duty. If he'd asked her to do something for him, something important, I believe that she would have done it, for that reason. I reckon that's probably what she did.' He glanced across at Ellen, then at Dan before continuing.

'We've had a quick look amongst Rose's things and we've found some pictures of them together as children. There aren't many really, just a few of them both, there are also some of them with their parents ...' He leaned forward and picked up a large envelope. 'We thought you might like to see them.' He handed the envelope to Ellen. She thought she might cry. She nodded solemnly and held the package close.

'Thank you, all of you. We've brought some things for you to look at too. Rosy brought them down from the house. There are some photograph albums ...' she smiled across at her daughters, then at the others, not apologising, just explaining ... 'it's what I do, I'm afraid. I put photographs in albums. I sort things, label things, keep things up together.' She laughed, at herself. 'I even label the albums. I put date labels on the spines too, so that we can keep them in order on the shelves.' They were all grinning in her direction now.

Maisy nodded. 'I do the same sort of thing. And I make lists. Dad teases me but I'm always making lists. It helps me to make decisions, to get my thoughts sorted out. It helps when I'm revising for exams, or planning for a trip ... anything like that.' She smiled at Ellen, sharing this knowledge, this part of herself ... the beginnings of relationship.

'We've left everything out in the car. We'll bring it all in then you can have a look through it all if you like.' Ellen made to get up but Dan stood quickly. His gesture made it clear that she should stay where she was.

'We'll go and carry things in for you if you just show us the way, won't we Frank.' He turned to Mara and jerked his head in the direction of the door. 'Come on then. Show us where it is.' He was smiling.

Mara felt herself blush. She was acutely aware that this was the first time today that he'd actually looked directly at her. After their initial easy friendliness, she'd sensed a strange distance growing between them, ever since that shocking revelation about their father. Embarrassment was not quite the right word, but there was an awkwardness, self-consciousness anyway. Something had definitely changed. She'd seen him chatting easily with Rosy. There didn't seem to be any problem there, and that relationship was potentially the same. For now she returned his smile as she rose to join the expedition.

'You wait here Mum, we'll go and sort things out and the men, and the youngsters, can carry it in.' Mara's tone was light. She sounded more like her old self.

Frank moved to unlock the French windows and Ellen was happy to see them all bundle out into the sunshine together. She could hear their voices, chatting easily in the distance as the warm smell of cut grass and growing things wafted in on the air. She looked down at the envelope, turned it over, opened the flap and put her hand inside. There seemed to be quite a collection of photographs, all different shapes and sizes. She drew out a small handful, holding them together between fingers and thumb. The large envelope made a table on her lap and she looked down at the array of images spread out there ... pictures, mostly in black and white, of her husband as a boy, with his family, pictures she had never seen before.

Little Theo in shorts; in a sailor suit; in a long white christening gown; dripping wet wrapped in a towel on the sand; scrambling barefoot on rocks; with arms around a large golden retriever; standing up straight for a formal pose with what she took to be his parents. In most of the photographs the curly-haired little boy was smiling at the camera. In all of them he was accompanied by a girl, a few years older than him, her mass of curls sometimes tied back, sometimes plaited. Ellen could see the family likeness; their mother's hair was full and curly. She was very pretty, smiling and engaging with the camera. Their father appeared more formal, quite tall, upright with smooth, short cut hair. Ellen picked up the family group and looked closer. She noticed the man's hand resting on his son's shoulder ... and the moustache. She smiled, remembering her husband's own moustache, his habit of twirling the ends when he was thinking.

Replacing the picture amongst the others, Ellen's eye was caught by an image she recognised – at least it was similar to one she had seen once before, a long time ago now, in Kenya. It was a photograph of the young brother and sister but this time they were standing either side of a tall black man she knew at once to be Jomo Kenyatta. The handsome young African in his long overcoat was looking straight at the camera, each of his hands held tight by the children of the photographer, his host, his new friend. She picked up the picture and looked on the back. In the man's own handwriting she saw the inscription: *'For an English Rose, Jambo from Jomo.'* followed by his signature. Ellen was well aware how much store Theo had set by his photograph of that day. If his story was to be believed it had even saved his life. Rose had clearly been keeping her own memories close too.

Browsing through the random collection of pictures, Ellen was gradually developing a clearer sense of the relationship that had existed between the brother and sister. They had played together like friends, shared adventures, marked each other's special days. There were some lovely shots with birthday cakes and one beside a Christmas tree when the children were quite small, scarcely more than toddlers, with their mother holding little Theo on her lap, pointing towards the camera. What a happy family they seemed to have been. But all of this just made it even harder for Ellen to understand why Theo had kept his own young family away.

Hearing the others in the garden and thinking that she had come to the end of the photographs here, she picked up the envelope and shook it upside down just to make sure that none were left inside. An old photograph that looked as if it had been folded fluttered out and fell facedown onto her lap. Ellen saw that someone had written on the back. Curious, she picked it up and read the inscription:

'My darling Rose, here is a new little sister for you to take care of. Her name is Njeri. With love from Mummy.'

Ellen turned the photograph over and looked closely at the little Kenyan girl, perhaps five or maybe six years of age, who was smiling back her. So this was Njeri. She was dressed in what Ellen took to be a school uniform: a checked, short-sleeved dress, ankle socks and dark shoes. Her thick curls were tied into small bunches; they stuck out like sunrays all over her head. As the photograph was in black and white she could get no sense of the colours. Njeri had figured quite prominently in the story that Theo had told her that time in the house in Nairobi. Ellen had never been quite sure if what he had told her that day had been the whole story. In the light of recent developments it obviously wasn't. She kept this picture of Njeri and the one of Kenyatta out on her lap. All the others she replaced in the envelope. As Frank and Dan came smiling in through the opened French windows each carrying a yellow box, followed by the three girls chatting easily, Ellen was closing the envelope, the two black and white images still on her lap.

'Sorry if we kept you waiting, Mum. Maisy was just showing us the old tree house. Dad used to tell us stories about his tree house. Strange to think that it was really here, all that time.' Rosy came across and sat down on the sofa beside her mother. Maisy made herself comfortable in the chair alongside. These two were clearly becoming friends. 'You've missed a few, Mum, look.' Rosy had spotted the pictures on Ellen's lap.

'I left those two out on purpose. I thought you and the others might like to look at them later.' She picked them up, holding them close, but made no attempt to offer them. Dan and Frank had brought the yellow crates to the circle of chairs – they were moving things about, trying to make space for one of the containers on the coffee table.

'Why don't we keep the surface clear? Bring the boxes round here, next to me, then we can take the things out and put them on the table. It'll be easier for people to look at them. What do you think?'

The two men paused, looked over at Ellen; she was smiling her question. They looked at each other, nodded and followed her suggestion. Mara came around with the boxes and began unloading the brightly coloured albums and some smaller packets onto the table. The large poster roll she carried back to her seat and set it on the floor by her feet. Dan and Frank took the chairs on either side of her and suddenly they were all seated around the coffee table with its piles of albums and packets. After all the easy activity, this strange stillness was disconcerting. It seemed that everything was ready – but ready for what? A note of tension had crept into the air. Rosy and Mara sat forward in their chairs, looked to their mother; Dan and Maisy looked towards Frank; Frank was looking at Ellen. Ellen smiled. She looked around at each of them in turn.

'This is beginning to feel a bit too much like a staff meeting'. Everyone laughed. 'Well, the Headmaster's not here, not yet anyway. It's strange ... I've been looking at these photos while you were gone. For me, Theo is a grown up. I never knew him as a boy, nor as a young man really. He was already in his forties before I even met him. Just seeing these pictures of him as a child, a boy, with his sister, his parents, with his dog, that beautiful Golden Retriever. I feel I'm getting to know him better. What about if we all have a look at some pictures of him ... pictures we haven't seen before. It might help ... before we go on to the more difficult bits. Girls, I think you should have a look at these ...' she held out the envelope. 'The rest of you might like to browse through these albums ... see what he was like ... some of the things he did. Try not to laugh at the pictures of me though.' She laughed. 'Most of them are labelled but I can tell you anything you want to know.'

It was Frank who answered for them all. 'Thanks Ellen, I reckon that's a great idea. Mara why don't you swap places with Maisy, you'll be able to look at the photos with Rosy then and Maisy will be with us – that should make this whole thing easier, what do you think?' Frank was happier now that there was a plan and so was Maisy. She stood up at once, ready to move to Mara's place between her uncle and her Dad. Dan hesitated. He was not sure if he was ready for all this yet, but he was beginning to trust Ellen. He reached out and took a pile of albums from the table.

'Come on then, let's get started. It's about time the phantom Headmaster joined the party.' Dan smiled at his daughter and invited her to choose one of the albums. He picked one for himself and carefully inspected the date on its spine, the label on the front, and the caption beneath each photograph. 'You weren't joking when you said you were well-organised, Ellen. You remember that interview you were going to have for my job? Well, you're hired!' He and Ellen shared the general laughter.

Still grinning, Frank reached out to take an album too but the pile he chose was precarious. It slid to the floor with a crash. Raising both hands and his eyebrows in apology, he collected up the fallen books and selected one at random – it looked older than the others, with a dark red leather cover.

'Aha! You missed this one.' Mischievous, he grinned at Ellen. 'Look – there's no label on this one, no date.' He opened the book, 'and no captions either. Are you still sure you want her for that job, Dan?'

Surprised, Ellen looked over at the book in his hand. She shook her head. 'I don't recognise it. I've never seen that one before Frank.' She reached out, curious. 'Do you mind if I take a look?'

'Sure.' He leaned across and handed over the leather album. The book opened randomly in her hands. Intrigued, Ellen looked down at the black and white images.

'Oh my goodness …'

Her hand flew to her mouth. Colour drained from her face.

'What is it, Mum? Are you alright?'

Concern was sharp in Mara's voice. Her mother was deathly pale.

'Oh Mara ...' Ellen looked up. Horrified, her eyes were drawn back to the book open on her lap. 'How could anyone do that?'

Ellen was clearly fighting back tears. She was staring aghast at the images on the page, shaking her head slowly from side to side. She looked towards her girls in shocked disbelief. The Headmaster's daughters dropped everything to be at their mother's side.

25

Kenya, Rift Valley – 1954

'Theo, we can't keep them here, not any more. This is a school. If we're discovered, hiding them, sheltering them here, I dread to think what would happen, to the children, to us all.'

It was almost a year since the violence first spilled into their settled existence that Christmas night of 1953. The night of the ambush, the night they almost lost Njeri, the night when Theo had finally told them about Kernowi. Crouched in the darkness, tending to the wounded, guarding the door in fear of their lives, Theo had told his friends of his decision to take a stand in the conflict that was engulfing the country.

The violence, the inhumane treatment he had witnessed in the camps had filled him with such horror that he could no longer look the other way, do nothing as so many did. The Mau Mau were undoubtedly savage and lawless and unthinkable atrocities could be attributed to their fighters and to their cause but this could not, should not, be used to justify the same kind of brutality by the British. These detention camps were a national shame. As his friends listened to his reasoning, Theo had shared with them in hushed tones his determination to keep records, to call the perpetrators to account, to demand justice and to rescue as many of the torture victims as they could, using Daniel's inside knowledge, helped by Njeri and by Jack and by a small band of trusted others. In fear of their own lives, they operated in secret.

Since then, Kernowi had become something of a legend, a name whispered in awe amongst those who needed his help, reviled by those who considered him a traitor to his own people.

Many scarred and traumatised individuals had been snatched to safety by Kernowi, and hidden in various safe houses, including an old outhouse at the school, before being moved on, for the moment at least, out of harm's way. But now, in the Headmaster's study Aunt Catherine was standing, hands clasped as if in prayer, pleading with the young man before her. Behind the heavy wooden desk, her husband sat with his shoulders bent, elbows planted on the polished desktop, hands supporting his greying head. His face was creased and careworn as he looked up at the young man he had come to think of as his son.

'Your Aunt's right, Theo. You know she is. So far we've been lucky out here. Those lawless bands of Mau Mau fighters ... they've left us alone up until now. The Army is in the area; we've managed to avoid conflict with the Colonial authorities; and we've been able to keep the students safe. All those rolls of barbed wire around the perimeter fence help but I don't know how long this can go on. Questions are being asked. If either side gets wind of what you're doing, if anyone links you or us with the activities of Kernowi ... we'll all be fair game. I can't let anything happen to your Aunt, Theo, I can't.' Charles paused. He swallowed hard, coughed to cover the passion these thoughts aroused in him.

Theo moved swiftly towards his Aunt. He dwarfed her, placed his strong hands on her shoulders and drew her towards him.

'Aunt Catherine, I'm so sorry. You are like a mother to me ... as dear. I would never wish to put you in danger, never. Of course we'll find another shelter for the last few. By tomorrow morning they will all be gone, don't worry. Most have already been moved on. Jack took several of the older men straight to the farm in Limuru under cover of darkness. He has a safe place there. Njeri is outback with Joyce, tending to the three we brought in here last night ...' He helped his Aunt back to her chair, turned to his Uncle.

'But Uncle Charles, you would not believe the horror in which these men, and hundreds, thousands like them, are kept. One of the men in your outhouse right now, he was pegged out on the ground, had been there for days lying in unspeakable filth, open wounds from goodness knows how many lashes ... festering

... covering his body ...' he glanced across to where his Aunt was covering her eyes to block out the awful image. 'For your sake Aunt Catherine I will not complete the picture. All I will say is that I was glad ... glad that Daniel could divert the guards, could direct us to the place, glad to be able to release this poor creature, to rescue him from that hell, along with the others. If only we could help them all. We can't. But we can, we must, help as many as is in our power to reach. We can't just sit by and do nothing! Remember that, Uncle Charles? '*All that it takes for evil to flourish is for good men do nothing ...*' or something like that.' Theo was exhausted. He slumped down in the armchair opposite his Aunt, his eyes filling with helpless tears.

His Uncle moved out from behind the desk, came around and leaned himself back against the strong oak tabletop.

'Edmund Burke. I remember that too, at least the sentiment if not all the words: '*All that is needful for evil to flourish is for good men to do nothing.*' Inspirational - and cautionary indeed. You are certainly a good man Theo. But from what I hear, the violence in those camps is not all being carried out by the Colonial forces, nor by the interrogators either. The Mau Mau are active in those places too ... strangling ... mutilations ... murders ...'

The dreadful words shuddered in the silence like boulders heaved into muddied waters. The Headmaster shook his head slowly from side to side as he went on. 'Reverend Cookson was telling me just the other day how it is. He's been writing letter after letter to the governor, to the government in England, trying to bring the true horrors of the situation to their attention. As a minister of the church he's recently visited the camps at Manyani, Langata and Gilgil. He was saying that aside from the actual brutality and violence the conditions inside those places are scandalous. Malnutrition is rife, sanitation is appalling, disease is of epidemic proportions and typhoid is sweeping through all of them. It brings shame on us all.'

Once more Charles paused, shook his heavy head against the dreadful images that sprang to his mind; the horror is almost more than he can bear. He looked towards the young man still slumped in the chair.

'Theo, you are like a son to me. I am truly glad for the man that you've become. I am sure that my dear friends, your late father and your mother, would have been proud of you, proud of Kernowi; proud that you have not turned away; proud that you are trying to be true to what you believe.'

On each utterance of the word 'proud' his big hand pounds the desk at his side. 'As far as I am concerned, every one of those poor souls that you can save from those disgusting places is a triumph in the face of disaster. But ... Theo ...' and here the older man paused, fixed the younger with his gaze, 'I must ask you to have a care to protect your Aunt, this school, all the things that you and I both hold dear. I have a friend. He has an outpost. It has been abandoned for a while. You can use that place. I'll show you on a map. But you must be careful. As soon as the men you rescue are able, they must take responsibility for themselves; move on; go back to their families perhaps. I don't know. I don't know what more to say ...' He stopped, unable to find the right words to express his sorrow. Theo came slowly to his feet, moved towards the door, turned back.

'We're taking pictures you know, keeping records ... of names, places, injuries inflicted, that sort of thing. Daniel recognises quite a few of the guards, some of the interrogators. It's true they're not all as bad, but the worst of them have become like savages. Somebody must be called to account for all this. They can't be allowed to get away with it ... cover it all up ... blame it all on someone else ... the rebels ... tribal civil wars. There have undoubtedly been atrocities carried out by both sides, no one can deny that. The barbarity of the massacres at Lari, with Kikuyu rebels slaughtering their own people because they were loyalists, the savagery of the reprisals, by the Home Guard, by ordinary settlers, by the Colonial forces ... all of that. Uncle Charles, if I hadn't seen some of it with my own eyes I would never have believed it. But these camps ... the interrogations, the beatings, the systemised torture ... Uncle Charles, these places are just like concentration camps. But this time it is we, the British who are responsible, we who must face the world, we who must take the blame.'

The horror of his words was written plain across the young man's face, across the faces of the headmaster and his wife, this loyal couple, greying now, who cared for him like their own, from boy to man. Theo was deeply moved. The embrace he offered each was heartily and gratefully returned.

'I need to get back now, to Njeri and Joyce. They're doing their best out there to deal with the injured. Joyce is a good nurse; she's such a brave woman. No one at the Kijabe mission can ever know about the work she does with us. Her colleagues there, they think that she is at a dinner party out here with friends, staying overnight. She says she actually thinks that most of them would support her if they did know ... but they can't be told, for their own safety. There is too much at stake. Njeri too. She's unbelievable – nurse, teacher, leader, foot soldier. She is right at the forefront of all of this. No one could be more determined to gain justice, Independence for the country as a whole, nor more careful for the wellbeing of each individual countryman or woman. You've raised her well Aunt Catherine. She really believes that she can make a difference. When this Colony finally gains its Independence she at least deserves a place at the table.'

'And speaking of the table, Theo ... don't forget to pick up that kikapu from the kitchen before you go back out there. I've put a few things in there for Njeri.' Aunt Catherine stepped forward and took his hand between hers. She reached up on tiptoe and kissed his cheek. They were smiling again as the young man finally took his leave, united in their love for the young woman Njeri, adopted daughter, sister, friend.

26

Kenya, Rift Valley – 1959

'Do you two want to take a break? I'm just going over to the dining room with the children before games. Somebody said there was Dundee cake with snack today. Shall I bring some out for you?'

In his open-neck shirt and light cotton jacket the young Mr Jack Davidson-Lea cut a dashing figure as he skipped down the veranda steps and strolled across the grass towards the young couple. Daniel had set up his wooden easel at the bottom of the sloping lawns, in the shade of the fringy eucalyptus trees. His model raised her hand to wave, breaking her pose. Laughing, the artist set down his brush.

'Tea would be good thanks Jack, and we all know what Njeri thinks of Aunt Catherine's Dundee cake.' The general hilarity showed that they did.

From the dining hall the sounds of children's after-school chatter drifted across to the schoolmaster and he made to continue his walk across the springy African grass. He was still smiling, hands in pockets, as he walked, relishing the sunshine, enjoying the sense of 'home' that this place gave him. 1959 – how time had flown. He loved it here, loved the people. They'd been through so much together – like family. He glanced back at the couple, chatting so easily now in the shade. It was so good to see Daniel up and about again after that incident in Nairobi, although the walking stick propped against the high stool that he has taken to using at the easel showed that there were still some problems with his balance.

Since Njeri's return from the long, rough trip up north to

Lodwar, where Jomo Kenyatta was now being held under house arrest, she had barely left Daniel's side. The nursing skills she had learned from long hours spent alongside her friend Joyce, tending the sick and wounded during the 'Emergency', those skills stood her in good stead as she had fought to save this man that those who knew her best had begun to suspect she loved. Lately, as her patient had become stronger, the two were often to be found outside together in the afternoons, usually seated on either side of Daniel's easel, at various vantage points around the school grounds. Jack smiled at the memory of Theo teasing them just yesterday morning, before he left for another of his reform meetings up in Nairobi. He'd made everyone laugh by saying that Njeri was Daniel's muse. She'd never heard the word before and, like an elder brother, he'd kept her guessing, until Daniel took pity on her and explained that she was ... that she'd inspired him to produce some of his best work yet. At this Njeri had blushed her embarrassment and boxed Theo on the arm. Jack heaved a sigh. If it hadn't been for Theo, Daniel might well have died.

Theo had been concerned about his friend's safety for a while ... they all had ... out there on the farm alone at nights, especially after the break-in a few weeks earlier. On that first occasion, Daniel had been eating dinner when he'd glanced up and spotted a rifle muzzle around the dining room door. Shots had been fired, and the houseboy had come screaming back in from the kitchen, but in all the confusion the intruder had escaped. Daniel had definitely been unnerved, and was on the brink of moving either into town or out to the school for a bit, but a decision was still pending when he failed to turn up for what he knew was a very important meeting.

The meeting had been arranged with one of Theo's contacts from the Kenyan Ministry of Defence. It seemed that, as independence was becoming inevitable, instructions had been coming through, from the office of the British Secretary of State for the Colonies, that thousands of files, sensitive files relating to the pre-independence period, the Mau Mau rebellion and the 'State of Emergency,' should be secretly migrated back to Britain, others reclassified, to avoid them being seen by subsequent administrations and others containing particularly incriminating evidence should be destroyed. Scandalised by this, one of the civil servants involved had heard about the 'reform' group meetings and had contacted Theo with the information. Theo had planned to meet up with Daniel on the terrace at the Norfolk Hotel first, before going on together to meet the man, who was keen to keep a low profile, for obvious reasons.

As Theo had explained later, after waiting around for a while in the busy bar area, he was just finishing off a beer when one of Daniel's neighbour's had spotted him and strolled over to pass the time of day. It had soon become clear that nobody had seen Daniel for a few days, perhaps even a week. Before the hour was out, secret meeting forgotten, Theo was driving at breakneck speed up the long stony drive, through the straggled forest of gum trees, past abandoned shambas, up to his friend's homestead. No guards, none of the usual Kikuyu staff rushing out to greet him, as he skidded to a halt at the bottom of the veranda, hurtled up the steps towards the wide-open doors. It was in the kitchen that he had found Daniel, lying dazed on the stone floor, beaten about the head, back and shoulders, dried blood matting his thick blonde hair, staining the leg of his khaki working trousers from what looked to be a slash wound across his thigh, probably from a panga. Horrified, Theo had described how he'd roused the weak and wounded man, brought him water, carried him to the vehicle and driven him straight to the mission hospital out at Kijabe, straight to Joyce.

Jack could only imagine what this journey must have been like for Theo and also for Daniel. Joyce had used all her expertise to revive the scarcely conscious man before her. After what seemed to be at least two days and nights lying alone on that kitchen floor Daniel was desperately sick, dehydrated and, Theo was certain, lucky to be alive.

As soon as he could be safely moved, they had brought Daniel out to the school, into the watchful care of his friends. The idea had never entered anyone's thoughts that he should be anywhere else. As far as Charles and Catherine were concerned, Daniel had become part of their extended family. This was a home for him for as long as he chose to stay. For the time being he was lodging in the guest room but Jack was aware that there are plans afoot to build on some additional accommodation. Daniel would be safer here. After the recent attack he was unlikely to be allowed to return to his farm anytime soon.

As he collected his tea and made for the staff table, Jack was still in a reflective mood. Sipping the tea, sinking his teeth into the slice of Dundee cake his thoughts returned to the attack and more significantly to the attackers. It seemed that Daniel had been taken completely by surprise … although as he had gradually been able to remember, he recalled being aware of a strange stillness in the yard, around the house, an absence of familiar noise that should have alerted him sooner. Then he described a sudden eruption, an onslaught of sound, of shouting, yelling, of screams, some of which were his own, as he struggled to shake off the attack from in front and behind. He remembered *pangas* and heavy wooden clubs swung at his head and back. Slashes and livid bruises on his arms and back were continuing reminders of his frantic efforts to defend himself. He remembered trying to reach the pistol that, like many other settlers he had lately become accustomed to wearing at his hip, but the clip was securely on the holster and the relentless beating had made it impossible for him to free his weapon. Looking back it seemed significant to him that no guns were fired this time. He had begun to think that his attackers were out for some kind of revenge, or perhaps to teach him a lesson, to warn him rather than to kill him. Another thing … he was determined that this was not a just Mau Mau attack. Whilst most of his assailants were definitely natives, most likely Kikuyu, he was certain that at least one of them was a white man. He remembered hearing an unmistakeably English voice amongst the shouts that surged around him as he sank into unconsciousness. None of the attackers whose faces he was able to glimpse were familiar to him, but he continued to be bothered by that voice. He reckoned that there was something familiar about it, a twang, perhaps, someone who might have spent time in South Africa. Also – and this is the thing that most concerned his friends – he recalled hearing the word

'*Kernowi*', not just once but several times during the course of the vicious attack.

Talking things over just a few nights ago, it was this linking of the name 'Kernowi' with Daniel that was on everyone's mind, as Jack and Theo were perched on the end of Daniel's bed, talking into the early hours. The three had become very close during the times of struggle, more like brothers … brothers in arms. When Theo had been captured in the bush a few years back it was Jack, with Daniel and a couple of trusted Kikuyu, who had outwitted the gang of Mau Mau fighters in a night raid on their encampment, had rescued their friend from the pit and rushed him to Kijabe where Joyce had cleaned his wounds and treated the welts and swellings all over his body from the savage biting of soldier ants.

During the 'State of Emergency' the name of Kernowi was widely whispered, but the identity of Kernowi remained a closely guarded secret. If Daniel's intuition was correct, it seemed that someone knew, or at least thought they knew, about his part in it all, perhaps even suspected that he was Kernowi himself. None of the friends were under any illusion; to those whom they rescued from squalid conditions, torture and likely death they were heroes, but to the authorities, people of their own kind, they were seen as traitors, fit only to be hunted down, brought to trial, or more likely dealt with some other way, probably shot, if they were lucky. Most dangerous of all now are those perpetrators of the violence who had reason to fear exposure, since rumours had begun to circulate that Kernowi was keeping accounts, collecting names, dates, evidence of atrocities.

Now that the colonial forces had effectively put down the worst of the Mau Mau rebellion, the struggle towards independence had become more political again. Conditions in the work camps and so-called 'protected villages' were still appalling but there had been fewer calls on Kernowi of late. In fact when Njeri had returned from Lodwar she had brought with her a word from Kenyatta suggesting that perhaps the time had come for Kernowi to fade into legend. Having escaped the eyes of the authorities this long, discovery for Kernowi and his men at this juncture would be unthinkable.

'Sir ... Sir ... We're ready. Everything is cleared away. Can we go and get changed now sir?'

Amongst the clatter of children's voices, their mugs and plates, Jack had been lost in his own thoughts. He turned and looked into the round, earnest gaze of James, one of the House Captains. The schoolmaster came to his feet, smiled around at the sea of eager faces awaiting his dismissal and gave the word. Released, their exit was quick and efficient. Knowing that his presence would soon be expected out on the games field, Jack moved swiftly to collect the promised tea for his friends. Balancing cups and plates of Dundee cake on a tray, he emerged, blinking, into the afternoon sunshine.

27

Cornwall, Old Rectory – 2008

'That was all a bit of a shock in there. Those awful photographs – the injuries – I've never seen anything like it. They seem to be some kind of a catalogue, some kind of record. I guess Theo must have taken them. Did you notice they're all numbered?'

When no reply was forthcoming, Dan continued talking to the silent woman's back, as he moved from the kitchen doorway towards the table.

'Your mother thinks there must be a list somewhere. She's got them all searching. She reckons that your father might have been keeping these pictures as evidence.' Again he paused for her comment, but receiving none, he went on. 'That he was intending to expose the perpetrators, bring them to justice – or something like that. I came to look for you.'

Dan's voice when he entered the kitchen had taken Mara by surprise. She did not want him to see her crying. He was at the table now. She heard the scrape of the heavy chair as he moved it back, preparing to sit. When she turned from her slow stirring to face him, her eyes were dry, but the tears had left their mark. She had already stirred three spoons of sugar into the mug of tea for her mother – somebody had said that hot sweet tea was the remedy for shock. Back in the sitting room, Ellen was actually re-covering well. Out here, looking at her daughter, Dan thought that Mara was more in need of the hot sweet tea than her mother.

'Sorry. I was just thinking about my dad ... those photo-graphs ... all the things I didn't know about him.' Caught unawares by the fresh tears, Mara brushed them away with the back of her hand. 'I'm so sorry. I seem to be doing this a lot lately.' Dan moved quickly towards her. His arm was around her shoulders as he guided her to a chair, encouraged her to sit at his mother's table.

'Come on – you'd better drink that tea. You need it. Go on. I'll make another one for your mother in a minute.' Pulling out the chair next to hers, he sat down himself. 'Go on. Drink the tea. Everybody says that hot sweet tea helps. I can't stand the idea myself, but come on. It's worth a try surely.' He grinned and pushed the mug towards her. She picked it up and took a sip, then another. She smiled.

'It's not too bad actually. It's quite nice. I can feel it working already.' She took another mouthful and set the mug back down on the table. 'Look, Dan, I'm so sorry – sorry about all of this actually. Everything is my fault. If I hadn't got myself so wound up about this Cornish thing, getting to the bottom of it. Trying to sort myself out too, I guess, find out about Dad, about our history, get my own story straight. I don't know.' She sighed and sipped at the tea. 'Dad could be so amazing, you know, but so frustrating. When we were kids, there were always 'no go' areas, questions he wouldn't answer, questions we were afraid to ask, if I'm honest. He could be really moody, withdrawn. It was miserable, hard to understand when you're little. It makes you feel like its all your fault, somehow. And he always seemed to be holding something back. I don't know how to explain it really. Anyway, I'm just so sorry – if I hadn't stirred everything up, then perhaps Mum wouldn't have been so excited about getting involved with your job, coming up here, messing up your lives.'

Now she was really crying, tears running in rivulets down her cheeks. Dan pulled a large, rather crumpled blue handkerchief from his pocket and offered it to her. Mara took it, wiping at her eyes and blowing her nose noisily. She grinned through the tears.

'Sorry.'

'It's all right. No, you keep it.' Dan laughed, shaking his head in mock horror as she tried to hand it back, his curls flopping forward onto his forehead. He leaned back in his chair, regarding her thoughtfully.

'Actually you know something, Mara? Believe it or believe it not, this is not all about you. You think that this is just your story … maybe yours and your Dad's. You couldn't be more wrong. You thought if you could do a little bit of investigation, write a neat little piece for your magazine … you could draw a tidy line underneath it all and that would be that. Well, I'm sorry to have to tell you this, but life is not like that. This is a much bigger story than that. All of us … we're not just bit players in your story we've all got stories of our own. We're each of us the stars of our own show.' He laughed. With both hands he brushed his hair back from his face, adjusted his spectacles behind his ears. Mara had almost finished the tea. She was calmer now, listening. He clearly had more he wanted to say.

'I am a Cornishman. I am Cornish because I have chosen to be. I was brought up here. It's the place I know, the people I know. I belong here. I do understand that you've only got to look at me to know that there's more to it than that … at least one of my parents was clearly not from Cornwall.' Smiling, he held out his brown hands, gestured to point out the dark colour of his skin. 'Genetically it is not hard to see that part of me is African, Kenyan, I know. But for me, up until now that is, that has not been the thing that has defined me. I had two fantastic parents who took care of me, loved me, a brother who played with me, protected me from bullies … all that sort of thing, the important stuff. I reckon I was lucky. Ok. They were not my birth parents, but they were here, have always been here for me. I belong here, with them. I chose … I still choose … all this.'

He paused. Mara's elbows were on the table. She was silent, waiting for him to continue, which he did.

'Now, it seems that your father, Theo, is quite probably my father too. So suddenly, out of the blue, I've got a sister, a half-sister anyway, since you and I obviously do not share the same mother. You've suddenly acquired a half-brother too … sorry about that.' They grinned ruefully at each other. 'I guess what I really feel like saying is sorry that we're related. I was quite getting to like you, if you know what I mean.' Now they both laughed. She took his meaning, had felt it too. He reached up and tucked his curls behind his ear; she did the same. Catching each other in the same gesture they laughed again.

'Do you mind then, about Dad, about Theo I mean? Are you interested in finding out about him, about your mother?' Mara was curious. If she was honest, somewhere in the midst of it all, she actually did feel betrayed by her father. She wanted to find out more about the woman with whom he seemed to have fathered a son. Dan had been abandoned by his father ... the same man. His mother had died. Whatever did that feel like?

'I do want to find out about him. For a long time I didn't. I think I'm ready now. I want to know more about my mother too ... not because I need too, but because I want to.' He nodded slowly, affirming his own very recent decision. He looked straight at Mara. 'For me, that's the most surprising thing about all this. Because I always had Rose ... she was my mother. I don't think I ever really thought more about it than that. But just lately I've been thinking more about this young Kenyan woman, whoever she was. She died. And I don't need another mother. It's just that I think that she needs someone to know about her. Actually I think that this is what is most important to my own daughter, to Maisy. Maisy has already begun to care about her. I think Maisy really needs to explore the Kenyan side of her heritage. That was my mistake really. Because for me it very soon became a non-issue ... as I said, I lived in a relatively small safe community and I expected it to be the same for Maisy, for her mother. My identity, my status if you like, was bound up with that of my family. I was black ... mixed-race I guess you'd say nowadays, but I was Edward and Rose's son, Frank's brother, we lived at the Old Rectory. Everybody here accepted me for who I was. Actually they accepted Maisy too, but her mother was worried that her little girl was the only mixed-race child in her school at the time, that there might be problems for her later if she wanted to live somewhere else.' He shrugged, shook his head. 'I don't know really; that's what she said ... but I guess she just didn't love me enough to stay.' He sighed, shrugging his shoulders again. 'Anyway, that's why she took her away back to London, so that Maisy would grow up in a more mixed community. It seems to have worked. She's a great girl, happy in her own skin as they say, totally relaxed about being who she is.' He smiled – a proud father. 'But she's been telling me that lately she has been wanting to explore her Kenyan side and I want her to be able to do that, support her, hence the sale of my goods and chattels which your Mum is going to help me with ... at least I hope she still is ... because I certainly don't have anything like her talent for organising things.' He grinned.

Mara was recovered enough to join him now. She nodded. 'Mum's great – she really is. She's great at getting things up together. She keeps everything organised for us too. She has always been the calm centre for Rosy and me. Nothing ever fazes her for long.' She was looking straight at Daniel now. Strange, but she felt comfortable, talking like this, with this man, this new brother. So she went on, sharing her thoughts just as they came.

'Dad was much less predictable for us girls. Sometimes he was fantastic, really relaxed and easy, playing with us, telling us his stories, but other times he could be quite detached, distant somehow. He would shut himself away in his study, or go off on his bird-watching trips, even when we were small. That kind of thing was quite hard for us ... especially since we always thought of him as some kind of hero ... everybody else's headmaster but our personal property, our wonderful Dad.' She grimaced. 'I think Mum understood our feelings, our frustrations, all those childish insecurities, even when we were grown-ups.' She was not proud – she chuckled now at her confessions. 'Mum was just always there to explain him to us, to interpret him we used to say to each other. I suppose what she did was, she kept us all safe.' Dan had been leaning forward, listening to her with his elbows on the table, chin resting on his cupped hand. Now he sat up straight and looked at his watch.

'Speaking of your Mother, I guess we should make her that cup of hot sweet tea ... although judging by the way she was already recovering that famous equilibrium, the way she had the others searching for more clues amongst the albums in there when

I left. I'm sure that nothing can keep her down for very long. The more I get to know her, the more I like her.'

He smiled and the new brother and sister rose from the table, Dan to put the kettle on once more and Mara to fetch down another one of Rose's coloured mugs. As she started all over again with a tea bag, she glanced across at the man who was at that moment rinsing out her blue mug under the cold tap. She smiled. She could say the same about him: the more she got to know him, the more she was coming to like him.

'Dad, you should see these paintings. They are really good. The artist who painted these faces has the same touch as you.'

Maisy was standing over by the piano, the cardboard tube at her feet, a pile of half-curling paintings on the piano stool beside her. She was holding up one of the paintings, like a scroll unrolled between her hands, showing the image which seemed to be a head-and-shoulders portrait of a young woman, an African woman, probably Kenyan. As Dan watched, she held the picture up alongside his own painting of her younger self.

'She looks a bit like me actually.' Maisy was smiling.

Dan carried the mug of sweet tea over to Ellen who now seemed quite recovered. She was looking carefully through one of the old leather albums. Beside her on the sofa was a list, a handwritten list on a piece of lined paper that looked as if it had been torn from an old exercise book. 'Did you find something interesting?' He set the mug down on the table.

Ellen looked up. She seemed preoccupied.

'Sorry Dan. Thank you for the tea. Yes, we did actually. This album is another one; just like the one we found earlier, only this one had a list tucked in the back. I was right. It is a bit like a catalogue. Look the pictures are all numbered and then this list ...' she held the list out to Dan, '...this list has all the numbers and a name next to each one. All of these photographs seem to have come from one of the detention camps ... look ... names ... dates ... I think someone was keeping documentary evidence of the conditions, injuries, some of them are awful, you could say atrocities. And, you know, I think that it must have been Theo. This writing on the list ... it's his, I'm certain of it.' In Ellen's eyes Dan saw first surprise, then curiosity, then pride.

He took the list and began to study it as she went on. There was something like excitement in her voice as a plan was forming.

'After the weekend, I think that we should look online; make some inquiries; try to find out about those cases that are being prepared – being brought against the British Government. These albums might be helpful. They are certainly evidence of mistreatment, of abuse; you could call it torture. They are all listed ... documented ... look, more people's names, dates, places ... this looks like the name of the detention camp. And here, look at this picture, these men with their rifles, they're in uniform, they're guards, officers maybe. Look, they've all been named. See these arrows that Theo's drawn to pick them out.'

She was running her index finger over the lines, tracing each of the arrows, linking names to faces. 'My goodness, this one's practically scratched right through the paper. It looks like someone's – like Theo's gone over and over it.' Ellen was a woman on a mission. 'And there are some comments he's scribbled here, look, in the margins. The writing's a bit small for me to read but somebody might be able to make it out.' Like Agatha Christie's Miss Marple on the case, she peered in close, tilted the page towards the light. 'It looks like ... 'Freeman' maybe. But I think this bit's in Swahili ... looks like ... yes, I think it says 'Uhuru???' right next to this arrow. But why all those question marks? It's almost like it's that man's name. But look here, at the picture ... that can't be right, can it? Uhuru – that means freedom, in Swahili, doesn't it? This man is not Kikuyu, not even Kenyan. How can it be a name?'

'Did you say 'Uhuru'? I know that name. I've heard it recently. It's the name of that guy from Kenya ... the one who's interested in buying some of my stuff. Here, let me have a look.' Dan reached down towards the album. Still pointing towards the image of the man in question, Ellen offered it up.

Rosy had been listening. She was as interested as Dan, keen

to see the photograph too. 'Just imagine ... I only picked these old albums out of the drawer, almost as an afterthought. I thought they might be diaries ... we know Dad kept diaries. I've found three more albums so far, with photographs, like the ones mum's got. There are more lists too.' She was on her knees, still going through the contents of the yellow boxes. She glanced over at Frank. 'The one Frank's looking at are just old photographs of groups of people, views of the Rift Valley, a few groups of school children ... that sort of thing.' Frank looked up, smiling. Mara moved across to look over his shoulder.

'Dad, come and look at these.' From the far side of the room, Maisy's voice was insistent now. 'These paintings, Dad, come and look at the paintings. This guy paints just like you and his name looks to be Daniel ... Daniel something or other. His signature is almost as bad as yours.' She laughed, awaiting her father's inspection as he passed the album into Rosy's outstretched hands and moved across the sitting room towards her.

Adjusting his spectacles on his nose, he took hold of the painting she offered and examined it closely. The pictures had clearly been rolled for a long time. This one seemed reluctant to be in the light, trying to roll back as soon as he let go of its corner. His daughter was right. The skill of the artist sang from the image ... the young woman's serenity, the light in her eyes, her warm smile, even the trace of a scar across her forehead to her eyebrow. It was all there, masterfully done. He looked again at the signature, tried to make it out ... Daniel ... yes it was definitely Daniel ... and the surname seemed to be Lind ... Daniel Lind. Whoever he was, he was good. An artist himself, Dan was certain of that.

'Do you think she looks a bit like me, Dad?' Maisy was grinning at him over another one of the paintings. 'Look, she's in this one too, and I think it was her in that one over there, but in that one she looks a bit different, her hair's different ... she's wearing traditional African costume.' She pointed over to a rolled painting on the piano stool.

Dan picked it up, unrolled it, and looked closely. It was definitely the same young woman. This time she was sitting on some steps leading to a veranda, festooned with colour, probably bougainvillea. He looked closely. Yes, he could see a likeness to his daughter, but that could just be the Kenyan influence. Maisy had picked up the portrait again. She was walking towards the circle of chairs, eager to show Uncle Frank, ask his opinion.

'Look, Uncle Frank. Aren't these paintings good? Do you think she looks a bit like me?' She knelt beside Frank's chair and he looked up from the album, the old photographs that had been weaving their spell, drawing him back into their world. 'Look, what do you think?' Maisy thrust the painting in front of him and he gave it his attention.

'She is a very beautiful woman … and … yes …' he looked from the painting to his niece then back again, considering; smiling; making her wait for his judgement. 'Yes, she is a bit like you. And the artist is nearly as good as your Dad.' He grinned. 'Actually, you know, I think I've seen her face before … in here … yes, look … here she is … and here. Look, here, with a very handsome young English man. He's got his arm around her shoulders … look …' he held the album out for Maisy to see. 'It's her, it's definitely her, and there's a caption look, it says '*Rift Valley, Daniel and Njeri. 1959.*' Frank and Maisy were clearly enjoying the detective work, the connections they were making.

Ellen had looked up from the album on her lap. She was watching them. 'Did you say 'Njeri'?' She had taken off her the reading glasses.

'Njeri. That's what the caption says. It's probably her name, the young woman in the paintings and in the photographs too.' Maisy was excited; it was in her eyes and in her voice. They were on the trail of the beautiful mystery woman.

'Njeri … Theo told me something about Njeri … a long time ago.' The older woman paused, nodding slowly. All eyes were fixed on her as she blinked, swallowed hard, breathed deep. Then, looking around her at the waiting faces as if seeing them after a long interval, Ellen smiled. She was gesturing as she spoke, waving her reading glasses like a conductor's baton. 'In that packet of photographs from Rose's study … there's a picture of her there … as a little girl. It's a picture sent to Rose, by her mother, Alexandra, when she and her husband were in Kenya, just before they were killed. Fetch me the envelope will you Mara. I'll show you.' They were making progress, unravelling the mysteries.

Dan had returned to the circle. He had an idea, a question too, a suggestion to make. 'The artist, the one who did these paintings ... his name looks to have been Daniel, Daniel Lind. Do you think that's him, the man with her in those photographs in the album? 'Daniel and Njeri' ... they seem close, friendly anyway ... it could be. What do you think?' Dan was standing behind his brother's chair now, looking over his shoulder at the photograph.

Mara handed her mother the envelope of Rose's photographs. She smiled across at Dan. 'It could be. It seems highly likely in the circumstances. Are there any more photographs of him, any with Dad? Although I suppose, if they are all Dad's photographs, that's a bit unlikely. He would have been behind the camera.' She turned to her sister. 'Where did you find all this stuff, Rosy, the old albums I mean? Was Dad keeping them somewhere private, somewhere where none of us would have been allowed to look? Were they hidden? I don't remember seeing them in his study ... not out on his shelves.'

'They were in his desk ... in the bottom drawer.' Rosy looked sheepishly across at her mother. 'Sorry Mum, but the drawer was locked. I searched for the key. It was at the back of the little narrow drawer, you know, the one in the middle. It was actually taped to the top if you know what I mean, like they do in the movies.' She grinned, childlike. 'I must admit I did feel a bit bad ... like Dad might come in at any time and catch me. I would never have done it before all this. It just seemed strange to find the drawer locked ... like I needed to find the key ... like it might be part of the mystery.'

'You know, I was thinking earlier, about all the things you lose when you die. Your right to privacy seems to be one of them.' Ellen sighed.

'Oh Mum, I'm so sorry. I didn't mean to upset you. I really didn't.' Rosy seemed suddenly deflated. It seemed as if she might cry.

Ellen raised her hand against the possibility. 'It's all right, Rosy, I'm fine. In the circumstances you did the right thing. Theo had secrets, probably for good reasons, knowing him, but those secrets have implications for the lives of all of us here, for Rose too I think. It's time now for things to be made clear. We need to know more than we do about Theo and about his past. His past is bound up with this family's future. Rosy you really mustn't worry about what you've done here. However, I do hope ...' Ellen looked around the circle as she spoke; suddenly serious; making eye contact with each one of them in turn, ' ... that as we try to unravel some of these things ... your father ... Theo ... will be treated with respect. He was a good man, and I feel sure that the things we discover will only confirm that.'

It was a significant moment. They all recognised it as such. Each one nodded their commitment ... commitment to the woman before them as much as to the man whose honour she still upheld.

'It's getting quite late. Is anybody else hungry? I'm beginning to feel peckish.' Frank called up the stairs as he emerged from Rose's study carrying a pile of about five or six coloured envelope-folders and made his way towards the sitting room door.

Dan and his daughter, assisted by Rosy, were still busy, bringing all of the boxes from his old bedroom, carrying them downstairs to be sorted by Ellen and Mara. While the girls were working, Dan had also ventured into the dusty attic storeroom and had begun to bring some things from there too.

Pushing the sitting room door open with his elbow, Frank paused on the threshold, smiling as he surveyed the scene. The comfy chairs were still clustered around the coffee table as before, but now the rest of the room had begun to resemble the packing centre for some up-market mail order company. Cardboard boxes of all shapes and sizes, some already opened, others still sealed with packing tape awaiting inspection, seemed to be arranged in different areas. Somebody obviously had a system. Ellen was kneeling over by the fireplace beside a pile of what looked like shoeboxes, a list in one hand and a pencil in the other. As Frank watched it soon became clear that Mara's job was to open each box, display the contents to her mother, who would then record each item on her list and the box was then allocated to the appropriate area. From where he stood Frank could not tell what the criteria were for the sorting process, but there seemed to be four distinct zones to which Mara was designated to carry each box.

'Talk about organised! You two are amazing.' Frank was teasing as he came into the room and deposited his files on the coffee table.

'It's not me. It's Mum. I'm just doing as I'm told.' Mara chuckled as she edged past him to add the current box to the collection that was already building behind the door.

'Did you find anything in Rose's study that might help us make sense of all this?' On the hearthrug, Ellen was now sitting back on her heels, her list and pencil set down beside her. She was smiling but Frank thought she looked tired as she lifted a hand to push her hair back from her forehead, massaging her temple with her fingers.

'I've brought a couple of things through for us to have a look at – but that's for later … another day, probably. I think it's about time we all stopped and took a break. I for one am feeling hungry. I don't know about you two … what would you say to fish and chips?'

'What a good idea.' Ellen reached out a hand to the fireside chair and used its support to come to her feet. She flexed her ankles, making circles. 'Oh, my old bones.' She grinned. 'I could certainly eat something, and fish and chips would do me nicely. Out of paper?'

'But of course!' Frank moved to take her arm, to help her across to the sofa where she settled herself, slipping off her sandals, then one at a time circling her ankles, first to the right then to the left. From where she stood, Mara watched her mother. She seemed comfortable, strangely at home.

'What about if we all drive down to Polperro? They do great fish and chips down there by the harbour. You could even have a

Cornish pasty, Mara, if you like. It's what all good Cornishwomen eat you know.' Frank joked in Mara's direction and she returned his grin. It occurred to him in that moment that he was really enjoying the company of these two women ... women he had only known for a matter of days but whom he already thought of as friends, almost like family.

'Did somebody mention fish and chips?' Rosy nudged her way into the room, balancing a pile of old books up to her chin. Close behind her Maisy was doing the same.

'I heard Cornish pasties.' Maisy grinned. 'We could leave all this until tomorrow ... head off to the seaside. Why don't we go down to Polperro? You could see Dad's studio. He could show you some of his paintings.' As she spoke, the young woman leaned forward deposited her dusty pile of books in a colourful cascade into the lap of the pink-flowered armchair.

Rosy smiled over the top of her own pile; 'Where do you want these Mum?'

'Oh sorry. I've messed up your system.' Maisy laughed guiltily and made to pick up her pile again.

Ellen was quick to stop her. 'Don't be silly, Maisy. Just put them anywhere you can find a place for now, Rosy. I'm done for the day ... and mine's a large cod and chips please.'

As Dan came in carrying what looked to be another armful of cardboard rolls of paintings, he found them all relaxing together; like family. He grinned and moved across to join them.

'I think I've found some more of his paintings ... Daniel Lind's that is ... up in the attic storeroom. I've just had a quick glance at a couple of them but I really do like his style. They're good, quite similar to the ones you've got. We can get them all out and have a proper look at them.' He glanced around at the others, 'But not now ... another day. Did I hear you say you were hungry, Frank?'

'Uncle Frank was suggesting that we all go down to Polperro for some fish and chips ... or pasties.' She grinned at Mara. 'What do you think, Dad? You could invite us all in for a drink at the studio afterwards, if you like.' Maisy shimmied across to her Dad and hung on his arm, wheedling, like she used to as a child. Grinning, he patted her curls, as if she were.

'I think that's an excellent idea.' He glanced down at his watch. 'If we go straightaway, they should still be open.' He looked around him, sensed a system. 'Where shall I put these?' He nodded down at the rolls from the attic, looked to Ellen. She had become the acknowledged organiser of effects.

'Just put them over there, by the piano with the others. Theo must have really admired that man's work, mustn't he? What with the ones Rosy's brought down from his study at home and the ones you've been discovering … we must have quite a lot … quite a body of work. It's really exciting. I can't wait to get them out and look at them all together. I wonder if Theo knew the artist well, if they were friends.' Ellen had been smiling; excited like the others, but now a shadow seemed to cross her face. She shook her head. 'I just don't understand why Theo never mentioned him, never had any of his work on display in our home … not in Nairobi nor back in England. Why ever did he keep this collection private?' Her obvious distress moved them all but it was Mara who reached her first, sat down beside her, took her hand.

'I'm afraid that's just one of many mysteries, Mum, and probably not the most important one either. To think that for all these years everybody thought he was just another boring old headmaster … whoever would have thought that he had such hidden depths … such a secret life.' She was trying to make her mother smile again, appealing to the sharp sense of humour that was never too far below the surface. 'Whatever would the parents have said? What if the students at school had found out that their Headmaster was such a master of deception … maybe even espionage … a spy … imagine the conspiracy theories …' Mara was warming to the subject, making herself smile. 'Imagine the headlines in the local papers … 'Double Life of Lind'n Lea Headmaster!' Remembering the increasingly staid persona of her husband, the Preparatory School Headmaster, Ellen nodded first, and then grinned broadly.

'Did you say 'Linden Lea Headmaster'? Was that the name

of the school, the school in Sussex where you were living until he retired?' Dan was standing by the piano, still clutching his collection of cardboard rolls. Like the others he had been listening to Mara's teasing characterisation of her dad, the staid headmaster, the master of espionage, the spy, and since this same man was his own father he was definitely interested, even in the detail.

'Lind'n Lea ... that was the name of both schools, the one in Nairobi and the one in Sussex. Everybody used to think it was Linden Lea, like in the old song,' Mara paused, smiled, before launching into a snatch of the William Barnes poem set to a tune by Ralph Vaughn Williams:

> 'And I be free to go abroad
> Or take again the homeward road
> To where for me, the apple tree
> Doth lean down low in Linden Lea.'

A spontaneous round of light-hearted applause greeted her low bow at the end of her performance.

'Uncle Frank, what do you think? Maybe you and Mara could be a double act?' Maisy was laughing. 'I'll design your costume Mara.'

'It's a good thought, Maisy, but I wouldn't be able to call myself a one-man band anymore then would I?' Frank was laughing too as he made his way over to help Dan offload the rolls of paintings and stack them carefully with the others.

While his brother took the rolls one at a time, Dan was still thinking about the name of the school. 'You said that people thought the school was named for the song 'Linden Lea' but that they were mistaken.'

'That's right. For some reason that Dad never really ever explained, the schools were called Lind'n Lea' and she spelt out the letters to him, stressing the apostrophe which often used to catch out even the most fastidious of new parents, until, that is, they became old timers themselves, and from then on took great delight in pointing out the mistake to newcomers. It had become one of the schools' traditions. 'An image of a Linden tree, in green, was actually on the school's logo which made it even more confusing and the song was always sung in assembly at the start and end of terms too. I think that people used to think it was all a ruse, creative use of language ... something to make people notice, to make them ask questions. Like they do in advertising, you know, like 'Beanz Meanz Heinz' ... that sort of thing.'

Mara was looking at Dan, watching him consider her explanation, raise his eyebrows and tip his head slowly from side-to-side as he appreciated the tactic. Frank reached out for the last cardboard roll to add to the stack and, hands free at last, Dan held it out towards him. As he did this the label on the tube caught his eye.

'Hey, what do you think of this?' He drew the roll back from his brother's grasp and inspected the label more carefully. He read it out to the others. 'Lake Naivasha – water colours, 1958. Lind, Daniel.' Dan looked up from the label, looked at the others, expecting some reaction. But they were still expectant, waiting for him to explain, to spell it out. 'Lind Daniel ... Lind Dan ... don't you see ... Lind Dan ... Lind'n?'

'You mean, you think that this might be the reason, the reason that the schools are called Lind'n Lea Schools.' Ellen was beginning to understand what he was suggesting. She looked at her daughters who were clearly also beginning to wonder if this might actually be right.

'You might be right, but why the 'Lea'? Perhaps it just sounded good, appealed to Dad's sense of humour. He always did like wordplay, didn't he?' Rosy and Mara looked at each other. It was definitely the sort of thing their father had enjoyed.

Ellen spoke slowly, as if she were giving voice to each new thought as it flowed into her thinking. 'Uncle Jack ... do you girls remember Uncle Jack? He was one of your father's oldest friends, out in Kenya. They knew each other since they were young men, when Theo first went out to Kenya. They were young teachers together, at the school out in the Rift Valley. I always knew that he was your father's business partner, but when I first arrived at the school Jack was more on the business side of things, like a bursar, if you know what I mean. I think he did coach the cricket team, if I remember rightly, but nothing else. It was only when your father left Kenya to set up the school in England that Uncle Jack took over as headmaster of Lind'n Lea in Nairobi.' She looked around at the others, settled on Mara then Rosy, then back to Mara. 'Uncle Jack's surname was Davidson-Lea.'

'Lea. That could be it ... the Lea in the school's name.' It made sense to Rosy and there was some agreement from the others.

Mara was looking less certain. 'I understand the Lea, and even the Lind'n makes some kind of sense, but what about Dad? I always thought that he and Uncle Jack were equal partners in the business, that they had raised the money together. I don't understand where this Daniel Lind – or Lind Daniel – comes into it.'

Even Ellen appeared mystified by this. 'Theo and I lost touch with Jack over the years after his wife died. When he eventually came back to Kenya, to take over from your Dad, to take up the Headship again in Nairobi ... I think it was in 1987 or 1988 ... that was when we came back to the school in England and your dad took over Lind'n-Lea back here again. Since then I never really saw Uncle Jack, though he and your Dad had meetings. Occasionally your Dad went out there for conferences and Jack came to England when the meetings were held here. But those meetings were always held in London. I stayed at home with you girls. We always exchanged Christmas cards though. I'm sure he's still alive. I think he lives somewhere near Chichester, Bosham I think was the name of the village. It's down by the sea. He was always a keen sailor. He used to have a boat on Lake Naivasha. I'm not sure if you girls will remember but we often used to go down there at weekends when we lived in Nairobi, to his boat, to the sailing club at Naivasha, out on Crescent Island. Your Dad used to take you out on the water in the Sunfish.' The memories were happy ones and she was smiling.

'Actually, yes. I do remember. You used to let us wander off with the other children, collecting treasures, pieces of that shiny black volcanic rock ... obsidian. Do you remember that, Mara?' Rosy was enjoying the memories too although she had only been small at the time. 'Do you remember fishing for crayfish there, down by the jetty?'

'I do, I remember we both got soaking wet … and muddy … and I remember that time when Dad was windsurfing out on the lake and we were watching from the beach on Crescent island. He suddenly dropped his sail and we were all wondering what he was doing, when we suddenly saw a hippo … the top of its head broke the surface of the water right in front of him.' Mara was speaking quickly, reliving the vivid childhood memory.

'What happened next? Hippos are really dangerous, aren't they?' Maisy's voice was eager. Like the others she was caught up in the excitement of the story.

'They certainly are, if they feel threatened or if you catch them by surprise. But thankfully this one just snorted then sank calmly back down while Dad waited. Then after a few minutes he lifted the sail up again and came back to shore.'

'He sounds like quite an action man your Dad.' Frank was impressed.

Ellen nodded. 'I guess he was when he was younger. Although when you think about it he was already in his fifties at the time. Living out in Africa though … being in the sun … I think that once you get used to the climate, it keeps you young. It's so much easier to play sports, that kind of thing when the weather is more predictable. We certainly missed the warm climate when we came back with the children. Birthday parties are so much more fun when the sunshine is guaranteed.' She was relaxed again, that earlier moment of sadness forgotten, as was her train of thought. 'But why did I start talking about Kenya. What was I saying?'

'You were saying about Uncle Jack, Mum, about him being a keen sailor; when we used to go sailing with him on Naivasha, remember?' Mara stepped in to put her back on track.

'Oh yes, that's it. I was thinking that tomorrow I might telephone him, if we can get hold of his number. Then we could ask him about the school's name couldn't we … tell him about what we were wondering? He would probably be able to tell us about this Daniel Lind too, I should think, perhaps he knew Njeri. Maybe he'll even be prepared to talk about those early days, the struggles before Independence … although if he's anything like Theo I doubt it. It might be worth a try though. What do you think?'

'I think that sounds like a very good idea Ellen. And since we've all got a lot to do tomorrow … phone calls to make, solicitors to speak to, unpacking all the stuff from Kenya that's stored in the old gardener's cottage, sorting out the attic storeroom … that sort of thing needs to be done now I think … I suggest we get ourselves off to the Fish and Chip shop in Polperro as soon as possible. I said I was peckish earlier. Now I'm starving.'

Frank was taking charge and they all began to move at his bidding, to close up windows, lock the doors, carry cups back to the kitchen … all the things that a family needs to do before they leave home.

As Maisy ran quickly up the stairs at her uncle's suggestion to check the bedroom windows, she was aware of the sounds of life below – Mara talking to her mother about what they should do with the lists, Dan whistling 'Linden Lea' on his way out to the kitchen, Rosy calling to ask Uncle Frank about the key for the French windows in the sitting room. In the stillness of the high galleried landing the young woman paused, one hand resting on the smooth bannister rail, listening. It sounded good, like the old house coming alive again. If only her grandmother could be here to welcome these new members of the family into her home. Maisy was certain that Rose would get on well with Ellen. They were quite alike in many ways. And she would definitely love Mara. Maisy pictured them both with their sandy curls. There would be no mistaking the family likeness. And then there was Rosy, her namesake. Maisy sighed. Tomorrow they would all go to see her down in Lostwithiel, and maybe, before too long, Grandma Rose would be herself again, well enough to come back home too.

28

Stifling a yawn, Ellen pushed back the curtains and looked out over the waking garden. She had not slept well; probably over-tired. It was past midnight by the time they'd got back from Polperro and she'd had a lot on her mind. Perhaps it was the fish and chips lying heavily that had disturbed her; she was not used to eating so late. Maybe it was the wine. She couldn't quite remember but she'd had at least a couple of glasses back in Dan's studio while they were all eating and chatting and looking around at his work. The wine had made her sleepy and once her head had hit the pillow she'd dropped off quickly but before long she'd jolted awake from some vivid dream, all in a sweat. After that it seemed to her that she had been awake most of the night.

Now barefoot in blue-striped pyjamas, Ellen padded across to the ensuite bathroom and on automatic pilot used the loo, pressed the flush, moved over to the sink, pressed for soap and water to wash her hands. Catching sight of herself, tousle-headed and bleary-eyed in the mirror, she leaned forward and stuck out her tongue. Not a pretty sight. She turned on the cold tap, filled the glass and padded back into the bedroom, sipping at the water as she made her way towards the bed. On the table beside the bed was the evidence of the night time reading that had been occupying her thinking since the early hours ... several of the leather albums which had caused such a stir the previous afternoon lay opened, one on top of the other. Beside those was a small stack of her husband's old diaries. One was lying open at the last pages she had been browsing; they were written towards the end of 1960.

'Christmas Eve in the Rift Valley ... Everyone, except Jack of course, here for supper ... even some carol singing, led by Uncle Charles of all people. He and Aunt Catherine are very happy. Daniel and Njeri have announced plans to be married in the New Year. Jim Cookson will do the business out here at the school. I'm to be best man! Njeri's mother and her uncles have given their permission, so all should be well. It should have been her father but he's still detained ... somewhere in the 'pipeline' we think ... no one is able to trace his exact whereabouts ... Njeri fears the worst.'

Daniel and Njeri ... Leafing through Theo's diaries it had soon become clear to Ellen that these two people were very close to her husband's heart ... Njeri like a sister, Daniel his dearest friend. Daniel was the artist. It was his work that they had all been admiring yesterday, his paintings of the beautiful Kenyan woman, of Njeri, that had sparked the interest of young Maisy, caused them all to spot a likeness. Daniel Lind ... so he and Njeri had been a couple, man and wife. If she was honest, yesterday, with all the talk about Njeri, Ellen had begun to think that Njeri and Theo ... Even in her mind she can scarcely allow the thought to settle, to take shape, the idea that Theo had loved, had fathered a son, with another woman ... and even worse, not told her about it, after all these years. But now, reading Theo's own words in his diary ... It was Daniel who had loved Njeri, been loved by her. The flood of relief, the wave-wash of it, had left her reeling.

As she clambered back up onto the comfortable bed, plumping the pillows behind her, shifting herself, settling back and pulling up the duvet around her waist, Ellen reached out and picked up the diary once more. Rosy had only brought down a few of the many that Theo had kept safe in his study. Ellen was thankful she had lighted on this one. No one had been allowed to see them in his lifetime, not even his wife. Now gently, almost reverently, she closed the book and held it against her with both hands. She lifted it to her face. For a moment it seemed she might kiss its soft leather cover. She breathed deep, searching for the scent of him, but smelled only the old leather. Theo was gone. These diaries were the only way she knew to discover his heart, to help his family understand the man they had lost. Still holding the book to her face she closed her eyes. His family ... what a difference these last days had made to those words.

Ellen opened her eyes. She lowered the book to her lap, drew in a deep breath through her nose and let it out softly through her lips. She was ready to begin again. This time the diary opened itself at somewhere near the halfway mark, earlier in that year. Ellen adjusted her glasses and began once more to read her husband's record of his life before they met.

'Last day of June ... overcast today but no rain ... only two weeks till end of term ... strange to think of summer holidays back home in Cornwall ... received Rose's letter yesterday ... bluebells in the beech woods, blue sea, breezy days along the beach ... like another world ... Kernow and Kenya ... meeting with CW tomorrow in Langata ... hoping for some new information regarding whereabouts of Njoroge ... also about destruction of files! Hope it's not too late!'

Ellen longed to be able to ask him about Njoroge ... and did CW turn up with the information? She shook her head, sighed a deep sigh and frowning flicked forward a few pages.

'October ... another mass meeting in Nairobi calling for Kenyatta's release ... heard that they might move him to Maralal with daughter Margaret early in the new year ... they'll have to let him go soon ... reform meeting ... talk of Lancaster House Conference in London to discuss future of colony ... can't come soon enough! Daniel still at school almost back to normal but still limping... he's refusing to use his stick! Njeri beats him with it ... haha!... teaching some classes... he's seriously thinking of selling the farm ... good idea! Still no news about Njoroge ...'

Njoroge again ... Njeri's father. Ellen turned on a few pages then stopped as she spotted Jack's name.

'Nearly the end of November ... still no sign of the short rains ... blue sky again ... very hot ... Aunt Catherine in bed all day yesterday ... quite frail, since Daniel's attack ... feverish in heat ... Joyce here tomorrow ... relief! Played cricket against Pembroke today ... victory!!! Njeri and Daniel out walking again ... reckon something's afoot! (ha,ha!) Jack heard today that his parents will not be returning to Kenya, selling up at Limuru ... his mother's health is reason ... he thinks there's more to it ... his father had a severe dose of malaria a few years back ... it keeps returning, worse each time. He's not been well lately ... Jack's planning to go back for Christmas.'

Poor Jack. Ellen already knew that his father had died of his fever and his mother soon after. The farm had been sold and Jack had used his inheritance to fund his share of the new Lind'n Lea School at Langata, the school that she herself remembered so well. Later, when the girls were up she would search through the things downstairs to see if she could find Jack's phone number at Bosham. If not she might try ringing the school office; someone there would probably be able to get hold of his phone number. The diaries were helping but there were still questions that only someone who was there at the time would be able to answer. If Theo really was Dan's father as he had been told, then someone must know something about his mother. Yesterday she, and perhaps the others too, had begun to think that Njeri might be the one, but now that she'd read the diary she didn't think so. So if it was not Njeri, then who? It couldn't have been Joyce, the American nurse. Dan's mother had obviously been a Kenyan. The diary for 1961 was not here. Maybe it was at home in Theo's study ... she hoped it was. Now that the questions had been raised, she desperately needed to know the answers.

Ellen turned her head towards the window and gazed out into the clear blue of the early summer sky. Who else might be able to help her? And then the idea came ... Rose ... his beloved sister Rose. Ellen was suddenly certain of it. The more she had heard about Rose and her relationship with her younger brother, the more it became clear that Rose would have known. It seemed that Theo had trusted Rose with his son ... he would definitely have trusted her with his secrets. But now, from what Rose's boys had said yesterday, it seemed that Rose herself might no longer remember. Later today they were all meeting up for coffee at the Community Centre and then the plan was that they would together to visit her. Frank and Dan would go in first with Maisy and if all seemed well then they would invite Ellen and her daughters to join them. This was, of course, as long as Rose's doctors thought that it would be all right. Ellen had her doubts. If Rose was already unwell, her doctor would be sure to say that it would all be too much for her. Ellen could understand that; it had been almost too much for her and she was fine. She reached for the glass and gulped the remaining water down in one. There again, Rose might be having a good day … she might take it all in … she might even know about them already … she might greet her new family with a hug and answer all the questions they needed to ask. In your dreams …

Ellen's blue-grey eyes flashed a sardonic smile at such silliness. She leaned across and set the diary back down on the table, flung back the rumpled duvet, swung her legs out over the side of the bed and shuffled her feet into her slippers. She listened. No sound from the girls yet. This morning for a change she would have breakfast quietly, by herself. These were surprising times. Who knew what each day would bring? She would need to be prepared for … no not for the worst … Ellen decided then and there that she would be prepared to expect the best! And here she used what seemed to be her late husband Theo's favourite punctuation: the exclamation mark.

29

Kenya, Rift Valley – 1961

'Don't look so worried, my friend. She'll be fine. She's still young and she's strong. She'll be back home soon. And the fact that she's carrying your child will guarantee that she's sensible, for a change.'

Grinning broadly, Theo nudged his old friend, new husband, soon to be father. But Daniel's nod was still distracted, his half-smile vague as they walked on in silence.

'You know, I've been thinking. If the child is a boy, you will be able to say that he is the light of your life: 'the African son.' Theo was not be deterred in his efforts to lift his companion's spirits. His tone was playful.

This time Daniel took the bait. 'Light of my life? African son? African sun? That's good, Theo. And you're fresh and smelling of cattle dung. 'Cornish heir/air'. Remember that one?' At last, a real smile. Now the two men were laughing together, like the school friends they had been. This game was one of the many things they'd shared.

'That's more like it. You need to relax. They'll take good care of her. Anyway, did you really think we could keep her here on a day like this?'

At last, the long-awaited day had come: August 1961 and Jomo Kenyatta had been released from detention. Despite her husband's protestations, Njeri had travelled to up to Gatundu with her father's sister and a group of her friends, among countless others from all over the country, to give their hero the welcome home that he deserved.

'I know. She'll be all right. And you're absolutely right.

There was no way she was going to miss this, not after all she's done for the cause, all the effort she's devoted to his release, to the party.' Daniel's smile belied the anxiety still lurking behind his eyes. 'I just wish I could have gone with her, that's all.' He shook his blonde head and the half-smile slipped from his lips. 'She's right though. If I had gone, I would have just attracted attention. I know I would have been more of a risk, a white man, and with all these rumours about *Kernowi*.' He reached out, touched the arm of his friend. 'There's talk that it's me you know. She's really worried, afraid that I'm a marked man. She was saying that someone she met in Nairobi just recently told her they'd heard a Kikuyu from the Home Guard bragging over his beer that there's an informer, that they've got it in for me, that I should be on my guard, that one of the *mzungus*, the white man who calls himself *Uhuru* is out to get me too.'

Theo has turned sharply at the mention of the words *mzungu* and *Uhuru* in this context. 'Did they really say a *mzungu*... a white man? Calling himself *Uhuru*? Who is he? Why's he calling himself *Uhuru* of all things? This is the first I've heard of him?'

'I'd never heard of him before. Apparently this *mzungu*'s got a really bad attitude and a reputation to match. Calls himself *Uhuru* ... uses the name as some kind of perverted battle cry for his machete-wielding gang of mercenaries ... freedom from any code of honour, from the rules of civilised society, freedom to do as they like. Who would ever have thought that word, *Uhuru*, could be associated with such savagery, such depravity? And yet, do you know something Theo. When I heard about him, how despicable his behaviour sounded, it made me think of ... I don't remember the names now, but you know, that father and son, the ones who were managing my Uncle's estates when I first got here. Oh, what was their name? John was the son's name ... that's it. I remember now. Freeman, that was it. Freeman. I sacked them both. Do you remember?'

With one hand leaning heavily on his walking stick – he had lately given up the fight with his vanity – Daniel had the appearance of a much older man. Lifting his free hand, he scooped his hair away from his face and scratched absentmindedly at the back of his head. To Theodore he seemed suddenly vulnerable.

'I do. I remember them and all the trouble you had. I don't know. There could be a connection, I suppose. With a name like *Freeman*, I guess there could be a link ... but at least now you're out here in the Rift Valley with us you're safer. No one in Nairobi knows where you are at the moment. After that trouble at the farm, some people think you've taken fright, gone back to England like the others. Old Bill Nunn was telling everyone at the Muthaiga club bar just the other day that he'd caught sight of you down in Mombasa. He reckons you must be staying down at the coast, lying low at your family's old place at Malindi. I certainly haven't said anything to contradict the idea, and none of the students here really knows much about you at all, except that you're now our very own Mr Njeri, the new art teacher.' Daniel grinned at this and Theodore smiled, relieved. 'They're unlikely to make any connections between anything they might overhear at home and you anyway. As far as the pupils are concerned, teachers live in pigeon-holes, no one ever imagines they have any kind of life out of the classroom, believe you me.'

The two men were enjoying a late afternoon stroll around the grounds, out by what passed for a cricket pitch on the tough African grass. The scuffing around the wicket and the deep russet-red track in the murram dust revived happy memories of last term's games won and lost, and the friends reminisced as they made their way around, back across the games field towards the main school buildings and the headmaster's house. The air was still warm, dry despite white cloud bubbling up high in the bottomless blue over the Great Rift Valley.

'Remember the last game of the term, against Pembroke House?' Theo slowed his pace, turned back to face his friend, caught the stumble, the quick grimace of pain. He waited, watched Daniel collect himself, before going on. 'That game was balanced on a knife edge, then young James came in twelfth man and just slogged the ball all around the ground. It was incredible! Remember his face? He was over the moon. Even Jack could hardly contain his excitement that day.' Both men were grinning at the memory. James Junior had become an overnight legend; saved the day; become everyone's hero.

'How could I ever forget?' Daniel had recovered. He was grateful for Theo's understanding.

'Jack has really worked wonders with the cricket team, hasn't he? He's turned out to be a natural on the sports field, a great games teacher and to think that when I first knew him he always used to insist he would only teach mathematics.' Theo's praise was accompanied by a phantom ball toss and a broad smile. Jack had made the long journey back to England again during the school holidays. Since his father's sudden death last Christmas, his mother was ailing and, as an only son, Jack was concerned about leaving her. The exact date of his return had been left uncertain. Everyone at the school was hoping against hope that he would be back in time for the start of the new term.

'Talking of Jack ... I forgot to mention it. I had a letter from him just the other day.' Daniel's news was a surprise. It captured Theo's attention as they approached the colourful gardens surrounding the school buildings. 'He must have written it soon after he left here. It seems that their farm up in Limuru has finally been sold. I don't know the details. He didn't say. But he was making that proposition again ... remember when we were all talking that night? He was suggesting that with the proceeds of the sale, he and I go into business together; that we should start our own school, nearer to Nairobi, probably somewhere out at Langata. He thinks that with Independence, when things settle down, there will be a lot of call for the kind of education we can provide. Not a boarding school though, a day school for people living in and around Nairobi. He wants you involved too of course ... international ... multi-national ... I don't know ... he didn't go into details. But he is clear about the name though.' Daniel broke off, laughing at Jack's certainties. 'He thinks we should call it 'Lind'n Lea.' What do you think? It sounds like Linden Lea.'

Theo was laughing too. 'It sounds just like Jack, if you ask me. It's not a bad idea though. What do you think about it? I can't make the kind of investment that you two can make at the moment but I'd want to be part of it. Especially now that it looks like Uncle Charles is starting to think about calling it a day out here.'

At the mention of Charles, their quick laughter faded. Both men were anxious for the couple they have come to think of as family. 'Before they left this time, Aunt Catherine was talking about staying on in England, up at their house in the Cotswolds – initially until Christmas. It's going to seem so strange without her. But her health has not been so good of late has it, not since the attack, you being so badly injured. It seems to have brought things a bit too close to home. I think she's lost her confidence out here. I don't think Uncle Charles will want to stay on too long without her.'

Walking and talking the men had reached the narrow stone pathway through the cascading purples and oranges, pinks and reds of the rampant bougainvillea, so much beloved of Charles and Catherine, into the small private garden of the headmaster's house. Daniel sank thankfully down onto the cushioned wooden seat, set back in the shade beside a table and a couple of side chairs. It was a favourite spot. Njeri and Catherine were often to be found here reading quietly or chatting together into the late afternoon.

'Do you fancy a drink ... a beer ... tea ... lemonade? I think Samson's round the back in the kitchen. I'll tell him we're back and see what we've got out there.'

Theo had moved into the main house while his Aunt and Uncle were away in England. Over the years it had become a tradition ... he was not really sure why. He sauntered around the outside now towards the back of the house, leaving his friend massaging his weak leg, recovering in peace.

As he entered the kitchen through the opened back door, Theo felt the sudden chill on his sun-warmed arms. The air was always colder out here, probably designed to be that way. He shivered as he moved towards the pantry cupboard. Everything in there had to be kept in sealed containers, covered basins and such-like, to keep out the creatures, the little sugar ants that got into everywhere, the cockroaches.

'Bwana Theo. I did not hear you. I did not know you were back.'

As Theo opened the door to the cupboard, Samson was looking up at him, eyes wide; the ravaged skin at the side of his face adding to the impression of horror. He came to his feet. He had been crouching down on the low stool that was always kept in the pantry so that Aunt Catherine could use it to help her reach the higher shelves. Both men were as shocked to see each other.

'What are you doing in here, Samson? Why are you in the cupboard? Is something wrong? You look worried. Come on out of there. What's the matter with you?' Theo ushered the older man out into the open kitchen, pulled out a chair from the table, invited him to sit.

'Some men came, while you were out walking with Bwana Daniel. They beat the *askari*. Moses let them in through the gate. They drove very fast into the compound.' His voice was shaking and he was close to tears. 'There was a lot of noise, sir, they were shouting, they had sticks. I hid in the cupboard, sir. I was afraid.'

'It's all right, Samson. There's no one here now. Everybody's safe. I'll go down and check on Moses in a minute. What did they do? There's no sign of damage. They don't seem to have come into the house. They must have left when they found no one here.' Theo looked around him, deciding what to do next. 'You stay here. I'll go and tell Daniel what's happened then I'll go down to the gate. You just wait here. Get yourself a drink of water.'

So saying, Theo left Samson alone in the kitchen and moved cautiously through to the front of the house. There was no sign of forced entry. Unlocking the front door from the inside, he stepped out onto the shaded veranda but was immediately stopped in his tracks. Spread out in front of him, on the top step was a flag; a flag he knew only too well; a black rectangle emblazoned with a white cross. It was the Cornish flag, the black and white flag of Kernow. It was Kernowi's flag. Theo froze. His mouth was dry. He reached out a hand, clutched at the wooden balustrade. Someone knew ... they had been here. But who were they? What did they know? Shaken, Theo sank down onto the wooden step beside the flag.

Still, hanging on to the wooden rail like a child he remained, knees hunched, staring out through the finials. Several long moments passed before the man stood, picked up the flag and folded it deliberately into quarters, then eighths. Setting the emblem to one side, Theo descended the remaining steps and strode out over the grass and down the gravel drive in the direction of the front gates.

At the far end of the drive the *askari's* hut was empty. There was no sign of Moses. The gates were wide open. Theo picked up the *askari's* heavy wooden club, presumably abandoned in the old man's haste to escape. It hung from his hand, dragging along the stony ground as he approached the breached gateway, passed through, out on to the murram track that led up to the road. He stood in the middle of the track, eyes sweeping to left and right, scouring the surrounding scrub and grassland for any sign of the intruders. Satisfied, he turned and headed back towards the gates. Whoever was here was long gone. All that remained for now was to secure the boundary, lock the gates, be on their guard.

With the heavy wooden gates locked and bolted, still carrying the askari's club, Theo made his way, briskly now, back up the winding driveway, through the copse of shaggy trees towards the house where Daniel and Samson were awaiting reassurance. In his haste to regain the relative safety of the compound Theo almost missed the slumped form deep in the shadows at the side of the track. It was the groan, more like a wild animal's throaty growl, that caught his ear, his eye, caused his blood to leap. He stopped, turned towards the sound, scanning the undergrowth for movement. He waited. There it was again, over there, by that tangle of scrambling lantana. The figure, for so it seemed, rolled over. Theo made out a face, grimed, bruised, bloodied.

'Who is it?'

Bending low, Theo scrambled towards the bundled body, reached it, saw it to be a man, a man who had been badly beaten, a man he knew well.

'Njoroge! Whatever has happened to you? Where have you been? How did you get here?'

He had so many questions but no prospect of answers ... not yet. The man's lips were parched and dry, swollen, split and bleeding from infected wounds. One eye had swelled beyond recognition. An ear had been sliced, but not cleanly, perhaps bitten. Dried blood and puss had dribbled in filthy runnels down his face and neck. Theo was sickened to his stomach.

'Who did this to you?'

The look of pleading in the poor creature's one good eye broke his heart. Never a big man, Njoroge had been reduced to skin and bones. Theo scooped him up in his arms and carried him like a child towards the house, thankful that Njeri was not there to see her father in such a pitiful state.

'Is that you Theo? What's going on? Where have you been? What have you got there?'

Daniel had been waiting all this time, relaxing in the garden, enjoying the quietness, unaware of the drama unfolding around him. Hearing scrunching along the driveway he emerged from the bougainvillea archway, through the wooden garden gates, to meet Theo face to face. His relaxed smile was transformed in an instant to a mask of horror as he recognised Njoroge, took in his injuries.

'Daniel ... I'm so sorry ... I forgot to come and tell you. We've been raided. Samson was hiding in the pantry. Moses has disappeared. It looks like somebody has dumped Njoroge's body from the back of a vehicle and left him to die at the roadside. He's been beaten, tortured. He needs help. Could you get pillows, cushions, sheets anything you think might be useful. Bring them round the back to the kitchen. I'm going to use the kitchen table.'

Daniel nodded and leaning heavily on his stick, made for the front veranda where the main door stood wide open, just as Theo had left it. Theo himself hurried around to the back of the house, calling out to Samson, cradling the old chief's broken body close against his chest.

Even as he entered the shady kitchen, waited while Samson hastily cleared his clay jars and cooking pans from the long wooden table, it was clear to Theo that it would be many days, weeks probably before Njoroge would be sufficiently recovered from these horrific injuries, before they would discover the answers to some, if not all of their questions. But the questions, like flash-floods in monsoon rains, were unstoppable, surging through his brain, pumping with each anxious heartbeat. The stark image of the black and white flag spread out across the step struck a chill, caused the hairs to rise on his arms, prickle at the back of his neck. A threat ... it was definitely a warning. These men, whoever they were, most likely the same men who had been holding Njoroge captive, starving and beating him, torturing him ... for what? For information? It must have been ... for information about Kernowi; about Kernowi's whereabouts ... that must be what this was all about. And they obviously thought they knew something now, or else why the flag? Why return Njoroge like this? But what had made them pick on the old chief in the first place? Somebody must have connected them, himself, the school, Daniel, Njeri ... perhaps someone had spotted Daniel at one of the cricket matches, some-one from one of the other schools. Apart from that he'd been more or less been in hiding.

Daniel appeared, as if on cue, from the darkening hallway, clutching an armful of grey blankets, a pillow and some old sheets. Without a word, Samson took the bundle from him and busied himself, preparing a bed on the cleared table now pushed in close against the wall. Nobody spoke; nobody knew what to say. At a nod from Samson, Theo moved forward to the table and between them they eased the old man's body onto the blankets, settled his grey head onto the creamy-white pillow. Njoroge's eyes were closed, his battered face expressionless. He seemed for all the world like a dead man.

It was Theo who took charge, carefully removing what re-mained of the torn and bloodied clothing; peeled off the layers of wrapped cloth; preserved as far as he could the dignity of the old chief, his old friend. As Samson lifted the body onto its side, Theo gasped. The extent of the raw flesh visible amongst the slash wounds, livid across the leathered skin of the man's scrawny back and buttocks were shocking even to one who had thought himself to have seen some of the worst that man could do to man. He glanced at Samson. Tears had left glistening trails down the cook's cheeks. They mirrored his own … tears of compassion, hot tears of rage. Daniel stepped forward and, tight-lipped, the men worked together to save their friend. Only later would they give rein to their feelings of shock and of anger. Only then would they take time to confront their fears, their worst nightmares and only then would they have to consider the future in which it seems they will each be called upon to face the full consequences of the decisions they had made.

30

Kenya, Kijabe – 1961

'Your father is a brave man, Njeri. He is not a young man any more...'

Here the Nurse paused dramatically, wagging a tantalising finger towards Chief Njoroge. Propped up in the cane chair, the old man was wrapped in a borrowed dressing gown, grimacing and shaking his head at her teasing.

'But he is as strong as a lion.'

At this Nurse Joyce threw back her head and let out a roar of laughter. The old man's good eye lit up. He beamed a lop-sided, gap-toothed grin, nodded his close-cropped head as if on a spring and lifted his right arm, shaking his fist in an exaggerated display of strength. But the gesture, though valiant, was sharply at variance with the frail figure that he cut, cocooned as he was in the over-large, dark blue gown.

Beside him on the hospital veranda, his youngest daughter was laughing too. She was tall for a Kikuyu, as rounded with her pregnancy, as her father was stick-thin. Her head was shaved close today and her scalp was shiny as polished mahogany. Her thick-lashed brown-black eyes were warm, her features fine. Often to be seen in western-style clothing, that afternoon found her more traditionally dressed in some kind of close-fitting dark top and wrapped around in kanga cloths, red and blue and green with a flash of yellow-gold. As she leaned forward to lay a hand on her father's bony shoulder and moved across to hug her friend, there was a certain radiance about her, a glow often spoken of, yet not so often found.

Today for the first time Njeri could feel it herself. Her husband was steadily regaining his spirit and her father his strength. All was well with her child ... she could feel him even now, pushing back against her hand as she rested it fondly atop her distended belly. Up here at Kijabe – 'Place of the winds' in the Masai language – at this mission hospital perched on the rim of the Great Rift Valley, she knew that those whom she loved had been healed, kept safe. Theodora Hospital named for the love of God and for the family of her friend Theo, would always be a safe place for her. It was her hope that her son ... for she was certain that her child would be a boy ... her son would be born here, though she was mindful that, for her own mother, the birthing had been so sudden, so quick, that she Njeri was born out in the bush. Kikuyu women were resourceful. Her mother had given birth alone. Looking up, she met and held Joyce's gaze. The two women had already discussed it. Njeri was resourceful too. She would know what to do. Her smile, her nod, confirmed her thanks and their friendship, before they returned once more to the mundane business of the day.

Njeri glanced fondly at the frail old man. 'As soon as Daniel and Theo have finished chatting with John in the office ... did I tell you... they're going over some changes to the plans for the new hospital buildings ... he'll bring the vehicle around to the front and we can load up and get going. I know that *mzee* my father is keen to get back to his home and to the welcome that is awaiting him.' Her hand on his shoulder was light. He had given them all such worry in the last months, such relief at his steady recovery.

The mention of John had brought a special warmth to Joyce's face. John was the young missionary priest who was also a doctor and a master-builder ... in fact he would turn his strong hands to anything that needed to be done on the station. It seemed he could cook too, and he had even been known to dig graves. Since his arrival about six months ago, he and Joyce had become close. Njeri had great hopes for her friends' future together. There had been a time when she had thought that Joyce and Theo might make a good couple but no. Theo's time had not yet come for that kind of happiness.

'*Jambo*, Sister Joyce, *Jambo Njeri. Habari?*' A young Kikuyu woman called up to them, waving a greeting from the narrow path below. From the look of her as she made her way up across the rough grass towards them, one hand at the base of her back the other resting atop her belly, it seemed that before very long her child would be age-mates with Njeri's own. The two women were already friends as was evident by the warmth of their greeting and the giggling chatter in the easy Kikuyu language they shared that was soon bubbling around them, temporarily excluding the others.

Joyce looked down at the quietly dozing old man, recalling his battered state, his brush with death, his gradual recovery. Compassionate, the Nurse reached out and touched her sun-freckled fingers onto the dark leathered skin of the old chief's hand. He opened his eyes with a start, took a moment to return from his dreams, before looking up at the nurse.

'So, you're leaving us then? After all we've done for you, you're just walking out?' Joyce was back in 'Matron' mode, rallying her patient, teasing again. It was her way, and those in her care loved her for it. Chief Njoroge drew up his face in what might be mistaken for a grimace but which was his way of returning her good humour. Despite the livid scarring puckered around his eye and at the corners of his mouth that gave him the fearsome look of an old devil, the twinkling in his good eye conveyed his warmth of feeling towards the nurse who had been like an angel in his hours of need. Words were impossible for him now. His tormenters had taken them away with his tongue.

31

Christmas Eve. The fat brown envelope is on the leather passenger-seat, like a gift beside him. But Theo's sideways glance is quick, almost furtive. He swallows hard, flicking his eyes back to the windscreen, his shoulders hunched over the steering wheel. For now he must force himself to focus on the driving. The old Land Rover is bouncing about all over this rough farm track, riddled with deep ruts and gullies. With a sigh of relief he spots the metalled road just up ahead.

As he pulls the vehicle out of the stony drive and up onto the road, the wheels grind and skid on the loose gravel, kicking up clouds of dust and he reaches out, scrabbling for the handle to wind up the window. Too late. The thick dust trail catches up with him, billows in through the gaps and he sneezes violently, coughing. One hand clutching at the steering wheel, he rubs his eyes with the other, clicks on the wipers to clear a path through the drifts of dust sprawling across the windscreen. The strip of road that stretches out before him has definitely seen better days. In places, the potholes have been filled with murram and stones, but the ride is rough and he grips the wheel tightly with both hands now, anticipating a long, hot journey back down over the escarpment into the rift, and out to the school. He glances anxiously at his wristwatch. All being well he should just about make it back before nightfall.

These meetings with CW – this is the third time now that they've met – have always left him feeling like this, edgy, exhausted somehow, yet strangely invigorated. When he first got wind of the existence of the 'W' or 'Watch' files, files never to be seen by African eyes, when he'd heard rumours of the secret pre-independence scrabble to destroy these files, along with masses of other documents and evidence of abuse and brutality, a destruction only to be carried out by 'servants of the Kenyan government who are British subjects of European descent,' he recalls his feelings of shame, of outrage, feelings that, he soon discovered, were shared by CW.

CW – he will not reveal his real name to Theo even now – was one of those government officials ordered to take part in the purge of incriminating files, warned to keep their red 'W' stamps in a safe place, threatened with prosecution should any paperwork be taken home or, even worse, leaked. He was also a man of conscience. After many sleepless nights and much soul-searching, he had come to the conclusion that someone should know about the 'Watch' files, be told about what was going on. Somehow – Theo was not exactly sure how – he made a connection with Theo. Gradually over the course of their secretive encounters, Theo has come into possession of information, and now, here in this envelope beside him, documentation, practical evidence that he will be able to use to challenge, to bring to light, the disgraceful practices of this colonial government.

The enormity of the responsibility; the dangers of the task ahead of him weigh heavily now across his hunched shoulders, sit like a stone in the pit of his stomach. One of the papers in the envelope springs to his mind, evidence of just how far the powers that be are prepared to go to get rid of the masses of incriminating files. He can hardly believe what he has read: '*It is permissible, as an alternative to the destruction by fire, for documents to be packed in weighted crates and dumped in very deep or current-free water, at maximum practicable distance from the coast*'. This information, along with other evidence, including one of the actual 'W' stamps, must, with all urgency, be put into the right hands. But whose hands? Theo is still pondering the question as he arrives at the edge of the escarpment. The view out over the Rift Valley from this point never ceases to thrill him. He lifts a hand from the wheel, glancing at his watch once more, pursing his lips at the lateness of the hour, yet slowing the vehicle to a halt anyway. Coming to a stop at the side of the road, he reaches forward onto the shelf below the dashboard and lifts out his binoculars.

As he scans the vista before him from left to right, in the light of this late afternoon the extinct volcanoes *Suswa* and *Longenot* rise ominous from the valley floor, their shaded craters clearly visible to his practised eye. Lake Naivasha, one of the only two freshwater lakes in the Great Rift Valley, glimmers in the distance. And stretching out for mile upon mile the plains dotted with Acacia trees, thorn bushes and scrub, grazed by zebra, impala, and giraffe and by wandering herds of Masai cattle, goats and donkeys. Despite himself he chuckles with a mixture of relief and amusement at the memory of the near miss when an old donkey had wandered out onto the road one afternoon, right into the path of the school bus returning with the cricket team after the game at Gilgil. The vehicle had screeched to a halt and the donkey had scarcely batted an eyelid at the children's loud insults as it ambled off into the bush on the opposite side of the road.

Wrapping the leather strap around the binoculars, he tucks them back safely on the shelf and restarts the engine. His friends back at the school will start to worry if he doesn't get a move on. In the current situation he knows it is not wise to be out after dark. Njeri was not really happy about him going out today at all. Daniel is very nervous about recent night attacks in the area. He has been unsettled by the rumours flying around about reprisals and Samson, the Kikuyu cook, has seemed really edgy in the last few days too. Since all that business with Njoroge, he just hasn't been the same, despite the fact that the old chief has recovered remarkably well from his appalling injuries. In fact, now that he comes to think about it, it seems to Theo that Samson and Njoroge have become even more wary of each other as the old man has become stronger. Just the other day Njoroge got into a real state when Samson had come in from the kitchen and it had taken all Njeri's efforts to calm her father down. His frustration at being unable to speak is only exacerbated by his inability to read or write which means that communication with him has to be with grunts and gestures.

Changing down to a low gear now for the descent, Theo is glad that Uncle Charles and Aunt Catherine were finally persuaded to make the journey back to England for Christmas this year. They will be sadly missed, especially for the festivities, but they both needed the break and Theo is hoping that they might decide to stay longer, perhaps until things quieten down a bit here. Once more he glances across at the envelope, dustier now, then sharply back to the business of negotiating yet another of the hairpin bends that mark the steep descent to the valley floor. The question of how best to deal with the contents of the envelope occupies his thoughts as the time slips by towards sunset over the plains. Miles pass by in a frown.

The going is marginally easier now and he passes the left-hand turning down to Narok with a quick glance and a wave to the old Masai, draped in a dusty red blanket, casting a long one-legged shadow at the windy junction. As he continues on his way, Theo is smiling, recalling his younger self, struggling to adopt that resting stance of the Masai. With one leg bent at the knee jutting out to the side with its foot resting against the other knee of the straight leg, the stance still seems to him impossible to describe let alone to hold in balance. Yet the Masai accomplish it with seeming ease; standing one-legged, ram-rod straight; with their hands holding either end of a walking stick balanced across the back of their necks. It's incredible. Just one of the many things that these people can do better than he can! He laughs out loud. The laughter revives his spirits and he recalls with a grin that this is Christmas Eve. A surge of nostalgia and optimism soon has him singing his way through his repertoire of snow-covered Christmas songs as the plains of East Africa slip by on either side. The occasional branch-browsing giraffe and grazing zebra raises a head to watch for a moment as the old Land Rover speeds onwards with its trail of dust.

Naivasha town and the turn-off to Gilgil well behind him now, Theo realises with a shock that his mind has been coasting for miles. He is nearing the end of his second or third rendition of 'Good King Wenceslas' as he pulls thankfully off the road and onto the bumpy murram track that leads out to the school. His progress is slower here and the unsolved problem of what to do with the envelope catches up with him again, as does the red dust swirling up around the vehicle. He flicks on the wipers in an effort to keep the dust from settling across the windscreen; like driving through the snowstorm in the carol. Peering out through the dust he is humming now; '*In his master's steps he trod, where the snow lay dinted … dah, dah, dah, du, dah, dah, da-ah ..* ' singing the rest of the words under his breath. It helps him concentrate on the tricky business of keeping the vehicle on the road; swerving around rocky outcrops; narrowly avoiding bottoming-out on ridges or jamming a wheel in one of the many deep ruts scarring the track.

He mustn't take his eyes off the road to check his watch, but he is certain that it will be dark soon. The sun is setting fast in a blaze of orange and gold but evenings are virtually non-existent out here, so close to the equator, not like in England. How he misses those long balmy evenings of a Cornish summer. A vision of the Old Rectory, his family home in Kernow, springs fully formed into his mind. Evening light on honey-gold stone, the walled garden, the smell of fresh cut grass and the fragrance of ripening fruit from the apples trees. In the picture his sister Rose is laughing, swinging high on the rope swing that their father had slung over the branches. So long ago, so far away … and in that moment of missing, he knows his problem is solved.

The box. The secret box that Rose gave him after their parents died. He will keep the envelope safe in his special box. When he returns to England at the end of this school year, as he now determines to do, he will be able to bring the evidence straight to the top himself. He has connections after all. Daniel has connections in high places too and Jack is already there. He knows people; he has contacts in parliament and in the press. Together they will expose the inadequacy, the corruption at the heart of this colonial government, challenge the British politicians and present the facts to the British people.

Relief at the decision made is intense, a physical sensation like a flash flood. Theo sighs – a deep shuddering sigh. He is suddenly exhausted, completely drained. Arching backwards in the driving seat, he extends his cramped arms. God, he is tired! Another image arises unbidden – condensation on a cold glass, water first, then a large beer. He swallows hard, draws in a long deep breath, filling his lungs and tries to hold it for a count of ten, or longer like he used to as a child. But the air in the car is dry and dust-laden; he erupts in a fit of coughing, all the while struggling to keep his eye on the strip of road that is blearily visible through the dust-streaked windscreen. Just up ahead he catches sight of the wooden sign that marks the schools boundary – not far to go now. He starts to plan a bath, perhaps a nap before dinner, then that drink. He is wondering what Samson might have prepared for their meal, as the entrance to the school's compound comes into view just beyond the copse of ragged gum trees.

The pick-up truck catches him completely unawares. As the Land Rover approaches the familiar turning, the unknown truck, piled high, bristling with men brandishing sticks and knives, comes flaring at top speed up out of the driveway from the direction of the school buildings, flings itself in a hail of dust and stones out onto the road and hurtles off in the opposite direction. Theo stands on the brake, bringing the Land Rover to a screeching halt. For a fraction of a second, he is caught between two opinions. Should he pursue, try to apprehend the vehicle which was clearly trying to escape or should he let them get away, turn into the school, find out what was going on? His hesitation is short lived. He restarts the engine and heads, as fast as the car will carry him, down the driveway towards the school, towards his home, towards the people who are dear as family, the people he feels certain now are in mortal danger.

32

Cornwall, Lostwithiel – 2008

They'd come in Rosy's car this morning. Mara's Clio had been left back at Duloe. Patting the bonnet as they left, she'd laughed and said the old fellow deserved a rest. Actually she was glad of the opportunity to be a passenger for a change, sitting in the back, letting someone else make all the decisions. Fields, hedgerows and passing traffic blurred beyond the glass as she allowed her thoughts to drift, just vaguely aware of her mother and her sister chatting in the front of the Scenic.

It was an unfamiliar experience for her these days, being a passenger. She was always in the driving seat, literally and metaphorically. She nodded as the idea settled in with a sigh and a rueful smile. The first child, the big sister, the sensible one, everything under control, a '*control freak*' she'd been branded at the wrong end of one memorable relationship. Mara grinned at her reflection in the window-glass beside her.

Mara – why on earth had they called her 'Mara'? With a name like that you had to be strong, you had to be able to stick up for yourself. You couldn't really be a wimp if you were going to explain to everyone you met that you were called after a game reserve in East Africa. That you were named after your parents had enjoyed a night of passion in a tent beside a dirty brown river of the same name, filled with cavorting hippopotami. Her father had had no sympathy. He said she should be proud of her name. She was special, his Kenyan beauty. Mara shifted in her seat. Him again. She breathed deep. Everything – her strengths, her weaknesses, her self-confidence, her insecurities ... everything came back to him. She was not grinning now, her lips were clenched in a tight line and she caught herself grinding her teeth again. Recalling the dentist's advice, she forced herself to relax her jaw. But it was true. She sighed a deep shuddering sigh.

'Are you alright back there?' Ellen turned her head, looked back over her shoulder at her older daughter.

'I'm fine, thanks.' Mara's quick smile was reassuring. An answering smile from her mother, a few moments of easy silence, then Ellen and Rosy were chatting once more and Mara settled back to her thoughts.

She had loved her Dad so much, knew she always would – but sometimes he had made her so mad that it hurt. Love – that's what she supposed it was. Love – but why did it have to be so painful? Why did loving someone have to be so complicated? At least, it was for her; seemed like it always had been. Other people seemed to manage it: to love someone, to let them love you back. For her it was just not possible. She couldn't seem to ... what? What was it she couldn't do? She could love ... yes, she could do that. But she could not let herself be loved ... let herself be vulnerable ... was that it? Just thinking about it, her pulse quickened and she felt the familiar tightness in her chest. Tim, the one who had called her a control freak, the one whose calls she kept refusing ... he reckoned he understood her. He'd said on more than one occasion that she was holding herself back, that she was taking it out on all men – whatever 'it' was – that it was all her father's fault, that she would never be able to love another man, that nobody would ever be able to live up to her precious father. That's what he'd called him *precious* ... *'your precious father.'* Was he right?

And now look where this precious father had brought her. Here she was, on the way to meet up with someone who was most probably her long lost brother, about to meet her father's sister for the very first time. Each day was bringing fresh revelations, new surprises. Take yesterday for instance ... those diaries, the paintings, those awful photographs. If only someone could explain it all, someone who was there at the time. Before they left this morning her mother had made contact with one of her old friends who used to be the secretary at the school, to try and get hold of Uncle Jack's phone number. She'd promised to find out what she could and get back in touch. Mara knew that her mother was hoping against hope that Rose would be able to talk to them, perhaps even answer some of their questions, but she herself was not feeling optimistic, based on what the others had been saying about the old lady's present condition. Looking at photographs of Rose as a young woman, it had been plain to see the family likeness: the sandy curls, the light in her eyes, the easy smile. The others had all commented on the similarity and Mara had been convinced. There was no longer any doubt in her mind. Cornwall, the Old Rectory, these people ... it was all part of her family's past and now, back in Lostwithiel, they were heading full-tilt towards its future.

'This is it, Rosy. This is the turning. Turn left. Yes ... yes here. That's it. Look Mara, this is where we parked before. That's the Community Centre, over there.'

Ellen's excitement dragged her daydreaming elder daughter back to the present and guided her younger daughter into the car park. 'It was so crowded when we were here the other day, Rosy. You wouldn't believe it, there were so many people, so many cars. There's plenty of space today though. Look you can park over there, right next to the path. There's the seat look. That's where I sat to wait for you, Mara, that's where I met Gladys.'

Rosy parked the Scenic easily, nose on to the curb, right in front of the seat that seemed to mean so much to her mother. Ellen was already unbuckling her seat belt. She was clearly eager to get out and sit on the bench again, this time with both of her daughters.

'Hang on Mum. Wait a minute. Let's get ourselves sorted out first, shall we? Is it okay to just leave these bags open on the back seat do you think, if we're going inside? Do you think we should put them in the boot, cover them up or something?' Mara was rummaging in the carrier bags that Ellen had loaded into the back of the car. 'What is all this you've brought anyway, Mum? Are these more of Dad's diaries? What's this in here?'

Curiosity piqued by the particularly angular package, Mara reached out for the over-sized, white plastic bag and pulled it over to her lap.

'I know this. It's Dad's box ... his special box isn't it?'

The bag had folded back to reveal an inlaid wooden box, rather like a smaller version of a pirate's treasure chest. 'I remember this. He used to keep it in his study when we were kids, didn't he? I haven't seen it lately though, not since he retired, not since you moved house.' She lifted it out from the bag and held the box with both hands. It was quite heavy. She gave it a shake; listened. It sounded like a lot of papers, perhaps letters, a book, maybe one of his diaries. It sounded quite full. And then there was that slight rattling noise, coming from somewhere in the base. She shook it again.

'I brought it to show Rose, to show the others. Maybe she'll recognise it. Maybe they'll be able to work out how to get it open because I can't. I've tried.' Ellen's frustration clouded her face, slipped into her voice. 'Your father kept a lot of his most precious, private things in there. I know he made up stories about it for you girls, but he never shared its secrets with anyone, not as far as I know. He certainly never opened it for me. I've no idea what's inside.'

'He'd had it since he was a boy ... at least that's what he told us. So you're right Mum, Rose might recognise it and it might help her to remember. It was a good idea.' Rosy reached across the front seat and patted her mother's knee. Ellen's hopeful smile returned.

Mara was settling the old box back into its bag. She nodded to her sister who was watching her from the rear view mirror. 'All right. I think this is really the only thing of value in there, the only thing that might catch a car thief's eye I suppose. The rest is mostly just old books, papers, nothing that would arouse anyone's interest. I could just take the box with us if you like, in this shopping bag. It's not too heavy – not heavy at all really compared to the piles of marking you used to carry home every evening, Mum.' She laughed.

Ellen was pleased with the suggestion. She was all optimism again, keen to move on now that they had come this far.

'Just put that jacket over the other bags if you want to cover them up, Mara, but if I was a thief I reckon that might make me even more interested. I should leave them as they are if I were you.' She smiled over her shoulder and Mara nodded her agreement.

'All right, we'll leave it like it is and I'll carry the box. Here pass me your bag, Mum. It's not too heavy at all. It'll be interesting to see what's inside certainly. Didn't you find a key or something, Rosy? It looks like there should be a key. Perhaps one of the men can pick the lock. It's the sort of thing men do isn't it?' Mara laughed. It seemed funny to her, but then what did she really know about men? She pulled on the handle and the car door opened, letting in a draft of fresh clean air. It smelled of mown grass and warm blossom, much better than the air conditioning inside. 'Come on then. Race you to the seat.' Settling the bag over her shoulder, Mara slammed the door and set off briskly in the direction of the wooden seat. She easily reached the bench first and sat beaming in the sunshine, while her mother and sister sorted themselves out, locked up the car and made their way over at a steadier pace to take their places, one on either side of her.

Maisy spotted them straight away as she and her Dad pulled off the main road and into the car park, closely followed by Uncle Frank.

'There they are ... there look ... on that bench. They look like the three wise monkeys, sitting in a row like that.' She glanced across at her Dad. He was concentrating on the parking. She carried on with her chatter. 'Not that I'm making fun of them or anything. I really like them actually. I hope Grandma is well enough to meet them later. If she was her normal self, I know that she would love them. Ellen seems to be a lot like her, don't you think?' She took a brief pause for a breath. 'Do you think she already knew about them, Dad?' Another glance at her Dad saw him raise his eyebrows as he pulled the car into the space next to the Scenic, but no answer was forthcoming. Waving through the windscreen at the women, Maisy was not yet ready to stem the flow of questions. 'Dad, do you think Grandma was in touch with her brother all the time? Do you think that she knew about everything? Do you think she knows all about this Daniel Lind ... about Njeri, the woman in all those pictures?'

Dan turned off the engine and they sat in the quick silence. He smiled out at the waiting women, waved, turned to his daughter. 'Maisy, you remember what Uncle Frank was telling us last night, after they'd left, what he'd found out about the house, how the Old Rectory actually belongs to Grandma's brother, how Rose and her brother have been talking to the agents for that holiday property company, planning to sell the old house ... all that sort of thing? Does that sound as if they've been in contact?' He waited only the briefest of moments before answering his own question. 'I've been thinking about it ... and I reckon it does. I've got a strong feeling that Rose knows about everything. She was the older sister after all. After their parents died, I think that she would have felt that it was her responsibility to take care of him, to protect him ... you know what she's like. At least, you know what she used to be like ... before this illness, or whatever it is, took hold. I really hope she's feeling good today, that she can talk with us, meet them.' Maisy looked across at her father, sensed the weight on his shoulders. She reached out and hugged him. The exercise was a bit awkward in the confines of the car and father and daughter were soon giggling together. Dan made a show of pushing her away. 'Come on ... less of this ... we need to get out. They'll be wondering what's going on in here.' Grinning, they did exactly that.

Frank was already up at the bench, chatting easily to the three women. They rose as Maisy and Dan approached and soon the group was moving off together in the direction of the community centre coffee shop.

'What's that you've got in the bag then? The way you're clutching it, keeping it close, it looks like a treasure chest or something. It looks interesting.' Dan and Mara were walking together behind the others. He was relaxed in her company. His question was filled with good humour, teasing her, like an older brother might have done. At least, that was the thought that occurred to him, and he grinned.

'Ah ... you'll just have to wait and see.' Mara responded in kind. They were inside now, through the shady foyer, past lively pin-boards covered with cards and posters, advertising events as varied as their colours, up the few steps, around to the left and the bustling coffee shop came into view. On the threshold she relented. 'Actually it's Dad's ... or it used to be. It's his special box, where he kept his treasures. Apparently he had done ever since he was a little boy. Mum thinks that Rose might recognise it, that she might even know how to open it, because we can't. We're thinking that it might contain something that will help to explain all this.' Here she spread her hands to include him and Maisy and Frank, all of them. He took her meaning.

They were following the others now towards a free table for six. 'I reckon it's worth a try. It seems like a good idea. If it is familiar to her, she might start remembering. She might come back to us ... tell us what this is all about.' Dan pulled out a chair and Mara sat as he finished talking, sitting himself down beside her.

As the pair joined the group again, it was Ellen who had some news. 'Frank was just telling us something else he's found out, Mara. It seems that Theo, your father, is officially the owner of The Old Rectory, not Rose.'

Mara's astonishment showed from across the table as Ellen went on. 'And apparently there are other properties too, The Old School House being the largest, then three smaller terraced cottages. It seems that he and Rose together have been talking to Estate Agents. They were intending to sell The Old School House and the cottages along with some other outbuildings and a couple of paddocks, probably to a development company.' She paused, flared her eyes for effect. 'Rose was to have had a cottage built specially for her and it seems that your father was planning to use the funds raised to refurbish the Old Rectory. It's not clear what he was planning to do after that, but the solicitor thought that Rose was thinking, at least hoping that her brother might be planning to move back in himself.' Ellen's lips were uncharacteristically tight at this point and she flared her eyes again.

'Your mother says 'they were intending' ... that's because I've told them, the solicitors and the agents that is, to put a hold on it all. Things are different now. Until we've had chance to take it all in, work out what's right for everyone, I thought it would be best.' Frank's tone was sympathetic. He could well understand that all this new information was a lot for the girls to take in.

Ellen continued, her tone was brisk and business-like now, though Mara could sense something else brewing – tension certainly, but impatience too, and irritation. If her Dad were here, he would definitely have some serious explaining to do.

'I'm going to talk to our solicitors later, to see what they know. Apparently your father has also been using an agent in London, an old family friend it seems, to handle his affairs as far as all his Cornish dealings are concerned. Frank and Daniel will talk to him initially. And then there's a local man who's been dealing with Rose's affairs. I just wish your father were still here. To be quite honest with you, I don't know what to make of it. What did he think he was doing? Why did he have to make everything so complicated? Why didn't he talk to me about it?' Ellen sat back in her chair, folded her arms across her chest, clearly confused and not a little exasperated.

This time it fell to Rosy to smooth her mother's ruffled feathers. 'Let it go, Mum. It won't do any of us any good to get all wound up about it, will it? You know what he was like. He wanted to protect you, to take responsibility for everything, to have everything under control. Who knows, perhaps he really was going to bring us all together at last at The Old Rectory. He must have had a plan. If he hadn't died so suddenly like he did in the end, I would think that he was hoping his plans would all come together ... just in the nick of time. He would never have wanted to upset you Mum. You know that. I'm sure that he intended it all for the best. We just have to try and figure out what his plan was, don't you think?' Shoulder to shoulder with her mother, Rosy leaned in close, like a nudge. She did it again, nudging, finally coaxing a smile. Mother and daughter shared a chuckle while the others looked on, relieved. They all needed Ellen to stay positive.

And she did, stay positive that is, all the way through the chatter over coffee and doughnuts, through the easy stroll down through the old town still decked with strings of multi-coloured festive flags, through the push-button release of the heavy white door into the carpeted stillness of Rose's care home, right up until the moment that Maisy came back to fetch them from the soft-white-painted waiting room.

That had been the plan. Dan and Frank and Maisy would go on ahead to see how Rose had slept, how she was that morning, how she was feeling, if she was alert. Perhaps they would try to talk to nurse Rachael. Then, once they were sure that Rose would be able to understand what was happening they would talk to her about Ellen and the girls. If she seemed comfortable, if she wanted to meet them, Maisy would come to collect them. And now she had. At that moment, Ellen's warm heart plummeted and she felt a shiver of something like panic, the panic she remembered as a child called into the dentist's surgery. Theo's sister. After all this time she was actually going to meet her husband's family ... his sister.

'Come on, Mum. We can do this.'

Ellen looked up into the encouraging faces of her daughters, her Kenyan beauty and her English rose. They had already come to their feet and were waiting, hands outstretched, to help her up, to support her every step of the way. She smiled and stood, taking a hand of each. In her other hand, Mara held the bag containing Theo's treasure box close in to her side as they moved out from the safety of the waiting room and followed in Maisy's wake through the quiet corridors towards her Grandma's room. At the door, Maisy rested a hand on Ellen's arm.

'Relax. She's much better today, quite like her old self. You'll be fine. She wants to meet you. Come on in.'

From the armchair in the corner, the welcome that Rose offered was in her eyes, in her open arms. Ellen glimpsed the man she'd lost, her daughters their father. His salt-and-pepper curls; his pale-lashed eyes, clear turquoise-grey, like summer sun through sea-glass; his lop-sided smile; the slight left-lean of his fond-remembered head, the tilt they'd teased him about, aped so often, all here in this little woman beckoning them into her warm pink room.

'Come on in … yes that's it … come along in and close the door behind you.'

Her voice was soft, delicate like old rose-petals. She paused, patient while the women entered. Ellen, smiling, accepted the seat that Dan offered. Mara, still clutching the wooden box in the carrier bag, joined her sister with Maisy perched like fledglings on a wall, along the edge of the single bed. The small room was crowded now but as the new arrivals settled themselves, the air stilled and all eyes turned towards Rose. Her smile was calm; she seemed to have been expecting them. Her voice was steady as she spoke.

'We have never met, but I feel I have always known you. I am Rose. Your husband, your father … Theo … he was my brother. He loved you, dear Ellen, and your lovely daughters, very much.'

As their eyes met hers, each felt her smile like a blessing. Nobody moved. For a long moment no one spoke, until once more Rose's quiet voice broke the silence that had settled on the room.

'He was my little brother, you know … we played in the orchard … up and down on the swing … see-saw, Margery daw …' Lowering her eyelids as if searching for the image, Rose began to sing the nursery rhyme over and then over again, singing on to herself in a light girlish voice, chuckling at a scene only she could see.

Maisy, concerned for her grandmother, looked towards her dad. Ellen caught the glance, raised her brows in the same question. Dan shook his head slowly, lifted a finger in caution. Just wait. Mara shifted in her seat, adjusted the bag on her lap. After a moment or two, the singing tailed off and Rose was quiet again, her eyes closed. Still no one spoke into the silence that was once again growing around them.

And then, just when it seemed that she might have slipped away into her own world of memories, Rose returned to the room. She looked up sharply, then at each one of them in turn, meeting their anxious eyes with her own. As if in response to some inner voice the old woman nodded. It was time to continue. With both hands she patted her lap and drew in a long breath before taking up once more with the story she seemed now determined to tell.

'When our mother and father died Theo was afraid ... of the dark ... of a lot of things ... mostly that we would be lost ... that Father Christmas would not find us ... I took care of him. I gave him my special box to keep him safe. It made him brave ... made him smile. It helped him to be happy again ... he kept our mother's letters in the box ... his treasures ... as if he kept her there ... with him always. I think he even used to talk to the box ... like he was talking to her ... something like praying I suppose ... Our father ... and our mother ... who art in heaven ...' The older sister, old woman now, chuckled, shaking her head.

Dan glanced across at the package on Mara's lap. She caught his unspoken question and turned towards Ellen. Mother and daughter exchanged a glance, a barely perceptible shake of the head, a frown. Later they would show her the box ... later ... not yet.

'Theo was always a good boy ... he tried very hard to be good ...' Rose was nodding now, buoyed on the tide of her memory. Thoughtful, she lifted a hand and tucked a stray curl back behind the clip at her ear. 'He wanted to be like our father, to be strong, to be the very best that he could be. That was what our mother used to call him ... her best little man.' She shifted in her chair, sat straighter. She smiled, fond, as if she saw him standing there, young, bright-faced, eager with news of blackbirds nesting in the apple tree, tousle-haired, cheeks flushed with success from the hundred yards dash at the school Sports Day. Her family watched, waited once more while Rose dawdled amongst her memories, drifting somewhere between then and now.

The quiet voice drew them back from their own wanderings.

'I think that for Theo, leaving our home was the hardest thing ... leaving Cornwall ... going away to school. He knew it was his duty to be brave but it was hard for him, for us both, at first. He never gave in you know. He worked hard. He wanted to please our father, to make our mother proud. I think he believed that they would still know.' She paused again, looked directly at Ellen. 'He grew to be a brave man, a good man. I was proud of him. I think our mother was too.' In that moment, his sister and his widow shared a look of understanding.

Nodding, Rose leaned back into her chair, her thin fingers smoothing the plum-coloured velvet arms. The motion, like rocking, was strangely soothing. Her listeners looked on as her hands slowed their stroking, stilled, settled. Her eyelids sank. The rise and fall of her breathing, snuffling, like a baby's, lulled the room. No one moved, no one spoke to disturb her slumber... as if the woman in the chair were the princess Beauty, cursed to sleep for a hundred years and they, her courtiers, bound by the same spell.

'Rose, my love' ...

The door swung open. Nurse Rachel's bright voice broke into the silence that had settled thick, like a cobweb veil. 'Oh, I'm so sorry. It was so quiet in here. I thought you'd all gone.' The young woman's startled eyes took in the scene; her first thought was that someone had pressed the 'pause' button, like on the TV back home. But then, as in slow motion, Frank rose from his seat and the others turned towards her. 'I just thought Rose might like a sandwich or something for her lunch ... that's all. I didn't mean to disturb you.' Rachel was blustering in the doorway, a warm pink flush colouring her cheeks.

'Oh no ... don't worry. It's alright, really Rachel.' Frank raised his hand. He was smiling now, reassuring. 'Mum is fine; she was happy, telling her story. She just dropped off to sleep a few minutes ago. We were letting her doze, waiting to see ... to see if she would wake again and want to continue or perhaps ... I don't know ... we want to do what's best for her ... what do you think? Should we just slip out and leave her sleeping?' Frank's voice was hushed, almost a whisper. He spoke for them all.

'It seems like your mother is going to answer for herself.' The young nurse was easy again, smiling, pointing towards the corner of the room where Rose was stirring in her chair, opening her eyes, remembering. The slow smile that dawned on the old woman's face as she looked around at her visitors, across to Rachel, was in her voice as she spoke.

'My family have come.'

There was contentment, perhaps pride, certainly no sadness, in the sigh that followed this declaration. To those who had loved this woman for the whole of their lives her words were a benediction. To Ellen, to her daughters, they were a welcome home.

'That's lovely, Rose. Well I'll just leave you then to enjoy your company. You can have your lunch a bit later ... after they've all gone.' The nurse turned to Frank. 'If you let me know when you're leaving, I'll pop back in and make sure everything's alright ... sort out some lunch for her ... she'll probably be ready for something by then.'

'Thanks, Rachel. That'll be great.' Frank nodded towards her. He was thankful that Rose had such a kind young woman to take care of her now. 'I shouldn't think we'd be staying much longer ... we don't want to overtire her. But it's lovely to see her so much brighter, more with-it today, more like the old Rose.' He grinned across at his mother and winked. Her smile was his reward.

As the heavy door closed itself quietly behind the nurse, Mara caught the smile that passed between mother and son. She made her own decision. The rustling of the carrier bag caught the attention of them all. Rose's sharp intake of breath as the box emerged from its wrapping caused Mara a brief moment of uncertainty. She hesitated. Had she made a mistake? The look on the old woman's face quickly allayed her fears.

'It's my box ... my secret box, Theo's treasure box.' Rose was wide-awake now, sitting bolt upright in her chair, reaching out. Her family looked on in astonishment as she beckoned with outstretched fingers, as if urging this long-lost friend to fly into her arms of its own accord.

Mara breathed deep, exhaled her relief through puckered lips. She rose from her perch on the single bed and lifted the box into Rose's welcoming embrace, settled it onto her lap. No lost kitten ever received a fonder homecoming. Smoothing its softened contours, stroking its inlaid patterns, inspecting with her finger-tips the marks and scratches of its long experience; Rose was lost to the lookers-on. Ellen watched in amazement, as her husband's sister upended the precious box, began feeling with her fingers over its base.

'Aha! There it is!' Finding what she sought, the old woman shrieked with delight as a panel flicked open to reveal a small compartment that had been hitherto concealed.

'Look! It was our secret ... the key.' Rose had lifted out the little silver key and now held it up for everyone to see. 'It was our secret, Theo's and mine; no one else knew; that's what made it so special. Look.' Rose was giggling now, a girl again, as she inserted the little key into a hole in the side of the box and turned it, twice. Like a spring released, the wooden base, which it seemed was actually the lid, jerked upwards. The box was open. Grinning broadly, Rose looked to her audience, anticipating applause. The wide eyes and open mouths did not disappoint. Satisfied, she chuckled, shaking her head from side to side as at some private joke and lifted the lid. She peered inside. Reaching into the box, she rummaged amongst her brother's treasures.

Spellbound, her family watched her sift through the contents, lift out a handful of envelopes. Three seemed quite new, rectangular, thick, cream in colour. Others looked older, tissue-paper thin, possibly airmail. A small black and white photograph slipped out from between them, fluttering to the floor, settling like a butterfly on Rose's pink slipper. Frank leaned forward and plucked it gently with his musician's fingers, handed it to his mother. It was of a young girl.

'Look. It's me. I gave it to him when he went off to school.' Rose held the old photograph out for them all to see. 'I knew he'd keep it in here.' The old woman's bright eyes were shining with quiet assurance. The bond between this brother and sister had been an enduring one. She held out the hand still clutching the envelopes towards her son. 'Here. You take these my dear.'

Frank reached forward and took the bundle from his mother. All eyes were now focused on the Music Man, as he settled back into his chair, fingering through the envelopes and papers like notes on his accordion. He hesitated; they saw the quick frown. Looking up, he met Ellen's gaze. The expression on his face was hard to read, almost solemn. Ellen paled as Frank picked out one of the thick cream envelopes; handed it to her. In her husband's familiar, perfectly formed cursive hand she saw her own name, in black ink across the front of the long, strangely formal envelope: '*My dear wife, Ellen.*'

33

Cornwall, Old Rectory – 2008

There had been three more envelopes, exactly like this one that Frank had passed to her, each addressed in Theo's flowing hand. Ellen had always admired, even envied, the skill of his penmanship. With her index finger she traced the black-ink curls of her name, picturing the golden nib of his fountain pen drawing the thick, confident line over the cream vellum. Then, more slowly, she re-traced her title – *'My dear wife'*. Lingering over the possessive pronoun her smile was tinged with something like regret. She had been, totally, completely his – but had he been hers, completely hers? She spoke it aloud: 'My dear husband ... Theodore.'

Earlier, in his sister's small bedroom, she had felt him so close. Impossible, yet it seemed as if he had known that his family would be there together; as if he had planned to be there too. Frank was his messenger. After Ellen had received her envelope, Theo had addressed their daughters: *'For Mara and Rosy – my beloved daughters.'* They were to share this final message from their father. Frank had offered the creamy envelope into Mara's opened hands.

As soon as it had become clear that there were others, Frank had suggested, and they had all agreed, that it would be better, more appropriate, if the envelopes were opened privately. These last communications with husband, father, brother, seemed to demand an intimacy, which would not be possible in the little room.

Like a child at a party, Rose had watched wide-eyed as they had received their gifts from the box, hopeful then crestfallen as what appeared to be the final letter was handed to Dan. *'For*

Daniel – my son.' In his warm, Cornishman's voice Frank had read the inscription. The words were simple, the message clear. Mara had glanced at her mother then, anxious. But Ellen's face was calm; she was watching Dan. As he accepted this first public affirmation from his father, the envelope from his brother, the younger man had seemed for a moment to be close to tears. Ellen had fought a strong urge to reach out, to comfort him as he lowered his head, taking the letter into his cupped hands, as if he were receiving an honour.

At this point, Ellen remembered that Frank had stood and made to lift the wooden box from his mother's lap. Rose had in-stinctively hugged the treasure close, raised her chin, looked up at her son with the merest hint of a challenge. Calmly he met her gaze, held it for a moment, before she let the box go with a little smile. Returning to his own chair, with the treasure chest wide open on his lap, Frank had made a show of scrutinising its remaining con-tents. After the briefest of pauses, he had winked at Rose, smiling as he drew out an identical envelope. Childlike, she grinned, taking his meaning. She was not forgotten. This one was for her.

Things had moved on quickly after that. Rose had been eager to open her letter, but Frank had urged her to wait until the others had left. He had promised then to come back and read it with her later, after she'd had some lunch and a rest. This idea was met with a frown, a shrug and then a sigh of resignation. When Rose had then gestured towards her old treasure box, he'd suggested that maybe he could first take everything else out of the box and put it in Mara's crumpled carrier bag, so that Ellen could take it all away with her to look through later. Rose could then keep the box, which she seemed to have reclaimed as her own. When no one raised any objections, he had promptly emptied the contents of the box into the carrier bag, which he'd handed to Ellen. His mother was happily caressing her treasure box as her family bid their farewells.

The carrier bag was lying on the sofa beside her now and Ellen reached across and touched the recyclable white plastic. It had sprawled sideways and some of the items inside had slipped over each other, spewing out onto the cushions in their rush to be picked first. Well, they would have to wait. She stood and moved away from the sofa, towards the bay window that gave out over the late afternoon garden.

They were at the Old Rectory. The morning's developments had taken everyone by surprise, left them all feeling a bit shell-shocked if truth were told. Like the others, Ellen's early concerns had all been for Rose, her health, her state of mind, how she might react to meeting these new members of her family. None of them had anticipated an encounter with Theo himself.

By the time they'd finally emerged from the quiet, carpeted corridors into the fresh air of the sunlit car park, Ellen had felt drained and she and the girls had been only too glad to go along with Frank's suggestion that they should all go back to the house together. He would pick up some bread and a few other bits for lunch on the way up through the town and then there would be time and space for them all to relax afterwards, to read their letters from Theo when they felt ready, to reflect on the past and to consider its implications for the present. It had seemed only natural that they should be here, in this house, in these gardens, to hear the last words that he'd wanted but for whatever reason had been unable to say face-to-face to those he had loved.

Looking out over the sloping lawns, through a drift of peonies and shoulder-high delphiniums, Ellen spotted her girls. Mara's arm was around her sister's shoulders as they sat close on the wooden bench. From this distance Ellen couldn't see for certain, but she guessed they were reading their father's letter.

'They get on well, don't they?'

Ellen turned quickly. She had not heard his approach but the look in her eyes told Frank his company was welcome.

'Yes, they do. They always have.' She smiled, watching them from a distance. 'They're as different as chalk and cheese but yes they get on well together. I'm glad that Theo's letter was for them both. They'll be able to help each other.'

'What about you? Have you opened yours yet?' Frank's tone was soft.

'No. Not yet. I don't know if I'm ready ...' her voice tailed off. She reached into the pocket of her linen trousers and drew out a tissue. 'I just don't know if I'm ready ...' again she was unable to finish the sentence and she dabbed at her nose with the crumpled tissue. She turned and looked straight at the man standing behind her, her face a picture of despair. 'I really don't know if I'm ready to listen to him yet. I just don't want to talk to him. Actually Frank, I know I shouldn't say this, but I feel so angry with him right now. In fact I don't think I want to see him or his letter; I don't want to talk to him at all!' Pent up tears flowed hot, unchecked, down over her cheeks, dripped from her chin. Frank reached out, pulled her towards him and she rested her head against his chest, crying quietly into the shoulder of this man whom she had barely met yet who had so quickly become a friend.

It was several minutes before Ellen pulled away, un-crumpling the tissue and blowing her nose. She wiped at her wet cheeks with the back of her hand as he watched her.

'I'm sorry about that.' Her hands were clasped in front of her now, still clutching the damp tissue as she looked up at Frank. 'I'm so sorry.' She lowered her eyes.

'Hey, come on ...you have nothing whatsoever to feel sorry for.' His hands were on her shoulders, reassuring. 'Look, why don't you just leave the letter for a bit? There's no rush is there? What about the other things, the things from the box? If you like, we could go through those together. It might be helpful ... you know ... having someone else to talk to, share it with. If you'd like to, that is ...' Just for a moment he hesitated.

'Frank, thank you.' The warmth was back in her eyes, her voice. 'I would like that. I'd like that very much.' She turned back towards the garden where her daughters were still on the bench, heads close, shades of gold amongst the pinks and blues. She was not needed out there. Frank was at her shoulder; he was watching them too. Ellen heard the sudden hesitation in his voice.

'Of course, you might prefer to leave it for now ... let them help you ... Mara and Rosy ... go through your husband's letters and things together. I could really understand that, if you wanted to do that, I mean.'

'I've thought about that, and, you know, I don't think I want to do it with them. Some things are too personal, even now. They might both be grown-ups, but to me, they are still my children. I just feel that perhaps this is one of those things I would like to do myself.' Ellen swallowed, looked down; she was twisting her wedding band as she spoke. 'Who knows what he might have kept in that box. He was a very private man. He certainly kept secrets.' She glanced up at the man beside her, his sister's son; just one of the many things that Theo had kept from her. Closing her eyes, she tried hard to conjure up an image of her husband's face as she went on, whether still speaking to Frank or simply giving voice to her thoughts was unclear. 'He was passionate too ... but he was really quite shy underneath it all. He was easily embarrassed. He loved his daughters very much, but even so I am sure that there would have been some things that he would still prefer to keep from them.' At the mention of his daughters, her thoughts flew to his son. She turned to Frank with her question. 'But what about Dan ... and Maisy ... are they all right? Shouldn't you be with them?'

He was on safer ground here and he was smiling as he answered. 'You know ... I think that Dan is fine, or at least he will be, once he's had a chance to take it all in. This letter from his father, being included like that, called 'my son' in front of you all. It took him by surprise.'

Without pausing for thought, Ellen interrupted him. Her tone was uncharacteristically sharp. 'It was a shock for my girls too, when you read out what Theo had written. It was like hearing it spoken in their dad's voice ... hearing that they really did have a brother ... three siblings instead of two ... sharing him ... all these years they'd thought he was theirs alone ...' she hesitated. She had not found it easy herself.

Frank nodded. He could scarcely imagine what Ellen had had to confront in these last days, about the man she'd loved, about their relationship. Looking at her now, he was amazed all over again at her composure, her compassion for others, and her complete lack of self-pity. This woman reminded him so much of his mother, of Rose when she was brighter, before this damned creeping dementia had begun to diminish her, to take her from them.

Sensing his eyes on her, Ellen looked up, smiled, embarrassed; 'I'm sorry, Frank. It's not your fault. I just feel so frustrated with Theo. How could he put them through this? And Dan? I'm sure he found it really hard, in front of everyone like that.' She was shaking her head from side to side, her eyes back on the garden.

It was Frank's turn to speak his thoughts. 'Actually, I thought that my brother ... that Dan ... seemed quite overwhelmed. It was as if he had finally heard his father's voice. To be honest I thought he might cry. I looked across at Maisy then and I'm sure she had the same thought. She's such a good girl. I think you'll really love her as you get to know her. She's got so much of her grandmother's good sense. She has what I've heard described as 'emotional intelligence' in spades. She'll be a big help to Dan over in the coming days. In many ways he's had this hanging over him his whole life. In fact I wouldn't mind betting he'll be glad to have everything out in the open at last. He's just kind of ignored his father, blanked him out; like he tried to pretend he didn't exist. But I reckon he might be ready now ... to face up to his past and deal with it, if you know what I mean. Maisy is really good for him. I heard her, you know. She just told him straight out to get on and read the letter by himself and then she would be there to talk it all over with him afterwards.'

Frank had turned and started to move away from the window as he spoke and Ellen was following him back into the room. He headed for the fireplace and she watched him reach out for the old photograph of her husband.

'That was before I even knew him, you know.' Ellen nodded. They were standing close, the young Englishman and the African chief staring back at them, unsmiling. 'Just look at him – so young, so eager. He looks every inch the idealistic young Englishman, don't you think?' She smiled, glanced up at Frank, before turning back to the photograph. 'I wonder what it was that happened to him, what it was that changed everything, that made him cut himself off so completely from this home, his family, from everything he knew, as far as I can tell.'

Again she looked up at Frank but this time she was no longer smiling. She shook her head. 'Something must have happened back then, I'm sure it did, something so dramatic, so dreadful that it could never be reconciled, not with his past in Cornwall, nor with his future life with me, with his daughters. Whatever could it be, Frank? Whatever could it be?' Her voice wavered. 'How could he live with that secret?'

Frank set the photograph back down on the mantelpiece; he had certainly not intended to upset her. He turned: 'Shall we?'

At her nod, with his hand at her elbow, he guided her gently towards the sofa and the waiting carrier bag. Who knows, perhaps here they would discover some of the answers to her many questions.

34

Kenya, Rift Valley - 1961

'Where is everyone?' Has he spoken the words aloud or are they just in his head?

The impossible silence, the stillness, the complete absence of life … the scene before him seems otherworldly, held as on a breath, his own indrawn breath. Rolling clouds of dust that have churned in the wake of his careering vehicle finally catch up. Driver's door flung wide, the car stands empty now as the insidious red dust billows inside, settles over the man. Like a spider with a fly, it enshrouds him, stealing into orifices, sealing his nostrils.

The sneeze is tumultuous. The shock of it shifts his feet, frees him from the spell. It kick-starts his senses and the scene is suddenly drenched with sound: scraping and screeching of cicadas; plinking of frogs, like pebbles flung into pools; whooping of monkeys, mournful through the darkening trees; countless other night noises that he could not have named. And then he catches it, the shrill ululating, the wailing, rising up with the wisps of acrid smoke from the native village. Something terrible has happened here.

He is running now, full tilt towards the schoolhouse, stumbling over the stones. He is bounding up the steps to the veranda, bursting through the hanging door, calling out their names:

'Daniel! Njeri!'

He is calling as he flings open other doors to other rooms, to the kitchen:

'Daniel! Njeri!'

He is calling their names as he crashes through the opened door from the kitchen to the blackness at the back of the house. He is calling their names into the echoing wall of night that blocks his path:

'Daniel! Njeri!'

Black fear is invading his thoughts. White terror is tightening in his chest. Dread is driving red through his veins, throbbing in his ears. They are not here. He steps back into the empty kitchen. For the first time he takes in the wreckage: pots and pans strewn across the wooden floor; chairs, stools up-ended; blood. He bends and dabs his finger into a sticky, black puddle. The sharp smell of iron fills his nostrils. Blood. Lots of blood.

Wheeling around, crashing heedless back through the house, he follows the gory trail along the unlit hallway, onto the veranda, down over the steps, veering off in the direction of the headmaster's garden. The trail is black, unmistakeable. Heart pounding, head swimming with each wheezing breath, he stops dead, pressing his hands against his heaving chest. Ahead of him Theo can just make out the bougainvillea-hung entrance to the garden, Aunt Catherine's precious haven of rest leached of its vivid colours now by this terrible night. The prim wooden gates have been wrenched from their hinges. They hang lopsided, sagging in shame, like a blouse ripped from the breasts of a woman ravaged. Beyond them the black hole gapes.

Slowly now, watchful, he moves towards this hellish gateway. Beneath the arching foliage, tentative he reaches out. His fingers come back stained with blood. He catches his breath as his searching foot nudges something soft, lumpish. It tilts away from him in the darkness. The stench is sickening. Fighting against his rising stomach he clutches one hand tight over his mouth, his nose. There is blood, so much blood. Murderous deeds have been done here. His eyes in the darkness make out more bloody lumps, haphazard over the black grass. In a flash he recalls the clustered pangas, the killing knives piled in the escaping vehicle. The body, or what is left of it, has been lashed to the thorn tree. He sees it: slashed; gashed; headless. Limbs, or parts of limbs are gone; organs dangle. Clothing has been rent but enough remains for Theodore to know his friend. This is Daniel.

The vomiting goes on and on. He fears it may never stop. He has witnessed savagery before, but none like this. This is the stuff of hell. Lurching blindly now, he makes his stumbling way back to the steps. He collapses against the veranda rail and slides down into blessed oblivion.

'*Bwana* Theo! Bwana Theo! *Kuja! Kuja hapa!*' Come! Come here! The young voice is urgent; the fingers clutching his arms are sharp. They dig into his flesh, dragging at his heavy limbs. His eyelids seem weighted down; he struggles to lift them. As his vision clears, he finds himself staring into the eyes of a boy from the village – his addled brain cannot find the boy's name but that is small matter now. '*Kuja! Kuja!*' The boy wants him to come. 'Njeri ... Njeri ... *Kuja!*' Finally Theo's head clears. It is Njeri. The boy wants to take him to Njeri.

Alert, he scrambles to his feet, struggling at first to find a balance on his cramped feet and in his seared stomach. He clutches a hand to his mouth. The boy grabs hard at his other hand, drags him towards the African village and Theo is conscious once more of that eerie sound, the shrill keening, ululating, loud and long into the night. The moon is up and the familiar mud and grass huts are silhouetted, stark against the arching sky. The stars look down. He remembers with a start that this is Christmas Eve.

As Theo enters through the low opening, comes upright inside the round hut, sharp smoke from the smouldering wood fire in the centre of the flattened-earth floor stings his nose, makes his eyes run. He is rubbing at them with his balled hands before he remembers the blood ... Daniel's blood. For a moment he thinks he might fall in a faint. Then he becomes aware of eyes watching him. This is Njoroge's hut. He is there, inscrutable, his youngest wife is beside him. Her large, round eyes are brimming with fear. Across from these two, slumped on a mattress, is Njeri. Her dark face seems grey in the firelight, gaunt. Her dress at the neck is ripped, the wrapped skirt torn. With her right hand she is pressing hard against her hip, against the side of her pregnant belly. There is blood oozing from a gash, a panga slash, long and deep across her left shoulder, onto her upper arm.

'What have they done?' He dreads her answer.

'You must take me, Theo. Daniel's son ... he is coming ... soon. You must take me to Joyce. You must take me to Kijabe.'

Her eyes hold his. She does not plead. She does not explain. This and this he must do. Her voice is empty, all passion spent. She attempts to rise and he moves towards her, takes her arm, eases her to her feet. She stumbles, refuses his hand.

'Wait outside. I will come.'

He lowers his head and is once more out in the vast African night, waiting, so small beneath the stars. Soon she emerges through the hut's low doorway, struggles to come upright but again she stumbles. This time she does not refuse his help. Without a word, he scoops her into his arms and strides back up towards the waiting vehicle.

It is not until they reach the junction with the road that she speaks again. Her silence has kept them safe, as the car's headlamps sliced through the darkness, making a tunnel of the long tree-fringed track. Theo's struggle to manage the desperate urgency of his mission with his desire to keep this woman safe has till now occupied all his thinking. Daniel is dead. He, Theodore, must bring Daniel's wife ... and his child ... to the hospital at Kijabe. His grip is tight on the steering wheel, knuckles sharp and white, nails biting hard into the heel of his hands as he swings the vehicle once more out onto the road.

'Samson. It was Samson.' Her voice is small beside him in the dark, but clear.

'Samson?' His eyes are staring straight ahead, straining onto the road.

'It was Samson who led them to him, who brought those men to kill Daniel.'

'What do you mean? Samson? Why would Samson want to kill Daniel? Why would anybody want to kill Daniel?' His pain, his confusion is thick in his voice.

'The oath. They had made Samson swear an oath. They forced him ... they wanted to find ... to kill Kernowi.' A sharp intake of breath. She winces, clutches the edge of the seat as the car strikes hard against the edge of a pothole.

'Sorry.'

'Don't worry, Theo. Just keep going, keep driving. I want to tell you. I want you to understand what happened … for Daniel's sake.' She pauses at the mention of her husband's name. 'Do you remember that night … it was Christmas … when I came late to the school … I was injured … with Samson? We were told he had been tortured. We rescued him. On the way back we were ambushed. He was badly hurt. I think I always had my suspicions … something about that night didn't seem quite right. It was part of their plan, to get him into the school … as a spy … a cook. Samson believed that Daniel was Kernowi.'

'What? But Daniel was not Kernowi. I know there were rumours around Nairobi … but why did Samson think that? Anyway, who are they, these men who made him swear? Is it Mau Mau? Or was someone else behind it? Who were these men that came tonight? Where did they come from with their killing madness? Who was their leader?' His questions tumble staccato, like shots sprayed into the dark between them.

'I don't know, Theo. I don't know. It all happened so fast. At first we thought it was you, back from Nairobi. We were ready to start the Christmas celebrations. I had gone to the guest-house to collect some gifts that I'd hidden there. It happened so quickly. There was so much yelling and shouting, whooping … war cries filling the air: *'Uhuru!'* Theo, I was stunned. I didn't know what to do.' The horror is in her voice. He hears the tears behind her words as she struggles to go on with the task she has set herself.

'Daniel was in the kitchen. I heard them burst in on him. They were beating him, shouting at him, they had clubs, pangas. They dragged him out into the darkness, to the garden, Theo. He was wounded, covered in blood … oh Theo … he was bleeding, bleeding. I saw him. The noise, Theo, there was so much noise. I ran out then, tried to get to him. Somebody grabbed me. They had tied Daniel to the thorn tree. They were cutting him, slashing at him. There were so many of them. His head had flopped forward, onto his chest. I thought he might be already dead.' She pauses.

Theo flicks his eyes from the road, glances across at the woman beside him. She seems shrunken. Njeri frowns, clutches at her side. She shifts herself in her seat. Blood is seeping from the wound at her shoulder, but she will go on with her story.

'One of them grabbed a handful of his hair ... his beautiful golden hair all bloodied from the beating ... they pulled his head upright. I could see his face. Theo, it was awful. Then Daniel, my Daniel, he lifted his eyelids. He was not dead. The blood-crazed man shouted into his face: 'You are *Kernowi!* You are *Kernowi!*' Now her hands are covering her face. Through her fingers, she continues, her voice barely above a whisper.

'For a moment ... I thought Daniel ... my beautiful Daniel ... I thought he smiled. But perhaps I was mistaken. Oh Theo, you'll never believe what he did next. His eyes looked awful, bloodied and swollen ... but he looked straight at me and he tried to sing. It was your song ... you know ... the one about Trelawney ... '*and shall Trelawney live, and shall Trelawney die ...*' he sang, Theo. He sang your song. He knew what he was doing. It made them mad ... they knew what it meant. It drove them to a frenzy. He sang your song.' She looks straight across into the eyes of the man to whom she has entrusted her life, her baby's life.

Theo's face is white in the car's half-light. He is close to exhaustion but he must forge on through this unspeakable night. There is far to go. Naivasha is still ahead and the hospital even farther. They pass a mile or two in silence but for the drone of the car's engine. Her dark head droops forwards. He thinks she might be sleeping.

'They killed him, Theo.'

She is suddenly awake, shifting in her seat, her hand pressing hard against her side. He catches the stifled cry of pain; the time must be near for the child to be born. His quick glance seems almost furtive. For a second, a fraction of a second, she meets his eyes before his focus flicks back to the road ahead. Her words are without expression. They cut him like a knife.

'Daniel wanted them to think that he was Kernowi, that he was you. He loved you, Theo ... like you were his brother.'

The man beside her is silent, caught up in a flood tide of memory. *'Greater love ...'* the words are in his head. He cannot trust himself to speak.

The road ahead glows white in the headlamps. Thorn trees catch the light, their feathered fronds white-dusted like snow, weaver bird's nests hanging from their branches like baubles. A group of late-grazing gazelles, caught in the glare, flick up their feet, white tails flashing to the safety of the dark. Night hunters lurk in the shadows.

Distraught, Theo strains forward, hunched over the wheel, urging the vehicle onward, as fast as the road will allow. He knows this journey well ... he has driven it not many hours ago in the opposite direction, but now everything seems different, more perilous, more fraught with dangers. Every bump and swerve, every skid over loose stones – his fear is for her, for the child. For several miles she is silent. He hopes against hope that she is dozing; that she is finding some relief in sleep.

'They would have killed me too.'

Something has roused her. She is pulling herself upright in the seat beside him. 'Samson saved me, Theo. They would have taken me, killed *Kernowi*'s son. Samson was brave. He pulled them off; he put himself in front of me. He yelled at them, told them this was not *Kernowi*'s son. He thought to lie. He did not know it ... but in that thing at least, he spoke the truth. He shouted that I was your wife, Theo. That the baby was your son.' Her hands are on her belly. 'He grabbed me, grabbed my arms. He pushed me away, begged me to run for my life, run to the village. He saved me, Theo. He saved my baby.'

Beside him in the darkness her thin voice has risen to a sharp crescendo. Nothing he can do or say will bring comfort. His silence along the road is all he can offer. He knows that she is crying quietly. Her quick sniffs, her thick breaths, these tell-tale sounds betray her private grief. After a while she falls silent, her hand resting light over the top of her belly, fingers tip-tapping in time with some rhythm that only she can hear. It seems to him she lulls her child. Her voice is calm when she speaks again.

'My baby ... I think we shall meet him soon. You must be his father now, Theodore. Daniel's son ... he will need you. You must keep him safe.'

35

'I remember this one.'

Perched on the edge of the sofa Ellen was sorting through the photographs from the carrier bag, from Theo's special box – the ones that he had counted as his treasures. With a quick smile of recognition, she selected one from the pile on her lap.

'Look at him, Frank. He looks every inch the proud father doesn't he? Look at that grin. Our friends used to laugh, you know, tease him about it. I remember when it was taken. There was another one, with us both in, but that one doesn't seem to be here.'

Ellen held the picture out for Frank to see. He took it, looked down at the man holding a baby, and looked back up at her. The tension that had clamped her lips and creased her forehead had vanished. He smiled. To oblige her, he looked more closely at the photograph. She was right. The man did look proud. His grin to the camera was broad, his cheeks glowing. The chubby, bald-headed baby was dribbling, wrapped in a lacy shawl, cradled in her father's smart-suited arms.

'It's Mara – our first daughter. She was such a delight.'

'Well, she certainly looks different without her curls.' He grinned, and so did Ellen. They were still chuckling when Mara herself appeared at the French doors, rattling on the handle. Her sister was at her side, peering in through the windows. Frank was in jovial mood as he turned the key and let the girls in.

'Aha, the lady herself.' He turned back to Ellen. 'I was right. She definitely looks better with hair.' His comment caused a further outbreak of mirth, leaving the girls bemused.

'Mother! What's been going on in here?'

'To think we were worrying about you, and here you are having all the fun.' Rosy held a straight face. It was her turn to tease.

'Oh, come on you two ... hardly that. Where's your sense of humour?' Ellen was smiling as she rose to greet her daughters. 'We've just been sorting through the things from your Dad's box. I've been looking at the photographs first, showing Frank your baby pictures, Mara.'

'Oh, I see ... and that's what has caused all this hilarity is it, pictures of me.' Mara was grinning now as she made to grab the photograph from Frank's hands. 'Come on then; let's have a look.' Quick as a flash he lifted it high above his head and laughing, skipped out of her reach. The resulting chase around the furniture was a moment of fun for them both and set the others laughing.

Rosy was soon joining in. 'Hey, Frank, I thought you were one of the grown-ups. Go on Mara ... I'll get him round this way ... that's it ...grab it!'

'Uncle Frank! What's all this noise? What are you doing with Rosy? Put her down!' Maisy burst into the sitting room from the hallway to find Frank battling with the two girls, and everyone shrieking with laughter.

'It's all their fault ... it's nothing to do with me ... honest, miss.' Frank disentangled himself, grinning. Leaving Mara and her sister poring over the photograph, he came back across to the sofa where Maisy had joined Ellen. The mood was lighter now and the piles of papers, old envelopes and various photographs set out on the long coffee table no longer seemed quite so intimidating. Ellen was busy explaining their strategy to the young woman who had settled down beside her.

'We decided to sort things out first, into piles. Some of those old airmail letters are really fragile ... look ... like tissue paper. They were sent to Theo and his sister, your Grandma, from Kenya. Look at the dates on the stamps. I think they're from his parents, when he was a little boy, when he and Rose were left back in England. I haven't looked at them yet. Look at the beautiful handwriting. It reminds me of Theo's.'

'These envelopes look more formal, more official, don't they? It looks like they might contain some important documents, or something like that.' Maisy had leaned forward and picked up a large, brown envelope. 'This one's got a solicitor's name on the back. Look ... and there's an address.' She shook it. 'It rattles. There is something inside. I can feel it.'

'Let's just leave the letters for now, shall we, especially the official ones ... do you mind?' There was an edge to Ellen's voice and she was frowning again, suddenly vulnerable. Frank heard it. He looked up quickly.

'Just leave it for now, Maisy. The time will come for detective work, don't you worry.' He was teasing. She caught his meaning as he glanced across at Ellen. The smile she gave him in return was warm: 'What a lovely man you are!' but with wisdom beyond her years she did not speak the thought aloud.

Frank drew her into the conversation. 'What's happened to that elusive brother of mine anyway, your father? Have you seen him recently?'

'I went up to his room to see how he was getting on. He was still reading the letter from his father. He said he was fine ... that he was nearly finished ... then he might to go down to the old gardener's cottage to look at some of the furniture and stuff there. Apparently his father had mentioned a few things particularly. I asked him if he wanted me to go with him but he said thanks ... he wanted to do this by himself if I didn't mind. I told him of course I didn't mind and that I would be down here with you lot when he was ready.' She looked from Frank to Ellen then across to the sisters.

'Are there any photographs of me there, Mum?' Rosy was ready to move on. She came over to kneel beside her mother at the coffee table. Mara followed.

Ellen looked from one to the other. 'Are you girls all right? Have you read your father's letter?'

Mara answered for them both. Her voice was soft and her hand was resting on her mother's knee. 'We're fine, Mum. Don't worry. It was good actually ... almost like listening to him ... as if he was talking to us. Mum he was so warm. It was like he was giving each of us his blessing. There were other things too, things that he explained, things that we'll talk to you about later, after you've read your letter. He said you would help us to understand ...'

Ellen covered her daughter's hand with her own. She leaned forward and planted a quick kiss on the top of her head. Then she opened her arms and both girls came into her embrace.

'Hey, I like this one. Is this you, Rosy, bathing in your birthday suit ... or should I say birthday-ing in your bathing suit?' Maisy was grinning now, teasing.

Rosy clambered up out of the group hug and her mother watched as the two young women huddled close, peering at the blonde-ponytailed little girl in the elasticated swimming costume. The child was frowning at the camera, or maybe at the sun, and behind her on what seemed to be a long, white beach was a woman, also wearing a bathing costume, holding a birthday cake complete with candles.

'Mum, look at this. Is this me? I reckon that's you holding the cake. Did I have my birthday down at Mombasa that year, when I was seven, judging by the candles? I can't remember.' Rosy was holding the photograph out towards her mother.

'You did. It was your last birthday in Kenya. I expect that was why your father kept that picture in his treasure box. We stayed at the Nyali Beach Hotel ... don't you remember? You girls and I went down on the train and your dad met us there? That's when you had your first pair of flippers if I remember rightly.' Ellen's memory was supplying more details as she spoke.

'I remember.' Mara interrupted her mother. 'That was the time when that man stole the lady's bag at the station and the crowd went mad. They were going to kill him. I was really scared. You kept us safe, behind the suitcase.'

'Can you really remember that?' Ellen had hoped her children had forgotten, though she herself never would. She shivered.

'I do remember the flippers and the mask. I loved those flippers. Look, I think I'm holding them ... yes there ... look ... that's them in the picture.' The moment had passed. Ellen was glad.

'It's funny, the things Dad chose to keep in his box, don't you think?' Mara had picked up the snapshots, was flicking through them. 'There are quite a few of us as children. I can't see any of us as grown-ups though. He had quite a few of you, Mum. Have you seen this one?' She held it out for her mother to see. It was of a young woman, smiling to the camera, hair brushed out long and loose, catching the sunlight. Behind her the looped back flaps of a safari tent. 'It's beautiful, Mum. You're beautiful.'

'That was when we went to the Masai Mara ... our first safari. I remember.'

Mara nodded, winked at her mum. 'Mmm ... from what I've heard about that trip ... I can guess why Dad kept that one!' They all laughed then and that was how Dan found them, a family, enjoying each other's company.

But, as he came across the room towards them, slumped himself down into the armchair, Dan was not smiling. Still without a word, he leaned forward and picking up the pile of photographs, began flicking through them. He seemed to know what he was looking for, to be searching for something. As the others watched him, he stopped, selected a postcard-sized black and white image and looked at it closely, then cradled it between his palms.

'Are you all right Dad? Is something wrong?' Maisy's concern was in her voice.

Her father looked up as from a distance. He met her eyes, held them for a moment before he spoke.

'Maisy, this is my mother, your grandmother.'

He held out the photograph for them all to see. They recognised the young woman from other photographs and from the paintings. There was no mistake. It was Njeri.

Ellen's hand went to her mouth as she drew in a sharp breath. She had been standing; now she lowered herself onto the arm of the sofa. Dan turned to face her. He saw her tight lips, her frown, the questions in her eyes. He understood.

'And Ellen ... all of you ... this man is my father.'

He was pointing now to the young man standing beside

Njeri. The man's face was lit by his smile; his arm was around the shoulders of the woman. His hair was blonde, straight, flopping forward across his broad forehead. He wore no moustache, no facial hair at all. This was not Theo.

'My birth father's name was Daniel. I was named for him. His name was Daniel, Daniel Lind.'

Dan paused and looked around at his audience. All eyes were wide, focused on him as he began to share with them some of what he had discovered in Theo's letter.

'My father was an artist, a teacher. He was Theo's closest friend. It seems that he was killed, murdered by what Theo described as an avenging mob ... possibly a hit squad ... at the school, out in the Rift Valley ... in the last days of the struggle for Kenyan Independence. My mother died later that same night ... Christmas night ... the night that I was born.' He stopped for a moment, visibly moved. He looked down at the photograph in his hands, looked up at his daughter. 'According to Theo's letter, your grandmother was a very brave, intelligent and beautiful young woman. She was his dear friend too ... like a sister he said.' He held the picture out towards Maisy. She took it from him.

While his listeners were still digesting this information, Dan continued. 'Those paintings we looked at before, the furniture, the jewellery ... all the antiques and other stuff stored down in the gardener's cottage ... it seems that it all came from my father's family and from his house in Malindi. Apparently there are other things that my father inherited from his grandfather's estate in England, all held in a bank, with solicitors. Theo organised everything. It seems that was what my father wanted.'

'But why did Theo leave you here in Cornwall. Why did he allow you to believe for so long that he was your father?' Ellen was finding it hard to comprehend what she was hearing.

'It seems that my mother committed me to him on the night she died. As she was dying, she begged him to take me into his family, to take me back with him to England. It seems that ever since she was a little girl, since she had first met the beautiful Alexandra – your grandmother, Mara – my mother thought that

England was as close to heaven as you could get on earth – those were Theo's words. And she thought that I would be safer there. Apparently there were people at the time, one man in particular, who wanted to kill me, just like they'd killed my father. They would have killed her.'

'But why? Why did they want to kill you? Why did they kill him? Why did they want to kill Njeri?' Maisy had so many questions.

He faced his daughter. 'I don't know all the answers yet, my love, not by any means. But Theo said something about Kernowi ... that these people thought that my father was Kernowi ... whatever that means ... and that amongst other things he had information that would cause big trouble for them, information about torture and brutality ... stuff to do with the government even ... 'Colonial cover-ups,' he called them. He also said that Ellen would be able to help us understand more about it all.' He glanced in her direction.

Ellen shook her head. 'I don't know what to say. Those were terrible times, those last days of the Colonial Government in Kenya. Of course I only know what I've been told, by Theo and others. A lot of very bad things happened ... on both sides as far as I can tell. Those diaries, the pictures we were looking at the other day ... it was dreadful. Theo didn't actually talk about it much. I got the impression he was trying to put it all behind him. But he did tell me a bit about Kernowi. They called him ... that is they called Theo, 'Kernowi' ... Kenyatta and his men ... because he told them he was Cornish, not English. He told them he came from Cornwall, from Kernow. He showed them the black and white Cornish flag. He even sang '*Trelawney*' when he met Kenyatta in the forest.' She watched them all struggling to take in what she was telling them, trying to make the connections.

'Kenyatta ... did you say Kenyatta? How did Theo know Kenyatta?' Frank was really interested. Kenyatta was a name he knew.

'He met him first in England, here in Cornwall actually, at the Old Rectory, when he was a boy, then again in Kenya.'

'So Theo was actually this 'Kernowi' but the mob thought

that it was Daniel?'

'It seems so.' Ellen nodded.

'In the letter, my father ...' Dan hesitated, scratched his head, coughed to clear his throat; 'I mean 'Theo' also mentioned a man, an old friend, called Jack ... oh and he said that there were things, letters and suchlike, in his treasure box and in his diaries that might help us to make sense of it all.' Again he glanced across at Ellen but this time she was looking at her daughters.

'Mara ... Rosy ... did your father say anything to you about all this in his letter, about a son, about Dan, about his friend Daniel?'

Her daughters were looking back at her, both nodding slowly.

'He did, Mum. He told us that he had taken on ... he might have said 'adopted' but I can't remember ... the baby son of his best friend Daniel. He said that he owed this to Daniel. That Daniel had died in his place ... had let his murderers think that he was 'Kernowi.' That was why they killed him.' Mara stopped speaking and glanced at Dan. He was staring into the distance. His face was expressionless.

It was Rosy who took up with the story, at least, as far as she could understand it. 'Dad said that he owed a debt of honour to Daniel and to Njeri's son. Reading between the lines, it seems to me, to us both actually ...' she glanced across to include her sister, 'that in some way Dad thought he was giving up his own former life in Cornwall in order to keep their son safe, so that none of the bad people would be able to trace the child. That's why he did nothing with all that evidence he'd collected. He said he wanted to put the past behind him. Above all he wanted their son to have 'a safe and happy life with Rose and her family at the Old Rectory.' Those were his exact words.' Theo's younger daughter stopped then and looked around at the others. It was her father's voice that echoed in the stillness.

'And I did.' Dan spoke into the lengthening silence. He sighed as he came to his feet. 'And maybe he was right, maybe it was all for the best.'

'Oh Dad.' Maisy was in his arms.

'Anyway, it seems to me that we've all found out a lot more than we expected to today. But, you know what ... I reckon this is just the beginning. There's so much more to discover, to learn about my family, about yours.' Dan was smiling now over his daughter's head at the others. He looked directly at Mara, 'and now that we're not brother and sister ...' He grinned broadly and she blushed.

Frank laughed then; punching the man he would always think of as his brother playfully on the arm. 'And on that note ... does anyone fancy a drink?'

36

Cornwall, Lostwithiel - 2010

'I've been thinking.' Muffled by the thick woollen scarf, Mara's words were scarcely decipherable. The bobble hat pulled down over her forehead and ears rendered her barely recognisable too. Her gloved hands were stuffed deep into the pockets of her overcoat, collar-up against the cold. Striding at her side, Dan had taken an almost identical approach for the late night walk through the lanes to the local village church. Mara had suggested it. It was Christmas Eve; she wanted to sing carols, and Dan had offered to accompany her.

Now, all carolling done, they were making their way back up to The Old Rectory. Around them the night was silent; their breath drifts of white smoke on the icy air. Stars littered the sky like diamonds flung on velvet and distant homesteads twinkled in the darkness. Up ahead, between the winter hedgerows the damp lane shimmered in the moonlight. The pair had been linked at the arm, but now Mara disengaged as she stopped, fumbled in her pocket for a tissue and blew her nose. The sound echoed, trumpet-loud in the stillness and Dan chuckled.

'Wow! You sound like the fanfare for the 'heavenly host!'

Mara giggled. 'Sorry.' Then she did it again, which was the cause of further hilarity.

'That's what I was thinking about actually, you know, at that moment, those exact words: 'the heavenly host.' Can't you just imagine it on a night like this?' She waved her gloved hands at the vast sky. 'Can't you just imagine 'the heavenly host' breaking through those stars, singing 'Glory to God in the highest and on earth peace ...' or something like that?' She grinned up at him behind her scarf. He could see it in her eyes. Arms linked once more, they walked on up the lane.

'So, you were thinking about angels?'

'No, not 'angels' really. Just thinking about Christmas and all those words that are so familiar we hardly notice them, like 'Glory be to the Father *and* to the Son.' Funny, but hearing that tonight in the church, it made me think again about Dad, 'the Father' ... and about you, 'the Son.' Glancing up at her companion, then back down at their steady-striding boots, Mara pictured them tied at the ankles, like kids at Sports Day. She chuckled then, warm and damp into the muffling wool.

Beside her, Dan was pensive. He waited for her to explain, as he knew she would. As they rounded the bend, the gateway offered a moonlit vista out over frosted fields to the horizon. Of the same mind, they slowed at the gate. This time it was Dan who fumbled for his handkerchief.

Gloved hands deep in her overcoat pockets, Mara was ready to share her thoughts. She spoke into the stillness.

'Actually it was the 'ands' I was thinking of really: *and* peace on earth ... *and* to the Son ... It made me think of all the all the 'ands' ... all the things I never knew about my Dad while I was growing up, while he was alive; all the things we've discovered since, keep on discovering; all the 'ands' that made him into the man he was ... that made us into the people we are.' She paused and he linked his arm through hers as she continued.

'He's been on my mind so much these last few days, leading up to Christmas. He loved Christmas, you know. He always made it special for us when we were small. But when I think about it ... he would often go off by himself, into his study. Sitting quietly in the dark I found him once. We were wrapping last minute presents with Mum. I ran to get something from upstairs when I saw him through the open door. He was sitting at his desk in a pool of lamplight, all alone, just staring at something in front of him. I thought at the time it was a photograph, I'm sure it was. He slipped it into his desk drawer when he noticed I was there, turned and smiled. I didn't understand then … but I think I do now. He was thinking about you … about your mother … about the night you were born.'

Her words moved him more than he could say. So he kept his peace as they stood in silence together.

When at last they turned away from the gate and walked on they were in step once more. The long tramp up the lane passed in comfortable, thoughtful silence.

As the entrance to the familiar driveway came into view up ahead, the pair increased their pace. They were nearly home. The Old Rectory that had been Theodore's childhood home had finally become home to his own family. Mara knew that her mother would be anticipating their return, probably with hot cocoa and mince pies by the fire. Rose would be sleeping peacefully already in the old gardener's cottage, renovated and restored especially for her. Rachel her nurse would most likely be sleeping too, in her own room across the hall. Having no family of her own, the young nurse had quickly become part of theirs. She and Rose would be spending Christmas day up at the house with the rest of them … at least for as long as Rose was comfortable, as long as her condition allowed.

Maisy would probably have finished the movie she'd been watching up in her room when they left. She would most likely be back downstairs again with Ellen by now. Those two had become really close; to Mara and Rosy she seemed more like a sister. Rosy would arrive with her young family in the morning and Frank would be there too. He always had an invitation to stay, and in truth he was up at The Old Rectory most days, helping with something or other since they'd all moved in. But 'Rock Cottage' was his own special place, and the one-man-band liked to be there, 'to make my own music in peace,' he laughingly insisted.

Gravel scrunched under their feet as they turned onto the drive and started on their way up towards the old house. They'd not gone far before Mara slowed her pace and they came to a stop, beside the door into to the walled garden. Withdrawing her arm from his, she turned to face him. Beneath the bobble hat, she was frowning.

'Dan … do you mind if I ask you something?'

Her tone was serious and he met her gaze, unsmiling. Presuming his permission she went on with what had clearly been bothering her. Her voice was strangely hesitant.

'You know what it's been like ... finding out about Dad's past ... the Mau Mau uprising ... the atrocities in the detention camps ... those awful pictures of torture victims that he took ... the records he kept ... the people he tried to help ... all the killing and fighting ... your father's murder ... the colonial cover-ups ... all the things he tried to protect us from, to keep hidden ... Dan, what do you think he would say if he knew what we've discovered? Do you think he'd be happy? Do you think it helps us now, to know all that, I mean?'

She searched his face for answers. Inscrutable, Dan breathed deep. Head down, he turned away, hands stuffed deep into the pockets of his overcoat. She watched in silence, waited till he turned back to face her. He was nodding as he spoke, slowly, thoughtfully.

'Mm, I reckon it does, help us that is, or it will, anyway. It makes me think of that line from Auden's poem, the one that we were talking about the other day: '*The winds must come from somewhere when they blow* ...' There is a reason for everything. It helps to make sense of things, to know. For me personally, I'm very glad to know now about my real father. I feel so close to him – so proud of the man he was, of his friendship with your father, of what he did. And my mother too – what a strong and brave woman she was. How much she loved my father ...' Dan closed his eyes over the images that were so hard to bear. He drew a deep breath of the icy air. It steadied him and he was able to continue.

'I'm looking forward to going out to Kenya, when we all go in the New Year. I'm looking forward to seeing where the school was, where my parents met and lived ... and died ... to seeing the Rift Valley and going to Kijabe where my mother is buried. Yes, I am certain that for me, and for Maisy, it has been very important to know, or at least to have the chance to gradually discover the truth. You know something Mara, I've come to respect Theo so much. He was truly an honourable man, a good man your father.'

Nodding on those words of affirmation, he looked into the eyes of Theo's daughter who was standing right beside him in the cold night air. She was nodding too, as with a gloved hand she wiped at a tear that had escaped onto her cheek. Taking her arm in his, Dan continued with the answers he knew she was waiting to hear.

'As to how he'd feel about all this ... your father was a man of integrity. I think that he must have found it hard ... a heavy burden to bear ... to keep silent for so long, especially to keep things from your mother. From what I can tell, I think he would be glad, relieved to have things out in the open at last. Who knows what might have happened, but I get the feeling that he was actually planning to do something about it himself. Otherwise why did he write those letters?'

Mara nodded again, thoughtful as she brought out into the open one more thing had been troubling her.

'Mm, I think you might be right about that. Maybe he did have a plan to do something about it all. Perhaps he really was planning to bring us all together at last. We'll never know for sure but it would certainly be very like him. He always had a plan.' She smiled ruefully, remembering his face.

'Dan, can I ask you something else? Do you really think we did the right thing, handing those records, the photographs, those documents, the 'w' stamp, Dad's diaries, all that stuff, over to the lawyers for those elderly Kenyans so that they could use it in their case against the British government, for their torture and abuse in those terrible detention camps?'

She waited, needing his reassurance. The responsibility had been weighing heavy on her mind. The decision had been her mother's.

This time his answer was quick in coming.

'Yes, I'm certain that was the right thing to do. As far as I can see, it was always Theo's – and my father's – intention that justice should be done, that the victims should not be forgotten, that people should be held to account. I'm sure it was only because of the commitment he made to my mother to protect me that he kept silent all these years.' Dan looked at Mara and she nodded, waiting for him to go on. 'All we can hope for now is that it happens, that 'Kernowi's' record-keeping will not be in vain and that there will be some kind of official recognition of the terrible abuse, the ill-treatment those people suffered at the hands of the Colonial administration and who knows, maybe an apology, financial compensation ... I don't know. How can anyone ever make it right? ... We'll have to wait and see what happens now. Anyway, I'm so glad that that man *Uhuru,* John Freeman, didn't get his hands on any of it.' Dan's voice held all the vehemence of his disdain for the man who had almost certainly been behind the murder of his father, the man who had been trying for so long to track down the son, the man who might have killed him too.

'Once everything was out there, out in the open, there was nothing that he could do. That was all down to your mother. What an amazing woman she is!'

Mara was bouncing up and down on her icy feet, but she was grinning now as she remembered. 'You're right. She is amazing. It was so lucky she'd read Dad's letter, read about your mother's last words, about '*Uhuru*' coming. After seeing those awful pictures, his name in the album with those arrows like that ... as soon as you told her the name of the man you were meeting, the man who was trying to get hold of your things, who had been 'waiting a long time' to find you, to get hold of them ... she put two and two together straightaway.'

They could laugh about it now but at the time the stakes had been high. Those days leading up to the meeting, to the broadcast, had been very tense indeed.

'Ellen was absolutely brilliant. Getting the local BBC news teams involved like that ... getting the cameras in. It was a stroke of pure genius. Inviting '*Uhuru*' to appear on BBC local news, on Spotlight, under his real name – and then when he finally turned up, expecting to talk about the antiques, the pieces of Lamu style furniture, the other items from Dad's collection that he was hoping to get hold of. I must admit that when I saw him, I was a bit surprised. I wasn't expecting such an old man. But those eyes ... like a snake ... there was so much hate, so much venom in those eyes. When he finally realised what it was all about ... the questions ... the evidence against him ... against his henchmen ... no wonder he scarpered.' Dan shuddered on the memory, at the awful presence of the man.

'Mum even got him to admit, live to camera, that his dad had once worked for your father. That he had been the manager on his farm in Kenya, for a while anyway, before he was sacked. The pair of them obviously hated Daniel ever since that time and then the whole Kernowi business. As he left he was still ranting about how Kernowi had killed his father, shot him ... 'after Lari,' that's what he said, and that Daniel was Kernowi. You know, Dan, I looked up Lari online after that. It sounded absolutely awful. The Mau Mau were massacring Kenyans who were loyal to the British, and then British forces were joining with the loyalists in the terrible revenge killings that followed. So much savagery had been unleashed! Killing Kernowi, murdering your father ... that was nothing at all to do with the Mau Mau though. Mau Mau was just a cover, just an excuse for him to take his personal revenge. What a dreadful, dreadful man!' She shook her head, shivered at the memory.

'And then he stormed out, pursued by that reporter with the microphone. Remember how he batted the camera out of the cameraman's hand?'

Noisily now, the pair recalled the man's bluster, deflated in the face of Ellen's certainties, the interviewer's probing questions, not about antique furniture, as he'd been expecting, but about links to allegations of brutality and torture during the Mau Mau uprising and in the Kenyan detention camps. The investigations would continue and at last Theo's records would be helping in the search for justice, for accountability.

Regardless of the spectacle they were making, Dan and Mara high-fived in their thick woollen gloves.

'Is that you? Mara ... Dan ... is that you, making all that noise out there?' It was Ellen, lit by a halo of golden light from the opened door behind her.

'It's all right, Mum. It's only some carol singers.' Mara's

words were lifted on the winds from somewhere across the valley. Laughter was in her voice. It was in her eyes as she turned back to Dan. 'It's past midnight you know ... Christmas day. It's your birthday.'

His smile was warm into the woollen scarf. Beneath the thick bobble hat his dark eyes glowed. He nodded, sniffed.

Mara's kiss on his cheek was soft.

'Happy Birthday, Dan.'

And as Ellen peered down the drive into the darkness, the carol singers made their way up towards her, arms linked, singing together at the top of their voices.

'It came upon a midnight clear, that glorious song of old ...'

POSTSCRIPT

Statement to Parliament on settlement of Mau Mau claims (6th June 2013) The Foreign Secretary made a statement to Parliament on the settlement of claims of Kenyan citizens relating to events during the period 1952 - 1963.

'With permission, Mr Speaker, I would like to make a statement on a legal settlement that the Government has reached concerning the claims of Kenyan citizens who lived through the Emergency Period and the Mau Mau insurgency from October 1952 to December 1963.

During the Emergency Period widespread violence was committed by both sides, and most of the victims were Kenyan. Many thousands of Mau Mau members were killed, while the Mau Mau themselves were responsible for the deaths of over 2,000 people including 200 casualties among the British regiments and police.

Emergency regulations were introduced: political organisations were banned; prohibited areas were created and provisions for detention without trial were enacted. The colonial authorities made unprecedented use of capital punishment and sanctioned harsh prison so-called 'rehabilitation' regimes. Many of those detained were never tried and the links of many with the Mau Mau were never proven. There was recognition at the time of the brutality of these repressive measures and the shocking level of violence, including an important debate in this House on the infamous events at Hola Camp in 1959.

We recognise that British personnel were called upon to serve in difficult and dangerous circumstances. Many members of the colonial service contributed to establishing the institutions that under-pin Kenya today and we acknowledge their contribution.

However I would like to make clear now and for the first time, on behalf of Her Majesty's Government, that we understand the pain and grievance felt by those who were involved in the events of the Emergency in Kenya. The British Government recognises that Kenyans were subject to torture and other forms of ill treatment at the hands of the colonial administration. The British government sincerely regrets that these abuses took place, and that they marred Kenya's progress towards independence. Torture and ill treatment are abhorrent violations of human dignity which we unreservedly condemn.

In October 2009 claims were first brought to the High Court by five individuals who were detained during the Emergency period regarding their treatment in detention.

In 2011 the High Court rejected the claimants' argument that the liabilities of the colonial administration transferred to the British Government on independence, but allowed the claims to proceed on the basis of other arguments.

In 2012 a further hearing took place to determine whether the cases should be allowed to proceed. The High Court ruled that three of the five cases could do so. The Court of Appeal was due to hear our appeal against that decision last month.

However, I can announce today that the Government has now reached an agreement with Leigh Day, the solicitors acting on behalf of the Claimants, in full and final settlement of their clients' claims.

The agreement includes payment of a settlement sum in respect of 5,228 claimants, as well as a gross costs sum, to the total value of £19.9 million. The Government will also support the construction of a memorial in Nairobi to the victims of torture and ill-treatment during the colonial era. The memorial will stand alongside *others that are already being established in Kenya as the country continues to heal the wounds of the past. And the British High Commissioner in Nairobi is also today making a public statement to members of the Mau Mau War Veterans Association in Kenya, explaining the settlement and expressing our regret for the events of the Emergency Period.*

Mr Speaker this settlement provides recognition of the suffering and injustice that took place in Kenya. The Government of Kenya, the Kenya Human Rights Commission and the Mau Mau War Veterans Association have long been in favour of a settlement, and it is my hope that the agreement now reached will receive wide support, will help draw a line under these events, and will support reconciliation.

We continue to deny liability on behalf of the Government and British taxpayers today for the actions of the colonial administration in respect of the claims, and indeed the courts have made no finding of liability against the Government in this case. We do not believe that claims relating to events that occurred overseas outside direct British jurisdiction more than fifty years ago can be resolved satisfactorily through the courts without the testimony of key witnesses that is no longer available. It is therefore right that the Government has defended the case to this point since 2009.

The settlement I am announcing today is part of a process of reconciliation. In December this year, Kenya will mark its 50th anniversary of independence and the country's future belongs to a post independence generation. We do not want our current and future relations with Kenya to be overshadowed by the past. Today we are bound together by commercial, security and personal links that benefit both our countries. We are working together closely to build a more stable region. Bilateral trade between the UK and Kenya amounts to £1 billion each year, and around 200,000 Britons visit Kenya annually.

Although we should never forget history and indeed must always seek to learn from it, we should also look to the future, strengthening a relationship that will promote the security and prosperity of both our nations. I trust that this settlement will support that process. The ability to recognise error in the past but also to build the strongest possible foundation for cooperation and friendship in the future are both hallmarks of our democracy.'

<u>www.gov.uk (6th June 2013):</u> The Foreign Secretary made a statement to Parliament on the settlement of claims of Kenyan citizens relating to events during the period 1952 – 1963.

Printed in Great Britain
by Amazon